INTO THE MAIDSTONE

SHANE TRUSZ
— AND —
DARRYL FRAYNE

To my parents for loving me.
Sorry there wasn't a parenting book in all the world
that could have prepared you.
And sorry for ditching the car that one time on Bradette Road.
Yes, that was me.
Shane

To Ian and Dylan.
You fill my days with love, joy, wonder,
and hope for a better tomorrow.
Darryl

CONTENTS

INTO THE MAIDSTONE

THE FOURWINDS
MAIDSTONE CHRONICLES MAP

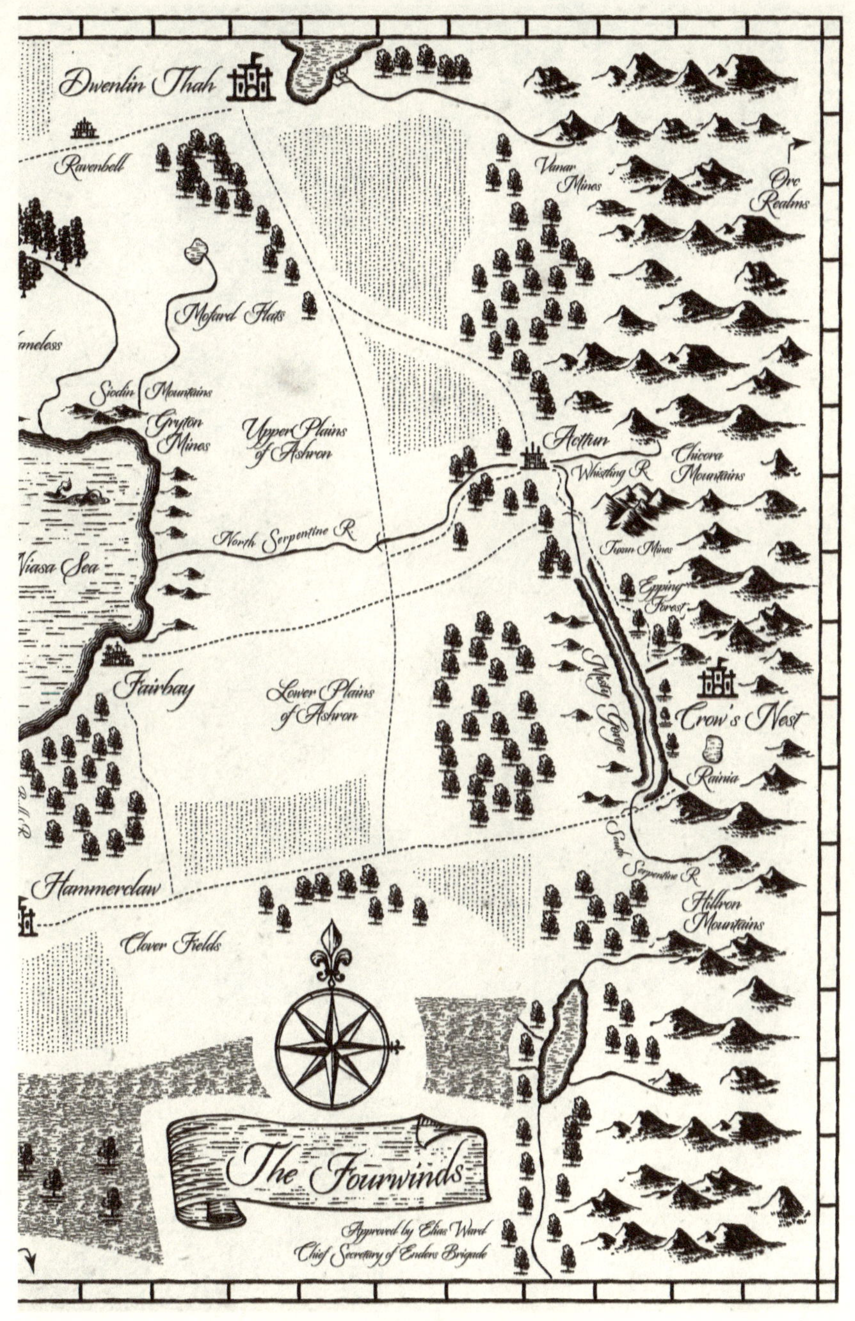

Dwenlin Thah
Ravenbell
Nameless
Mosard Flats
Sjodin Mountains
Gryfton Mines
Upper Plains of Ashron
Viasa Sea
North Serpentine R
Fairbay
Lower Plains of Ashron
Hammerclaw
Clover Fields
Vanar Mines
Orc Realms
Aettun
Whistling R
Chicora Mountains
Tyran Mines
Epping Forest
Misty Gorge
Crow's Nest
Rainia
South Serpentine R
Hillron Mountains
The Fourwinds
Approved by Elias Ward
Chief Secretary of Enders Brigade

Prologue

NEVADA, USA — A northwesterly wind crested the rugged Nevada peaks and swept into the rocky, arid valley commonly known as Area 51. Far beneath the surface, a highly classified "black project" came to an unexpected conclusion. Four US Air Force officers had been attending a demonstration by a team of weapons engineers from Lockheed Martin's Skunk Works division. One of the officers was a lieutenant general from the US Department of Defense. In less than eight hours, he was expected to provide a full report to a special task force that included the president of the United States.

Two harvesters disguised as Air Force privates entered the meeting room to clean up the dishes, cups, and glasses they had brought in a few hours earlier for the team's coffee break. The harvesters had tainted the food and drinks with an elixir known as Phyriad, and they wanted to ensure that every officer had partaken. But there was no need for close examination. Judging by all the groans and coughing, everyone in the room was already infected.

An hour later, the harvesters grinned as they watched a plane marked with the colorful Department of Defense logo taxi toward one of the longest runways in the world. On board and doing his best to suppress his sudden flu-like symptoms was the lieutenant general. He downed two extra-strength Tylenol pills, determined not to miss his opportunity to present his report in person to the president. The jet roared down the runway and disappeared into the night sky, bound for Washington, DC.

BAKU, AZERBAIJAN — At an important crossroads between Europe and Asia, a harvester stood atop the twelfth-century Maiden Tower in the old city of Baku. It was quiet here, away from the city's busy nightlife, which had dwindled well after midnight. Footsteps shuffled across the time-worn cobblestones below. A woman's soft laughter faded as a couple disappeared down a narrow alley. The ancient tower was closed to tourists now, providing a private place where the harvester could shift into its native skin. The creature inhaled a raspy breath as a steady breeze off the Caspian Sea cooled its dark, scaly hide.

Recent shifts in commercial trade winds had opened opportunities for the Port of Baku, dramatically reducing the time needed for goods to travel between Europe and China. The harvester had spent the day disguised as a wealthy businessman supervising two shipments. Among the two hundred steel containers aboard a ship bound for China, one carried three thousand tins marked as Italian olive oil. A second ship had arrived from the east with ten containers that were transferred to a freight train bound for London, England. On that ship, the container of primary importance to the harvester carried 350 cartons of tea.

Infusing olive oil tins and cartons of loose-leaf tea with Phyriad had been tedious but quite simple; port workers on night shifts were quick to accept bribes for a side job to cash in on the New Silk Road.

The harvester growled contentedly. This new road would serve its master's purposes, dramatically reducing the time to spread his influence across this vulnerable land.

⁂

TORONTO, CANADA — Two harvesters emerged from the Arden Forest into the warmth of a quiet Sunday afternoon. Anyone in the nearby town of Cochrane would have recognized the pair of shape-shifters as fencing world champion Morgan Finley and her mother, the nurse Julie. But the troubled town was not the harvesters' immediate destination.

The harvester disguised as Morgan slung a leather satchel over its shoulder and noticed an abandoned Buick Century parked on the side of the Arden Road. The other harvester retrieved the car key that the real Julie Finley had hidden under the floor mat, and within minutes, they were heading south on Highway 11. Eight hours later, they pulled into a weekly parking lot at Toronto's Pearson International Airport.

The disguised harvesters followed a small group of Air Canada workers into the employee locker room. Given the high turnover rate among cabin service and cleaning attendants, no one questioned the presence of two new faces. Everyone was too busy preparing for the busy overnight shift, donning rubber gloves and orange safety vests, and checking cleaning supplies. The harvester disguised as Morgan carefully removed a glass flask from the leather satchel and added a few drops to two plastic spray bottles.

Twenty minutes later, the harvesters joined a cleaning crew aboard a Boeing 787 scheduled to leave for Amsterdam within two hours. As cabin crew staff vacuumed floors, restocked pillows and blankets, and scrubbed windows, the two harvesters pulled up their rubber gloves, adjusted their face masks, and proceeded to spray and wipe every seat-belt buckle, armrest, tray table, and lavatory door handle.

By the time dawn broke at the end of their shift, the harvesters had infected airplanes bound for Amsterdam, Barcelona, Beijing, Dubai, Sao Paulo, and Sydney. When they checked the level of Phyriad remaining in the flask, they realized there would be enough for another work shift.

<hr>

ACTTUN, THE FOURWINDS — While most residents in the strange city of Acttun slept, a harvester crossed a bridge and followed an overgrown, deserted road to the dilapidated main gates of the asylum. The creature clutched a small glass flask and huffed as it stared up at the five-story structure, now sealed like a derelict mausoleum. The assignment from the Iron Dragon made no sense to the harvester. What good was an old abandoned building? Despite its hesitation, the creature carefully pocketed the flask and climbed the ladder to the roof. As it passed bricked-over windows, bizarre sounds—too muffled and faint to recognize—permeated the weathered wall.

The harvester crept across the expansive flat roof toward a small access building. An iron fence that resembled a giant birdcage surrounded the structure, and the only way through the fence was a single locked gate. With a dexterous clawed hand, the harvester retrieved a large key from a chain around its neck and opened the pitted lock. The gate resisted but swung slowly open, its rusty hinges squealing. Two thick metal slabs barred the top and bottom of the roof access door.

Hearing nothing beyond the door, the harvester removed the metal bars and waited. The night was silent, save for the distant laughter of drunken men on the streets below leaving the Cauldron's Stew. The harvester jiggled the door handle, and the latch gave way. A waft of dank air emerged, carrying the pungent odor of feces, rotting flesh, and unfamiliar things.

The harvester clutched the flask, took a deep breath, and pulled the door open a few inches. Something slammed against the other side of the door, pushing it open a few more inches. Reflexively, the harvester stopped the door with its foot. In the blink of an eye, it tossed the flask inside, then threw its weight against the door, barely keeping it from flying open.

There was a sudden eruption of shrieks and raking claws inside, but the harvester managed to close the door. Something pounded on the other side as though desperate to escape. The harvester fumbled with the iron slabs, replacing them as best it could. The key trembled in its clawed hands, but the creature quickly relocked the iron gate. Beyond the sealed door, the chaos inside struck a fevered pitch.

❧❀❧

DWENLIN THAH, THE FOURWINDS — It was early morning when the two-wheeled one-horse cart rolled through the quiet streets on its way out of Dwenlin Thah. Most people these days were trying to get into the city, but the cart was now empty, its purpose here complete. The largest city in the Fourwinds would normally be active by this time of day, especially near the main gates. But the streets were unusually quiet this morning. The steady clip-clopping of the horse pulling the cart down the main cobblestone street was broken only by the persistent coughing of the soldiers guarding the main gates.

From the driver's seat, the elderly male driver and the woman next to him nodded to the soldiers on duty but did not slow. Two children sat in the empty cart, waving at the soldiers as they passed. On the back of the cart hung a crooked sign that read *Maple Syrup Candy*.

A soldier caught the girl's eye. "Anything left? I could use something to soothe this nasty cough."

The girl lifted empty hands and shrugged. "Sorry."

A half mile down the road, the cart took a small path to the top of a forested hill. The old man pulled the cart to a stop near a rocky ledge overlooking the city. Sheltered now among the trees, the four harvesters shed their human disguises. The creature that had been driving the cart stretched its muscular neck and purred like a contented bear. The others grinned and scratched their scaly hides with long, clawed fingers.

As the sun peeked between passing clouds, the harvesters gathered to observe the results of their two-day effort to spread the Phyriad-infused candies throughout the capital city.

The main gates and the streets remained relatively quiet for the rest of that day and throughout the next. The harvesters grew impatient. But as midnight struck to mark the third day, the city was transformed.

CHAPTER 1
DRAGON SIGHTING

Will Owens dabbed his forehead with a damp, dirty rag. It was filthy, in fact, but at least it was cool. The afternoon sun was merciless, and the breeze atop the North Crow Gate was far from refreshing—it was more like standing in front of a furnace exhaust fan. Fortunately, his Trannalun cloak—the distinctive magical garment worn by all Callum Sages—helped to protect him from the elements. Even so, the persistent heat showed no favoritism.

Will blinked several times, trying to stay focused. He'd rather be diving off his dock on Rainia Lake—enjoying a private swim with his new bride, Ryowyn—but such pleasures would have to wait until he finished his work here. His unique ability to see shape-shifting demons known as harvesters made him solely responsible for identifying the evil creatures in the crowd of refugees below.

Too many harvesters had already entered the well-protected Rainia Valley long before Will had arrived in the Fourwinds. A few had entered the Crow's Nest castle, ascended to the Records of Time tower, and passed through the Gateway to Will's hometown of Cochrane, Ontario. As servants of Natas, the Iron Dragon, the harvesters had been spreading a strange contagion known simply as Phyriad. The elixir transformed those infected into the reptilian image of Natas, creating more servants to extend the spread of Phyriad. As a result, refugees from across the Fourwinds had been seeking shelter in the secluded valley.

Like all who worked to protect the North Crow Gate, Will took his daily task seriously, but today the bright sun and constant interruptions made the tedious process of searching for harvesters more challenging.

Tonna, the first messenger of Enders Brigade, approached and stood before Will and the other two red-cloaked Callum Sages. Lines of sweat streaked the messenger's forehead as he glanced at Will and Morgan before addressing Rowe of the Nest.

"The remnant of our troops should be here by tomorrow, sir," Tonna said.

Will pulled his cloak tighter. News of Enders Brigade's imminent arrival was a relief, but he preferred to leave military affairs to his two friends. Rowe was far more experienced in military strategy than either Will or Morgan, and after the battle at the South Crow Gate, Morgan was practically a seasoned war vet. So, Will returned to his simple yet vital task of scanning the refugees awaiting clearance to enter the valley. He had already singled out one harvester today, and that was one too many for his liking.

"Thank you, Tonna," Rowe said. "I appreciate the update and the risks you took. Please give a full report to Brigadier Henowing at the Crow's Nest so he can make an announcement at the gathering tonight. Many anxious families are awaiting this news."

"What about the survivors from the North Gnome Army?" Morgan asked.

Tonna shuffled his feet. "Well, uh…Captain Culthison said they waited for Commander Yossar and his gnome army at the Mofard Flats, as Brigadier Bayard commanded. But…Yossar never arrived."

"Do you think they were overcome by Phyriad like the rest of their army?" Morgan asked.

This caught Will's attention. He turned and studied Tonna's face. The trusted messenger was withholding something, but Will didn't know what. Or why. Will met Rowe's eye and realized he'd noticed it too.

"Is there something more, Tonna?" Rowe asked.

The messenger sighed deeply. "The captain told me they were unable to wait longer than an hour, sir. They had to flee from…"

"From what?" Will asked.

"A horde of wild and sickly gnomes attacked from the Nameless Forest. The captain didn't see Commander Yossar among them and feared all the gnomes had been infected with Phyriad. The gnomes were slow-moving, but our men were battle-weary. It would have ended much worse if not for—I'm sorry, sir—" Tonna swallowed hard. "A dragon came and killed most of the gnomes and routed the rest."

"A dragon?" Morgan said. "Why would Natas destroy those he infected to be part of his army?"

Tonna shook his head. "Not Natas—at least if rumors of the Iron Dragon are true. This dragon was red."

Rowe's piercing-blue eyes brightened. "That would be General Raric. Johanissan said he had transformed into the Red Dragon. Raric destroyed Uluk, and now he's fighting the infected armies of Natas."

Again, Tonna shook his head. "I wish that were true, sir. But the dragon also attacked Enders Brigade. The gnomes got the worst of it, but we lost some good soldiers in the flames."

Will waited for Rowe to respond, hoping he would have some insight or wisdom gleaned from his vast knowledge of the Histories. But Rowe was silent.

"Where's Rar—er, the Red Dragon now, Tonna?" Morgan asked. "And how did Enders Brigade escape?"

"The dragon flew past them and continued east, which allowed Enders Brigade to travel south through the Plains of Ashron."

Rowe's brow wrinkled. "East? Where would it be going? To Acttun? Or—"

"To us," Will said, turning his back to them. He leaned against the parapet and gazed over the trees of the Epping Forest into the clear late-afternoon sky. The others joined him and, after several long minutes of scanning the sky, Will pointed. Despite the lack of clouds, there was a distant rumble.

"That couldn't be thunder," Morgan said.

About three miles out, the Red Dragon soared above the Misty Gorge. It appeared to be heading due south and, although its flight pattern was far from direct, it made no move toward the Rainia Valley. The dragon dipped into the gorge and out of sight almost as quickly as it had appeared.

Will looked at the others, then at the soldiers and workers along the wall. The sawing, hammering, and conversations continued as if nothing had happened. On the ground below the outer wall, workers continued to help refugees. A sense of urgency remained all around, but no one else seemed to have noticed the dragon.

"And I thought Natas was big," Morgan said, her voice cracking.

"I believe that Scarlas is the largest dragon in history," Rowe said. "And the only one ever defeated by humans. Raric destroyed

Scarlas in the Dragon War, but it seems the Red Dragon has re-turned for its revenge."

"Is it coming back here?" Tonna asked.

"It's heading south," Rowe answered, shielding his eyes as he peered into the bright sky. "So, I imagine it will encounter the South Gnome Army. Twelve thousand bush gnomes ought to keep it busy for a while."

"And give us more time to secure our defenses," Morgan added.

Will let out a slight snort but was not amused. "How can we defend against *that?*" He turned to Rowe. "No offense, partner. After hearing how you guys fought at the South Crow Gate, I don't doubt your ability to defend this wall—especially with reinforce-ments coming. But a gnome army attack is one thing. How do we stop dragons from thundering into the valley from above?"

Rowe scratched his stubbly chin. "Thundering…" he mused. "The Histories tell of a powerful weapon capable of disorienting and bringing down a dragon. It's called a thunderclap. I've read that Marlay Bonicle created a few dozen and kept some in a large vault at the asylum in Acttun. If they're still there—"

"I'm not going back to that place," Morgan said. "Besides, we have enough to do here, caring for refugees and preparing for Enders Brigade, and possibly whatever's left of the North Gnome Army."

"And eventually," Tonna added, "those infected with Phyriad will find their way to these gates."

"Yes," Morgan said. Her hazel eyes sparkled as she bobbed her head. "And we need to quarantine them, and care for as many as we can."

Rowe tilted his head at Morgan as if she were suggesting that they care for a pack of injured wolves, hoping they would one day make nice pets.

"With respect, Morgan," Rowe said, "if we do not protect this valley from dragon attacks, it will not be a safe place for anyone."

"And I agree, but—" Morgan began.

Rowe held up his hands in defense. "I'm not saying caring for refugees is not important. I've spent years working with Gloriana to find homes for people in the Crow's Nest and in Rainia. You know that. But as long as Natas lives and dragons threaten the Fourwinds, the strongest walls will not protect us."

"Not all dragons are our enemies, right?" Will interjected.

Rowe paused with a confused look on his face but, after a moment, nodded. "That's true, Will. The Ice Dragon has helped us in the past. But I've not seen her since she rescued us from the Waerdreath. We could have used her help defending the South Crow Gate, but I understand that her ways often differ from ours."

Will glanced at Morgan but resisted saying more with Tonna present. When the Ice Dragon had rescued the three of them from the Waerdreath castle—with General Raric and Bremer—Will had been unconscious. He had tried to get more information from Rowe and Morgan, who had both seen the Ice Dragon at the Waerdreath and, earlier in their journey, in the Tuxan Mines on their way to Acttun. Whenever Will asked for details, Rowe and Morgan changed the subject. But Rowe had just used feminine pronouns to refer to the Ice Dragon. That was new.

"Okay," Morgan said with a heavy sigh. "Who will you send to Acttun?"

Rowe held Morgan's gaze a moment. "I need to go," he said. "I know where the thunderclaps are and how to find them."

Morgan pursed her lips for an uncomfortable moment as if she were trying to control her emotions or choose her next words. Will was glad when Tonna used the pause to speak first.

"With your leave, sir, I will go report to the brigadier now."

As Tonna left, the setting sun painted the sky a soft blend of pale blue and orange. The breeze, finally cool with the waning day, ruffled the red Trannalun cloaks of the three Callum Sages, but no one moved. The bustle of activity on the wall dwindled as workers finished for the day.

"If you're sure that dragon isn't returning soon," Will said, breaking the awkward silence, "shall we head to Rainia for the gathering?"

The way Rowe and Morgan continued to look at each other reminded Will of unspoken arguments his parents used to have. Rowe puffed his chest, and Morgan squared her shoulders. Neither appeared ready to finish the conversation.

"If you're going to Acttun," Morgan said, "then Will and I are going with you. I thought we agreed to stick together from now on."

Rowe turned to face the sunset. "As you said, Morgan, there is still much to do to protect this wall. I do not like the idea of separating either, but I would prefer to leave at least one Callum Sage here. There's only three of us. I need to go to Acttun. Morgan, you're the one who set up protocols for entry here, and you and your mother are an indispensable team. You should stay. We need Will to watch for harvesters here, but I might need him in Acttun to look for harvesters. We'll have to discuss that later."

Morgan watched Rowe in silence, but Rowe avoided eye contact. After all they had been through together at the South Crow Gate, Will understood why they would be reluctant to be apart. Now that he was reunited with Ryowyn, Will would do anything to keep her close. At the same time, he understood that if they didn't protect the valley, there would be no future for them.

Morgan's shoulders relaxed slightly as she nodded, reflecting the sense of resignation that Will felt. He didn't like the idea either, but there seemed to be no other choice. He wrung his hands. "Apparently, we have some important decisions to make, and I think we could use some advice from Joe."

CHAPTER 2
THE GATHERING

Four major roads connected the burgeoning city of Rainia to various points throughout the valley. Along the two smaller roads, farmers herded the recent influx of cattle, sheep, and goats. On the other two roads, people arrived from the Crow's Nest, from the newly formed town of Little Hammerclaw, and from rural farms. They poured into Rainia on foot, on horseback, and in horse-drawn wagons. Young and old, rich and poor, joyous and grieving: they all gathered for a common purpose.

Although many people hoped to celebrate the victory at the South Crow Gate this night, most realized their treasured valley home was still under threat. The gathering provided an opportunity to learn what new life in the valley might look like given the influx of refugees, soldiers, half-orcs, and mer.

The legendary sea folk were an exciting addition, but rumors of highland gnomes now seeking clemency and sanctuary in the valley made most people uncomfortable. Others spoke of a strange plague spreading across the Fourwinds. A few older women told tales of Natas, the fabled creature of chaos, daring to suggest that the dragon was behind the warring, displacement, and disease. There was one question on almost everyone's lips: Who would lead the way forward and protect the remnant flocking to the Rainia Valley?

Will, Morgan, and Rowe slowed their horses as they approached the outskirts of town. Dozens of partially framed houses, hostels, and barns fringed the border, expanding the city limits every day. When the Callum Sages reached the city center, near the northern shores of Rainia Lake, they dismounted beside a large stable.

A young, lanky boy—probably not yet ten years old—rushed to take the reins of Rowe's horse.

"For the night, sir?" the boy asked in a high-pitched voice.

Rowe shook his head. "We're just here for the gathering."

"Very good, sir," the boy said as Will pressed three coins into his palm. The boy looked down at his hand, then flashed a wide grin. "Thank you, sir!"

Two more boys joined the lad, and each took one of the three horses and led them into the stable.

Next to the stable stood the newly constructed framework of a larger barn. The sound of hammering drew Will's eyes upward where at least half a dozen men, young and old, secured cedar shakes to the sheathing on the roof. Rowe stopped to speak to a man on the ground, who quickly called for work to stop for the day.

Will and Morgan followed Rowe down a narrow path to a row of cottages along the sprawling beach. From a fishery building up on the bank, an impressive wooden pier stretched across the beach and out into the deeper waters of Rainia Lake. Several fishing trawlers, moored along each side of the pier, bobbed in the small, rolling waves. The sound of clanking rigging and creaking ropes reminded Will of the town of Fairbay beside the Niasa Sea.

As clusters of people strolled onto the beach, he couldn't help but think of the night of celebration after they had rescued Fairbay from the dark elf Onathe Wyeth and Sidara's slave runners. That night was hard to forget. But Fairbay had survived only to fall to a greater enemy a few weeks later when the Niasa Sea was overrun by Phyriad-infected creatures. Despite thoughts of that horrific day, Will held on to the memory of that first night of celebration when he had met the beautiful mer princess, Ryowyn, now the love of his life.

The scene also reminded Will of the Recovery Ale House and Inn, which then reminded him how thirsty he was now.

An elderly man emerged from a cottage carrying two large mugs in one hand and a small bottle in the other. "It's about time you three showed up." He wore light tan-colored cotton pants and a flowing white shirt that exposed part of his brown, nearly hairless chest. Contrasting with his weathered face, his smooth, long white hair was braided tightly behind his head. His welcoming smile was a sight that Will cherished.

"Joe!" Will waved as Rowe and Morgan followed. "Sorry I missed you in Little Hammerclaw today."

"Well, I waited for a while but figured something was up." He handed the mugs to Will and Rowe, and the bottle to Morgan. "Jessman and the boys at the new Recovery send their regards."

"Thank you, Johanissan," Rowe said.

Morgan tapped her bottle against Will's mug. "Yes, thanks, Joe."

Rowe took a long drink from his mug, then started toward the pier. "I'll head up now. Meet me there in a few minutes."

From the pier, a bard began strumming his lute. Another bard picked up the tune as he walked along the beach. Two more joined them from the crowd, and when they were all together on the pier, they began singing a somber folk song.

Joe leaned toward Will and Morgan and lowered his voice. "This is a popular song called 'Days of Dreams.'"

Down from the ruins she led us
To green pastures and clear flowin' streams
Up from the ashes she pulled us
To silence the cries and the screams

Another musician on the pier joined in with a handheld drum that reminded Will of an Irish bodhrán. A woman in a long dress with colors that rivaled the sunset danced to the music. A few others ventured to sway and move their feet, but a melancholy mood dominated the crowd. Even so, many joined in the familiar chorus.

There're days I'll always remember
There're nights I'd rather forget
But the hours I spend dreamin' of home, dear
Are moments I'll never regret

On the other side of the pier, the merpeople gathered, already transformed to walk on land. The remnant from the great kingdom of the Niasa Sea was dressed in preparation for mingling with the humans. Their clothing represented the variety of blues and greens of the Niasa, woven from a rare flowering seaweed. The mer stood out like irises in the desert. But it was not their clothing that differentiated them from the humans; their smooth teal skin marked them as strangers in this remote corner of the Fourwinds.

The mermaids were tall, with flowing white hair and lean figures that swayed to the music. Many appeared to be in mourning. One look at the disproportion of mermaid to merman revealed the reason for the sadness. Most of the mer soldiers had been lost in the recent attack on the Niasa Sea. The few mermen that remained stood tall and strong, with muscles rippling like the sea after a storm.

Will spotted Ryowyn surrounded by mer soldiers clad in coral-crafted armor and armed with long tridents. The princess's influence was growing daily. She was speaking with an older mermaid, who leaned forward and nodded as if absorbing every word. Ryowyn's wild white hair was tied up in an intricate twist, displaying her elegant shoulders and neckline. A simple light-blue dress covered most of her tropical-sea-toned skin.

The graceful Queen Almithara stood several steps away beside Ryowyn's broad-shouldered father, Ryodan Ayoust.

"Come on, Will," Morgan said, tugging his cloak sleeve. "Let's head to the pier before the crowd gets too thick."

At the bottom of the pier stairs, they met Morgan's mother, Julie, and Gloriana, who together shared responsibility for all refugee affairs.

Will smiled as Morgan and Julie embraced. A moment later, he flinched as a gentle hand touched his back.

"There you are," Ryowyn said.

Will spun and wrapped her in his arms. From the corner of his eye, he noticed a few people whispering to one another as they watched the red-cloaked man and the teal-skinned mermaid embrace. He was aware of the varied opinions and, in fact, had wrestled with the implications of marriage to a mermaid. But she was worth the fight. He had almost lost her once when she had sacrificed her life to save his. Such love had carried him into the

Maidstone to find the legendary horn of Thaudas, the winged unicorn. And the healing power of Thaudas had saved her. Despite the differences between Will and Ryowyn, no one could deny their incredible bond.

Ryowyn trembled as she squeezed him tighter, as if refusing to let dissenters or death come so close to separating them again.

Most of the human population in the Rainia Valley had only heard stories about the mer. Very few had ever seen one, let alone spoken with or befriended one. Tonight's gathering would provide that opportunity.

"Did you know there would be music?" Ryowyn asked. "I used to love listening to the bards in Fairbay."

Will took her hands as she moved to the music. "I'm not sure what to expect tonight, but I'm hoping for the beginning of something good."

Warm, light-hearted conversations rose around them, punctuated by an occasional outburst of laughter. People waved at acquaintances or called out greetings, and almost everyone cast glances at the pier as a general sense of anticipation filled the evening air. A light breeze pushed away clouds of sorrow that hovered over so many people who had lost so much.

Will stood in the sand as Ryowyn swayed and danced around him. He spun her around once, then twice, before noticing Ryodan and Almithara joining Rowe on the pier.

"It's time," Will said to Ryowyn.

As the couple climbed the short set of steps with Julie and Gloriana, the bards brought their song to a wondrous finish. The woman in the bright-colored dress stopped dancing, and the colors in the material seemed to fade into twilight. She sang the closing stanza solo.

Though shadows and death o'ertake us
'Tis never as bad as it seems
For out of the darkness we'll shine, dear
Returning to days of dreams

Tears stung Will's eyes as most of the crowd joined in unison to sing the chorus a cappella.

There're days I'll always remember
There're nights I'd rather forget
But the hours I spend dreamin' of home, dear
Are moments I'll never regret

The first few evening stars twinkled in silence as crickets began their own nightly chorus from the tall grasses along the shoreline. Steady waves lapped the smooth rocks and pitch-coated posts of the pier. Flames from several beach fires crackled and popped. No one moved.

CHAPTER 3

UNEXPECTED COMPANY

After a moment of silence, Rowe cleared his throat and stepped forward to the edge of the pier, several feet above the crowd on the beach. His red cloak shimmered in the firelight, making him appear larger than life. He swept the hair from his brow and addressed the gathering.

"Tonight, we've laid down our tools." Rowe raised his mug of ale, and a few others raised theirs in salute. "Our tireless toil—building homes for the homeless, providing food for the hungry, and loving those who have lost loved ones—is the spirit that will carry us in the coming days."

Many people nodded in agreement and began talking to one another. Rowe waited for the murmur to subside.

"Friends, we've been at war for a long time, and I know you're looking for news. We will get to that. But I first want to address the changes we have all experienced over the past few weeks."

A few outbursts rose from the crowd, and Rowe raised his hands to quiet them.

"As most of you are aware, the Niasa Sea has been lost to an outbreak of the plague known as Phyriad. Besides losing the only homeland they've ever known, the mer experienced heavy losses in the outbreak. Because Rainia Lake is the nearest body of salt water—and the safest—we insisted upon sharing our valley.

"For most of you, this is the first time you've seen the mer. Your children will point and ask questions. That's normal. But as we get to know one another, those differences will fade until one day they will no longer be noticeable. Until that time, I implore you: Talk to one another. Ask your questions. Make your observations. But open your hearts to those who are different from you."

Rowe turned to the crowd of mer. "And it needs to go both ways. Although the mer have lived alongside humans in Fairbay, the people of Rainia are strangers to you. It will take time to adjust, but you are welcome here."

Another rush of chatter spread through the crowd as a few humans and mer ventured from their comfort zones and moved closer to each other. But most remained where they stood.

Rowe nodded at Ryowyn, and Will felt her body tense. He squeezed her hand, then let go. She took a deep breath and stepped forward.

"My name is Ryowyn Ayoust, daughter of Ryodan and Almithara Ayoust, king and queen of the mer." She did not have to point to her parents, whose presence dominated the pier. "I come to you this night with a heavy heart. Our people have lost so much. But hope remains in my heart because, like many of you, we have found a new home here in this valley. You have greeted us with open arms. For that, we have no words to convey our gratitude. We will never forget those we leave behind, but we will move forward together toward healing, toward feeling whole again. Tears will one day be replaced with laughter. I believe this to be true with all my heart."

The crowd responded more favorably to her words than to Rowe's. There were voices of agreement and blessing, and many heads nodded. The space between mer and human grew smaller. Ryowyn bowed before moving away from the edge, then stood next to Will.

Without hesitation, a towering figure in a pressed uniform of blue and gold stepped forward. He walked along the pier for a few yards, hands tucked behind his back. His tangled gray eyebrows knit together as he studied the crowd. After a gravelly cough, he smoothed a hand over his trimmed but thinning gray hair and projected his powerful voice as only a lifelong military man could.

"My name is Brigadier Twell Henowing, commander of the Marauders. Many of you are hoping for news from Enders Brigade." He paused as if waiting for complete attention, but it was unnecessary. "We received an update this afternoon. About a week ago, Enders Brigade met the North Gnome Army for battle near the Nameless Forest. But the battle did not go as expected. It appears we were wrong about some of the gnome armies, namely the highland gnomes. Queen Sidara and Uluk the Shadowfallen deceived them. The highland gnomes thought they were fighting for their land, but they were mere pawns to spread Phyriad and poison the Fourwinds. After learning of Uluk's plans to infect all races—including gnomes—Brigadier Bayard and the gnome commander tried to negotiate terms of peace. Unfortunately, the gnome army had already been infected. The few who survived were supposed to meet a contingent of Enders Brigade and come here."

Shouts of defiance burst from the crowd. Twell clamped his mouth tight and folded his thick arms across his broad chest. Will understood the commander's agitation but also sympathized with the crowd; he, too, had resisted the news when he'd first heard it.

He had seen firsthand how cruel the gnomes could be when he was a prisoner in the Clover Fields. But he had also witnessed the compassion and generosity of highland gnomes. The stark contrast between his experience of both suffering and mercy filled him with uncertainty. How could he forgive those who tortured him? On the other hand, how could he turn a blind eye to victims of a merciless dictator?

Twell waited for a minute, then turned to Rowe and lowered his voice. "I've said enough, Rowe. Back to you."

Rowe stepped forward, and the people grew quiet again.

"Please remember," Rowe said, "unity is vital to our survival and applies to all races, including gnomes. And…" he added, pointing to Dench and his companions sitting on a grassy bank away from the crowds, "half-orcs. Remember how difficult it was to welcome them. But after their heroic efforts at the South Crow Gate, I am glad we did. Someday, we might say the same of gnomes."

There were still a few grumbling complaints, but there were more nods of agreement—or at least resignation.

"Enders Brigade will arrive at the North Crow Gate by tomorrow evening," Rowe continued. "We will first need to clear them to ensure none are infected with Phyriad, but after that, they will be free to reunite with those of you who have awaited their safe arrival."

Rowe glanced at Morgan and Will, then concluded his speech.

"One last word about the safety and security of this valley. There are now greater threats to the Fourwinds than war. Beyond this valley, the sickness that we call Phyriad is ravaging the land. If it has infected the population of Dwenlin Thah *and* the highland gnomes that Brigadier Henowing referred to, then it is only a matter of time before we see the infected at our doorstep. We must be ready to protect this valley at all costs. It is possible that we are the genesis of a new era in the Fourwinds."

Will expected a barrage of questions—his own mind was swimming with them—but a spirit of quiet acquiescence settled over the gathering.

Rowe offered a few final words. "For everything you have endured recently, for your hard work defending and rebuilding this valley…and for your work in the uncertain days ahead, I offer my gratitude. I wish this night could be one of celebration, but that night will have to wait. Tonight's gathering is an opportunity to cease our labor and come together to remind each other of the importance of this great, unified work."

Rowe stepped away from the edge of the pier to scattered applause, and people resumed their mingling. He joined Will, Morgan, and Ryowyn as the mer soldiers escorted their king and queen from the pier. Twell had already disappeared.

"Did that go as expected?" Will asked Rowe.

"Slightly better, actually."

"I'm glad you didn't say anything about the dragon," Will said.

Ryowyn was wide-eyed. "Dragon?"

Will took her hand and lowered his voice. "This afternoon, the three of us saw a dragon fly above the Misty Gorge. It was heading south, so we think we're safe for now."

"Natas?" Ryowyn breathed.

Will shook his head. "We think it was the Red Dragon, or what used to be General Raric."

"But what if it attacks the valley?" Ryowyn said. "Even a heavily fortified wall cannot stop a dragon."

"I believe there is a way—" Rowe began.

"I thought we had agreed to discuss this with Joe," Morgan interrupted.

"Yes, we did," Will said with a small sigh. "In fact, here he is now."

Joe reached the top of the stairs and joined the two couples. "Well done, Rowe. I sense that your words were well received… for the most part."

Will wanted to get straight to the point. "Joe, something happened this afternoon, and we need your input." He scanned the busy beach, then turned around. "Maybe we could all go to the end of the pier where it's not so crowded?"

After hearing the account of the dragon sighting, Joe stood leaning against his walking stick. He seemed to be more interested in the small waves splashing the posts that supported the pier—and maybe he was—but then he looked at each of the young faces watching him.

"We have no shortage of enemies and a glaring lack of resources," he said.

"Johanissan, are you familiar with the stories of thunderclaps hidden in Acttun?" Rowe asked.

Joe offered a single nod as his eyes narrowed.

Rowe rested a hand on the hilt of his sword. "I believe we should leave immediately to find the thunderclaps and bring them here to defend against a potential dragon attack."

"We still have refugees arriving at the gates," Morgan added, her words tumbling over each other. "Enders Brigade should be here by this time tomorrow. And we can *hope* the gnomes are untouched by Phyriad, but what if we're faced with an epidemic at our doorstep?"

Rowe crossed his arms and moved his feet apart slightly. "We will be ready to defend the North Crow Gate, especially if we have Enders Brigade to help us."

"What if that dragon attacks the valley?" Will asked, turning to Rowe. "Could we shoot it down?"

Rowe was shaking his head. "Even the best archers could not penetrate dragon hide. We need more powerful weapons. I could take a small team to Acttun and be back within five days."

"A lot can happen in five days," Morgan countered. "Look what happened at the South Crow Gate in *three* days! We almost lost *everything*."

Will stared at Morgan, sharing her frustration. They were backed into a corner, and if they didn't act soon, Natas would continue to have the upper hand. He turned to Joe. "What do you think?"

Joe was silent a moment, then pointed back down the pier. "I think this messenger might help us decide."

A young soldier wearing the blue-and-gold uniform of the Marauders Brigade approached, closely followed by two people wearing dark cloaks. The messenger's face was red and flustered, but the strangers' hoods were up, masking their faces.

Rowe shot a glance at Will, who quickly reassured him: "No harvesters."

"Excuse the interruption, sir," the messenger said to Rowe. "These two were among the last group of refugees we cleared from quarantine this evening. We told them they needed to go to the Crow's Nest with the others, but the man insisted on speaking with you immediately. I'm sorry, sir; he was…quite persuasive."

The couple remained in the shadows as the taller one spoke: "Pretty tight security around here, Rowe." He brushed past the messenger and pulled back his hood. "And you started a meeting without me?"

The stranger's name burst from Will's and Morgan's lips in unison: "Bremer!"

Rowe clasped the rogue's outstretched hand.

Will's breath caught in his throat. He hadn't been able to thank Bremer for saving his life and rescuing him from the Clover Fields, and now wanted to reach out and hug him. But Bremer wasn't one for hugs, and this wasn't the right moment. He fixed a somber gaze on Rowe.

"Actually, your timing is perfect, as usual," Rowe said. "We just received news from the battlefront and were discussing our next steps." He dismissed the soldier. "Thank you, that will be all."

"Well, you'll want to hear what I have to say," Bremer said. "I've just come from Dwenlin Thah. The capital is no more."

The group let out a collective groan. Joe inhaled sharply, and Rowe placed a hand on the railing as if to steady himself.

"What does that mean?" Will asked. "What happened?"

"Well, kid, after you and I were separated at the Clover Fields, a gnome guard who preferred to keep his life told me that the North Gnome Army was transporting Phyriad in a small cart. I started tracking them. By the time I discovered that they'd taken the cart to the capital under cover of darkness, I was too late. When I got there, the city was already infected."

"And you managed to escape," Rowe said. "But not alone, I see."

Bremer turned to the other cloaked figure, who stepped forward and pulled back her hood.

"It's good to see you again, Rowe," the elderly woman said. "We have an interesting story to tell you."

CHAPTER 4
FOUR DAYS EARLIER

Deep within Dwenlin Thah's castle keep, in a small room atop the highest tower, the queen's governess, Brynlee Mason, slowly emerged from a cavernous sleep. She lay still for long quiet moments, not wanting to move her old bones just yet. The city outside was dead calm, and the lack of noise made her feel like she was the last person in the Fourwinds.

A second later, she awakened fully to the sound of a distant wailing moan. Deep coughing followed, and in that moment, Brynlee realized that life as she had always known it would soon become a memory.

She sat up in her bed and pieced together events from the past few days. A brief meeting with Queen Alarra had gone poorly. Brynlee knew she had overstepped the boundaries of her station as governess by suggesting that the queen's brother, General Raric, would be coming for her head after he finished with Uluk the Shadowfallen. But when soldiers from Raric's army arrived to warn of a two-wheeled cart full of poisoned maple syrup candy, Brynlee had confronted Alarra again.

"That family…" Brynlee had said, gasping. "D-distributing candy on the streets! They've poisoned the city! Alarra, you must do something!"

In response, the queen had offered a dismissive hand and a chilling voice: "Lock down the castle."

News of the order had spread through the city like a midsummer brushfire.

Brynlee had simply stared, helpless. Her despair was almost complete. All her efforts to raise Alarra from a curious child to a compassionate ruler had failed. The great city of Dwenlin Thah was doomed.

Later that night, Brynlee and a few of her close friends from the kitchen had tried to escape, but the lockdown proved too tight. Furious upon hearing the news, Alarra had imprisoned the kitchen workers in the dungeons to await trial for treason. Because of Brynlee's years of faithful service, the queen ordered that her governess be locked in her quarters with an armed guard outside her door. Alarra had spared Brynlee's life, but the charge of treason hung over her head, nonetheless.

Now, as the sounds of coughing, wailing, and pleas for royal aid rose from beyond the keep, Brynlee resigned herself to her fate. Even if she survived the plague, the penalty for treason was death. She rolled over onto her back and sighed. *So be it.*

The clamor outside subsided for a moment, and she sensed a presence in the room. Her body stiffened. She lowered her eyes, peering over her small bed into the shadows across the tiny room. Beside a small armoire, a man stood with hands tucked behind his back, watching her.

Brynlee inhaled sharply and froze. The man stepped into the dim light shining through the window. His face was hidden beneath the cowl of a deep hood, but his long cloak was open in the front. He was clad entirely in black. Across his broad chest was a leather vest, cinched tight with a belt that held half a dozen throwing knives. He wore a sword on each hip, with a bow slung over one shoulder.

As Brynlee leaned closer, trying to see his face, the man pushed back his hood. He was bald and clean-shaven, his scalp and face weathered and scarred. Despite his dangerous appearance, he was handsome, Brynlee thought, and…familiar.

"Mother," he breathed.

Brynlee inhaled sharply, fully awake now, and fully alive.

"Bremer?" she whispered. "Can it really be you?" She had dreamed of him so often through the years, and now that her dreams had darkened, she doubted what she was seeing.

"Here I am, Mother," he whispered, kneeling at her bedside. He took her hand into his own as they stared at one another.

"My son," she said. "How did you find me?" She glanced at the door. "How did you get into the castle?"

"Too many questions and too little time, Mother." He gave her frail hand a gentle squeeze. "I'm getting you out of here. To the safety of the Crow's Nest."

"Has the valley suffered the same fate as Dwenlin Thah?"

Bremer shook his head. "Rainia is sound. I will take you there."

"Are the Callum Sages still with us?"

He smiled but hung his head and averted her eyes. "They are few, but strong."

"Can they stave off this darkness spreading across the Fourwinds?"

"I believe they can. But we have more urgent matters to consider. People in this city are leaving their dwellings, but they're no longer human."

Brynlee brought a hand to her mouth. "Wh-what are they? What's happened? Is it true what Raric's messengers said about—"

"Phyriad. I'm afraid so." Bremer stood and glanced at the small armoire. "I need you to get dressed and ready now, Mother. No fancy court dresses for you today. Do you still have riding pants and boots?"

She nodded.

"Very good. Wear a light chemise because the days are hot. And bring a warm riding cloak for the cool evenings."

"But how will we make it through the city if the streets are unsafe?"

"The manner in which Phyriad passes from one person to another is unclear, but I do know we need to stay away from anyone we think is infected. Bring a kerchief to wear around your nose and mouth, and I'll keep us as far away from them as possible. I will not lie to you: it will be difficult leaving the city."

"There's a guard posted at my door… How will we—"

Bremer leaned down and placed a finger on her lips. "Do not concern yourself with such things." He stood and moved to the door, turning his back to her. "Please get dressed now, Mother."

When Brynlee was ready, she tugged Bremer's cloak. Without turning, he pulled his hood over his head and slowly opened the door. As they entered the quiet hallway, Brynlee touched the doorjamb and, feeling something wet, pulled away to see fresh blood on her fingertips.

Bremer took her hand and wiped the blood clean with his sleeve. "When I left this place, you were a mother to the queen. Now I find you under lock and key, with an armed guard stationed at your door. What happened?"

She nodded and smiled despite the thumping in her chest. "Does your tongue ever get you into trouble, son?"

Bremer led the way down the hall toward the stairwell. "All the time."

"Well, I hate to break it to you, but you won't be outgrowing that. It's in your blood."

Bremer chuckled as they descended the winding steps. "But I don't understand what risk you could pose, Mother…to anyone."

"I know too much. I know Alarra's past, her secrets, her plans, and her deepest fears. I've seen the trail of blood she's left, and I know where all the bodies are buried."

Bremer paused on a step. "But you've been caring for her longer than I've been alive."

"As you know, power can change people. And now that she knows my faith in her leadership is gone, she's terrified that I will betray her. That's why—"

The sound of shuffling footsteps in the stairwell far below interrupted her.

"Come," Bremer whispered. "We're out of time."

A narrow doorway opened in the wall where Bremer had pushed, and before she could react, he pulled her inside. She bent low and stepped in beside him. The locking mechanism clicked as the door closed.

"I've used this stairwell so many times," Brynlee whispered in the dark. "I had no idea…"

A small spark flared, lighting the secret passage. Brynlee raised her eyebrows when she saw the sunstone in Bremer's hand.

"I *was* a Callum Sage, Mother."

"Yes, I remember. Keepers of secrets."

Bremer led them through a rough-walled passage so narrow

they had to walk sideways through most of it. When they came to an apparent dead end, Brynlee peered past her son but could see nothing within the glow of the sunstone.

"How are you with ladders?" Bremer asked, stretching out his hand.

A few steps in front of him was an iron ladder bolted to the wall and leading down into a narrow opening in the floor.

"If it means getting out of this place, I'll be fine."

"This ladder will take us straight down into the catacombs. It's a long way down, and some of these walls are thin, so we must remain as quiet as possible. And there are cracks in the mortar, so I'll need to put out the light."

Brynlee nodded, and without warning, he turned and wrapped his bulky arms around her frail form. He held her in a tight embrace for a long, quiet moment. She hugged him back, surprised by the show of affection, but breathing deep the sweet aroma of hope.

After close to an hour navigating the underbelly of the castle, Bremer and Brynlee approached what looked like another dead end. Bremer released a lock hidden near the floor and placed his ear against the stone wall. After listening for a moment, he pushed, and a doorway opened. A rush of musty air greeted them.

The light of a single lantern hanging from a low beam in the center of the small room revealed a hay-covered floor, old wagon wheels, and an assortment of rusty farm tools linked by cobwebs. A thick film of dust covered everything. Bremer took his mother's hand and walked toward the door on the opposite side of the room.

"Where in the Fourwinds are we?" she said.

"This is the rear storage room of the Wild Blossom Stables."

"Amazing," Brynlee said. "That's about eight blocks from the castle."

Beyond the door, a horse huffed. Bremer stopped. "This is as close to the curtain wall as we can get underground. From here, we must ride through the open streets to one of the small service gates. Do you think you can—"

"I may look a hundred years old to you, young man, but I can still ride a horse."

Bremer nodded slowly, studying her determined gaze. "Very well. But I'll need you in the saddle with me lest we become separated."

She jabbed a forefinger into his side and smiled. "Aww, that's sweet. You just want your mother close to you."

When they reached the far door, Bremer pulled it open a crack and saw someone lying in a pile of hay near the first in a series of horse stalls. The person wheezed between a bout of barking coughs. Bremer stepped back to see his mother tying a long blue kerchief around her neck and over her mouth and nose.

"Wait here," he said.

Bremer was fairly certain he was looking at the stable hand he had paid handsomely to have a certain mare ready to go. Sweat soaked the man's hair and gray tunic. A dark rash covered the back of his neck. Having already encountered those infected with Phyriad, Bremer sensed the danger. His experience at the Stoneberg wall on the way to the Waerdreath had taught him about the vicious, unpredictable nature of someone transformed by Phyriad. He drew a dagger from his belt and approached with caution.

The stable hand turned his head enough for Bremer to see that it was, in fact, the person he had paid. But now crusted phlegm smeared the man's face. Some was dripping from his nose. Even his eyes, red and drawn, were oozing as they glared at Bremer.

The man lunged for Bremer's feet with extraordinary speed considering how sick he looked. Bremer threw the dagger and followed with another for good measure. The man's horrible wheezing stopped instantly, and he collapsed on the floor.

Bremer grabbed a pitchfork, tossed some hay over the body, and rushed to check the horse stalls. He sighed in relief when he found the large brown mare wearing a tandem saddle. At least the stable hand had finished his task.

Bremer ran to the main stable gate and peeked through the cracks. Several people stumbled past, their wheezing loud and gruesome. He eased the gate open just enough to allow a horse to pass through.

When he rushed back to the horse, Bremer was surprised to see his aged mother resting comfortably in the saddle. "I thought I told you—"

"Stop wasting time and get up here!"

He pulled himself up in the seat in front of her. "The next few minutes could prove interesting." He reached for a long spear leaning against the wall, then nudged the mare forward through the gate.

Outside, three people hobbled down the center of the street. Two looked sickly, with rashes on their exposed skin. They clawed at themselves with talon-like fingernails. The third person walked in a straighter line than the others, although his bare arms were covered in a dark, scaly rash. He also seemed much stronger, and when he glanced at Bremer, his eyes flickered fiery red.

The horrors of the three beasts that Bremer had killed at the Stoneberg crucifixions flashed in his memory. But there was no time to fight now. A dozen crazed people crashed through doors and windows into the street, instantly giving chase to the horse and riders like a pack of starving wolves.

Bremer kicked the horse's flanks to spur it into a gallop, but the mare had already responded to the threat. Infected people poured from the surrounding buildings. Forced to turn down a cross street to avoid the growing numbers, Bremer yanked the reins so fast that the mare almost lost her footing on the cobblestone lane. He swung the spear like a club, striking several people who snatched at his legs. No matter how fast the horse moved, people emerged from buildings all around. Bremer knew if he stopped even for a few seconds, there would be no escaping this nightmare.

He turned left down another street, then charged toward a small gate in the curtain wall, shouting at the top of his lungs, "Open the gate! Open the gate!"

Bremer's goblin companion reversed the gate controls and worked the cranks as quickly as his small arms would allow. The mare galloped through the opening. A dozen people slipped through before Urk could close the gate, but it didn't matter because, outside the city walls, hundreds of people stumbled around like diseased cattle.

Bremer refused to slow until they were far from the crowds.

"How did so many—" He turned in his saddle to see the massive main gates open wide. Some of the infected were attacking the scores of refugees camped outside the city, while others moved south.

"Look at them all," Brynlee breathed as she loosened her tight grip around Bremer's waist. "Where are they going?"

High above the rolling hills, an enormous iron-gray dragon led the infected masses through the forested lowlands.

"Almost looks like Natas is leading them toward Acttun," Bremer said. "If so, we'll need to burn up the miles to keep ahead of them because that's the route we're taking. The main road through Acttun is the fastest route to the Rainia Valley."

Bremer slapped the reins, and the mare resumed a gallop. He rode in silence, focused on the path ahead. Now that Phyriad was spreading throughout the Fourwinds, events would spiral out of control. He had not planned to rescue his mother, but lately, very few things were going according to plan. He tossed aside every thought beyond getting her to safety and warning his old friend Rowe.

CHAPTER 5

THUNDERCLAPS

The flame of a lantern on the mantel fluttered softly as Bremer and his mother concluded their story. When Brynlee had begun the story of their escape from Dwenlin Thah, Rowe stopped her, saying that the pier was not the best environment for such a conversation. The security of the valley was critical, and he was not sure everyone in Rainia was trustworthy. A secluded room on the second floor of the old mill, recently renovated to accommodate the new Recovery Ale House and Inn, would be more suitable.

Will stood in silence beside Rowe, guarding the door. Joe sat in a chair next to them, staring at the floor. On the simple four-poster bed, Morgan, Julie, and Ryowyn leaned forward, listening to the incredible account. Bremer stood by the fireplace, his hand resting on his mother's shoulder as she shifted in the stuffed leather armchair. The room was warm, but Brynlee was still shaking.

"Had another hour gone by," Bremer said, "there would have been no way to escape Dwenlin Thah." He paused as Brynlee reached to her shoulder and patted his hand. "I knew there was only one place for us to go. We would have arrived much sooner, but—"

Three sharp taps on the door interrupted Bremer, and Rowe quickly opened the door. Gloriana entered carrying a large platter filled with goblets and small bowls, a loaf of bread, a large pitcher of water, and a pot of what smelled like Hansla's famous chowder. She placed the platter on the small table in the middle of the room and filled the goblets with water. Will and Morgan helped pass them to the others while Julie sliced the bread.

Rowe sipped some water and swallowed hard. "Thank you, Gloriana. You were saying, Bremer?"

Gloriana handed a bowl of chowder to Brynlee as Bremer continued.

"Near the Mofard Flats, we saw a dragon strafing a section of forest with fire from its mouth. A *red* dragon. We had to stay hidden for a few hours. Any idea where that thing came from?"

Joe stood from his chair and stretched his back. "I can answer that."

"You remember Johanissan, Bremer," Rowe said.

"Of course. I heard rumors you had returned, but…" Bremer trailed off as Joe took a slice of bread and moved across the room to the curtained window.

"I returned to the Fourwinds just in time to assist the druid Margrave," Joe said. "General Raric—the Dragon Killer, some call him—wanted a way to defeat Uluk the Shadowfallen. So, he came to Margrave seeking the hide of Scarlas as armor."

"Dragon melding," Bremer said. "But that's—"

"Impossible?" Joe shook his head. "Improbable, yes. But Margrave agreed, and the melding was…somewhat successful. We are still unsure whether Raric's soul will be strong enough to survive in his new form."

"Was the dragon attacking people, Bremer?" Rowe asked.

Bremer shrugged. "We were too far away. But whatever was in that forest is no more."

"Did you notice what direction it flew off in?" Will asked.

Bremer shook his head. "We were long gone before it finished with the forest, but I can tell you it looked half asleep the way it was flying. It dropped several times, banking wildly as if it momentarily forgot how to fly. Even the way it gained altitude was strange. Its wings worked far too hard for what it was trying to do. Every movement seemed strained and uncertain."

"Raric still fights for survival," Joe said.

The room went quiet again.

"Please," Gloriana said after a moment. "You all need to eat."

No one spoke as Morgan and Julie filled bowls and handed them to the others.

Rowe stirred his chowder idly, gazing into the bowl as he outlined the implications of Bremer and Brynlee's story.

"Dwenlin Thah has fallen. Hammerclaw is already destroyed. Fairbay and the Niasa Sea are uninhabitable. Now, General Raric could become a threat. The destructive power of Natas is spreading east, leaving the Crow's Nest as the last remaining stronghold in the Fourwinds. The Iron Dragon has reached every major city except…" Rowe looked up at Bremer. "We must go to Acttun. And we must leave at dawn."

"Acttun?" Bremer brushed some bread crumbs from his bottom lip. "Why would you want to go back there? It's bad enough at the best of times, but who knows how long it will be before part of that infected horde reaches the city. We intentionally went around it on our way here."

"We must protect this valley, Bremer," Rowe said. "The North

Crow Gate is strong, but we are vulnerable should a dragon attack from above."

Bremer's face darkened. "What do you have in mind?"

"The wizard, Marlay Bonicle, may have left some thunderclaps in a vault in his study," Rowe said. "I've been trying to figure out how to open the vault."

Bremer nodded slowly. "Thunderclaps could work against a dragon. And I've never met a lock I couldn't pick."

"The lock could be magically sealed," Rowe said. "I have an alchemist named Dadore who's been working on a way to open it. But he is uncertain if it will work without knowing what type of vault we would be dealing with."

Bremer huffed. "Shades, Rowe! The vault could be the least of your worries. Who knows what lies in the asylum? I've spent time nosing around that place. There's something inside those walls. And, as far as I could tell, some of the infected horde from Dwenlin Thah was heading for Acttun."

Morgan's bowl clattered on the table as she set it down. "Don't you think going to Acttun is risky?"

"Sure, it's risky," Bremer said, "but so's being here in the valley."

Rowe sighed. "I am confident we will find thunderclaps in the asylum."

Morgan opened her mouth to speak, but Rowe held up his hands. "It's late. Tomorrow morning, we will all meet at the North Crow Gate to discuss our options."

"I agree," Brynlee said. The leather chair creaked as she leaned forward, and Bremer helped her to her feet. "I've had enough adventure lately, and these old bones are in desperate need of a soft bed."

CHAPTER 6
Alyssa Returns

It was almost midnight when Will and Ryowyn arrived at their new home, an old cottage on the northeastern shore of Rainia Lake. Its previous owner, a loyal friend of Rowe's named Tranas, had died in the battle to defend the South Crow Gate. Rowe had spoken of fond memories fishing off the dock with Tranas. But he told Will that fresh memories have a way of honoring old ones, and that Tranas would want someone like Will living there.

The cottage was the ideal location for Will and Ryowyn. Will needed a quiet place to recuperate after the horrors of the Waerdreath, imprisonment in the Clover Fields, a journey to the Maidstone, and a narrow escape from the destruction of Fairbay. The cottage also provided proximity to Ryowyn's people and family. The mer would need stability and strong leadership in the days ahead.

Will dismounted from the horse and helped Ryowyn down. After riding for almost two hours with her body pressed against his back, he was glad to see her face again. The full moon made her dazzling blue eyes sparkle.

Ryowyn wrapped her arms around him. "You've told me about Acttun, but what do *you* think of Rowe's plan?"

A shiver raced down Will's back. He wasn't sure if it was the thrill of her touch or the fear of going back to Acttun. "I don't want to leave you."

"That was not my question."

Will pulled her closer as he sifted through the options that scrambled in his head. "Part of me would like to go with Rowe. And if Bremer went, there'd be no lack of adventure. We still have so much to do before any of us can think about a normal life again…whatever that is. And I *am* a Callum Sage, after all. I know I've changed since coming to the Fourwinds. I'm not the guy I was back home in Cochrane, but…" He gazed up at the clear, starry night. "I feel so small, Ryowyn. And…afraid."

Her head tilted back, and her hair spilled over her shoulders. She flashed a smile. "I still have difficulty believing you were frightened when you rescued me in that barn back in Fairbay."

Will chuckled. "Terrified, Ryowyn. I was terrified."

"And yet, you saw my need and fought the slave runners. And here we are, alive and well. Together."

"Sometimes I feel like I have more luck than brains. And definitely more luck than brawn."

She took his face in her hands and kissed him softly. "Fortune smiles on you, my Will. Despite the trouble, pain, and sorrow we have experienced. Despite what many say about the gods forsaking the Fourwinds. And despite your doubts and fears. We are not alone, and we will get through this together."

Will shook his head in wonder. "How did I ever—"

Ryowyn pressed her fingers to his lips and smiled again. "You are more than enough for me. And…I say we still have time for a swim before bed."

She ran toward the back porch that spanned the length of the cottage and disappeared under the overhanging roof. Will led the horse to the small stable for a well-deserved drink and a bucket of oats.

Less than ten yards from the lake, Will draped his cloak over a split-rail fence. He gazed out at the calm water, then removed his shirt.

Ryowyn returned with a cup of water just as Will kicked off his second boot. He pulled off his sweaty socks and tossed them next to his boots. As he enjoyed a long drink, Ryowyn tugged his belt, urging him onto the dock. Her bare feet slapped the planks, and a moment later, there was a soft splash.

Ryowyn was as comfortable naked as she was clothed, which Will assumed was quite natural for a mermaid. But despite how confident he was around her, he still glanced self-consciously at the dark shores as he slipped off his pants. He took a few quick steps, drew in a breath, and dove off the end of the dock. Ryowyn swam around him as he floated lazily to the surface.

Will swam out about fifty yards, then returned to the dock. He pulled himself up just as Ryowyn sailed over his head and landed with a gentle thump. Water glistened off her teal skin as she transformed and stood on her feet again. The seamless change still baffled Will, and he often wondered if being on land for too long affected her. For now, she appeared to be healthy in or out of the water. And as long as they were together, Will was content to set aside his wondering.

Ryowyn held out her hand, and he followed her into the cottage as weariness overtook him.

Early-morning sunlight streamed through the wooden shutters of the large window in Will and Ryowyn's bedroom. Outside, a crow landed on the edge of the roof and cawed three times, then flew away. Will squinted at the window, rolled over, and closed his eyes again. He wanted a few more minutes to enjoy his dream where he and Ryowyn were jumping off the dock and swimming with all their friends. But as the dream resurfaced, he was suddenly alone. The scene darkened. He leapt off the dock to search for Ryowyn, but instead of splashing into the water, he crashed through a thin layer of ice.

Will shot from his sleep, gasping for breath. The dream that had haunted him back in Cochrane had not visited him for weeks, and he refused now to let it back into his subconscious. He lay in silence as his pulse slowed. The bedroom was still, the only sound coming from Ryowyn's steady breathing as she slept undisturbed. That was strange, he thought; she was normally a very light sleeper. But something had woken him, something more than a nightmare or a crow.

He scanned the bedroom. Beyond the footboard of their bed, the seven-foot-tall armoire was open enough for him to see that nothing was hiding in it. The long dresser on Ryowyn's side of the bed was undisturbed, decorated with mementos from the Niasa Sea: shells, fossils, and dried flowers. On Will's side, his shotgun leaned against the bedside table where his loaded Springfield 1911 handgun rested.

Will slipped from beneath the thin sheet and pulled on his trousers and T-shirt that he had folded on a chair last night. He grabbed the shotgun and tiptoed from the bedroom to the large open area that made up most of the cabin. There was no sign of an intruder. In the kitchen, pots and pans hung from the rough-hewn beams above the iron stove. The handcrafted cupboards along the far wall were all closed. A stack of dishes that Will had left on the slate countertop waited to be put away. In the living room lined with shelves buckling under the weight of books and artifacts, a few chairs and two brightly upholstered settees sat empty and unruffled. The cabin was empty. But the sense of something out of the ordinary would not let Will rest.

He walked out the back door and paused when he spied two people out on the dock. Shielding his eyes from the bright sun, he set the shotgun down on the porch when he recognized Morgan, seated in a deck chair facing him. The other woman, with dark hair cascading over her shoulders, sat in a chair with her back to Will.

He stepped onto the dock, and the woman turned. Her icy-blue eyes and powerful presence drew him closer. She rose from the chair and smiled, smoothing her plain sky-blue gown. Morgan also stood, nodding and wearing a broad smile.

"Mom?" Will breathed, wondering if he was still dreaming.

"Here I am," Alyssa said with outstretched arms.

Will rushed into her embrace. No one spoke as he held her tight. Hot tears, mingled with joy, sadness, confusion, and other indescribable emotions, soaked her dress. After a few minutes, his mother placed her hands firmly on his shoulders and inched him back to arm's length. Will stared through teary eyes, sniffling several times.

"Yes, it's really me," she said.

"How…? Where've you…?" Will's heart was thumping. "I've missed you so much."

A pang of regret flashed in her eyes. "I'm so sorry, Will."

"No, Mom. Don't blame yourself for doing what you had to do. I've often wondered if our meeting at the Waerdreath was real or a dream. I had hoped to see you again when I was near death in the Clover Fields, or when I went to the Maidstone." He glanced at Morgan and out at the lake. "And maybe this is just another dream—"

"This is no dream, Will," Morgan said. "She's really here."

"I'm so sorry I wasn't there in your times of need," Alyssa said, lowering her hands. "But it was too risky for me. It still is. But times are changing. Our enemy has grown stronger and bolder. The fate of the Fourwinds hangs in the balance."

Will took her hands in his own. "It's okay, Mom. I survived, thanks to Morgan and our new friends. And a little help from a flying unicorn named Thaudas." He glanced back at the cottage. "And I married a princess, Mom, an actual princess. Almost a fairy tale if not for the fact that there's no happy ending in sight…yet."

Alyssa grinned. "I've seen what you've become, son, and I'm so proud of you. But I fear our time is short."

"What do you mean?"

"Sit with me," she said, motioning to a third chair.

Will dragged the chair next to his mother's, and they all sat.

"The Iron Dragon, Natas, will not attack as long as I remain in hiding," Alyssa said.

"I don't understand."

"Natas fears reprisal from me."

"You could kill Natas?" Will quickly scanned her delicate features, her smooth skin, and thin arms. "No offense, but…how?"

"A few years ago, Natas returned and threatened to destroy the Fourwinds. Around that time, I crashed through the frozen Frederick House River back in Cochrane. When I understood the chaos that Natas was creating, I had to leave you and your father, trusting that you'd be well. I'm sorry for the hardship that caused. But the need here was too great. Although I cannot stop the Iron Dragon's evil influence, my presence prevents complete destruction and gives strength to those who fight for good."

Will blinked several times. He recognized the outward appearance of his mother, but she spoke like a complete stranger. "Who *are* you?"

Alyssa laughed softly. "I wish I could say more, but my time is short today. We have a problem, Will. The Red Dragon has returned to the Fourwinds."

"I know. We saw him yesterday, from a distance. Joe thinks Raric might still be in there somehow."

"As do I. When General Raric accepted the dragon melding, he risked unleashing the full power of Scarlas. If Raric cannot control the soul of the Red Dragon, Scarlas will win the inner battle and join forces with Natas. And I cannot ward off both dragons."

"There might be another way," Will said. "Rowe is trying to find something called a thunderclap in the asylum in Acttun. He wants to go there today, but we haven't decided who's going with him." He flicked his eyes in Morgan's direction, but she said nothing.

Alyssa nodded. "Morgan and I have already discussed your dilemma. Rowe is correct: there are three boxes of thunderclaps in a vault in Marlay's office on the top floor. They must be brought to this valley as soon as possible. And you must go with him, Will."

Will leaned back in his chair and met Morgan's gaze. He wondered how she felt about this and if she still wanted to join them.

Morgan sat up straight. "I don't want either of you to go Acttun, Will. It's a dangerous place. But I also understand that the thunderclaps could help us defend the valley."

"Rowe of the Nest plays an important role here," Alyssa said. "The Callum Sages are needed to defeat Natas, but they cannot do so alone. None of us can. It will take a unified effort from a diverse and unexpected group. You two have been brought to the Fourwinds for a reason. Both of you are vital to the healing of this land."

Will looked at Morgan, who was staring at his mother. Clearly, this was news to her as well.

"We need you both," Alyssa continued. "The two of you have been called into this story, and you must work together. But if one should fall, the other must take up the banner."

Will lowered his head and massaged his leg. The fracture he had suffered while in the Clover Fields had healed, but the memory remained. He knew what it was like to fall and be knocked out of the action.

"I've always trusted you, Will," Morgan said. "And I trust Rowe with my life. I'm willing to stand with you guys, whatever happens."

Will scratched his bare arm, trying to erase the sudden goose bumps. "Thanks, Morgan. And I trust both you and Rowe. I appreciate what you said, Mom, but I'm not sure I'm ready for another adventure on my own. I couldn't have survived the Clover Fields and the Maidstone without help."

Morgan nodded. "I don't know where we'd be without Rowe's leadership defending the South Crow Gate."

The three sat in silence for a moment before Alyssa stood. "The dragons must be fought," she said. "And there's still work to do to secure the valley. But as I said, our time is short. Will, what would you advise?"

Will looked at her, wondering if she was speaking to the right guy. He was the one who needed advice. He was a follower, not a leader. But here was his mother and one of his best friends waiting for his direction.

"Well…I could go with Rowe to Acttun, and, Morgan, you could stay at the North Crow Gate with Dench, Twell, and the Marauders. We need you there to maintain the protocols." He glanced at the sword at her side. "And if needed, you could help protect the valley better than I would."

Morgan stood next to Alyssa. "I really don't want us to be separated again," she said, "but I understand that we all have strengths and need to do whatever we can."

Will wiped his clammy hands on his thighs, trying to calm his jittery nerves. Planning an adventure was not his strength. But there was more to it than that. He worried for his friends. All the stress of the past few weeks threatened to break apart the bonds they'd formed on their first trip across the Fourwinds.

"You have to promise me something, Morgan," he said. "You need to tell Rowe how you're feeling. If you're really concerned about him going to Acttun…well, let him know. Life's too fragile."

Morgan's shoulders slumped as she nodded. "You're right. Is it that obvious?"

"As plain as that dragon we saw."

Alyssa smiled. "I have confidence in both of you. Now, go. Awaken Ryowyn and leave for the North Crow Gate immediately. I'd love to meet my new daughter-in-law, but that'll have to wait for another day."

CHAPTER 7

FOR BETTER OR FOR WORSE

From sunrise to sunset, the North Crow Gate was a loud place to be. Between the incessant sawing, hammering, yelling back and forth, and the high-pitched ringing of iron and steel from the blacksmith shops, it was not a peaceful setting. But the workers pressed on, determined to restore peace to their beloved valley.

Will, Ryowyn, and Morgan rode through the passage between the two walls, weaving their way toward the gatehouse for their morning meeting with Rowe. Clouds of dust drifted among the bustle, never quite finding a place to settle until the activity finished for the day. Workers had started building the roof over the first wall using wooden beams and cedar shakes, but after yesterday's dragon sighting, they were replacing wood with steel. A crane arm operated by four barrel-chested men swung overhead, carrying one of four new ballistae to be mounted atop the second wall. Each ballista was constructed of iron and steel, and only the swing arms were made of wood.

Will stood in his stirrups to see over a crowd of workers. Gray-haired craftsmen with calloused hands and a fierce work ethic were assembling another ballista. Around them, workers carried large metal plates to be mounted in front of the weapons. Will was curious how well those defenses would protect the shooters from the flames of a dragon's breath weapon. But these days left no room for doubt or indecision, only action.

After leaving their horses at the main stable, Will, Ryowyn, and Morgan made their way up the stone stairway to the gatehouse. Dench met them outside the door. The large half-orc stood with thick arms folded across his expansive chest. His battle-ax leaned against the wall within arm's reach.

"Good morning, Dench," Morgan said. "Is the gatehouse locked?"

"Rowe said you t'ree and Joe de only odder people allowed in." Dench knocked twice, stepped aside, and swung the thick wooden door open for them.

Julie sat in an armless chair at a simple table surrounded by five empty chairs. Rowe stood by a window holding a large leather-bound volume. The look on his face reminded Will of his old math teacher, who used to lecture him on his tardiness.

"I'm sorry we're late," Will said. "We had an unexpected visitor early this morning."

"I was about to send someone to haul you from your bed," Rowe said with a casual smile.

"Where's Joe and Bremer?" Will asked.

"Johanissan went to visit Dadore. I wanted to meet with him—Dadore, that is—last night, but he wasn't in the mood for visitors. Johanissan said he gained experience in your world talking with people who have gone through loss and trauma, so he went to Dadore's wagon this morning. He should be joining us soon.

"And Bremer was in the Crow's Nest earlier this morning making sure his mother is settled and looked after. I hope he comes, but you know Bremer. He's on his own schedule."

Will smiled, nodding. "I can vouch for Joe's care. He was a big support to me when I first met him in Cochrane—when I thought he was only a cop."

"Who was your visitor?" Rowe asked.

Will looked at Julie, then back at Rowe. "My mom." He fidgeted with his hands, still processing their conversation on the dock. "I'm not sure how she got there, or where she went after, but—"

"Your mom?" Julie said. "But I thought she… How could she—"

"No," Morgan said. "Will's mom didn't die in that snowmobile accident back in Cochrane. She came back here to the Fourwinds where she's originally from."

Rowe closed the book. His eyes darted from Morgan to Julie, then back to Will. Apparently, news of Will's mom had caught Rowe off guard. "What…uh, what did she look like?"

"What do you mean? She looked like my mom."

Morgan cleared her throat the way people do to get someone's attention. She was looking at Rowe as if he were hiding something behind his back and it was time to reveal the secret.

Will removed his Trannalun cloak and draped it over the back of a chair. "Before we discuss anything more, I'd like some answers. I should know more about my mom than any of you, but it seems like some of you know more about her than I do. And this morning, she talked like…like she was someone bigger than just my mom." He brushed a hand through his hair. "Rowe, you said you'd tell me more someday. I think today's the day."

"I agree," Morgan said.

Julie nodded with her eyes on Rowe as he walked to the table.

"Yes," Rowe said, speaking slowly. "You're right, Will; she *is* someone bigger than just your mom. When she appeared to you in the flames at the Waerdreath, she took her human form. But Alyssa has a more common form here in the Fourwinds. She chose that form when she appeared to Morgan and me in the Tuxan Mines, and when she rescued us from the Waerdreath. Alyssa—your mother—is the Ice Dragon."

"Dra-dragon?" Julie stammered.

"It's okay, Mom," Morgan said. "I know it's a lot to take in. But she's…uh…a *good* dragon."

Julie gaped at Morgan, scrunching her brow and slowly shaking her head.

Will leaned against the chair for support. Of all the incredible challenges he'd faced since coming to the Fourwinds, this was a curveball he had not expected. Yet, despite the enormous implications, the news did not shock him as much as it would have a month ago. Rather than surprise, Will felt relief. In fact, it filled him with a sense of hope and renewed purpose. And that surprised him even more.

"Okay," he said, nodding as he paced the floor. "You told me when we first met that she was powerful and unique. And that she might have returned to the Fourwinds three years ago to stand against Natas. I've often wondered what you meant. I saw a glimpse of who she really is when she appeared to me in the flames at the Waerdreath. But I…I should be shocked to hear that my mother's a dragon, but…I'm okay." He thought for another moment. "This explains why she left me three years ago, why she appeared to me in the Waerdreath, and how she protected me from Sidara's fire. And why she told me this morning about her power over Natas. It's weird and mind-blowing, but it's starting to make sense now."

Rowe raised his eyebrows. Apparently, he wasn't expecting that response. "So…what did she tell you this morning?"

"She's the reason Natas hasn't attacked. But she can't protect us from both Natas and whatever Raric has become. She said that you were right about the thunderclaps being in the asylum, and that we can't get them here quickly enough."

"How much time do we have?" Rowe asked.

Will shrugged. "Not long. She said Natas is leading a group of infected people to Acttun. The Red Dragon has been spending most of his time above the Hollowtangle until he showed up around here yesterday."

"Is there anything else?" Rowe asked.

Will nodded slowly. "She said I need to go with you to Acttun, and that Morgan should stay here at the gates."

"Agreed," Rowe said without hesitation. "The number of refugees coming to the valley has dropped significantly. It's possible that any threat of harvesters might be shifting to Acttun. I think we'll need your eyes more there than here." He scratched his scruffy cheek as he stifled a yawn. His eyes were bloodshot.

"You look bushed," Will said.

"I assume that means tired," Rowe said. "Yes. I was up late last night meeting with Ryodan. After that, Bremer and I met with Twell. Ryodan has offered four of his best mer soldiers to accompany us to Acttun. They will travel up the Serpentine River to avoid any potential confrontations along the way. Twell cannot afford to lose anyone from Marauders Brigade. And I agree; we need soldiers here at the gate, especially since we don't know how many of Enders Brigade will be fit for battle."

"Speaking of Enders Brigade," Julie said. "I would also like to keep Ryowyn here, Will." She addressed Ryowyn. "I could use your healing skills when the wounded soldiers arrive."

Ryowyn nodded enthusiastically. "I've been busy helping to get my people settled, but as soon as the soldiers arrive, please send for me, and I will bring others to help with the wounded."

"We've also asked Dadore to join us in Acttun," Rowe said. "He can help us get into Marlay's vault. Apparently, he has a potion that can dissolve the hinges. The problem is that he only has enough for two hinges, and I don't know if the vault has two or three. The Histories are unclear on the matter."

Will raised an eyebrow. "I don't know how you keep all those facts straight, Rowe. But…I really appreciate your leadership, especially after all you've been through the past few weeks." The last line came out a bit awkwardly, but he also remembered the pressure Rowe was under, and the tough choices he had to make daily. "I can't imagine going to Acttun without you."

"Is Dadore up for that kind of trip?" Morgan asked. "He doesn't seem too eager to go anywhere beyond his wagon."

Rowe sighed as he massaged his forehead. "Dadore is hurting. He lost his best friend, Kydaris, on the final night of the battle at the South Crow Gate. They were inseparable. And although he didn't always see eye to eye with Illious, he mourns the loss of his teacher, who also died that night." Rowe scraped a chair away from the table and sunk into it. "Dadore is struggling to figure out what life looks like without the only family he ever knew. I've visited him almost every day, as have Morgan and Joe. The only thing I can say with certainty is that Dadore, and only Dadore, can decide how to press on without Kydaris—without tevan root to ease the pain."

"Perhaps joining in this quest would renew his sense of purpose," Ryowyn suggested.

"I was thinking the same thing, Ryowyn," Julie said. "He needs to know that others care for him, but he also needs another opportunity to care for others."

"To be loved and to offer love," Morgan added. She looked at her mother. "Dad used to say that."

Julie nodded. "What about you, Will? You went through some difficult times when you lost your parents. What helped you get through?"

Will pulled out two chairs for himself and Ryowyn, and they sat close together. "Well, it's a miracle I didn't take my own life… like Dad did. I think back to all the confusion in my head and can't believe I made it through. Every day was dismal and gray. It wasn't until I met Morgan and Joe that I started to see color again. Simply knowing that someone accepted me for who I am… it made all the difference.

"Then we came to the Fourwinds, and I realized that my ability to see harvesters wasn't some freaky thing that scared people away; it was a gift. I could help save lives. Talk about a sense of purpose!

"So, did the rapid-fire adventures help the healing process? Who knows? It's all such a blur now. All I can say for sure is I'd be lost without my friends." Will paused. "But Dadore seems worse than I was, even in my darkest times."

Rowe nodded. "I hope Johanissan can get through to him."

"The thing about being such a mess in the head like I was," Will continued, "is that you don't understand what you need. Your mind gets whipped up into a frenzy, and common sense becomes a fleeting friend. You go with the flow because you're too tired to keep swimming upstream. Dadore's grasping for something to hold on to, as if he's desperate to get out of the rushing river."

Rowe lowered his head, wringing his hands in front of him. "It's my fault. I shouldn't have put so much responsibility on his shoulders at the South Crow Gate. He's so young…"

Morgan clicked her tongue. "You realize you're not the general manager of the universe, right?"

"What does that mean?" Rowe asked.

"If your ability to lead is determined by things beyond your control…well, how could anyone live under that kind of pressure?"

"You're right, Morgan. I know it up here," he said, tapping his temple, "but this is where the problem lies." He lowered his hand over his heart.

Before anyone could respond, there were two sharp knocks, and the door swung open. Joe entered, leaning on his staff and looking older than ever. His face, usually etched in some form of a smile, was slack, and his eyes were red around the edges.

His voice cracked when he spoke. "He's gone."

A knot tightened in Will's stomach.

"Who's gone?" Rowe asked, but the tremor in his voice suggested he already knew the answer.

"I went to see Dadore this morning, but he was not in his wagon. I found him in Kydaris's wagon. He…he took his own life."

Ryowyn gasped. Julie rose to hug Joe and help him into a chair. Morgan reached out and took Rowe's hand, pulling him down to sit beside her. Will didn't move.

"He was so lost," Joe said in a subdued voice. "I really thought he was doing better. Now he's gone."

A numbness crept over Will as the word rang in his ears. *Gone.* Because he didn't know Dadore well, he didn't feel the pain of loss as deeply as the others. Instead, it was as if an unseen enemy had infiltrated the valley, threatening those he loved. Despite all their efforts to protect themselves from outside attacks, they had failed to stop the enemy that lurked inside the false security of their defenses. For Will, the door to a protected room in his heart suddenly opened, and the pain imprisoned within took a step into the light. Memories of the day his father took his own life surfaced in perfect clarity as if it were only yesterday. But he slammed the door, refusing to let the pain out.

Rowe stood and inhaled deeply, puffing his chest out as if doing so might shield his heart. Maybe he, too, was trying to keep his pain locked away.

"We will mourn his death in the days ahead," he said. "And when peace reigns in this valley, we will celebrate his life and the lives spared by the gifts he offered. As Julie said, we all have our roles to play. We must protect those who live and fight against the spread of evil and death."

Morgan sniffled as a few tears spilled from her eyes.

Will marveled at the contrast between reactions. Rowe masked his sorrow, choosing to be a rock for others—but at what cost? Morgan, on the other hand, seemed to lower her defenses and embrace the pain. Which reaction was stronger?

"So, what does this mean for the trip to Acttun?" Will asked, knowing that they needed the thunderclaps.

"Bremer knows of an alchemist in Acttun who could help if we cannot breach the vault. But that would require going deeper into the city than I'd like." Rowe sat down again and thumbed the corner of his book. "I have no right to ask any of you to sacrifice—"

"Easy there, General Manager of the Universe," Will interjected. "No one has asked anything of us. We're all volunteering to do our parts—whether we stay or go." He glanced around the table and the others were nodding. "I choose to go because I love you like a brother, Rowe. Because all of you are my family."

"I'd like to remember Dadore in that way," Morgan said quietly. "Like family. He gave his life and his skills out of love for the only family he knew. Unfortunately, he never got to know his new family. Let's not let that happen to us. We've been through so much already. And who knows what lies ahead?"

After a moment's pause, Julie spoke. "Dadore represents those who endure the wounds of war that often go deeper and last longer than cuts and broken bones. We treat physical injuries right away, but we can't forget to care for their minds and hearts long after the battles end."

"Yes," Will agreed. "We're in this together for the long haul—even if it means being physically separated for a while. For better or worse…sickness and health, and all that other stuff, right?"

He put his arm around Ryowyn and ventured a glimpse at Morgan. She was watching Rowe, who had pushed his book aside and was staring at his folded hands. As if sensing her eyes on him, Rowe looked up and held her gaze for a moment. There was a spark between them, but Will couldn't tell if it was longing, sadness, or something else.

Julie reached over and squeezed Morgan's hand. Everyone nodded or voiced their agreement with Will, but Rowe sat quietly, gazing out the window opening that overlooked the Epping Forest.

The room grew quiet, and all eyes turned to Rowe. "Then it begins," he said, rising to his feet. "As soon as we know that Enders Brigade is free of Phyriad and harvesters, we will set out for Acttun."

CHAPTER 8

ENDERS BRIGADE ARRIVES

Morgan followed Rowe as he brushed past Dench without a word, leading the group from the gatehouse. She knew that, under normal circumstances, Rowe was a planner and preferred time to prepare for a dangerous journey. But time was already working against him. She sensed his frustration but knew what had to be done. The details would come together along the way. Will and Bremer were trusted companions for Rowe, and the North Crow Gate would be in the capable hands of Twell and Dench.

Morgan caught Rowe's arm, trying to pull him aside. "Rowe, can we talk?"

He stopped and addressed the others. "Thank you, everyone, for the meeting. Can you give us a minute?"

"Of course," Will said as he, Ryowyn, and Julie continued walking along the wall.

When Rowe and Morgan were alone, he turned to face her. "What is it, Morgan?"

His cold, businesslike manner took her by surprise. She remembered the kindness in his smile and the tenderness of his

◄ 63 ►

words when they had snuck away for a few minutes together at the South Crow Gate. She remembered the warmth of his body, the slight trembling of his hands, and his lips lingering against hers as if they had all the time in the world. Now, he seemed rushed and impatient as if she were another distraction. It had been less than a month since they had confessed their love for one another, but now the memory seemed as distant as a summer day in midwinter.

He touched her arm, and a hint of warmth returned. "I'm sorry. That didn't come out right."

"I'm sorry too," she said. "I…um, about Dadore, I mean." She hadn't thought this conversation through, and knew their time was short. "But also, about us. We've been so busy and focused on everyone else. I know it's been a stressful time for you. But I've been thinking…and I wanted you to know—"

Tonna appeared, stumbling on the top step in his haste.

"Enders Brigade is less than six hours away, sir." The messenger took a moment to catch his breath.

Rowe glanced at Morgan.

She hung her head. "It's okay. We can talk later."

"Go on, Tonna," Rowe said as they joined Will, Ryowyn, and Julie.

"They're traveling in small squads, sir. There's been no sign of sickness, but the number of wounded is greater than we expected. They have requested assistance to make the final leg."

"Wounded?" Rowe hung his head and rubbed the back of his neck. "Burns?"

Tonna nodded as his dark eyebrows knit together, and his jaw muscles flexed.

Rowe faced the others. "Morgan, how long before you and a team can be ready to ride out to them?"

"We have two wagons packed and ready, but I'm not sure about medical supplies." She turned to her mother.

"We already have enough clean bandages," Julie said. "If we can collect a few kegs of white vinegar and some raw honey to soothe minor burns, we should be ready to go by noon."

"There's a type of seaweed in the lake that's full of healing properties," Ryowyn added. "I know of a large patch off the coast of Little Hammerclaw. We could fill a covered cart within an hour or two."

"Twell can provide a troop from the Marauders to escort all of you safely there and back," Rowe said. "I'll stay here with Will to prepare for our trip to Acttun. If all goes well, you should be back with Enders Brigade before dark. Will can check for harvesters among them. After that, we will leave them in your capable hands and set out for Acttun." He paused for a quick glance at their faces. "I appreciate each one of you and all you are doing."

When Morgan and Julie were ready with the wagons, they joined Tonna and about fifty volunteers and soldiers along the north road out of the Rainia Valley. Most rode on horseback, except for a dozen volunteers in two horse-drawn wagons stocked with food and medical supplies.

Ryowyn was the last to arrive with a dozen mermaids, a troop of mer soldiers, and a pair of horse-drawn, two-wheeled carts loaded with large clay pots. The pot lids clattered as the carts rolled along the bumpy road. The horses came to a stop, and the watery contents sloshed inside the pots. Morgan breathed in the pungent, briny odor of seaweed.

"I'm sorry we took so long," Ryowyn said. "The seaweed was easy to collect, but it was difficult finding containers to keep it from drying under the sun."

Morgan held up her hands. "No apology needed, Ryowyn. We're ready to leave."

It was midafternoon when they met the first in a lengthy line of soldiers approaching on horseback. The sorrowful sight took Morgan's breath away. Even the horses appeared weary and defeated as they plodded along.

Some soldiers were so badly burned, they could hardly stay in their saddles. Many had hands wrapped in dirty, blood-soaked cloths and rode with their arms hanging at their sides and reins resting across their laps. The faces of despair were overwhelming. Their eyes reflected a range of emotions: half closed as they winced in pain, or wide with terror as they searched the clear sky—fearing dragons, Morgan assumed—and then a glimmer of hope when they saw the caravan riding toward them.

A soldier wearing smoke-blackened plate armor approached Morgan. He wore no helmet, and a scorch mark scarred his right cheek. He slouched in his saddle, leaning to one side as he brought his mare to a stop.

"Have you come from the North Crow Gate, Callum Sage?" He was unable to hide the desperation in his voice. "Is the valley sound?"

Morgan nodded. "Many of your families are anxious for your return."

The man breathed a prolonged sigh as if Morgan had just poured cool water over his head. "We were terrified that the valley had been sacked. Where—where would we have gone?"

"No need to worry about such things. We're here to care for your wounded until we get you to the valley. There's a large group of healers preparing the infirmaries in the Crow's Nest as we speak."

The line of soldiers rode past in crestfallen silence, eyes to the ground. Terrible burns marked their heads and bodies.

The armored soldier removed his gloves. "Begging your pardon, my lady," he said, extending a hand in greeting. "My name is Captain Culthison, now in command of Enders Brigade."

Morgan squeezed his hand and, feeling little strength to his grip, let go. "I'm Morgan Finley, and this is my mother, Julie, our most seasoned…healer." It sounded odd to hear herself use such terms to describe her mother, but she was trying hard to make this as comfortable as possible for the captain. "With us in the wagons is Ryowyn Ayoust and a contingent of mer healers. Rest assured, Captain, what we lack in number, we make up for in strength of purpose."

"The line of riders is about half a mile long," Culthison said, turning his horse. "There are few who escaped injury, but those needing immediate attention are in the wagons bringing up the rear. Come, I'll take you."

"Would you mind telling us what happened?" Morgan asked.

Culthison was quiet as his moist eyes gazed at his fellow soldiers. "We had an understanding—an accord—with Commander Yossar of the North Gnome Army. We learned that Phyriad had been unleashed west of the Stoneberg. Yossar didn't believe it, but when his scouts confirmed our report, we suddenly had more in common with the highland gnomes than we had differences. As we hatched a plan to combine forces against Uluk the Shadowfallen, we discovered that half the gnome army had just been infected through their food supply. Then Uluk showed up. We engaged in what looked like a futile attack. Then General Raric arrived—or what was left of him." Culthison's voice became raspy. "Raric somehow transformed into a full-size red dragon and tore the Shadowfallen limb from limb.

"We were amazed and hopeful for victory, but then Raric—or the dragon—attacked the gnomes with fire. The Nameless Forest erupted into flames. It looked like the dragon was intent on destroying the gnomes but then overshot one of its fiery runs and burned up dozens of our men. Through all the smoke and flames, I guess the dragon got confused, and started blowing fire everywhere. The screams…"

"I'm so sorry," Julie said.

"Before the fighting started," Culthison continued, "Brigadier Bayard told Commander Yossar of the possibility of coming to live with us in the Rainia Valley because they'd lost their homeland. If any gnomes survived, they were supposed to wait for our invitation near the Hennen Outpost."

"Do you know if any gnomes escaped being infected by Phyriad?" Morgan asked.

"We instructed the gnomes and our men to break off into small groups in case anyone was exposed. Anyone showing signs of coughing or fever was to be segregated. But that said, who can say?" The captain clenched his jaw. "Good soldiers don't forsake their comrades, no matter how sick or wounded."

"Today we will care for your men, Captain," Morgan said. "And tomorrow you can discuss the highland gnomes with those overseeing the valley. Our job is to care for your injured and bring you safely to the Rainia Valley."

⁂

The covered wagon that Julie and Ryowyn had been working in came to a slow stop outside the North Crow Gate. Morgan peeked in to tell them they had arrived. The lanterns hanging from the bows above swung back and forth, and the light flickered across a soldier's still body as Julie finished stitching a gash below his left ribs.

"Back home," Julie told Morgan, "in a sterile environment, this would have been a routine procedure." She stood and stretched her back as Morgan pushed aside the canvas covering the rear entrance to the wagon.

Ryowyn's hands were coated with a light-green gel from the seaweed that she and the mer healers had used to clean and dress burns.

The setting sun ignited the sparse clouds in shades of pink and orange. Morgan inhaled deeply and allowed the moment to seep into her weary mind. The vibrant beauty above her contrasted with the ugly task of caring for the soldiers.

Julie grimaced as she stepped gingerly from the wagon. There was no part of her apron left unbloodied.

At the North Crow Gate, the process of double-checking Enders Brigade for signs of Phyriad had already begun. It was important but somewhat redundant. Shortly after meeting Captain Culthison, Julie had set up protocols to deal with anyone showings signs of a cough, fever, or skin rash, but there had been no suspicious cases. Initially, Morgan was concerned for her mother's safety but knew she was a professional and confident caregiver through and through.

Noticing a clean spot on the back of her hand, Morgan used it to brush aside some stray hairs that clung to her forehead. She scanned the caravan of wagons. Volunteers emerged, one by one, wearing expressions of exhaustion on their faces. Many stretched their arms and flexed stiff hands and fingers. Each one had spent hours cleaning and dressing terrible wounds.

"How are you, Julie?" Ryowyn's soft voice permeated the chatter of excited soldiers as she touched Julie's arm.

Julie flinched and looked down at her arm.

Ryowyn touched Morgan's cheek, and a rush of energy washed from her face through her body, giving her the strength to press on. She glanced at Ryowyn, unable to hide her smile.

"The touch of a mer healer can alleviate invisible pains," Ryowyn said. "As long as they are not too deep."

"It's beautiful," Julie said. "Thank you. And to answer your question: besides being terrified of a dragon attack…I'm good."

Ryowyn lowered her voice. "How many survived?"

"Less than a thousand," Morgan said. "A few days ago, Enders Brigade was five thousand strong. Before heading off to follow General Raric, many of the soldiers had sent their families from Dwenlin Thah to the Crow's Nest. They were afraid of reprisal when the queen discovered they were serving General Raric." She let a tear roll freely. "All those mothers, wives, and children waiting on the other side of this wall will also need your healing gift."

Ryowyn placed her hand on Morgan's arm. Breathing the evening air was refreshing, but the mer princess's touch was like someone lifting her soul out of a dark cavern.

"It's like a combination of sedatives and narcotics," Julie said to Morgan. "It's truly amazing."

Captain Culthison approached, slumping forward in his saddle. His eyes were dark and drawn.

"Thank you, Julie Finley," he said.

Julie gave the captain a weary smile as the line of wagons moved a few dozen feet before stopping again. Without another word, he continued riding toward the stronghold now illuminated by the flickering flames of watch fires.

"I'll head to the front to guide the wagons to the Crow's Nest," Morgan told Julie. "Once we get inside the curtain wall, make sure you're in the lead wagon so you can meet up with Gloriana to get these people sorted. I need to find Rowe."

Among the crowd of volunteers helping the remnant of Enders Brigade, Will was there studying those on foot who had formed a single line. A wagon rolled past, and he looked inside. It might have appeared strange to some, but Morgan knew he was searching for harvesters in disguise.

"Come and find me at the infirmary when you're done here," Ryowyn called to Will.

"I'll be there," Will answered as he continued to scan the soldiers. "I love you."

"And I you, my Will!"

Their genuine expressions of affection convinced Morgan that she needed to finish her conversation with Rowe. She climbed the stairs to the gatehouse and found him with Bremer. On the table, they had spread out various items of food, cooking supplies, coils of rope, blanket rolls, and a few leather packs. The men paused in their conversation to acknowledge Morgan.

Rowe offered a nod in her direction. "I'll just be another minute, Morgan." He turned back to Bremer. "I would feel better if we had an extra rope for Will."

"No problem," Bremer said. "I'll go over to the barn."

He left immediately, leaving Morgan and Rowe alone.

She removed her cloak and laid it over a chair as Rowe fidgeted with some cooking utensils on the table. His left side was toward her, and he cast only a single glance in her direction as he worked.

"I had a brief word with Captain Culthison," he said. "They have lost so many, but he's grateful for what you and your mother have already done for them. I wish I could do more, but I need to go to Acttun." He leaned over the table and grabbed a metal cup.

As he shoved supplies into a well-worn leather backpack, Morgan walked up and wrapped her arms around him, resting her cheek against his back. "You're an excellent leader, Rowe. So competent at many things. But you're also one man, and there are limits to how much a person can handle. I'm concerned about you taking on so many burdens."

He relaxed slightly and rotated to face her. She kept her arms around him despite his nervous glance at the door.

"I'm responsible for the Crow's Nest, Morgan. I'm grateful for the council that has assumed leadership after I killed the duke, but I also carry the weight of this valley."

"You don't have to carry that burden alone."

"I know that, but—"

She touched his lips with her fingertips. "No buts. We're in this together, and I…I've missed you, Rowe. I miss the way you laugh. It's been days since I've seen you smile."

He massaged his forehead. "I know. I can't seem to shake this recurring headache."

She pulled him closer, and his arms had nowhere to go but around her. "And I miss…*this*. Just being near you."

His hands trickled down the back of her chemise and folded together. She watched his weary eyes in silence, waiting for him to open his heart.

"I'm sorry I've been so…" He trailed off.

"Distant? Preoccupied? Brooding? Disinterested?"

He pushed back a few inches and flashed a smile. "All that?"

"There's the smile." She leaned in again and kissed his mouth.

"I wish you didn't have to go." She lowered her gaze and traced a finger along the edge of his collar.

He smiled again. "Don't worry; we'll be gone less than a week."

"Traveling a land threatened by infected creatures, harvesters, and two dragons." She stepped away but held his hands. "Please be careful."

Rowe furrowed his brow. "I've learned not to make promises of safe returns. But as much as is in my power, we'll be back in five days with the thunderclaps. Then, we'll spend more time together."

CHAPTER 9
JOURNEY TO ACTTUN

Will's eyes shot open. The cold, mossy-smelling air awakened his senses to an entirely different reality. Dark shadows surrounded him. A few scattered leaves swished and scuffled across the ground. The horse beneath him shifted, and the saddle creaked. Will clutched the reins. A shiver shook his body, and he remembered that they were traveling to Acttun.

He and Rowe had been on the road for two days now, pausing only for a few brief rests for the horses' sake. Will had no idea how long they'd been traveling since their last stop, but his backside was sore, and his legs were stiff.

He could see only a few yards ahead, and even then, shadows veiled everything. The surrounding treetops traced a faint outline against the night sky. Heavy clouds had rolled in before sunset and now blocked out the moon, the stars, and any hint of dawn. Will cocked his head but could hear nothing. Even the crickets were asleep at this hour.

He took a few deep breaths to settle himself from the fright of waking up in a dark forest. Rowe's horse clopped along a few yards ahead, but Will could not see it. A twig snapped to his left, followed by the sound of soft footsteps behind him. Will spun his head, and a branch slapped his cheek. The footsteps drew closer. Now fully awake, Will slid his 1911 from the holster on his right hip.

"Will, it's me," Rowe whispered.

Will huffed a loud sigh of relief and returned the gun to its holster. "Oh, thank goodness!" He rubbed his eyes and tried to focus. "I thought you were riding ahead of me."

"We drifted from the main trail a short way back." Rowe walked past Will to collect his horse and guided it around a large tree. Will's mare followed.

"Can you keep a secret?" Will asked as Rowe climbed into his saddle.

Rowe stifled a yawn.

"I hate riding horses," Will said in a monotone voice.

"You would honestly prefer traveling in that loud horseless machine of yours?"

"You mean my Land Cruiser? One hundred percent! We'd be done in Acttun and back at the Crow's Nest by now."

Rowe harrumphed. "Shades! The moment you made that thing roar… I've never been so frightened in my life. Julie's carriage was no less terrifying to be trapped in. A horse might be slower, but at least I'm in the open while riding. I can dismount anytime I choose. And I'm in control…for the most part."

"You'd never ride a horse again if you ever got used to driving a truck. And if you prefer the open air, man, getting you on a steel horse would be pretty funny."

"Steel horse?"

"Yeah, it's what we call a motorcycle."

Rowe snorted a laugh. "Thanks, that clears things up."

Strange, distant sounds from the north swelled with the breeze. Rowe was instantly silent, and Will strained his ears to discern what he was hearing. A long, low whistle caused him to start and pull back on the reins. A few yards ahead, Bremer's horse stood still and nickered as they approached. A second later, Bremer materialized from the dark forest.

"You won't believe our timing," he said. "The horde from Dwenlin Thah is just starting to arrive."

Rowe slid from his saddle. "Can we make it to the asylum?"

"The main group is a few miles away, so time is still on our side." Bremer turned and disappeared into the forest. Will scrambled from his saddle and tied his reins to the first tree he found.

"Keep it loose," Rowe said.

"Why?"

Rowe didn't answer but followed Bremer into the forest. It didn't take long for Will to figure out that keeping the reins loose was necessary in case they didn't return. At least then the horses could go free.

The strange sounds grew louder, piercing the dead calm.

"What's that noise?" Will asked.

"The sounds of war," Bremer answered. "Mixed with magic spells and other unimaginable things."

Will rubbed his sweaty hands on his cloak as he followed Rowe's faint outline. He tried not to step on branches but made more noise than Rowe and Bremer combined. His heart raced as he stole glances through the canopy of darkness. Although the sounds were still far away, he had a growing sense that something was watching them, something so evil his skin crawled. He wanted to ask Rowe if he could feel it too, but he couldn't imagine him *not* feeling it, so he remained silent.

The sounds became more distinct. Thunderous explosions intermixed with long, crackling *pops*, sparking a low buzzing in Will's ears. Memories of his short time in Acttun flooded his mind, and his stomach tightened. The evil presence drew nearer. Will raised his shotgun from beneath his cloak and crouched low. Suddenly, Rowe grabbed Will and yanked him to the ground.

The evil presence changed from a vague sensation to a terrifying reality. A rush of warm air followed a deep *whooshing* sound. Will, Bremer, and Rowe huddled on the ground. Will lifted his head and caught a glimpse of a huge dragon shape darkening the sky in a shadow deeper than Will thought possible. Even so, he was surprised at how far away the dragon was from them.

Bremer stood and crept down the narrow trail.

"Relax, Will," Rowe said. "I doubt that Natas is looking for us, and most of those sounds are coming from the far side of Acttun. We should be fine."

"Nothing feels right," Will said. "It's freaking me out."

"Remember, Acttun is a city of magic. It can create powerful sensations in normal times, but now that the residents are rising to defend themselves, the warding spells will be more tangible."

"How on earth does Bremer know where to find all these backwoods trails?" Will said, trying to calm his nerves.

Rowe shrugged. "I've come to stop asking questions where Bremer is concerned."

A few minutes later, the trio stopped next to an old maple tree.

"Watch your step," Bremer said, pointing at the knotted tree roots along the edge of a sheer cliff.

Will stopped a few feet from the tree and peered over the edge. A few hundred feet below, the city of Acttun sprawled out in all her splendor. The skyline was so bright that, for a split second,

Will thought he was looking at a city powered by electricity. But that was impossible.

"I've never seen a city so bright in the Fourwinds," Will said.

"The quest for light sources in Acttun has evolved through the years into a dark competition," Rowe explained. "Almost every building has custom-crafted lanterns. I've seen some lined with crystals or mirrors that amplify the light."

Bremer pointed west where a single road from the narrow valley beyond led to a bridge that provided the only western entrance into Acttun. Massive watch fires burned along the riverbank and were noticeably larger at the wide stone bridge that spanned the river.

"The residents have created a collective spell, drawing magic from throughout the city," Bremer explained.

Three horizontal streaks of light formed what looked like a cattle fence across the far side of the bridge. Brighter than a welder's flash, the barrier crackled with power. Several dozen people were running down the road toward the bridge. A few of them tumbled as much as ran while rushing the magical gate with reckless abandon. Will leaned forward for a closer look at the people emerging from the darkness, but Bremer jerked him to the side.

"Here's your rope, kid," he said, shoving a coiled bundle against Will's chest. "Listen. We're going over a two-hundred-foot cliff here, so pay attention. I knotted your rope every few feet to make the descent easier for you. Every fifty feet or so is a thick knot, so you'll be able to stand on them to rest if need be. Got it?"

Will nodded quickly and smiled despite the terror rising in his throat. "At least this time you brought rope," he said, thinking back to the time when he and Bremer leapt over a cliff into the Serpentine River.

"That was unexpected," Bremer said. "And this time we're not being chased by a pack of angry holgs."

Will peeked over the edge and grew light-headed. He raised his eyebrows at Bremer and Rowe, thinking they were crazy to even consider going down that way. But he knew better than to question Bremer. Instead, he tried to think of something to keep from cracking under the pressure.

Bremer shifted the longbow on his back and tightened the small, rune-marked leather quiver. The magical bow was the perfect distraction. Will had won it after killing the infamous dark elf, Onathe Wyeth, in Fairbay. Bremer had said it was worth a fully furnished castle. But before they'd left the Crow's Nest two days ago, Will had offered the priceless bow to Bremer. Will thought it a suitable gift, considering what Bremer had done to rescue him from the Clover Fields. Initially, Bremer had declined the offer, thinking Will mad. But with Rowe's encouragement, Bremer grudgingly accepted the gift.

"That's a pretty nice bow, Bremer," Will said. "Where'd you get it?"

Rowe chuckled as he tested his rope.

Bremer looked at Will as if he were suddenly doubting his sanity. He clasped his hands around Will's shoulders and gave him a gentle shake.

"Look, kid, I know this is hard for you, so stay focused and take it slow. If you can survive a fall into the Misty Gorge, help slay a dark elf, defeat an evil queen, fly beyond the Hollowtangle on a winged unicorn, and…whatever other crazy things you've done, you can do this." He slapped Will's shoulder and, with a wink, added: "Just make sure that if you fall, you keep your cloak beneath you. If luck won't save you, maybe the cloak will."

Bremer tugged his rope to test Rowe's knot, leaned back, and started rappelling down the dark cliff face. Rowe was next over the edge, leaving Will momentarily alone with his thoughts.

Looking out over the city, he marveled at the haphazard design around the two rivers that carved it up into a series of wildly different islands. He concentrated on a dark section of the city that he hadn't noticed earlier. There wasn't a single light on the entire island, giving it a sinister look—and doubly so with the imposing asylum at its center.

Will shook his arms, rolled his shoulders, and took a deep breath. With trembling hands, he clutched the rope and knelt near the edge. He shuffled his feet back, keeping his chest close to the ground. Easing himself over the ledge, the rope twisted as he transferred his weight. His feet scrambled in a moment of panic until they found a knot. His right elbow stung, and he knew the rough surface had broken skin. All the way down, he struggled, bouncing off the rock and collecting numerous scrapes and bruises.

By the time he reached the forest floor, his hands were raw, and his biceps were so spent, he could barely lift his arms. But there was no time to complain or rest; Rowe and Bremer were on the move the second Will hit the ground.

Now that they were closer to the city, shouts and explosions filled the air. A tingling sensation raced up Will's body, and his scalp prickled with static electricity. Rowe's hair was standing on end. Moving through the trees, they plunged headlong into a sea of magical energy that guarded the city limits.

Rowe and Will caught up to Bremer, and the static subsided. The rogue was whispering to someone in the shadows on the bank of the Serpentine River. Will recognized the stranger as Kalmar, the mer soldier who had taken over as captain after the death of

Prince Wrathan. Kalmar melted into the river, and Bremer stepped into a small rowboat.

As soon as Will and Rowe were seated, the boat started moving. Pulled by four mer soldiers, the boat cut quickly through the dark water between islands. Peals of thunderous explosions rippled through the air in rapid succession, but they sounded like they were still outside the western border.

The boat passed beneath three bridges. A few frantic voices shouted from the streets, but no one noticed the trespassers on the river. After the fourth bridge, the boat drifted to the water's edge and struck the muddy shore of a dark island.

Bremer sprang from the hull and charged up the short embankment.

"This boat could be useful in transporting the thunderclaps," Rowe said.

Kalmar tied a mooring rope to the trunk of a small willow. "The water is high, so when you're ready, we can take the river all the way back to the Rainia Valley."

Rowe nodded as he started up the long embankment, and Will and Kalmar followed with barely a sound.

Bremer led the way around large patches of blackberry bushes that had overtaken the island. Scattered copses of tag alders and numerous short pine trees obscured the trail until Bremer burst into a clearing. He crossed the field and stopped before a massive dark wall.

An explosion from the west lit the night sky and illuminated the most haunting place Will had ever seen. Even the Waerdreath castle was more inviting than the Acttun asylum. Smaller red bricks, tightly mortared together, filled in the numerous doorways and embrasures in the five-story wall. The building was deathly still, like a massive tomb towering above them.

A shiver ran down Will's back, and he unconsciously reached beneath his cloak and unclipped the short-barreled shotgun from his shoulder holster.

"Only if things get really serious," Rowe whispered in Will's ear as they followed Bremer and Kalmar along the front of the building. Despite the darkness, Will felt exposed and vulnerable—serious enough to keep the shotgun ready.

Bremer stopped at the corner and peeked around the chipped, moss-covered block wall. The violence on the western front faded into an eerie quiet. In the tall grasses and tag alders at the perimeter of the asylum property, nothing moved. Bremer led the way along the side of the building, passing stone relics of times long forgotten. He stopped at a rickety set of wooden scaffolding that reached all the way to the roof.

"I wasn't sure how we'd get up there," Bremer said. "But this should work."

Will gazed up the length of the scaffolding. The first two levels appeared sound, but there were many broken poles and boards farther up.

"We're not climbing that thing, are we?" Will asked as he holstered the shotgun.

Rowe removed a few boards from the base of the scaffolding and uncovered an iron ladder bolted to the wall. The scaffolding had been built around the ladder, so it was initially hard to see.

Will stood near Rowe against the wall and watched the sky. Although the battle sounds had faded, he almost preferred them to the quiet. "He's out there, isn't he?"

"Don't worry about the Iron Dragon sneaking up on us," Rowe

said. "You'll feel his presence long before you see him." He grabbed an iron rung and started climbing.

Bremer nudged Will toward the ladder. "You're next, kid. I'll be right behind you."

Will shot a glance upward, and the dizzy sensation he had felt earlier at the top of the cliff returned. But this time, he had to go up instead of down. He took a few breaths, then noticed Kalmar watching him, his stern brow furrowed.

Will remembered Kalmar's face from the altercation in Fairbay with the king's son. Wrathan and his fellow soldiers had been ready to skewer Will with their tridents after learning that Wrathan's sister, Ryowyn, was bound by a life debt to Will—a mere human— because he had saved her life. That custom had dashed the hopes of many mer soldiers who had dreamed of winning the beautiful princess's heart. Perhaps Kalmar, a close friend of Wrathan's, had even expected to one day marry Ryowyn. But Wrathan had been consumed by the vicious spread of Phyriad released by the gnome army into the Niasa Sea. In his place, Kalmar controlled the surviving soldiers. If he carried any bitterness over the loss of Ryowyn and Wrathan—despite Rowe's unity speech at the gathering in Rainia—Will knew there was little he could do to stand against such a seasoned soldier.

"I'm ready," Will told Bremer. "I don't know what's up there, but I'm not staying down here."

"Just keep looking up," Bremer said. "And while you're at it, watch out for Natas."

Will glared at him. "So, there's nothing in that quiver to bring down a dragon?"

Bremer looked at Will as if he hadn't heard him correctly. "Do you have a problem with Natas?"

Will reared slightly at the question. "What do you mean?"

Bremer flashed a rare grin and punched Will's shoulder. "Relax, kid. We all have a problem with that creature; that's why we're here."

From the roof, Rowe whistled and waved for the next person to follow. Will started up before he lost his nerve altogether.

"I hope Natas doesn't show up in the next minute or two," Bremer said, unable to hide his grin.

Will crouched slightly from the second rung to look Bremer square in the face. "There ain't enough room in the Fourwinds for both me and that dragon. And I plan on staying."

Bremer's smile broadened. "Had it been anyone else to threaten Natas, I would have scoffed. But I've been around you long enough to know better than to bet against you."

Will turned and scaled the ladder without slowing. At the top, the wind gusted, carrying with it the sounds of battle from the western front. Rowe reached out a hand and pulled him onto the flat roof. Will sunk to his knees, taking deep breaths.

Rowe signaled for Bremer to come up, then dropped to Will's side. "You all right?"

Will shook his head. "Did you hear those sounds as you climbed?"

Rowe nodded before Will could explain what he meant. "There can be no question now. Something's alive in there."

"It was…like…like something was clawing at the blocked window openings to get to me." Will reached for his shotgun, expecting one of those *somethings* to attack. But the only other thing at the top of the building was a solitary roof access building.

Rowe stood and pointed to the western sky. "Look at that!"

Six massive fireballs were spinning and winding around the bridge like a snake, burning to ash the few attackers who survived the magic fence. The light of the protective fence was fading, likely due to the sheer number of Phyriad-infected people throwing themselves at the barrier. The strands of magical light had already sliced dozens of attackers. Will's stomach clenched, and he turned away after seeing the scattered body parts. But he was unable to tune out the high-pitched shrieks as the horde rushed the bridge. Those who survived the weakening fence were bursting into flames long before the fireballs touched them.

Adding to the defense, streaks of lightning arced from the city, crackling above the road beyond the bridge. Some of the horde was struck down by the bolts before they reached the bridge. The defensive power of Acttun seemed limitless, but the masses pressed forward, and Will doubted. "Do you think they can hold them off?"

Rowe shrugged. "Acttun has no lack of cosmic descryers, sorcerers, spell casters, warlocks, and witches. They are a diverse group, but they've joined together to protect their beloved city."

Bremer stepped from the ladder and whistled for Kalmar to join them. He glanced at the bridge but was unfazed by the activity. Instead, he ran to the roof access building, and Rowe and Will followed.

The iron fence surrounding the structure was old and pockmarked, but the gate's padlock was shiny and smooth. Bremer knelt beside it and removed a small package from a pocket. Before he could attempt to pick the lock, the gravel behind the structure crunched, and a large creature stepped around the corner.

"Holy crap!" Will shouted.

Rowe's blade rang as he unsheathed his sword. Bremer sprang to his feet, and the magic bow was readied and nocked with an arrow before Will was able to pull his shotgun out.

The harvester paused and emitted a growl as deep as thunder. The giant lizard-like creature flashed a sharp-fanged grin, took one step, then roared in pain as Bremer's magic arrow plunged into its broad chest. The impact lifted the creature off its feet and knocked it to the ground.

Rowe seized the opportunity and leapt forward, narrowly avoiding the long, swiping tail. Despite the gaping chest wound, the demon snarled and started to rise. Rowe lunged, driving his sword deep into the creature's side. The blade's magic crackled and burned the creature from the inside.

Kalmar joined them as Rowe stood above the dead harvester. "What's that in its claw?" Kalmar asked.

Rowe slipped the tip of his sword through a large metal key ring and lifted it from the creature's loose grip. "Was it planning to open that door?"

"Why would it want to go inside?" Will asked.

Rowe let the key ring fall into Bremer's hands.

"Something isn't right," Bremer said as he freed the lock. He pushed through the gate and put his ear to the steel door. "I can't hear anything, but I sure heard noises on the way up."

"What are you thinking?" Rowe asked.

"Nothing good, so let's get this over with."

As they approached the door, a deep whooshing came from the forest that surrounded the city.

"Cover!" Rowe snapped as he sheathed his sword.

Everyone dove behind the small structure, and the evil presence Will had sensed in the forest returned.

The Iron Dragon dropped toward the city, banking sharply. Its head pointed at the asylum, and Will expected a ball of fire to burst from the beast's massive mouth. Instead, a rush of static energy whirled around the asylum like a cyclone. Will covered his ears as a terrific explosion shook the building. For a moment, he was sure the entire asylum would collapse. Instead, many of the sealed windows and doors on the ground level blew open, scattering shards of brick across the courtyard with so much force that some splashed into the river. Dust billowed to the roof, forcing those on it to close their eyes and cover their faces.

After a moment, the air cleared. Rowe, Bremer, and Kalmar stood tentatively, searching the sky as if expecting another attack. But there was no sign of the Iron Dragon. Will stood next to Rowe, tugging his ears in an attempt to unplug them. The ringing subsided but was replaced by wicked, snarling sounds from below.

Rowe drew his sword again, Bremer nocked another arrow, and Kalmar readied his trident. Together, they walked to the edge of the roof and peered over.

Will lifted his shotgun from beneath his cloak. He tried to prepare himself for the worst but fell far short of the nightmare escaping from the asylum.

CHAPTER 10
DRAGON ATTACK

Morgan reached the top step of the North Crow Gate's main stairway just before the sun dipped behind the treetops of the Epping Forest. The air was still, but she shook off a shiver and closed the gap at the front of her Trannalun cloak. Only two days had passed since Rowe, Will, and the others had left for Acttun. To Morgan, it felt like a month.

Time had slowed as life at the North Crow Gate transformed. Twenty-four hours ago, the stronghold was buzzing with construction and renovations. Morgan had grown accustomed to the noise and the constant challenge of maneuvering around workers and piles of stone and lumber. She had spent most of her time supervising the construction of four separate buildings where refugees would be quarantined to limit the potential spread of infection. That work had consumed so much of her days that she hadn't noticed the fortification of the wall.

The stonemasons had finished the expansion and repairs of both walls. Carpenters had completed renovations on the wall walk, effectively doubling its width and protecting it with a sturdy metal roof. A team of burly blacksmiths had installed the giant ballistae, which now gleamed in the evening sun like armored guards stationed at their posts, ready for active duty. Although construction was finished, the North Crow Gate was not abandoned. In fact, Morgan recognized many faces among the gathering soldiers. The workers had traded tools for weapons as a new reality settled over the stronghold. They had survived the reconstruction phase without major incident or outside attack. But they all knew that couldn't last forever.

Morgan found a quiet spot at the edge of the wall walk overlooking the entrance to the main gate. The large open area and wide thoroughfare cutting through the Epping Forest was desolate. It was a strange sight. Until recently, a steady line of refugees had converged upon the only remaining entrance into the Rainia Valley, seeking what might be the last safe haven in the Fourwinds. But after the remnant of Enders Brigade had arrived and Rowe and the others set off for Acttun, there had been no new refugees.

On the one hand, the sight was a relief. It meant that Morgan and the others had done their jobs, providing new homes for hundreds of displaced people. Will had worked to ensure that no disguised harvesters found their way into the valley. And Julie had joined Gloriana in leading the effort to care for the sick and wounded.

But on the other hand, the empty thoroughfare troubled Morgan. Had they helped everyone they could? Or were there still more people out there, homeless and helpless in the face of the evil and danger that now reigned in the land? And what about the gnome soldiers that Captain Culthison spoke of? Would they arrive soon, assuming any survived?

The shiver returned, and Morgan rubbed her arms to settle her unraveling nerves. She knew her thoughts were spiraling to a dark place. But she couldn't bear the thought of dragons and Phyriad-infected creatures roaming freely while she remained relatively safe and secure behind a well-defended wall. Rowe and Will were taking action—marching into the heart of danger—while she remained, wishing she could do more to help.

"Good evening, Morgan." Commander Twell Henowing's deep and gentle voice interrupted her thoughts.

"Evening, Commander." Morgan stood straight as the tall brigadier stepped beside her.

Twell smiled and ran a hand over his close-cropped gray hair. Dressed in a short-sleeved tunic, he looked like a worker out for a casual stroll after a full day's work. His keen eyes twinkled in the setting sunlight as he studied the thoroughfare. Despite his age and calm demeanor, he was as solid as an oak and always a commanding presence.

He faced Morgan. "How are things at the infirmary?"

"It was a good day. We didn't lose as many as yesterday, and the rest should make it."

"I visited the infirmary before leaving the Crow's Nest last night. I'm impressed by the level of care. Your mother's organizational skills match her ability to treat the wounded. The sheer number of wash stations alone is like nothing I've ever seen."

Morgan flashed a smile as a surge of pride swelled in her heart. "My mother has dedicated her life to the study of medi—of the healing arts…and to managing the recovery process. She's also thankful for the healing magic that Ryowyn and her people bring. Their seaweed salves are helping to heal the burns and stave off infection. So, all things considered, most of the soldiers will make full recoveries."

Twell retrieved a well-used pipe from the small satchel at his side. "That is encouraging news. We will need their skills here in the coming days."

Morgan noticed a few soldiers watching their conversation. As their commander lit his pipe, the tension along the wall relaxed, as if each soldier were lighting up with him. She marveled at the effect he had on them.

"I've been wondering, Commander. We haven't seen any refugees for a few days. But there have to be more people out there still unaffected by Phyriad, right?"

Twell rested his forearms on the parapet and blew out a stream of smoke. "I wish I knew for certain, Morgan. The last scouts to return a few hours ago reported seeing small groups of infected people west of the Misty Gorge. So, they're still some distance away." He paused for a few puffs. "They seem to be traveling in packs…or herds. They move like cattle grazing in a lush field. When they see something to chase down, they behave more like a pack of wolves. A moment later, they return to what looks like aimless wandering. It's all very strange."

Morgan gazed at the forest. "That's what bothers me most. Assuming the reports are accurate, when people become infected, they lose their ability to reason. They're like wild animals. Then, as they transform and a rash spreads over their bodies, it sounds like their ability to think *increases*. If Natas can organize and command armies of gnomes, what could he do with an army of creatures transformed into his likeness?"

Twell's calm demeanor darkened. "You don't want to know, Morgan. I fought in the Dragon War. They are powerful, intelligent creatures. But under an evil commander, they can be dangerous and unpredictable. If this new breed evolves into a race that can think and work together, there could come a day when they construct siege machines to take down this wall." He gazed up into the evening sky. "And if they learned to fly like their master…"

Morgan studied the evening sky. "Until then, we'll make sure the infection doesn't breach this wall."

When Twell didn't respond, she turned to see him standing tall and tense. She followed his gaze, looking out over the trees to the rugged, beautiful cliffs beyond. Initially, she saw nothing to give him cause for concern. But then it appeared. A red dragon soared northward along the sharp cliffs of the Misty Gorge.

"Dragon!" Twell bellowed, his thundering voice launching everyone into motion as he dashed toward the gatehouse.

Along the wall, soldiers in banded leather armor scrambled to the ballista stations. The massive gears creaked and clicked as skilled soldiers pointed the weapons skyward. More soldiers carrying thick longbows and arrows reinforced with a dark alloy positioned themselves along the battlement.

Morgan tracked the Red Dragon as it rose and fell from sight between a pair of mountain peaks north of the Crow's Nest. How easily it could have bypassed the North Crow Gate to attack the castle before sweeping into the helpless valley! Her heart pounded as she thought of her mother in the Crow's Nest and Ryowyn at Rainia Lake. She drew her sword, then glanced down at the weapon in her hand, a mere toy compared to the power of a dragon. When she looked up, she spotted the beast as it circled another mountain peak—only, this time, the dragon was flying away from them. It came around again, apparently in no great hurry and with no sense of direction.

"Is it coming closer, Morgan?" Twell shouted from inside the gatehouse.

"I…I don't think so," Morgan answered while drawing her Trannalun cloak around her.

The dragon flew farther north, and Morgan's imagination ran wild. Was it heading to Acttun? Had Rowe and the others made it safely? With no stronghold to hide behind or heavy weapons to defend themselves, they would be powerless to stand against such a creature. Or maybe they had already found the thunderclaps?

As panic and fear threatened to immobilize Morgan, Twell returned wearing a heavy leather chest plate that also covered most of his shoulders. Studded leather reinforced with metal plates protected his forearms, shins, and thighs. In his gloved hands, the powerful commander hefted a longbow as he strode along the wall with his eyes to the sky.

A hush fell over the soldiers. For a few seconds, Morgan dared to hope that the dragon had left and would not find Rowe and Will either. But it reappeared around a snow-covered peak. The dragon dropped, soaring straight down along the towering cliffs, picking up speed. Seconds before it crashed into the forested lowlands, the Red Dragon pulled from the dive, easing its angle of attack just above the canopy of trees. It disappeared behind the trees for a few seconds, but there was no denying that it was flying at breakneck speed toward the North Crow Gate. It reappeared, much closer, popping over a tree-covered ridge before dropping again from sight.

"Ready your bows!" Twell shouted.

Morgan stared at the top of the trees only a few hundred yards away. Her heart was racing, and her mind screamed at her to run, but her legs were frozen with terror.

"We've all been to this show before," Twell yelled to the soldiers. "You know what to do!"

The dragon sailed over the last patch of forest. No matter how many of these soldiers had fought in the Dragon War, nothing could have prepared them for the intensity of this beast. Dropping low, it crashed over the treetops and leveled its long neck toward the North Crow Gate, opening wide its sharp-toothed maw. A blast of fire roared down the thoroughfare and slammed against the wall. Soldiers dropped to their knees behind the battlement as the flames exploded along the North Crow Gate.

Morgan screamed and clutched her ears as she cowered behind a merlon. Flames shot over Twell's back and forced him to his stomach. Considering the speed of the dragon, Morgan expected the creature to fly past, but it didn't. Instead, the great beast flared its massive wings, which fanned the flames into a firestorm that enveloped the North Crow Gate. In doing so, the dragon bled off all its speed and landed so hard it shook the stronghold.

Shouts filled the air. The initial blast subsided, but it had ignited several small fires along the wall. Twell loosed an arrow, which pinged off the dragon's armored neck. He ran to help two soldiers ready a ballista. Farther down the wall, a fire threatened to engulf another ballista. Morgan scurried toward it. She bumped into several soldiers dodging flames and seeking a safe vantage point from which to shoot at the dragon. Their armor and her cloak were keeping them alive, but neither would last if the dragon approached an undefended wall.

Reaching the base of the weapon, Morgan pulled her hood tight over her head and turned away from the dragon. She took a deep breath and rose to her full height as the heat grew more intense. The dragon shifted its head to burn the far side of the wall. As it did, Morgan turned and peeked through an opening in her hood.

"Grab the firing chain!" a soldier cried out as he aimed the ballista at the dragon, then dove for cover as another blast of fire swept past.

Morgan crouched again beneath the safety of her Trannalun cloak but maintained her grip on the firing chain. Unable to breathe or bear the heat any longer, she pulled the chain, hoping the soldier's aim was true.

The weapon kicked back. Morgan ventured a glance and saw the reinforced bolt shoot through the air and strike the dragon's right leg. At close range, the sheer force behind the ballista drove the heavy bolt through the dragon's scaly hide. The creature's leg gave out, and it shrieked. Enormous wings stretched out above the wall. The dragon roared, and as it took to the air, it launched another blast of fire that missed the wall completely. By the time Morgan risked peering over the wall, the dragon had disappeared beyond the trees.

The soldier that Morgan was helping loaded another bolt and cranked the winch in a spinning blur. All around them, soldiers labored to douse fires and reload weapons. The roar of the dragon echoed in Morgan's ears, but after several moments, she realized that the beast was not returning.

"That'll smarten it up," said the soldier manning the ballista next to Twell.

"Yes, that's the problem," Twell said as he stared in the direction the dragon had flown. "*That* is the problem: a smarter dragon."

Morgan tied her hair back in a ponytail and for the next hour worked side by side with soldiers and others who had seen the fire and raced to form a bucket brigade. Flames had only scorched stone and metal, so the effort centered around wooden planks, supports, and the gatehouse. Fortunately, the dragon blasts were so strong that most flames passed over the wall and died out in the wide-open, dirt-packed clearing inside the wall. Three supply wagons were consumed, and a few soldiers were taken to the infirmary with burns, but no one had perished.

When she had done all she could, Morgan walked slowly to join Twell, wringing her hands to stop them from shaking. "Do you think it'll be back?"

Twell shook his head. "We've seen the last of the Red Dragon for today. As for you…you are skilled at more than swordplay. I'm impressed at how you kept your wits about you."

Morgan lowered her eyes and brushed some ash from her cloak.

"This is not a time for humility or for pride, Morgan. We all do our part. Sometimes a single soldier rises to the forefront, but no one can do so without a unified effort. That said, if you hadn't fired the bolt when you did, we could all be ash right now." He clapped her shoulder. "All in a day's work, soldier."

Morgan nodded, then shuffled her feet toward the stairs as if waking from a nightmare. Twell was right; being in battle was nothing like the one-on-one fencing competitions she had participated in. Coach had taught her that after all her training and input from others, she alone must face her opponent. That philosophy had taken her all the way to the World Fencing Championships. She had no desire to be a hero or a popular athlete, but fighting her own battles was all she knew.

And what she had learned in competition, she carried into her personal life. When her father lost interest in her fencing career, she had battled her inner demons one by one. And when she eventually understood that an actual demon—a harvester—had taken her father's life, Morgan had fought and killed it too.

In the Fourwinds, if anyone dismissed her as a feeble girl, she took it as a challenge not only to her ability but also to her loyalty.

But hadn't she already proven herself? She had single-handedly killed a death knight in the Arden Forest. In the Crow's Nest, she had slain harvesters and then outlasted veteran soldiers at the South Crow Gate battle. To be sure, she wielded a powerful, magical sword. But the sword was in *her* hands; it was *hers* to control.

As she drifted down the stairs past soldiers, firefighters, and busy carpenters, the weight of Twell's comment settled over her. Had she really fought all her battles on her own? Deep down, she knew that wasn't true. World Fencing Championships weren't won without the support of coaches, parents, and friends. And she would never have survived in the Fourwinds without Rowe, Will, Bremer, and many others. But she had never thought of herself as part of a team, as one member of something much larger than herself. Instead, everyone around her was there to help her achieve her personal goals. But what if there was more to it than that?

Morgan mounted her horse and scanned the faces around her. Everyone was giving their best effort to secure this valley, to welcome strangers into their homes, and to stand against Natas and the spread of Phyriad. No one expected to do so alone. They weren't working for her or for Rowe or for any individual. They worked for the person to their left and the person to their right in a united effort to build a lasting community.

That work had taken a heavy toll on many lives, particularly Rowe's. He had dedicated his life to the safety and well-being of the Fourwinds long before Morgan met him. In the short time she had known him, she rarely saw him slow down, despite constant demands, threats, and a violent battle at the South Crow Gate. If Morgan was growing tired of the relentless barrage, what must he be enduring? Through it all—and perhaps now more than ever—the people looked to Rowe to help lead the way forward.

A thought occurred to her and settled in her stomach like a stone. Could part of her concern about Rowe and Will going to Acttun be *envy*? She had always wanted to be a winner, to be part of the action, to play a part that felt significant. But was the work of finding thunderclaps more important than that of the carpenter in front of her replacing a charred beam? Was her mother's work in the infirmary more valuable than the efforts of the cooks who fed the volunteers or the work of those who cleaned up after everyone had finished eating?

A stable boy walked up to Morgan and offered a lantern. "I think you'll need this, Lady Morgan. Daylight is fading."

The boy turned before Morgan could offer thanks. He was just one more person doing his part.

She tightened her ponytail and let the evening breeze cool her neck. The horse pawed the ground, and a cloud of dust and ash rose around them. Morgan clicked her tongue and flicked the reins, guiding the mare eastward. She and her mother had planned to meet at Ryowyn's cottage for an evening meal, which was probably cooking already. If she pushed it, she had a solid hour of riding ahead of her.

As she turned for another look at the North Crow Gate and those working and watching the skies for further attacks, she caught Twell's eye and exchanged a wave. "All in a day's work," she mumbled to herself.

CHAPTER 11
Into the Asylum

From his first and only trip to Acttun, Will knew there were many strange people and creatures in the multifarious city. His time there had been brief but unforgettable. As he recovered from his fall with Bremer into the Misty Gorge, Will had spent hours in front of the window of his room in the Cauldron's Stew scanning the crowds for harvesters so Bremer could kill them. Only one harvester had passed by, but scores of sorcerers and wizards in all shapes, sizes, and races walked the streets that day. As shocking as some of them were to Will, nothing compared to the terrifying creatures he now saw pouring from the asylum.

Hairless and lanky, they skittered along on four almost equally long arms and legs. The creatures might have been human at one time, but they moved like spiders with half their legs missing. Intricate tattoos inked the nearly translucent skin of their oversized heads. Between snarls, many were sneezing and spraying mucus, which also dripped into their toothy mouths that looked more canine than human. They kept their heads low, often cowering and shielding their eyes from bright flashes lighting the sky above the western front. Will counted at least a dozen of the ugly creatures, but more followed.

Over scattered brick and debris, the sickly little monsters climbed, then raised their heads, sniffing the air with large nostrils. With every distant explosion, they flinched. The flashes of light revealed something Will had not seen initially: each emaciated body was covered in a dark, scaly rash.

Will realized his mouth was hanging open, and he licked his dry lips. "What are those things?"

Rowe and Bremer looked almost as shocked as Will felt.

"Judging from the tattoos on their heads," Rowe said, "they must be Shalem priests…or at least they were at one time."

"And I recognize those scales on their backs," Will said. "But how could Phyriad infect them when they were locked inside the asylum?"

Rowe shrugged a shoulder. "They were in there a long time. Maybe—"

"Wait!" Bremer interrupted. "The lock on that gate was replaced recently."

Most of the creatures scurried toward the action on the western front. A few trailed behind and followed the river until one stopped at the bridge and sniffed. It made a strange guttural noise as if summoning the others to follow. Three creatures joined it and rushed across the bridge, sniffing the air as they went. They moved as a pack, picking up speed as they approached the small boat that the mer soldiers had been guarding. But now the boat looked abandoned.

The first Shalem priest to reach the riverbank sniffed around and stopped at the edge of the water. The other creatures scooted around the other side of the boat, faces low to the ground. Will gasped. If the creatures destroyed the boat, they would need to find another way to transport the thunderclaps.

Bremer made a move to climb down the ladder, but the three mer soldiers burst from the knee-deep water behind the boat. The Shalem priests hissed and reared. Tridents came around in wide arches, splitting three skulls. The fourth creature sprang back several yards, barely raising its head before a large spike shot from a trident and pierced its neck. The soldiers slipped beneath the surface, and the shoreline was quiet again.

Kalmar pointed to a new flurry of activity on the western front. "We need to hurry," he said.

The infected horde was trickling into the city. For every three that the magical bolts of lightning stopped, one slipped past unharmed. The group of Shalem priests would soon join the battle.

"Acttun may fall," Rowe said.

"Never thought I'd see this day," Bremer added, his voice despondent.

"There's nothing we can do to save the city," Rowe said. "Our job is to find the thunderclaps and get out of here."

He led the way back to the roof access building. The rusty gate hinges surrounding the structure squealed as he pushed it open and studied the door.

"Most of the security bars around the frame are loose," Bremer said. He looked down at the dead harvester. "Someone was here before us."

Bremer tested the door handle. It creaked and shifted, and the latch slid free. He held the door shut with his foot jammed against it, took a deep breath, and turned his head. For a split second, Will thought Bremer appeared nervous, but the rogue caught his eye and winked. Will shook his head. Would he ever be as fearless as Bremer? Did he even want to be?

Will lifted his shotgun from beneath his cloak and clicked on the flashlight mounted to the rail beneath the barrel. He had preloaded the gun with eight double-aught buckshot, each containing nine ball bearings he hoped would tear through the thickest, scaliest hide of whatever creature might still be inside the asylum.

Rowe and Bremer had seen the weapon several times, but the brightness of the flashlight surprised Kalmar, who stepped back. The mer captain glared at Will and shot his hand out, creating a sharp snap and a bright flash of light. A long, menacing trident appeared in his hand. This time, it was Will who stepped back as Kalmar lowered his weapon past Will's head and pointed it at the door. Kalmar planted his feet, gripped the trident shaft, and narrowed his deep-set eyes. Will remembered being terrified of Ryowyn's brother, Wrathan, but the mer prince was a minnow compared to this deadly shark.

Will had only seen a trident once when Wrathan and his soldiers had surprised him on the beach in Fairbay. He had always thought of the weapon as a simple three-pronged spear, but Kalmar's was nothing of the sort. The long shaft was made of dark-blue coral. Besides the three gleaming prongs at the top, a series of razor-sharp blades curved downward in the opposite direction, giving Kalmar the ability to kill when thrusting or pulling back. Two more six-inch blades surrounded the other end of the shaft.

Rowe drew his sword and stepped between Will and Kalmar. "The steps lead down into a short hallway. We turn left at the junction, then look for the third door on the right, the final door before the hallway turns left again. That will be Marlay's study." He gave a sharp nod to Bremer. "Let's make this fast."

Bremer pulled the handle, but the door didn't budge. He used both hands and tugged again until it screeched open an inch. A gust of dank air surged from the crack. Bremer slammed the door shut, stumbled sideways, and vomited. Will stepped in the opposite direction and did the same. Rowe shot back a step, burying his nose and mouth in his sleeve.

Kalmar lowered his trident. "I assume there is a vile odor inside?"

Will wiped his mouth. "That was awful! What's in there?"

Bremer gulped the outside air. "Rotting flesh, sewage, mold, experiments gone bad…"

"Or worse!" Will added, clenching his stomach.

Bremer pulled the sweaty handkerchief from around his neck and used it to cover his nose and mouth.

"I'm not sure how we'll breathe in there," Rowe said. "How long will you need to get the vault unlocked, Bremer?"

"I'll know in short order…if I can even do it."

Will opened the leather satchel he wore beneath his cloak and pulled out a linen shirt. With his boot knife, he sliced off a sleeve and tied it around his nose and mouth. Cutting off the second sleeve, he tossed it to Rowe, who did likewise.

Bremer braced himself in front of the door. This time, he yanked the door open all the way, then shifted to the side and drew a sword.

With weapons poised, they all stared at the dark opening, but only the rotten odor came out. The makeshift face masks helped, but Will still gagged. After a minute, the stench subsided as it mingled with the outside air.

Bremer stepped inside. Will shone his flashlight around the narrow stairwell beyond the door and followed to illuminate the way. Rowe and Kalmar were right behind.

It was calm inside except for an occasional rush of humid air.

Sweat tickled Will's forehead, and his hands became clammy. By the time they reached the bottom step, Bremer was wheezing. Will breathed through his mouth, fighting the growing itch in his throat. Something in the air irritated his eyes too, and blinking provided only minor relief. Rowe was rubbing his eyes, but Kalmar seemed unaffected; in fact, the mer captain seemed comfortable in the dark and damp environment.

At the bottom of the stairs, the floor was a thick blanket of moss. Large mushrooms grew in patches along the edges of the hallway. Near the center, narrow strips of moss had been peeled away to reveal dark hardwood planks beneath. Fresh splinters and chunks of cleaner wood indicated that something had recently gone mad in this place, gouging the moist, aged wood.

Will shone the flashlight against a stone wall slick with layers of dark mold. He traced a liquid stain to the floor where he saw the shattered pieces of a glass container.

Rowe grabbed Will's shoulder. "Don't go near that!" He kept his voice low. "It looks freshly broken. It could be the flask that the harvester used to infect this place with Phyriad. Let's keep moving."

Rowe led the way down the short hallway, taking slow, cautious steps. As they walked, the wooden floor beneath the carpet of torn-up moss flexed. Excessive moisture and water damage seemed to have compromised the floor's stability. At a junction, they turned left. Will's flashlight revealed three doors on the left and three on the right. The only closed door was the third one on the right.

"There's Marlay's study," Rowe said in a hushed voice, pointing at the closed door. "But be on guard as we pass the other rooms."

Muffled shouts and groans sounded from deep within the asylum. It was difficult to tell if the noises were coming from the top floor or one of the lower levels, but the danger seemed far enough away to proceed down the hall without incident.

The first two rooms on the left and right were pitch black. Mortared bricks sealed the window openings. Will shone his flashlight into the second room on the right and saw large objects hanging from dusty, cobwebbed wooden beams. He started to move his gun away to search the rest of the room, but Bremer grabbed the end of the barrel and held the light on one of the hanging objects. It resembled a giant cocoon with thick braided cords. A dark-green vine wrapped around the cocoon and connected it to the ceiling beam. Pale-yellow leaves grew along the vine and clung to the cords. It was a living thing, and Will shuddered to think what might be inside. Bremer released his grip on the gun barrel, and Will scanned the room. A half dozen more cocoons had been ripped open and were strewn across the room. They were all empty.

Rowe urged everyone on. "Nothing here to trouble us. Let's make sure that last room is empty before we open Marlay's study."

In the third room on the left, they found more cocoons, but these were much smaller and smoother. Most had fallen to the mossy floor where they had either burst open on impact or something had ripped them apart.

"What are those things?" Will asked. "It almost looks like skin."

Rowe raised an eyebrow with a look that suggested he was happy he didn't have to explain what Will had figured out on his own.

A slight movement and squishing sound deeper in the room caught Will's attention. He shone the light against the back wall. Large sluglike creatures the size of human toddlers recoiled from the light. Will couldn't point the flashlight away fast enough, and they headed toward the last door.

Bremer stepped into the middle of the hall, and the soft floor sank. He quickly shifted his weight closer to the wall. The others followed, stepping over the soft area, and gathered around the solid oak door to Marlay's study. Bremer stretched out his hand for the door handle but flinched when a loud, distant explosion came from outside. The battle raging along the western front had reached at a fevered pitch.

"We need to hurry," Rowe whispered. "But I don't know what might be waiting behind this door. Be careful."

Bremer put his ear to the door as the sounds from outside faded. He wiped his forehead and took a raspy breath. Will was also finding it difficult to breathe, as though the asylum were slowly suffocating them. Bremer tested the handle and found it unlocked. The heavy door swung open without a sound. He stepped to the side as Will aimed the shotgun into the room, his finger hovering close to the trigger. They both gasped at the same time.

Iron chains bound four bodies to metal bed frames with no mattresses or blankets. The stench of decay and feces was unbearable. The bodies resembled the creatures they had seen escaping the asylum, only these were covered in well-developed gray scales. Chains held their clawed hands to the bedposts. Deep gashes marred their limbs, and dried pools of blood stained the well-worn hardwood floor beneath each bed frame. Will noted that no moss grew in this room.

"These must have been among the first Shalem priests infected with Phyriad," Rowe said.

Kalmar moved about the room with his trident in front of him. Bremer poked with his sword at what looked like a lifeless body on a bed frame. The creature's eyes shot open, and it hissed through jagged fangs, rattling the chains against the metal frame as if trying to break free and attack. Bremer drew back, then drove his sword into the creature's head.

Will shone his flashlight at the other three beds, but none of those creatures moved. To be on the safe side, Bremer stabbed each one. A shiver shook Will's body, and he pointed the light away from the dead monsters.

Along the back wall was a long counter filled with stacks of old books, small flasks, and bowls of moss, dried leaves, and mushrooms. Sharp tools and broken glass littered the floor. An enormous armoire stood against another wall, its doors shut tight. Broken chairs lay near an empty table at the center of the room.

Rowe walked toward an open closet. "Bring the light over here, Will."

Bremer rushed to Rowe's side. The three men stood for a moment, their breathing now a dissonant wheezing.

Inside the closet was a large metal vault.

"This is it," Rowe whispered.

Will shone the light at the iron padlock, but Bremer pushed the gun barrel away.

"That's too bright," Bremer said. "I need something more direct. Rowe, use your sunstone."

Rowe reached into a pocket inside his cloak and held out the sunstone. The soft light illuminated the lock, and Bremer knelt to examine it.

Will stifled a cough, but it was louder than he'd expected. "Are we still worried about making too much noise?"

Bremer glared at him. "Only if you want to get out of here alive."

Will tried to suppress the tickle in his throat, but it was a losing battle. He coughed lightly into his elbow. Sweat saturated his back and armpits, and he assumed his face looked as ashen as Bremer's and Rowe's. His stomach grumbled, and his head swam.

Bremer's eyes were red and puffy. "Stand guard with Kalmar, kid. If you see anything moving—besides us—don't hesitate to use that thing."

Rowe tapped Bremer's shoulder. "Just get this open so we can get out of here." There was an uncharacteristically impatient edge to his voice.

Will leveled the flashlight across the room, checking the scattered debris for any sign of danger. He avoided Kalmar and the reach of his menacing trident.

Out in the hallway, a floorboard creaked. Kalmar was nearest the door, and he spun around, bringing his trident around waist height. Had anyone stepped into the room, the weapon would have cut them in two. Everyone froze, staring at the open door.

"I just need another minute," Bremer hissed.

"I'll check it out," Will whispered.

He stepped past Kalmar and eased the barrel of the shotgun into the hallway. The flashlight paused in front of each door, then stopped at the end of the hall. Will almost dropped the shotgun when he saw the Shalem priest.

The creature stood on all fours and lowered its chest inches from the floor. Its eyes were a solid glassy white, its dark face masked in scales. An irritated hiss leaked through its terrible teeth as the creature spun to avoid the light. It shuffled from one side of the hallway to the other, hissing constantly. Will trained the light on it, hoping for a clean shot, but the Shalem priest was too quick. It pivoted, then scurried toward Will in a crab-like movement. He stumbled backward.

The creature was less than six feet away when Kalmar leapt into the hallway. He threw his trident, but the creature moved too fast. The three prongs sank into the floor. The creature rushed past the weapon and sprang at Kalmar. Will shouted, unable to fire with the mer captain between him and the creature. But Kalmar was faster. He kicked the Shalem priest beneath the chin with enough force to send it crashing over onto its back. As the creature struggled to draw a breath, Kalmar jerked his trident from the floor and drove it into the scaly chest.

Rowe came to the doorway, sword raised, just as another Shalem priest dropped from the ceiling. The creature crashed onto Kalmar, who went down hard. He rolled over, forcing it from his back. It tumbled toward the doorway, and Rowe drove his sword into its skull.

"Got it!" Bremer called.

Rowe ran back into the room just as Will shouted, "Kalmar! Above you!"

Three more Shalem priests scampered across the ceiling like humanoid spiders.

"Cover your ears," Will said as he raised the gun barrel and took aim.

The report sounded like a cannon in the tight hallway, and a bright flash shot from the barrel. The ball bearings slammed into the nearest creature, splattering most of its chest into the ceiling. Its lifeless body landed next to Kalmar, who was clutching at his ears as he scrambled to the doorway behind Will.

The two remaining creatures fell to the floor from the shot's impact. Will pumped another round into the chamber and lowered the shotgun. He squeezed the trigger a second time, and another Shalem priest flew down the hallway in pieces. A few ball bearings clipped the third priest, raking its head.

Will was about to fire another shot when something reached out from the darkness for his face. He cried out in pain as claws scratched his neck. Before the creature dug deep, Kalmar leapt to his feet, twisted his trident, and a spike pierced its eye. The creature writhed and hissed for only a second before two more blades sunk into its neck.

Will spun around to see two creatures scurrying down from the ceiling. He fired another shot, and the broken remains of the Shalem priests crashed down. The hallway floor sagged under the weight of the mounting bodies.

Rowe appeared at the door beside Kalmar. "Will, you're bleeding!"

"No!" Will shouted. "Wait!"

Rowe stepped into the hallway, reaching to help Will, and the floor gave out beneath his stride. They both flailed their arms, grasping for the safety of Marlay's study, but the hallway floor collapsed into the darkness below, taking the two Callum Sages with it.

CHAPTER 12
FIRESIDE MEETING

Morgan was well past Little Hammerclaw when she turned to address the two soldiers from Marauders Brigade. She had noticed them riding behind her about ten minutes after she left the North Crow Gate. Their presence had irked her initially, but she understood Twell's concern for her safety. With a dragon threatening, it was unwise for anyone to be riding alone after dark.

"I'll find my own way from here. Thank you, gentlemen."

The soldiers brought their horses to a halt but did not turn back.

The lamplight cast a steady glow on the trail as Morgan continued to Will and Ryowyn's cottage. After a moment, she questioned her attitude toward the soldiers. Why did their presence bother her? In all likelihood, Twell had sent them not because he thought her weak but because he valued her and genuinely cared for her. So, why did she resist their help? Why did she have this need to convince others she was capable and resilient?

She realized now that she often responded to Rowe in the same way. Whenever she perceived that he doubted her ability or became overprotective, she worked harder to be strong. It was as if she were trying to prove herself worthy of his love or to demonstrate her love for him. Or both.

Morgan squeezed her eyes shut and rubbed her temple. All this self-examination was giving her a headache. Or maybe it was the sum of inhaling smoke from the fire at the North Crow Gate, the lack of sleep from worrying about Rowe, and the persistent grumbling in her stomach.

The smell of an outdoor barbecue and the sound of women's voices awakened her senses. Her mare went straight to the barn as if following its own nose toward the comfort of oats and shelter. Morgan stabled the horse and wandered past the cottage, which was lit only by a single lantern in the kitchen area. Out near the dock, a campfire illuminated the grass and trees. But where she had expected to find only her mother and Ryowyn, Morgan was surprised to see three other figures around the fire. Everyone was so engaged in lively conversation that they failed to see Morgan until she was about twenty feet from the fire.

"Is the wine chilled?" Morgan called out, startling her mother so much that she spilled part of her glass of wine.

"There she is!" Julie ran to embrace her daughter. "We were starting to worry."

"Sorry, I was…delayed. There was—"

"No need for excuses, kiddo. I hope you don't mind, but we have a few guests. I invited Gloriana, and she insisted on cooking for us."

"Come and eat, Morgan," Gloriana said as she pulled a cedar plank topped with a bright-red fillet from the fire. She pointed to a reclining beach chair where a small child lay sleeping under a thick blanket. "When Lillie discovered where I was going, she insisted on joining me. As you know, she's a hard one to refuse.

Ryowyn brought some mer younglings for her to play with, and there you have it," she said. "She's worn out after swimming and jumping off that new dock."

"They all loved her, of course," Ryowyn said. "And I hope it's no trouble, but I invited my mother."

Morgan bowed her head slightly when she met Almithara's eyes. Even without her royal dress, the mer queen was elegant and stunningly beautiful.

"It is good to see you again, Morgan Finley." A brilliant smile spread across Almithara's face.

Gloriana set a large iron skillet onto a grill above some glowing coals. The pan sizzled in a puff of steam when she tossed in a slab of butter. She stirred in the fresh-cut potatoes, carrots, onions, asparagus, and a wonderful blend of seasonings.

Morgan smiled back at the queen and inhaled the fusion of smells.

"And you remember Bremer's mother, Brynlee," Julie said. "She's been cooped up in the Crow's Nest, and I thought she was ready to see a bit more of this beautiful valley."

"I hope I'm not intruding on your evening plans," Brynlee said in a quiet voice.

The elderly woman seemed sad to Morgan, or perhaps a little frightened. She wondered if she would ever hear Brynlee's full story. The governess of Queen Alarra and mother of Bremer Mason must have lived an incredible life.

"Not at all," Morgan said. She shook Brynlee's hand, then stood by the fire to get the blood circulating in her legs after her ride. "I'm glad you're here, Brynlee." She looked around the circle of smiling faces. "And all of you."

Gloriana handed Morgan a cup of wine. "After the week you've had, this will do you good."

Morgan knelt in front of Lillie's chair and kissed the top of her head, hoping she would wake. The little orphaned girl's hair smelled like a fresh summer's day at the beach. Morgan's mind flooded with childhood memories of camping with her parents. She glanced at her mother, who cocked her head slightly, but the glint in her eye suggested she had a sense of what her daughter was feeling. Those were wonderful years, growing up in the safety of a loving family and a land unthreatened by war.

Lillie could not say the same. Her childhood was notably different, separated from a family she would never see again. Morgan touched the girl's clean, soft cheek and prayed that Lillie's dreams were all about her horse, Blackie. "Sleep in peace," she whispered.

Gloriana was smiling at Morgan with a twinkle in her eye. "She fell asleep the minute she finished eating."

"She tried to stay awake," Julie added with a wink. "But you know how a day at the lake can wear out a little girl."

Morgan smiled at her mother, shaking her head in wonder. How could a mother's love be so unconditional, so astute, so complete?

Almithara put her arm around Ryowyn. "Forgive me, Julie, but I think we both have little girls who never seem to tire."

Everyone laughed as Gloriana refilled wine goblets. Even Brynlee wore a closed-lipped smile, although the longing in her eyes was unmistakable.

Morgan raised her glass. "To mothers and their unshakeable love."

"And to their tireless daughters," Julie added.

The fire crackled and sent glowing sparks into the warm night air, and a gentle breeze carried them above the lakeshore where they dissolved into the starry sky.

"So, tell us what kept you at the wall this evening?" Julie asked. "When you left the infirmary earlier, you said you were just checking in with Commander Henowing."

Morgan tensed and shivered as if someone had just poured a bucket of water on the fire. "I think the burn marks will eventually fade." She accepted a bowl of fish and vegetables from Gloriana.

"What? What burn marks?" Julie asked. She knelt next to Morgan, examining her face, hands, and arms.

"I'm okay, Mom. Now don't freak out, but…the Red Dragon attacked." The statement was so plain that Morgan was not surprised by the incredulous looks on each face. She shoveled a spoonful of warm, moist fish into her mouth.

"You're serious!" Julie said.

Morgan nodded as she set her bowl next to the fire. "It was the craziest sixty seconds of my life—and I've had my share of crazy moments."

The other five women stood in rapt attention as Morgan recounted the traumatic tale. She was thankful that Lillie slept through it; the girl had been through enough terror already. When Morgan finished, the fire needed another log. The wine was all gone. A few yards away, the gentle waves lapped the shore.

"The minute I take my eyes off you…" Julie said, releasing a loud huff.

Morgan retrieved her bowl and took a small bite. "Trust me, Mom, I wish I'd come straight here with you guys. I just wanted to see if there was any news from Rowe and Will. I know it's too soon, but…" Morgan trailed off as hunger got the best of her. She downed two more spoonfuls.

"It was fortunate for us all that you were there," Almithara said.

"I can't believe how lucky we were. The wall is strong, and the soldiers are brave, but I don't know how we'll survive a sustained attack from the sky. It's like the Red Dragon was toying with us."

"Sounds like those thunderclaps might come in handy," Gloriana said. "I hope Rowe and the others arrived safely."

"They should have reached Acttun by now," Morgan said. "Feels like they've been gone a month."

"The thunderclaps might help us," Almithara said. "But do not be so quick to dismiss the gifts that already exist in this valley." Her eyes narrowed as she looked at Morgan as if trying to discern something unclear to her. "Or the strength that already lies within this circle of friends."

Morgan swallowed hard. All eyes were on her now. She lowered her head, her gaze flitting from her bowl to the fire to Lillie curled up in the chair.

Before anyone spoke further, the little girl stirred and let out a loud yawn. When she lifted her head off the chair and saw Morgan, her face came alive.

"Wait, wait, wait." Morgan quickly set her bowl down and scooped up the little girl. She kissed Lillie's tummy several times, then tickled her toes. "I don't want those clean little feet getting all dirty."

Lillie wrestled to defend herself, pulling her linen sleeping shirt down over her feet. Her giggles ignited smiles and soft laughter from the others. She clung to Morgan and buried her face in the Trannalun cloak. Morgan snatched the blanket from the chair and sat, bunching the warm fabric across Lillie's legs. The child climbed up and, after shifting a few times, settled into Morgan's lap.

The mer queen was smiling with the others, but she locked her eyes on Morgan. "Strength of a warrior in battle and heart of a compassionate friend…"

Morgan stifled a chuckle, feeling her cheeks warm. "I…I just did what I could today. Everyone did. Just like we all did at the South Crow Gate. I'd be dead if not for Twell and his soldiers. And Rowe, Dench, and the others." She turned to her mother. "And without the tireless work of Mom and Gloriana."

"Well, I knew you were special the day I met you," Gloriana announced. "One minute, you were stooping to notice the little ones—especially Lillie—and the next, you were flashing that sword and slaying harvesters. The South Crow Gate was no different. You helped us care for the wounded, and when the battle got worse, you fought right next to Rowe."

Ryowyn was bobbing her head as she responded to Gloriana's comments. "In Fairbay, while Rowe and Bremer fought slave runners, Morgan defended the captured children, killing a few slave runners to help free the little ones."

Lillie was wide-eyed, stroking Morgan's hair as she listened to the stories.

"She's always been like that," Julie added. "In competitions, she'd fight for the win as if her life depended on it. But her true strength lies deeper than that. Morgan's a caring friend and family member. She befriended Will when many people in our town shunned him. And she refused to give up on her father until…" Julie choked on a sob.

A tear trickled down Morgan's cheek as she watched her mother reopen the wound of losing her husband.

Almithara folded her arms across her chest as if daring Morgan to deny the compliments.

"Well…I…um, thank you for the kind words," Morgan said. "But I don't know where I'd be without each of you…and Rowe. And it doesn't hurt to have a magic cloak and sword."

"It was no accident of fate that brought you to the Fourwinds," Almithara said. "Do not take lightly the cloak you wear or the sword you carry."

"I've learned a bit about the Trannalun cloaks through experience and from Rowe," Morgan said as the questions she'd been collecting now spilled from her lips. "But I've wondered about the sword. How did it end up in our house? Where did Dad get it? And why didn't it burn my hands when I picked it up like it did Mom's? Why do I feel like I can't control its power?"

"The cloak is part of your heritage," Brynlee said. The older woman had been so quiet that Morgan had almost forgotten she was there. "Whether you accept or reject it," Brynlee continued, "a Callum Sage will always be a Callum Sage. But the sword of Avarthrill is another matter."

All heads turned to Brynlee.

"How—how do you know…" Morgan stammered. "The—the sword of…"

"Avarthrill," Brynlee said, looking at the confused expressions around the fire. "I am surprised Rowe has not already told you about it, but I imagine he has his reasons. It is a long story, and the hour is late. But I will be glad to share it with you someday, Morgan. And how do I know such things? I may be a simple old woman, but I learned a few things serving the royal family in Dwenlin Thah. And remember: my son was—or is—a Callum Sage. There is more to my family line than this feeble representative you see before you."

Morgan gaped at Brynlee.

"You should know," Brynlee said, "that the sword will not respond to just any warrior. Not even the bravest, most loyal, and trustworthy Callum Sage."

"I—I'm not a brave warrior," Morgan stammered. "I'm just trying to do the best I can. But I do want to be loyal and trustworthy."

Julie knelt beside Morgan's chair and touched her arm. "I may be biased speaking as your mother, Morgan, but I think everyone here trusts you completely. You don't need to prove yourself to us."

Ryowyn was smiling at Morgan with glistening eyes. "My brother was the warrior in our family. But I would fight by your side if you were the last Callum Sage standing."

A small tear spilled from Morgan's eye as she took the mer princess's hand. "Thank you, Ryowyn. Let's pray that day never comes."

CHAPTER 13
INFECTED

Will lay on his back surrounded by shattered floorboards and Shalem priest carcasses. He gazed up through the dimly lit hole that he and Rowe had fallen through, wondering if he had broken any bones. His vision was blurry, but he was unharmed. Somehow, between the magic of his Trannalun cloak and the thick cushion of moss in the fourth-floor hallway, he was still in one piece.

His shotgun had slipped from his hands when he landed and was lying next to him. The flashlight was still on, half buried in the mossy floor.

Rowe stood, his sword in front of him as he turned a quick circle before noticing Will on his back. "Easy, Will. Cover your mouth and slow your breathing."

Will sat up and grabbed the shotgun. As he rose to his feet, he shone the flashlight above and at the surrounding walls. The mold was much thicker on this level. He gagged and readjusted the tunic sleeve cloth over his nose and mouth. He drew a deeper breath, then launched into a short coughing fit.

Above them, Kalmar and Bremer appeared in the doorway to Marlay's study.

"Do you have any rope?" Rowe asked.

Bremer wagged his head. "Used it all climbing down the cliff, but I'll see if I can find something."

Will glanced around, following the light cast by the shotgun. Nothing moved, but farther down the hall, a Shalem priest hid in the mossy ceiling. It cowered when the light passed over it.

"Rowe," Will said, pointing to the creature. "We've got company."

The Shalem priest hissed and crept toward them, its hands and feet clutching the moss. The others had attacked quickly, but this one hesitated, averting its eyes from the light.

"There's no time, Bremer," Rowe said. "Collect the thunderclaps and get to the roof. We'll find another way out."

Will spun around, pointing the flashlight all around to make sure nothing else was about to leap from the shadows. He let out a slow breath; the creature on the ceiling was alone. Will struggled to suppress his coughing to help steady his aim. Between the noxious odor and his strained nerves, his stomach churned. They had to get out of the asylum before the mold and mildew did permanent damage to their lungs.

The Shalem priest inched closer. Will inhaled and held his aim. Rowe cringed to cover his ears. The explosion filled the small hallway and rang in Will's ears. The shot blew another smaller hole in the ceiling, and the creature's sloppy remains spilled to the floor.

"Sorry about the hole, Bremer," Will muttered.

Another Shalem priest approached from the shadows down the hallway.

Rowe grabbed Will's cloak and pulled him away. They turned right at the first junction but nearly collided with a wall of broken bed frames. Rowe let out a wheezy cough and kicked the tangled barrier in frustration.

"We'll have to go the other way," he said.

Will kept the flashlight pointed in front of them as they ran in the opposite direction. A few seconds later, he bumped into Rowe, who kicked at something slithering back into the spiral stairwell leading down.

Before Will could illuminate the top step, Rowe cried out, "Something just bit my leg!"

Will shone the light down in time to see Rowe kick the air, narrowly missing a small creature as it scurried down the stairs among the moss.

Rowe rubbed his leg. "You go first with the light."

Will stepped into the stairwell and saw something that looked like one of the Shalem priests, only much smaller. Not at all curious as to why it was different, Will lowered the barrel and fired without slowing, forcing them to walk through the bloody mess.

Will craned his neck to see around the bend in the stairwell. He and Rowe would be easy prey if there were more creatures lurking in the narrow confines. Thankfully, he saw nothing else until they reached the first floor where the stairs ended. Will ventured into the hallway, scanning the mess of rubble and moss. They were alone, but he could hear footfalls from the level above and from down the hall. It sounded as if all the creatures remaining in the asylum were converging upon them.

At the end of the hall, the dim moonlight shone through a window that had blasted open when Natas attacked. Will picked up his pace. A glimmer of hope spurred him forward, but Rowe jerked him back, saving him from a Shalem priest that dropped right in front of them. Before Will could react, Rowe lunged past and stabbed the creature as it spun to attack.

Will shifted the gun around in short, frantic motions, making it difficult to see more creatures blending into the moss and shadows around them. There were too many to fight. Will longed for the freedom offered by the open window. In his haste, he stepped on the leg of a small Shalem priest hidden in the moss. He felt the creature underfoot, and when he looked down, it sprang up and grabbed his ankle. Will cried out as it yanked his leg, nearly taking him down. The creature held tight and bit his ankle once, twice, three times, in rapid succession before Will shook it off. He fired point-blank and obliterated the creature.

"I can't breathe," Will gasped as his chest tightened.

"Keep moving," Rowe shouted, his voice raspy.

A cluster of Shalem priests appeared at the end of the hallway, blocking the way to the window. They shuffled among themselves and did not attack, as if aware of the danger the two intruders posed.

"There's too many!" Rowe said. "We have to find another way out."

Will dropped to his knees, whipped out his satchel, and pulled out a green box marked *Slugger High Velocity*. His hands trembled as he loaded eight shells into the shotgun.

"Get me to an outside wall or a window opening that's still bricked up."

Rushing back toward the stairs, they rounded a corner and stopped before a blocked window that spanned nearly floor to ceiling.

Will had never fired a one-ounce slug, nor had he ever tried to blast his way through a brick wall, but he was suffocating and desperate. Bending his knees slightly, he leaned back with the gun at his waist.

"Cover your ears!" Without waiting for Rowe's response, Will closed his eyes and pumped eight rounds into the wall in rapid succession.

The powerful blasts had the desired effect. Rowe kicked away loose bricks around a four-foot hole as Will loaded his shotgun with more double-aught buckshot should they need to fight their way to the river.

He shone the flashlight through the hole. Across the clearing, the three mer soldiers were near the boat killing two Shalem priests. Will slid through the opening, lowering himself as much as he could before dropping to the ground. He stepped to the side and Rowe landed next to him. Will started toward the boat to help the mer soldiers, but Rowe held his arm out, blocking his way.

"Stay back, Will," Rowe said. He pushed him away from the asylum but kept his distance from the boat.

"What is it?" Will shifted the light all around, expecting an attack from the shadows.

Rowe grimaced as he looked at Will's neck. "Your scratches… and the bites… We could be—"

Will inhaled through his teeth as he finished the thought.

Infected.

Rowe might as well have punched him in the gut. He wanted to deny it, but something told him Rowe was right: they were infected with Phyriad.

A distant explosion followed by a series of lightning flashes lit up the night sky. The battle raging on the western front had grown more intense while Will and Rowe were fighting their way through the asylum. The blasts and shouting sounded close.

Expecting a direct attack on the asylum, Will looked up into the sky. Silhouetted on top of the five-story building, Bremer stepped over the edge of the flat roof and started his descent down the ladder. Strapped to his back was a wooden box about two feet long and one foot wide.

When Bremer reached the bottom, he handed the box to Kalmar, who carried it into the boat.

"That's the last of them," Bremer told the mer captain. He turned to Rowe and Will. "Good to see you two made it out. Not surprised, given your luck."

Rowe held up a hand as Bremer walked toward them. "Not as lucky as you think. Don't come too close. We've both been bitten by Shalem priests and may be infected."

Bremer stopped in his tracks, his eyes growing wide. "You guys don't look so good. Take some deep breaths to get that poisonous air out of you."

Will coughed and hacked, struggling for a clean breath of fresh air. "I don't *feel* so good."

"Well," Bremer said, "you don't look near as bad as when I found you at the Clover Fields, all broken and feverish." His tone was hopeful, but the skeptical look on his face betrayed his true opinion.

"We need to get these thunderclaps back—" Rowe bent over as a dry cough broke his words.

"Hold on, Rowe," Bremer said. "You two are in no condition to reenter the valley. I'm putting you on that boat so Kalmar and his soldiers can take you back to the North Crow Gate for quarantine. The mer should be able to keep their distance from you by pulling the mooring ropes."

Rowe hung his head, wearing a look of resignation. "I know, I know. But I want you to do something for us."

"Anything."

"It's possible that Marlay is still alive and somewhere in the city. Someone had been working in his study before we got there. Things were in disarray as if someone were experimenting and had to leave in a hurry. It could have been Marlay. If you can find the wizard, he might know of an antidote or some spell to stop Phyriad from spreading."

"Sounds like a long shot," Bremer said. "But I'll try. Now, get in the boat and get back to the valley. You'll have a better chance of fighting this sickness there." He pointed to their Trannalun cloaks. "Those things have brought you back from near-death experiences more than once. Maybe they can keep the infection from spreading."

He let out an exasperated huff as he led Rowe and Will to the boat. "I'll see if I can find Meagan at the Cauldron's Stew. I could use a drink or three, although I doubt she's open for business. She might know how to help me find Marlay."

Kalmar and the three mer soldiers were already in the water, ropes in hand.

In the center of the boat, three wooden boxes were nestled together, tied to the middle seat. As Will stepped inside, he wondered what a thunderclap looked like and how to use one as a weapon. But he was too weary to ask, so he curled up in the stern. As he lay still, his Trannalun cloak warmed and gave him a degree of comfort. The scratches in his neck throbbed, and his leg burned where the Shalem priest had bitten him. Before he closed his eyes, he saw Rowe finding a place to lie down in the bow. The boat lurched forward and skimmed across the smooth river.

Will fell asleep remembering the pain and sickness he had battled while captive in the Clover Fields. He grit his teeth. Why was it that every time he had an opportunity to help, his weaknesses rose to defy him? He should be on the front lines, but now he needed rescuing again. The thought of letting down the three women he cared for most—Ryowyn, his mother, and Morgan—was unbearable. And if Rowe was too sick to help, who would lead the survivors in the Rainia Valley in the fight against Natas?

CHAPTER 14

A NEW PLAN

It was almost midnight when Ryowyn led Brynlee inside to sleep in the cottage's spare bedroom. Gloriana followed, taking Lillie inside so they could stretch out together in Will and Ryowyn's bed. It was far too late for anyone to go back to the Crow's Nest, so Ryowyn had volunteered to give up her bed and spend the night with her parents in the lake. Morgan and Julie were happy to roll out mats and blankets in the loft.

But Morgan was not sleepy. The food, wine, fresh air, and intriguing conversation had given her an extra boost. She added a few more logs to the fire and pondered Brynlee's words. *The sword of Avarthrill.* Morgan knew it was special, but the thought of needing to be a brave, trustworthy warrior made her uncomfortable. She watched her mother and Almithara engaged in quiet conversation. They were the leaders, not her.

Ryowyn returned alone and filled Almithara's cup with white wine. The queen raised the cup to her lips, then paused. Something near the lake caught her attention. Her bright-blue eyes sparkled in the firelight as she turned her head. Morgan followed her gaze and saw someone standing at the end of the dock watching them.

"Who is it, Mother?" Ryowyn asked as she and Julie peered through the darkness. "Did someone come while I was inside?"

Almithara was shaking her head. "No one could have swum undetected past my guard."

The queen took the first step toward the dock, and the other three women followed. Morgan's hand rested on her sword pommel.

The figure on the dock strode to meet them.

"Alyssa," Morgan breathed, recognizing Will's mother.

"I know you," Ryowyn said. "I look into those eyes every day. You are the mother of my Will."

Julie gripped Morgan's arm. "Alyssa Owens?" Her eyes were wide as if she were seeing a ghost. "So, it's true…"

"I'm sorry to startle you," Alyssa said.

"Remember what Rowe said, Mom. Alyssa, Will's mom, is—"

"The Ice Dragon," Almithara said. "I have heard the stories, and I must say, this is quite an intriguing evening."

Alyssa wore a gown of soft pure-white fabric that flowed as she walked barefoot. Her porcelain skin glowed and her cool blue eyes softened as they settled on Ryowyn.

"Yes," Alyssa said in a somber tone. "I am Will's mother. And I bring news."

Morgan's heart leapt to her throat, and Ryowyn gasped.

Alyssa inhaled a deep breath. "May I join you?"

"Of course," Almithara said as she stepped back toward the fire. "You are welcome here."

Ryowyn opened her arms and embraced Alyssa. Morgan raised her eyebrows, surprised by the princess's boldness. Alyssa was unfazed and smiled as she held her tight.

"It is good to finally meet you, Ryowyn."

Morgan put her arm around Julie and led her to a chair. Ryowyn and Almithara returned to their chairs by the light and warmth of the fire, but Alyssa kept her distance from the flames.

"Last night," Alyssa explained, "Will and the others secured the thunderclaps from the asylum. Kalmar and his soldiers are on their way back as we speak, transporting the thunderclaps in a small boat. But there was an unexpected confrontation inside the asylum. During that struggle, Rowe and Will became infected with Phyriad."

Morgan and Ryowyn shot from their chairs.

"They are safe," Alyssa said, raising her hands to calm them. "They were riding in the boat with the thunderclaps when I came to them under cover of darkness." She turned to Almithara. "I'm sorry, Your Majesty, but I frightened your soldiers despite my every effort. I carried Will and Rowe to the outpost cabin just beyond the caverns in the mountains beyond the Crow's Nest."

Tears clouded Morgan's vision despite her efforts to contain them. "That's where we spent our first night away from the Crow's Nest. Rowe loved that place."

"Will they be all right?" Ryowyn asked. "Can we help them?"

"When they awoke in the cabin," Alyssa continued, "they had no idea how they had arrived there. I locked boundary collars on them so they cannot travel more than a dozen yards from the cabin. If their condition worsens, we cannot have them wandering off."

"What do you mean, '*if* it worsens'?" Almithara said. "We saw what Phyriad did to our people."

"Their Trannalun cloaks seem to be slowing the spread of the sickness," Alyssa said. "But I'm not sure if the magic will be enough to restore them."

Morgan's legs trembled, and she slumped back into the chair. Conversation continued around her, but her heart was aching for Rowe. She knew the thunderclaps were important to protect the valley, but she wished there was another way or that someone else could've gone. But it was too late for wishing; her worst fears had come true. Despair pulled her lower until Alyssa's words lifted her spirits.

"There might be another option," she said.

Ryowyn leaned forward, her wide eyes glistening with hope. "Anything," she said. "What can we do?"

Alyssa took a moment to study their faces. "As you probably know, Phyriad originated in the Maidstone. What you may not know is that it was Sidara who created *part* of it. The worst part."

"I thought her alchemists created it," Morgan said.

"Partly true," Alyssa continued. "As a child, Sidara was invited to study at the Acttun Academy, and she quickly set herself apart from the other students."

"Wait a second," Julie interjected. "Sidara? I thought Rowe said her name was Nyrianne." Julie spoke slowly, as if trying to assemble a puzzle in her head with pieces that didn't fit. "She's the strange old woman I met during the battle at the South Crow Gate."

"That's right," Morgan said. "So how did the Dark Queen become that old woman?"

"That's an interesting question," Alyssa answered. "Will bested her in the Waerdreath, triggering her warding magic that transported her away. But the damage was done, and the Dark Queen had to expend a tremendous amount of magic to stay alive. In fact, she could no longer fend off the aging process, as she had done for many years. And so, in a matter of days, she became the old woman you saw at the South Crow Gate."

Morgan rubbed her eyes with the palms of her hands. "The Dark Queen, Sidara—aka Nyrianne—almost killed us at the Waerdreath. But as far as we know, the old woman, Nyrianne, *saved* us by destroying the southern passage beyond the South Crow Gate. I'm confused."

Alyssa nodded as she sat in the chair between Julie and Morgan. "Let me tell you more of her story. When Nyrianne's potential at the Academy came to light, one of her teachers—Addolay Bonicle—took advantage of her gifts. He tapped into her power and stole it from her. His methods were tortuous and brutal, especially for a small child. It was several years before Addolay's brother, Marlay, discovered what Addolay was doing to the girl. To protect Nyrianne, Marlay stole her away to the Maidstone for safekeeping.

"A small group of alchemists and sorcerers had discovered a way into the ancient tower and set up residence in a massive underground laboratory beneath the Maidstone. They agreed to protect the child and care for her until Marlay returned. But he never did.

"The two brothers conjured powerful magic in their famous confrontation. In the end, Addolay was killed and the Academy was razed to its foundations. Grief and shame overwhelmed Marlay. So, he sent some older students to join Nyrianne at the Maidstone and locked himself in his tower home in Acttun."

"And…did the students care for Nyrianne?" Julie asked.

Alyssa sighed. "I cannot say for certain. My guess is that she never forgave Marlay for abandoning her, or the Academy for abusing her. When Nyrianne eventually asserted herself as the one in charge of the Maidstone, she established a working relationship with Natas. Together, they took over the underground laboratory. To the best of my knowledge, Natas manipulated her. She became an unwilling participant in the development of Phyriad, working with some of the extremely contagious viruses found deep inside the Maidstone."

"But, why would Nyrianne help with something like Phyriad?" Morgan asked.

Alyssa nodded slowly. "After the abuse at the Acttun Academy, Nyrianne's broken heart hardened in her quest for power. Clouded by revenge, she agreed to leave the entire team of alchemists at the Maidstone to continue the experiments in exchange for the Waerdreath throne. To this day, I do not believe that she truly understood the purpose of Phyriad. She did, however, understand how contagious it was, and so she created an antidote at her labs in the Waerdreath. My understanding is that the antidote was stored in both the Waerdreath and the Maidstone."

Julie sat upright, gripping the arms of her chair as if waking from a dream. "Is it a vaccine or a cure?"

Alyssa shrugged. "I don't know."

"Would they create a vaccine without creating a cure?" Morgan asked.

Julie shook her head. "Not sure. But I would be surprised if people smart enough to develop something like Phyriad would not also create a cure. Accidents happen in lab experiments all the time."

"We need to go there—at once!" Ryowyn said.

The bright eyes and nods of the others suggested unanimous agreement with Ryowyn. But Morgan stared into the fire, wondering who would make such a journey. Rowe was best qualified to lead, but that was impossible.

Julie leaned in and touched Morgan's cheek. "I recognize the turmoil in your eyes. It's the way you looked before facing Larionoff at the World Championships. Confidence, determination, and doubt all mixed up inside you. But you did it, Morgan. And I believe we can do this too."

"We?" Morgan said.

Julie nodded.

"I'm going too," Ryowyn said. She turned to her mother.

Almithara's eyes were glassy. Morgan couldn't imagine the grief the queen must have felt losing her son, Wrathan, and now she faced releasing her daughter to risk a similar fate.

Morgan stifled a laugh. "So, three women charging the gates of hell?"

"Better make that *four*," Alyssa said. "With the Red Dragon's arrival, the time of my hiding is over. But doing so will force a confrontation with Natas."

Morgan drained her cup and swallowed hard. Will had described his brief journey into the mysterious tower, a place she had hoped never to enter. But now it seemed inevitable. And adding to her fear of the Red Dragon, Alyssa was suggesting that they also faced the possibility of an encounter with the Iron Dragon.

"How will we know where to find the antidote once we're inside?" Julie asked. "Will mentioned several hallways and stairs, and you said there's an underground lab. We could be searching for a needle in a haystack."

"There is someone else who must journey with us," Alyssa said. "Someone who knows how to navigate the Maidstone, and how to find what we're looking for."

The circle was silent for only a moment before Morgan understood. "As far as we know, Alyssa, Nyrianne died when she brought the mountain down on the gnome army at the South Crow Gate. No one has seen her since."

Alyssa shook her head. "Nyrianne lives. And we have already discussed the possibility of finding the antidote inside the Maidstone. She agreed to go, but her strength is failing. To complicate matters, her mind is slipping. I suspect that her instability has something to do with her loss of anti-aging magic and all the trauma she's been through in her troubled life. It's finally catching up with her. She might not be one hundred percent reliable, but if we need a guide—and I believe we do—then she's our best option."

"Will said there were…*things* in there," Ryowyn said. "Creatures he could not see clearly as he fled with the horn of Thaudas."

Alyssa stood and placed her hands on her hips. "This will be a journey fraught with danger. But if we succeed, imagine how many lives we can save."

"How do we find Nyrianne?" Julie asked.

Alyssa smiled at her. "Nyrianne spoke highly of you, Julie. And she told me that *she* would find *you*."

"What about Rowe and Will?" Ryowyn asked. "Who will care for them until we return?"

"I will take them water and supplies in the morning," Alyssa said. "And I will leave instructions with Gloriana and Joe. We need to leave tomorrow—or I suppose it's late enough now to say *today*. I want to arrive at the Maidstone by the evening."

"How many nights should we plan for?" Ryowyn asked.

"It's a four-hour flight, but I cannot say how long it will take to find what we need. Hopefully within a day, then a four-hour flight home."

"I will speak with Ryodan at once," Almithara said. She walked to the end of the dock and dove into the water.

"It's late," Alyssa announced. "You three get some sleep. I'll be back by midmorning to help prepare for our journey."

CHAPTER 15

Marlay Bonicle

Bremer watched as the small boat carrying Rowe and Will skimmed along the Serpentine River and disappeared into the night. Throughout Acttun, terrified shrieks pierced the shouting and explosions. The Shalem priests that had escaped from the asylum were wreaking havoc in the city. Bremer wanted to burn the cursed building to the ground but knew that, if he did, more creatures would flee through the reopened windows. Better to let them remain inside as long as possible. Instead, he ran toward the city in search of vengeance and a thread of hope for Rowe and Will.

Across the first bridge, he saw a Shalem priest covered in gray scales scurrying from a cottage. Fresh blood ran down its face. Bremer drew a knife from his chest brace and threw it as he rushed forward. The knife struck the creature in an armpit, dropping it into a heap of flailing limbs. Bremer silenced it with one swing of his sword.

He dropped to his knees, slipped off his quiver, and used his finger to trace a series of lines that began as one and ended in a dozen points. A single arrow materialized, longer and twice as thick as an average one. Bremer pulled the arrow from the quiver and casually drove the tip into the dead priest's chest, soaking the arrowhead in thick, dark blood. He didn't know how the arrow would respond when launched from the magical bow that once belonged to a dark elf, but there was only one way to find out.

He nocked the large arrow, and the bow vibrated and hummed. Without another thought, Bremer aimed the arrow skyward above the city and released it. The bow bucked hard and might have broken his wrist had he not been ready. The arrow shot into the night sky and broke apart into twenty-one individual arrows, complete with fletchings and hunting tips. Fresh blood on the arrowheads directed each one to Shalem priests scattered throughout the city. Sixteen arrows pierced the hearts of creatures in the open streets, pinning them to the hard ground. The other five arrows plunged through rooftops, killing Shalem priests that had crept into cottages to find helpless victims.

Bremer sprinted across another bridge to an island inhabited by spell casters. Many were out in the streets, their colorful robes and bright sashes flowing as they waved their arms and directed their energy toward the western border of the city. Everyone ignored Bremer as he ran past on his way to another bridge.

On the next island, brown-robed alchemists congregated in the center market around a large trebuchet. Three alchemists filled strange leather sacks with a coarse blue crystal. When they were ready, a man released the trebuchet, launching the leather sacks in a high arc above the only bridge into the city. The sacks burst open on the main road into Acttun where the Phyriad-infected horde gathered, seeking passage across the guarded bridge. A single flaming arrow followed the sacks. When it struck the ground, the crystals exploded into an inferno of light-blue flames.

Bremer shielded his eyes from the intense light and ran along a row of cottages. His chest heaved, and his lungs burned from smoke and the aftereffects of the toxic asylum air. He spotted a Shalem priest crawling into a broken window and drew a single arrow. The creature was only thirty feet away, but people were running across Bremer's path, blocking a clear shot. A narrow gap in the crowd opened, and the arrow took flight, pinning the Shalem priest's head to the window frame. Inside the cottage, a woman screamed.

Bremer rounded a corner and stepped into the most popular street in the city, right across from the Cauldron's Stew. A man and a woman were nailing wooden planks across the inn's front windows. Bremer called out to the woman, but shouts and explosions only a few blocks away muffled his voice. He shot another arrow at a Shalem priest climbing up the tavern wall. The woman spun around.

"Meagan!" Bremer yelled.

"Good heavens, lad, why am I not surprised to see you here!" Meagan's eyes lit up as she flashed a smile despite the chaos around them. "You're a touch late, I'm afraid."

"I'm always here at closing."

Meagan clutched him in a tight embrace. "I meant for saving the city. Those fireballs protecting the bridge will soon fail. We need to leave!"

"No," Bremer growled as he held her shoulders and looked into her eyes. "I have to find the wizard. Rowe's been infected, and there's only one person in this city powerful enough to help him."

Meagan stared as if Bremer were crazy. He didn't need to say the famous wizard's name, even though no one had seen him for years. But after a moment, Meagan's cheeks went slack.

"You're serious," she said.

"Never been more so, Meagan."

She huffed. "Shortly after the first defense went up at the main bridge, a young man came into the Stew and said he'd seen the wizard. Everyone laughed at him…"

"Where?" Bremer said, shaking her slightly. "Did he say where he saw him?"

Meagan pointed toward the river. "Beyond the bridge, there's a—"

Before she could finish, Bremer dashed down the street, dodging people fleeing in the opposite direction. He stopped near a small bridge leading to the western entrance.

On the other side of the bridge, a host of sorcerers and wizards gathered in six circles, with two wizards and four sorcerers forming each circle. They were floating several feet above the ground, the wizards with their arms skyward, heads back, while reciting a long and complex spell. The sorcerers were in kneeling positions, singing as their hands danced around them. Many of the words in the song sounded similar to the words in the wizard's spell, but Bremer understood none of it. Off to the side, a sizeable group of alchemists was preparing to launch the largest display of fireworks he'd ever seen.

As he crossed the small bridge, another fireball protecting the main bridge snuffed out, leaving only one to orbit the bridge. The wizards and sorcerers increased their volume and rose a few inches higher. Bremer exchanged his bow for two swords as he stepped off the bridge. If the collective power of these magicians could not protect the city, maybe it was time for some brute force. He passed beneath the six circles of magicians and almost bumped into a tall man emerging from the shadows.

Dressed in a finely crafted green robe, the man wore a small orange hat that barely covered the top of his stubby white-haired head. His face was freshly shaved, except for a long white beard trailing from his pointy chin. There was a timelessness about him, and a sadness in his eyes as he stared across the main bridge at the Phyriad-infected horde.

The group of floating magicians grew silent and lowered to the ground. All eyes focused on the tall stranger. By their reverence, Bremer knew he had found the wizard he was seeking.

"Marlay Bonicle," he breathed.

"Who roused me?" Marlay mumbled, his lips pursed in an angry grimace. Without waiting for a response, he adjusted his robes and walked toward the main bridge.

A cluster of Shalem priests, crawling low to the ground like spiders, darted through the shadows and encircled Marlay. Two broke from the group to attack Bremer. When they were close enough to leap at him, Bremer slashed both swords, severing two heads at once. He sheathed the swords and readied his bow. But before he could shoot a single arrow, Marlay waved a hand at the Shalem priests. Their frail bodies tumbled through the air in various directions, slamming into buildings with bone-cracking force.

With a loud blast, the alchemists released their fireworks. Bright streaks sailed over the main bridge and into the night sky. Seconds later, and a half mile beyond the forest, massive explosions shook the earth. The noise and flashes drew some of the horde away from the city.

Marlay moved forward, and Bremer followed a few yards behind. A gathering crowd joined the thirty-six wizards and sorcerers, all staring in awe at the infamous wizard.

The final fireball orbiting the main bridge faltered and went dark. Marlay continued toward the bridge, swinging his arms back and forth in an underhand motion as he widened his stride.

A wave of Phyriad-infected attackers swarmed the bridge as the wizard started his approach. Marlay's arms flew back and forth, suddenly releasing globs of thick green slime in a high arc toward the bridge. Each one landed in a violent explosion. Within minutes, liquid fire doused the entire road all the way up the hill. Screams filled the hillside as Phyriad-infected victims found themselves trapped in the growing inferno. Marlay continued to launch green globs around the hillside, burning everything within a hundred yards of the main bridge.

When the wizard finally stopped his attack, only the sound of sizzling and crackling remained. The steep road leading into the city was a sea of green fire.

Bremer stood with the others, gaping. Acttun had been spared… for now.

Marlay stretched his arms and let out a long, full yawn. He scratched his cheek and jolted when he saw Bremer standing so close. The other wizards and sorcerers stepped back, but Marlay casually turned his gaze back to the road as though admiring his work.

"I have two questions. First, how long have I been asleep?" he asked, his voice pitchy. "And second, where can I get a drink at this hour?"

The next day, Bremer awoke in a patch of grass near the main bridge. The afternoon sun blazed in his eyes. His arm shot up in defense, and two empty wine bottles clinked beside him. He swallowed dryly and pushed himself into a sitting position. As his eyes adjusted to the brightness, he found himself sitting a dozen feet from Marlay Bonicle. A crowd of people was staring at Bremer, but he soon realized that they were all gathered around the wizard, who sat in a padded chair in the middle of a manicured lawn.

Bremer scrambled to his feet, brushing himself off. A thin bright-yellow scarf was tied loosely around his waist. He pulled it off, tossed it aside, and rubbed his aching head, smirking as last night's memories came rushing back. The details were foggy, but the women in Acttun were, as always, unforgettable.

After Marlay had destroyed the attacking horde and saved the city, a lively celebration ensued. No one could sleep after terror turned to relief and joy. Everyone wanted to see the great wizard, and he had not failed to delight and entertain. In the light of day, Marlay appeared quite common, despite his above-average height and funny orange cap. He met Bremer's gaze and scratched his chin.

"Now, that was a night," Bremer said, smacking his lips. He really needed a drink.

Marlay raised his bushy gray eyebrows. "Definitely worth waking for."

A wave of gratitude, punctuated by laughter, swept through the crowd.

Bremer lowered his eyes and kicked an empty bottle. "That stuff makes tevan root seem like an herb for children." He scratched away some sleep crusted in the corner of his eye. "Speaking of things that ease pain and cure sickness—"

"Yes, yes," Marlay interrupted. "You spoke of your two friends last night."

Bremer rubbed the back of his neck. Some memories were fuzzier than others. "I did?"

"You did. And you told me how, why, and *where* they became infected. How dare they break into my office and steal my thunderclaps! It serves them right. Never thought we might need thunderclaps here in Acttun, did they? Could've used them last night against the Iron Dragon!"

Bremer hung his head. He was still getting used to the old wizard's odd mannerisms and didn't know if he was genuinely angry or just trying to draw attention to himself. "We thought the Rainia Valley was more vulnerable than Acttun."

"Of course you did. And it might be." Marlay leaned forward, his eyes narrowing. "Did they happen to leave any thunderclaps?"

Bremer winced. "We took them all."

Marlay clicked his tongue and wagged his head. "Shame. Well, I might need to make more, then, but it's a tedious process." He removed his hat and scratched the top of his head.

Bremer waited a moment, but his patience was growing thin. "About my two friends…"

Marlay glared at Bremer. "I'm sorry to say, but from what I saw of that infected horde, your friends are in for a rough go."

"I was hoping you'd have something to help them."

Marlay slapped both hands on his knees and stood. "You were right to look for me; there are few who can match my abilities. I'm not boasting, just stating the truth. But there's not a wizard alive who could conjure a cure for what you called Phyriad."

Bremer felt his shoulders slump.

Marlay stepped closer and lowered his voice so only Bremer could hear. "However, I do know someone who should be able to help. But he's not a wizard." He wrapped his arm around Bremer's shoulder and led him toward the riverbank. "Have you ever been to the Druid Forest?"

So Many Questions

"Someone kill me," Will said as he rolled his eyes to see Rowe entering the cabin.

Rowe tugged on the collar chafing his neck. "You look terrible."

"Take a look in the mirror, buddy. You don't look so good yourself." Will coughed. "How far did you get?"

Rowe sniffed. "No matter which direction I try, the collar prevents me from going more than twenty paces from the front door."

The cabin was warm, and morning sunlight beamed through the large front window with the promise of comfort. But a feverish chill crept over Will, and he pulled his Trannalun cloak around his shoulders. "But why would someone constrain us? I'm too sick to go anywhere."

Rowe dropped into in a wide, padded chair. "Are you serious?"

Will closed his eyes and groaned against his pounding headache before shaking his head. "About what?"

"Once our condition deteriorates…well, they don't want us running off."

Will wiped his runny nose with his sleeve. "But this isn't the quarantine area Morgan and Julie set up. This is prison. Man! I wish I remembered how we got here."

"I think our case is different, Will. As bad as we feel, our cloaks might be slowing the process. Whoever brought us here seems to have a plan, and we have to trust them. There's not much we can do to help ourselves, except hold on to hope."

"I'll drink to that," Will said with his arm draped over his eyes.

"Speaking of which, you still aren't drinking enough water."

"My head's killing me," Will groaned.

Rowe thrust a canteen into Will's hands. "So, drink!"

After a long nap, Will awoke to discover his headache had subsided. His lungs felt marginally better. He took a few deep breaths and stretched. The cloak's fabric was as hot as it had been after his escape from the Clover Fields prison camp. From that experience, he knew that the magic was responding to his sickness. But would it be enough to restore him as it had before?

He sat up on the edge of the bed. Although he couldn't say what day it was, he figured it was around noon. He stood and stretched his arms above his head, which induced a brief coughing fit. Rowe lay fast asleep in the next bunk and didn't stir.

Will stepped outside and nearly shouted at the sight of someone sitting in the chair beside the door, quietly gazing at the picturesque view from the ridge.

"Mom?" Will said.

Alyssa stood and took him into a tight embrace. They held each other for a long while until Will sniffled several times and pulled away.

"I'm contagious!" he said.

"Don't worry; Phyriad cannot infect me."

Will sighed. "So, it's true." He wiped a tear from his cheek. "Rowe told me you're the Ice Dragon."

Alyssa nodded and motioned for him to sit.

"Did you…*fly* us here?"

She smiled. "Being a dragon has its advantages."

"How did you know where to find us? Did you know we were infected?"

"Natas led the attack on Acttun. And he is responsible for the spread of Phyriad in the asylum. He has come into the open, and now I must do likewise should we have any hope of standing against him." The stern expression on her face reminded Will of the time she'd spoken to his principal after an unsuccessful fight Will had gotten into with a bully in the third grade.

"I'm leaving for the Maidstone today," she continued, "but Ryowyn wanted me to bring you two a box of food and clothes." She inhaled and smiled again. "And I needed to see you."

"The Maidstone?" Will asked. "Why are you going there?"

"Shortly after Phyriad was discovered there, Sidara's alchemists developed an antidote. I'm hoping it's still there."

"Too bad I didn't know that a couple weeks ago; I could've picked it up while I was there."

Alyssa chuckled. "I'm afraid it's not that simple. And from what I understand, you barely escaped with the horn of Thaudas."

She pulled the front door closed and lowered her voice. "I'm glad Rowe is sleeping. He would not like my plan." She crouched next to Will. "I'm taking a team with me: Morgan, Julie, Nyrianne, and…Ryowyn."

Will sputtered and coughed, trying to sit up. "What? No! We're going with you!"

"Stay calm, Will. Remember what I told you and Morgan: if one of you falls…"

Will slouched back in the chair. "The other must take up the banner." The pounding in his head resumed. "But why am I always the one to fall?"

Alyssa laughed softly. "Because you're the best at getting up again. You've done exceptional things in the Fourwinds, and if we can find a cure for Phyriad in the Maidstone, you will do great things again. But you and Rowe must stay here to allow your cloaks to slow the spread of the sickness."

"But why does Ryowyn need to go? It's too dangerous."

"She is stronger than you think, Will. And fiercely determined. You know from experience not to underestimate the love of a mer. It will carry her through the darkest times. We also may need to call upon her healing arts. And she will be a good companion for Morgan."

Will lifted a canteen from the box Alyssa had brought. He took a few sips and wiped his mouth. "You'll look out for them? It's an evil place, Mom."

"I understand, and I will. But I need you to do something for me, Will. Can you tell Rowe what we're doing?"

Will glanced at the door and nodded. "He's not gonna like it, but he'll understand. How long will it take?"

"If all goes well, I should be back here with the antidote in two days."

"Two days." Will massaged his forehead. "I hope we're still human by then."

Inside the Crow's Nest, Julie said goodbye to Gloriana, Brynlee, and Lillie. They had all risen at dawn, and Julie agreed to help them safely from the cottage back to the castle. The urge to check in with the staff at the infirmary was strong, but Julie resisted. She knew if she went there, she'd be working for hours. The infirmary was in capable hands, and Will and Rowe depended on her and the others to find the antidote. Alyssa would be waiting at the cottage, and Julie still needed to go to Little Hammerclaw for a few supplies…and for Nyrianne.

Julie walked the halls of the castle, marveling at the history. A few years ago, she had spent two weeks in London while her husband, Grant, attended a conference on church growth strategies. While Grant was in meetings, Julie had explored historic sites such as Windsor Castle, St. Paul's Cathedral, and the Tower of London. But none of those buildings compared to the ancient quality of the Crow's Nest. The narrow passages, the sprawling great hall, and the colorful handcrafted tapestries adorning the inside walls created a sense of being part of something larger than herself. But the thought of being in a different world or time made her head spin.

She traced a finger along the stone wall as she made her way down a long, spiraling stairwell. The hard soles of her tall leather boots echoed off the walls as she stepped into the busy keep where people were already bustling about their various duties.

During her brief time in the Rainia Valley, Julie had already made a name for herself. She had worked with Gloriana at the South Crow Gate battle, and then in the infirmary caring for the wounded. Even so, she felt out of place when she saw the strange medieval-style clothes everyone wore. She glanced down at her light tunic tucked into her riding pants and realized she wasn't all that different. She smiled as people offered her friendly nods and curtsies. Everyone valued health-care workers—or *healers*, as they were called here. Julie wasn't used to the attention, nor did she particularly enjoy it. But she loved people and happily returned each greeting.

She crossed the broad courtyard to the main stables and retrieved her horse. It was an easy ride to Little Hammerclaw, but long enough for Julie to plan the supplies needed for the trip to the Maidstone. She had left the food planning to Morgan and Ryowyn, so she would only need clean strips of cloth and a few herbs Gloriana had told her to look for. The local medicine would complement the kit she had brought from Cochrane.

In Little Hammerclaw, she rode past crews of workers building houses and shops for the exploding population. She followed a smaller road a dozen yards from the shores of Rainia Lake. The crowd thinned, and Julie was startled to see someone suddenly walking beside her mare.

The old woman walked with a hunched back and a distinct limp. Despite layers of clothing and the warm morning sun, she wrapped her woolen shawl tighter and hugged her body. Julie recognized the woman instantly and brought her horse to a halt.

"Oh, child, you mustn't be frightened of me," Nyrianne said with a mischievous smile as she patted the mare. "Were you not expecting me?" She chuckled, which came out more like a cackle. "Yes, yes. But perhaps a younger version of old Nyrianne?"

It was true, Julie realized. The woman looked much older than the last time they'd met, which made no sense because not even a month had passed.

"What—what happened to you?" Julie asked.

Nyrianne squinted as she gazed out at the lake. "Now, what

kind of question is that to ask an old woman? But no matter. Truth be told…I'm trying to figure it out myself."

"Alyssa said you would find me."

"Ah yes…Alyssa." Nyrianne's eyes became glassy as if recalling a painful memory. "There was once an evil queen in a dark castle who tried to do terrible things to Alyssa's family. But when Alyssa's son came to face the evil queen, the queen tried to kill him. But he survived her worst efforts. And instead of retaliating, the son spoke of love and forgiveness." She smiled. "He was so naive. The boy actually tried to offer the queen forgiveness. As it turned out, such love was too powerful. All that remained of the mighty dark queen was a tired old woman wandering the Fourwinds in search of redemption. And perhaps it was wishful thinking, but she also longed for a peaceful place to live out the last of her days."

"Were you that queen, Nyrianne?"

The old woman turned to face Julie but avoided the question. "I understand that the same boy is now very sick."

Julie nodded. "His name is Will. Will Owens."

Nyrianne raised her eyebrows and straightened her back slightly. "Yes. His name is Will Owens. And I must help him. The love he offered the queen can never be repaid, but such love deserves to live on, don't you think?"

Julie swallowed hard, thinking of the fierce love she had for Morgan. "Did Alyssa tell you where we're going?"

"Well, the Maidstone, of course."

"Will you help us find the antidote for Phyriad?"

Nyrianne hobbled on ahead of Julie, then turned her head slightly. "If it is still there, I know where to find it…or so the story goes."

Julie gave her a hard look, unsure if that comment was intended to instill encouragement or doubt.

After an hour with little helpful conversation—besides Nyrianne's complaining of her old bones despite her refusals to Julie's persistent offers to let her ride instead of walk—they strolled up to Will and Ryowyn's cottage.

Morgan greeted them at the door, and they joined her inside.

Out on the dock, Ryowyn was speaking with her father, Ryodan.

"They've been talking for over an hour," Morgan said as she cinched the top of a leather backpack. "Good to see you again, Nyrianne."

The old woman smiled. "And you also, Morgan Finley."

"Alyssa should be back soon," Morgan said as she fumbled with the pack. "She took food and supplies to the cabin for Rowe and Will. I–I begged her to take me, but there's just so much to do here."

Julie offered a hug. "Morgan, you don't have to hide your pain."

Morgan sniffled. "I've seen how people transform, Mom. It's like their DNA changes. What if we're too late? What if the antidote doesn't work? What if he's never the same again?"

Julie kissed Morgan's forehead. "Well, there's only one way to find out, kiddo."

"Oh, the antidote works, child," Nyrianne said. "But there are so many questions. Will we find it? Will Natas be waiting for us? What else will we find inside that cursed place? And yes, what if we're too late?" She wandered the cottage, casually studying the many paintings that Tranas, the previous owner, had collected. Some were of landscapes, while others were portraits of soldiers who were likely the councilman's ancestors.

"Is she up for the journey?" Morgan whispered to Julie.

Julie raised her eyebrows. "I certainly hope so."

Ryowyn walked through the back door and held it open. "Julie, my father would like a moment of your time."

Julie glanced at Morgan, who shrugged, then brushed past Ryowyn. Shielding her eyes against the sunlight, Julie crossed the sand to the dock.

Ryodan Ayoust's presence commanded respect even in humble settings. He stood on the end of the dock, statue-still and shrouded in jagged coral armor that was a deep shade of blue. He held a staff that seemed small in his hand.

Julie swallowed when she noticed his penetrating eyes.

"My daughter is every bit as stubborn as her father, and even more persuasive than her mother," Ryodan said. "We are reluctant to let her go but understand the necessity."

"I appreciate the pain of letting a child go to face their own journey. I will care for Ryowyn as though she were my own daughter."

"As any loving parent would," Ryodan said as he stepped closer. "I understand you have dedicated your life to the healing arts, and that your knowledge will be useful in finding an antidote for Phyriad. Almithara and I would give anything to heal our Will, but I'm afraid we've had no success in such matters."

He lowered his eyes. "I wish to offer a gift, something to keep you safe if things become dark." He raised the staff, which was about a foot shorter than Julie, and placed it in her hands. It was a dull green, like time-weathered copper, and rough to the touch. The end was tipped with a piece of roughly cut oval-shaped obsidian. Despite its ordinary appearance, Julie knew she was holding something very important to Ryodan.

"This is a warden rod," he said. "It has been in my family for many generations, so please consider it on loan."

"It's—it's beautiful," Julie stammered as she studied the exotic object. She raised her head to ask about its purpose, but the mer king was already gone, leaving only a widening circle of ripples on the smooth lake, and waves of questions in Julie's mind.

CHAPTER 17

THUNDERCLAPS

Morgan rose early the next morning to report to Twell at the North Crow Gate. She had promised Alyssa she would be back at the cottage by noon so they could leave together and arrive at the Maidstone before dark. Alyssa had explained that she preferred to fly at night when she would be unseen, but time was short. Will and Rowe were fighting for their lives, and Phyriad was winning. If Morgan and the others could find a cure, maybe they could stop the spread of the strange disease. If they failed, life in the Fourwinds would never be the same.

A knot tightened in Morgan's stomach every time she thought of the journey ahead. And since it was almost all she could think of, her stomach always ached. Staying in the Rainia Valley wasn't a safe option, but it was better than the prospect of going to the Maidstone. There was only one option now, however, and she owed it to Twell and Dench to tell them she was leaving.

She had rehearsed the story in her head many times, but no matter how Morgan sugarcoated it, she couldn't imagine the commander understanding why she would take such a risk.

154

Rowe and Will are infected with Phyriad, she would tell him. *So, I'm going to the Maidstone to look for a cure.*

But how will you get there? Twell might ask.

Well, the Ice Dragon is flying us, Morgan would say.

If the conversation continued, Twell would want to send Dench or some soldiers to help her.

Well, Morgan would argue, *that's unnecessary. You see, the Ice Dragon is going with us into the Maidstone. And I have the sword of Avarthrill. And my mom has the warden rod, given to her personally by the mer king. Ryowyn is coming too, and she's a powerful healer. Oh, and we also have Nyrianne, who used to be the Dark Queen Sidara but now is the old woman who single-handedly stopped the gnome army from getting through the South Crow Gate.*

Morgan sighed. If it sounded crazy to her, what would Twell say?

As she rode past the northern edge of Rainia, she seriously considered turning back to Ryowyn's cottage. Before she could decide what to do, four riders approached from the west. Morgan recognized Kalmar, captain of the mer guard, and assumed the others were mer soldiers. Despite knowing the present condition and location of Will and Rowe, her heart sank to see the soldiers returning without them.

Kalmar slowed to a stop next to Morgan. "I'm sorry, but—"

"I know what happened to Will and Rowe," Morgan said.

"But how—"

"It doesn't matter." She pointed to the box a soldier carried. "Are those the thunderclaps?"

Kalmar nodded. "There was nothing we could do. We watched as the dragon carried Rowe and Will out of the Misty Gorge and into the darkness above the Chicora Mountains. I realized that it was our responsibility to get the thunderclaps back to the valley.

Although we travel fast by river, it was another full day and night before we arrived at the North Crow Gate. Twell was sad to hear of Rowe and Will, of course, but he was glad to see the thunderclaps."

"What about Bremer?" Morgan asked.

"He stayed in Acttun. He said he needed to find someone there. I'm truly sorry about your friends, Morgan, but there was something about this dragon… I cannot help but think that it wanted to help rather than harm them."

Morgan nodded. "I think you're right. Don't worry about them."

"The commander instructed us to leave one box of thunderclaps with him in case the Red Dragon attacks the gates. We sent another box to the Crow's Nest, and this box is for Rainia. I don't know if the dragon will attack, but we'll be ready if it does."

"It already did," Morgan said. "While you were gone." She realized now that there was no time to go to the North Crow Gate.

They rode together into the city and were greeted by men from the Marauders Brigade. Kalmar slid from his saddle and grasped the wooden box from another rider. He set the box on the ground as Morgan and the mer and human soldiers gathered around. Using a short knife, Kalmar pried open the lid.

Thick red velvet padding held four strange devices snugly inside. Kalmar grasped one by its short metal rod and carefully lifted it from the box. The head of the weapon consisted of a smooth, melon-size ball made from a semitransparent silver-blue alloy. Several holes in the ball opened to channels that ran through it. An oval-shaped connector between the rod and the ball held small ball bearings that allowed the ball to spin freely. The connector was etched with shallow corkscrew grooves that had a mesmerizing effect as the ball spun.

"What do we do with them?" a soldier asked. "How do they work?"

Kalmar turned the weapon in his hands. "Bremer only knew basic instructions, and there was no time to get details from Rowe. This iron rod slides into one of our ballista bolts. We twist the tip here, which mixes some chemicals inside. When launched from the ballista, the wind rushes through these channels. We're to shoot it as close as possible to a dragon, and…that is all I know."

Kalmar sent soldiers with the other thunderclaps to the watchtowers at the other three compass points around the city. As they sped away, Morgan followed Kalmar as he carried their thunderclap up the steep set of steps to the deck of the recently constructed northern watchtower.

At the top, a giant ballista was mounted on a short pole, allowing a soldier to rotate it 360 degrees. Another mechanism helped lock the ballista at various angles, including straight up. The bow arm was about eight feet long. Iron plates in front of the ballista provided a small layer of protection for the operators.

Three soldiers helped Kalmar load the thunderclap into an iron bolt. He breathed a sigh of relief when the thunderclap fit perfectly into the hollowed shaft, making the weapon nearly five feet long.

"It doesn't look like much," Kalmar said.

A moment later, trumpet blasts rang out throughout the city. People rushed about as they shot terrified glances at the sky.

The Red Dragon soared high above the rocky peaks north of the Crow's Nest. More trumpets blasted throughout Rainia, and every available soldier in the city scrambled to find armor and weapons. Parents gathered children from the streets and huddled in their homes. At the four watchtowers, soldiers cranked back each ballista's bowstring and aimed the thunderclaps at the approaching dragon.

High in the Hillron Mountains, the Red Dragon disappeared behind a jagged peak. A heartbeat later, the massive creature dropped into a nosedive, following a sheer cliff toward the Crow's Nest. Several hundred feet above the castle, it gained speed until it was little more than a blur. Morgan waited for someone to launch a thunderclap from the massive curtain wall. Instead, the dragon banked sharply and soared directly toward Rainia.

"Crank it faster!" Kalmar shouted as a pair of soldiers wrenched the levers to get the bowstring pulled all the way back. The trigger clicked into the ready position. Kalmar set the thunderclap in place, and the soldiers maneuvered the ballista with trembling hands, tracking the dragon.

Other than a few dips in altitude, the dragon showed no sign of slowing or deviating from its course. Screams and shouts of warning spread along the northern border of the city. Kalmar seized the loader and adjusted the ballista's trajectory. He peered down the long bolt and held his breath. The dragon leveled out about thirty yards above the ground and opened its huge jaws.

"I hope this works," Kalmar whispered.

He was about to release the bolt when the dragon veered. Again, its jaws opened as it neared the eastern watchtower. A long bolt shot toward it, and those at the northern watchtower held their breath. But midflight, the thunderclap fell away from the bolt, and the two sections tumbled downward.

The dragon enveloped the eastern watchtower in a fiery nightmare.

Morgan groaned.

"Make sure our thunderclap is securely mounted to the bolt!" Kalmar shouted.

"It's good," a soldier answered. "It'll hold."

The dragon streaked over the city like a firework. Kalmar tracked the dragon but couldn't get the ballista around fast enough for a shot. The dragon sped past the western watchtower, but for some reason, the soldiers there did not launch a thunderclap. For a moment, Morgan thought the dragon was leaving the valley. But high above the Misty Gorge, it changed course.

Kalmar repositioned the ballista. "That's it…come around nice and wide."

Morgan watched the dragon, trying to tune out the cries, shouts, and roaring flames as several buildings ignited around the eastern watchtower. If they allowed the beast to attack again, it would level the city.

Instead of returning to the city, the dragon flew toward the Crow's Nest. When it was dangerously close to the castle, a bolt shot up from the curtain wall. The weapon sailed into the sky, missing the dragon by at least fifty yards. The bolt stayed intact, but as soon as it peaked, it dropped to the ground halfway between the Crow's Nest and Rainia.

A soldier next to Kalmar gasped. "Nothing happened!"

The dragon altered its course and increased speed toward the northern watchtower.

"This one will work," Kalmar said as he lowered the back of the ballista to get the angle just right. "Keep coming…"

The dragon leveled, its fiery eyes combing the landscape as if searching for potential threats.

"Arm the thunderclap," Kalmar ordered.

A soldier twisted the tip, and the head crackled.

Kalmar held the ballista steady.

The dragon raced closer, and its red eyes flashed as it opened its jaws.

Morgan braced herself.

"Release," Kalmar breathed.

The soldier beside him pulled the chain and leapt to safety. Kalmar stumbled backward from the powerful recoil. The thunderclap head spun wildly, faster and faster, as the bolt took flight. The tiny holes glowed and emitted bursts of bright-blue fire and a violent screeching sound. Morgan, Kalmar, and the soldiers covered their ears.

A sharp explosion split the sky, followed by a brief peal of thunder. A stifling wind rushed into the city, kicking up dust and knocking over scaffolding from a building next to the watchtower. Morgan covered her face to protect her eyes. As the wind blew past, a painful tingling sensation surged through her body, making her arm hairs stand on end. When she looked back into the sky, the dragon was gone.

A second later, the ground outside the city limits shook as the enormous creature crashed down. Dust and debris scattered from the impact.

Kalmar grabbed the ballista to steady himself. A soldier reset the ballista, cranking back the drawstring as someone else loaded an iron bolt with a barbed hook that glistened in the sunlight. They aimed the weapon at the dragon as it lay facedown in the dirt, unmoving.

Morgan waited, hoping it was already dead.

CHAPTER 18
THE RED DRAGON FALLS

Thunder rolled above Rainia Lake. Despite the sunny morning, an ominous dark cloud now gathered above the water. Screams and shouts spread across the southern stretches of the city.

At the northern watchtower, Morgan scrambled down the steps.

"Don't go out there!" Kalmar shouted. "The dragon might not be dead."

"I'm not; I'm going to the lake!" She wanted to stay with Kalmar to see what happened to the Red Dragon, but she had to check on Ryowyn and her family.

Confused crowds wandered the streets of Rainia. The eastern side of the city was ablaze, a dragon attacked the north, and a mysterious storm was brewing over the lake to the south. Morgan worked her way through the pandemonium to the shoreline, where she saw Ryodan and a company of mer soldiers near the main pier.

Queen Almithara and several mermaids formed a line on the shore facing the lake as they raised their arms and swayed in a united dance. They moved their hands in tight circles and began a soft chant.

Far out in the lake, the water churned. At first, it bubbled, then a large surface area spiraled in a wide circle. The whirlpool picked up speed as Almithara and the mermaids worked through an ancient spell, their movements smooth and calculated.

The wind picked up off the lake, whipping the mermaids' hair in tangled wisps, but still, they danced and sang.

A giant waterspout emerged from the lake, stretching into the sky. Dark clouds accumulated. Wind gusted. Bright flashes of lightning lit up the raging torrent of water swirling and rising from the lake. A moment later, the waterspout twisted into a massive tornado-like column and rose above the surface.

The growing crowd around Morgan cried out but remained frozen with fear. There was nowhere left to run. The mermaids remained in position but increased the intensity of their dancing and singing as the water column moved toward the shoreline.

Almithara reached out to the waterspout and directed it toward the eastern section of the city. As it passed above the shoreline, torrents of rain soaked those watching in terror. When it swirled above the burning buildings, Almithara straightened her arms, splaying her fingers. The queen waved her arms, and a wind whistled through the streets and whipped around the column of water. She bent her knees and thrust her arms toward the sky. The intense wind gathered and rushed upward. The waterspout exploded, and a torrential rain doused the city below. A moment later, the fires died. Smoke and steam billowed.

Morgan stood in awe, but Ryodan was unfazed as he strode toward her.

"What happened to the dragon?" he shouted.

"We shot it down!"

Together, they raced up the main road through the city and came to an abrupt stop when they reached the northern watchtower.

The dragon lay sprawled in a large field north of the city, about halfway between Rainia and the Crow's Nest. Kalmar and his men were watching from the tower. Out in the field, the only thing that moved was a single rider.

Tonna, the first messenger of Enders Brigade, rode out from the city at a full gallop on his mare, Interrupted. He rode in broad zigzag patterns, then came to a halt when he located the thunderclap from the first shot taken from the Crow's Nest. Tonna flew from his saddle, rolling twice through the tall grass. He snatched up the thunderclap, then leapt back into his saddle, turning Interrupted around in a tight circle.

The dragon let out a loud huff, and a cloud of smoke rose from its snout.

Tonna froze as if unsure whether to return to the city or flee to the castle.

In the northern watchtower, Kalmar readied the ballista.

A soldier grasped the trigger chain. "Ready when you are, sir."

"Not yet," Kalmar said. "Make sure Tonna is safe."

The dragon's eyes flickered open.

Tonna kicked Interrupted's flanks, and the mare galloped in a wide semicircle around the monstrous creature, straight toward the northern watchtower.

"Get me another hollowed bolt!" Kalmar shouted as he rushed to remove the regular bolt from the ballista.

The dragon huffed a second time and raised its head a few inches off the ground.

Tonna sped onward, raising the undetonated thunderclap.

"He's not gonna make it," a soldier cried.

As everyone else waited, Ryodan ran from the city toward the fallen dragon, followed by six mer soldiers. The king's feet thundered with massive strides, and a trident appeared in his hands. As he approached Tonna, the dragon breathed a blast of fire at them.

The mer soldiers produced tridents of their own and, following their king, brought them up in a quick sweeping motion. The tridents flashed as one, and the dragon fire shot straight up into the air as if it had hit an invisible wall. Ryodan spun his trident in a blur, and the fire dissipated in the sky.

While the king and his soldiers worked to stop the fiery blast, Tonna sped past them and handed the thunderclap to Morgan, who raced up the watchtower steps. Kalmar grasped the weapon and mounted it in the hollowed bolt waiting in the drawn ballista.

"It's already armed," he said, rushing behind the ballista. He took careful aim.

The dragon huffed again, and a giant red eye opened.

"Release," Kalmar whispered.

A soldier jerked the chain that released the trigger, and the drawstring snapped forward. The thunderclap spun and glowed, brighter and louder as it flew, but the trajectory appeared to be well above the dragon.

Kalmar sucked air through his teeth, cursed, and pounded the ballista with a fist.

Morgan also thought the weapon had missed, but as the dragon reared its long neck to dodge it, the thunderclap disappeared inside the dragon's gaping maw.

Its scaly head shook wildly, and one leg pushed off the ground and stumbled. The dragon made another attempt to rise, then its red eyes rolled back, and the great creature collapsed. When its head struck the ground, a terrible flash engulfed the dragon and nearly blinded those staring at the scene.

Morgan rubbed tears from her stinging eyes and stared in shock at the human figure lying on the ground where the dragon had just been.

After a few silent moments, two riders approached from the west. Morgan recognized them as Twell and Joe, and she started toward the steps.

"Maybe we should bring that last thunderclap," she said, "just in case."

Kalmar grabbed the wooden box and followed Morgan down the watchtower stairs and out to the field where they met the two men near the still figure.

Joe was the first to kneel. Carefully, he removed the red helmet from the sweat-soaked head. "It's you," he said, wide-eyed.

Twell gasped. "General Raric?"

"Wh-what…" Raric stammered, pausing for a few short breaths. "What happened?"

Joe helped him into a sitting position. "I think you won the battle of souls, General."

Morgan had heard the story of Raric transforming into the Red Dragon. Now, the dragon had transformed back into the general. Joe had told them that Raric's soul was battling the soul of Scarlas, the Red Dragon, and that only one could survive. It all seemed impossible, but if Alyssa could change into the Ice Dragon and back again, maybe the same was true for Raric—assuming he had actually won the inner battle and could now transform at will.

"I'm thirsty," Raric said in a raspy voice.

Joe chuckled. "I bet you are."

Twell stared at his commander general, who was back from the dead for the second time.

"Come," Joe said. "Let's get you fed and watered."

He and Twell helped Raric to his feet. Despite the trauma the general had endured, he moved with ease. He appeared un-injured, although he favored his right leg. Morgan lowered her eyes, knowing she was partly responsible for wounding the Red Dragon two days ago.

"Johanissan." Raric's voice was weak but lucid. "The dragon melding…it worked."

Joe squared to face him. "You might say that. Since I left you on that block of wood in the Druid Forest, you've been battling the soul of Scarlas."

Raric looked at those gathered around him, then gazed at the castle. "Where is Rowe of the Nest?"

"Rowe and Will were infected with Phyriad," Kalmar said. "I brought them back from Acttun…most of the way."

"Acttun?" Raric's eyes brightened. "I—I remember now. I was flying over that area before I came here. Acttun was in shambles, but the people appeared to be celebrating." He rubbed a shoulder, which appeared to have been badly scraped when the dragon fell. "I also saw two men walking past the scorched hillside west of the city toward the Plains of Ashron. One was dressed in black, and the other wore a bright-orange hat and a long cloak."

"The man in black could be Bremer," Morgan suggested.

Joe appeared deep in thought. "*Mm-hmm.* Orange hat?" He leaned on his staff. "There once was a famous wizard at the Acttun Academy who wore an orange hat. Could it be…"

Ryodan stepped forward. "Could this wizard help our Will… and Rowe?"

"I owe my life to Rowe," Raric said. "He risked everything to rescue me from the Waerdreath." He turned to Joe. "Could I fly back there to get this wizard?"

Joe shrugged. "It's possible. When you turned into a full-size dragon, I believe you became Scarlas for a time. Now that you've returned to your human form, I think you've won. You might now have the ability to transform at will. But I don't know if you can return to dragon form and still be…you."

"If I cannot find the wizard, I need to get back to the druid Margrave. Maybe he can help me control the dragon."

Morgan listened quietly, reluctant to tell the others of Alyssa's plan. This wizard might be able to help Rowe and Will, but Alyssa seemed confident that an antidote could be found inside the Maidstone. Then again, getting the wizard to produce some kind of magical spell would be far easier. Maybe he could wave his wand or say a magic spell and restore Will and Rowe to perfect health. It often worked in storybooks and movies. But something told her that was too easy. Alyssa had been quite clear, and the other women had expressed their confidence in Morgan's ability to lead them into the Maidstone.

She noticed Ryodan watching her as if reading her inward struggle. He knew about the planned journey and would back her. She stepped toward Joe.

"We're going to the Maidstone in search of an antidote," she blurted.

All eyes locked on her. Her heart throbbed in her ears.

Joe raised an eyebrow. "We?"

"Me, my mom, Ryowyn, Nyrianne, and—"

"The Maidstone is no place for humans," Raric growled.

"So I've heard. But Alyssa—the Ice Dragon—is going with us."

Twell finally dismounted. "What makes you think I'm going to allow a small group of women to head off and—"

Ryodan thrust his trident into the ground and glared at Twell. "That is not for you to decide, Commander."

Twell stepped back, glancing at Morgan. "I didn't mean… I—I've seen Morgan in battle, Your Majesty. I also have confidence in her."

"As do I," Joe added, winking at Morgan. "I've known of her skills with a sword for years, watching her from afar." He turned to Twell. "Besides, who else could make such a journey? We need you at the North Crow Gate. Ryodan's people need him. And neither of you can spare soldiers. I'm preparing to receive a remnant of the gnome army, which could arrive any day. I will need Dench's help; he understands what it's like to be a foreigner in this valley. As for Raric…"

The general nodded wearily. "I don't know why you'd trust a dragon after today, Morgan. But I do know that you helped rescue me from Sidara's prison. If you can do that, you might make the journey to the Maidstone. And if the Ice Dragon is with you, you are in good hands." He stretched his back and yawned. "But now, I need to sleep."

Morgan stood beside Joe as Twell and a few soldiers escorted General Raric to the Crow's Nest. Kalmar stepped next to her, holding the thunderclap box in front of him.

"I think you should take this with you," he said. "The Red Dragon may no longer be a threat, but the Iron Dragon is still out there. We have the other thunderclaps to defend the valley."

Morgan stared at the box, terrified at the thought of coming as close to Natas as she had come to the Red Dragon. "But—but how would I launch it, even if I could?"

Kalmar lifted the box closer until she took the handle from his grasp. "You've seen how it works, Morgan. The ballista helped us today, but the thunderclap is lighter than it looks. You could use a bow—if you're close enough."

"But I—"

Joe put his arm around her shoulder. "I hope you will not need it, Morgan. But it's not a bad idea to take it with you. And you will have Alyssa to guide you. Trust her wisdom."

Pockets of curious people ventured from their homes and shops in Rainia. This day would end another exciting chapter in a larger story that had shaken their simple lives.

For Morgan, the story was only beginning. The Red Dragon was a mere hiccup in the battle against the spread of Phyriad. Natas's plan to rule the Fourwinds was moving full speed ahead. He had backed his opponents into a corner where they now huddled in the valley. And he had worked his way into her world—her old world—through two harvesters who had slipped past her through the Gateway. For all she knew, Phyriad had spread through Cochrane and into the rest of the world. Her life back there—fencing competitions, Yale, a great career—was over.

The only ones remaining from her old life were Joe, her mother, and Will. But each day carried Will and Rowe closer to darkness and further from her life. She had already lost her father to Natas's plan; she would not lose her friend and…what was Rowe to her? Surely more than a friend. They had confessed their love for one another at the South Crow Gate. But was that a chance encounter, the result of heightened emotions in the heat of battle? Or maybe a final passionate flame, knowing that a single gnome dart could snuff out either of their lives? After the battle, Morgan had expected to spend more time with Rowe, but he threw himself into the work of restoring the North Crow Gate. Instead of deepening their relationship, Rowe seemed to be distancing himself from her. She barely knew him, she realized, barely understood his world and her new place in it. But there was something there, and the longing to be with him refused to die.

Her introspective headache returned. She pushed aside such thoughts and set her mind on taking action. She needed to return to Ryowyn's cottage and meet up with the others. It was time to shift from a defensive strategy to a bold offensive.

CHAPTER 19

FLIGHT INTO THE UNKNOWN

Morgan returned to the cottage well past noon and paused at the front door. Her mother and Ryowyn were speaking in hushed tones as they filled a small leather backpack with wrapped cheese, bread, dried meat, and nuts. Nyrianne was sleeping in a large padded chair, her feet resting on a wooden stool. Her hands were folded together on her belly, which rose and fell with each deep breath that teetered on the threshold of a snore. Sunlight streamed through the living room window and across the old woman's legs. The peaceful cottage welcomed Morgan in from the flurry of activity brought on by the Red Dragon's attack in Rainia.

Alyssa met her at the front door with a cup of cold water.

"We were beginning to wonder when you'd be back," she said.

Ryowyn stopped packing and looked up as Morgan gulped down the water. "We heard about the Red Dragon," she said. "My father hadn't returned by the time I left to come here, so we didn't hear the details." She pointed to the wooden box Morgan carried. "What's that?"

"Kalmar used the thunderclaps to bring down the dragon,"

❧ 171 ❧

Morgan explained. "When the dragon hit the ground, it transformed into General Raric. Since the Red Dragon might be on our side now, Kalmar suggested we take a thunderclap with us."

Alyssa flinched and took a step back.

Morgan set the box on the floor. "Oh, I'm sorry, Alyssa. I was only thinking about Natas, not how the thunderclap might affect you."

"It's fine, Morgan. The thought of it just startled me a bit. A thunderclap would bring the Ice Dragon down as it did the Red Dragon. But it needs to be triggered and then launched to be effective. I will encase it in ice and carry it with me in this satchel for safekeeping. I can quickly thaw it if needed."

Julie folded her arms in front of her. "I still can't get my head around the idea of real dragons, let alone the notion that you can transform into one, Alyssa. It sounds like a fairy tale."

Alyssa smiled. "I was just explaining a bit more to your mother, Morgan. It will be a shock to see me as a dragon, but we have little choice. Riding to the Maidstone on horseback or by wagon would take too long. Every hour we delay, Rowe and Will grow sicker. We have no better option but to fly, and I will need to push hard."

"I have to admit," Julie added, "I'm having trouble with many things here in the Fourwinds, but the notion of someone I knew from Cochrane transforming into a dragon is by far the craziest thing I've heard."

Morgan sat in a chair by the table, and Alyssa brought her a bowl of stew.

"We've all eaten, so dig in," Alyssa said, sitting in a chair next to her. "Julie, have you ever experienced culture shock?"

Julie leaned against the table and nodded slowly. "I'll never forget stepping off that plane in Nigeria. The humidity hit me like a wall. I felt like we'd landed on another planet. Many things about the airport were familiar, but once we left the city, it was like another world."

"I'm not saying the Fourwinds is the same thing," Alyssa said. "But it might help you to remember that you are capable of transitioning into a life that is foreign to you and adapting to ways that are unfamiliar."

Morgan sipped the warm broth from a spoon as she watched her mother's expression change.

Julie's eyes brightened, and her cheeks lifted slightly. "Don't get me wrong. As crazy as it's been since I got here, I prefer the simple ways and how people here actually have time for one another. Life back home is so hectic, making us so driven and self-centered."

Morgan nodded. "Even in our small town."

"This might surprise you," Julie continued, "but I'm actually excited about our trip today. I've traveled by just about every possible means known to man, so why not riding on a dragon?" Her tone was genuine, but she finished with a soft laugh and a quiver of her brow. Morgan was familiar with her mother's trademark nervous expression; she had seen it every time they left for a fencing tournament.

"I'm feeling anxious, to be honest," Ryowyn said. "Traveling by land for long distances is challenging for me, but I've never traveled through the air. I don't know how I'll respond."

"I will do my best to keep you all safe," Alyssa said. "And if the currents are with us, you will even be quite comfortable."

Ryowyn walked around from behind the table. She was wearing a dark-blue coral-studded suit that clung to her body. The material looked coarse to the touch but moved as a soft fabric. Sharp jagged ridges ran from the top of both her shoulders down the back of her arms to her wrists. Her slim, toned legs were lined with similar armor.

Morgan raised her eyebrows. "I think I'd be feeling pretty confident if I were wearing *that* suit."

Ryowyn looked down, examining her arms and legs. When she looked up with confusion in her eyes, the other women laughed.

"Don't worry; you look great, Ryowyn," Morgan said.

Nyrianne let out a sudden snort and opened her eyes. "Are we finally ready?" She stretched her arms and yawned. "I've been waiting all morning."

The others burst into laughter again, and this time, Ryowyn joined in.

"Yes, Nyrianne," Alyssa said as she picked up the satchel containing the thunderclap. "I think we're almost ready. Ryowyn, please bring these four blanket rolls when you come. I'll meet you all down by the dock in a few minutes."

The front door closed behind Alyssa, and Julie helped stack the four blankets in Ryowyn's arms. Morgan finished the last few bites of stew and grabbed the supply pack. It was surprisingly light, which gave her a measure of hope; she had no desire to make this an extended trip.

Julie sighed as she gazed at the door. "Ready or not...here we go."

Out near the dock, where Alyssa had first explained the necessity of traveling to the Maidstone, the Ice Dragon waited. Morgan had seen the majestic creature only once, atop the Waerdreath castle, but it had been dark that terrifying night, and events had happened quickly. Now, as the afternoon sun pierced the leafy canopy of a massive willow, Morgan marveled at the size and beauty of the dragon standing in the dappled shade. Alyssa stood on all fours but hunched to the ground as if trying to appear smaller than she was. Although unlike any earthly creature Morgan had seen, the dragon would have cast a shadow over an entire adult male elephant. The Ice Dragon was stunning. Even in the muted light, her ice-blue and white hide sparkled as she shifted her long tail behind the tree trunk.

Julie gasped and tightened her grip on Morgan's arm. "Lord, have mercy!"

Nyrianne strode up to the dragon, who lowered her massive horn-studded head. "Is she not the most beautiful creature you've ever seen?"

"Thank you, Nyrianne." Alyssa's voice sounded like that of her human form but deeper—almost like a growl yet more of a low, disarming purr.

Morgan had a sudden memory of the night the Ice Dragon had carried her, Will, Rowe, Bremer, and Raric from the Waerdreath to the elven healing camp. She had stepped into the safety of the dragon's claw as easily as climbing into the back seat of a small car. But they had only two options that night: escape with the Ice Dragon or stay to face the wrath of a moonwalker. Now that she had a moment to examine the rough claws and sharp talons, Morgan was having second thoughts about flying with her again.

"So, are we riding in your claws again?" she asked.

Alyssa flashed her sharp teeth in what was probably meant to be a smile. "Not this time, Morgan. That was an emergency rescue at the Waerdreath; no time for elven saddles on that night."

"Elven saddles?" Morgan said. She quickly surveyed the area but saw nothing that resembled a saddle.

"You'll find it easier to believe if I show you." Alyssa crouched low with her expansive belly to the ground. "Ryowyn, climb onto my back."

Ryowyn set the blankets down near the dock and worked her way up the dragon's side. She pulled herself up like an agile rock climber, gripping the edges of the smooth scales. There appeared to be plenty of room on the dragon's back for all four women to sit, but Morgan couldn't imagine how they would avoid falling off once Alyssa took to the air. They might be able to cling to one of the dragon horns for a short distance, but the thought made her stomach flip.

"Now, Morgan," Alyssa explained, "throw one of the blanket rolls to Ryowyn."

A single string bound the blankets, making it easy to toss up to Ryowyn.

"Good. Spread the blanket on my back, Ryowyn. It doesn't need to be perfect."

Ryowyn opened the blanket over the dragon's back as if she were spreading a comforter over a queen-size bed. For a second, the blanket looked about as useful as a tablecloth on the roof of an airplane. Then it fluttered as if a sudden gust of wind had come off the lake—except the air was still. The blanket clung to Alyssa's back, then shifted and contorted until it had reformed into the distinct shape of a high-backed saddle.

As Morgan studied it, she noticed slight indentations on both sides that a rider might comfortably use as stirrups. The backrest looked like it could provide ample support when sitting upright. There were also various places for armrests and handholds whether a rider leaned forward or sat straight. It was more than a saddle, but she understood why Alyssa would call it one. Anything in the Fourwinds meant to carry a passenger on a horse's or other creature's back would be referred to as a saddle. But the color and texture were so similar to the dragon's hide that it was difficult to see where saddle ended and hide began.

Morgan gaped. "It's so…it's like it's part of you."

"In a way, that's true," Alyssa said. "The fabric is elven crafted, making it both light and incredibly durable. But it took a clever druid to learn that by weaving in dragon horn fibers, the blanket could meld to a dragon's hide. The saddle looks like part of me because I willingly offered my own horn. Go ahead, Ryowyn, have a seat."

Ryowyn put her foot in a stirrup. "I've never been too comfortable in a saddle, although I'm getting better riding with Will."

"I won't take offense to that comment because horses are magnificent creatures," Alyssa said. "But I think you'll find this a very unique experience."

The mer princess sat in the saddle and tucked her feet into both stirrups. She leaned forward and gripped the handholds. The way she fit comfortably in the saddle reminded Morgan of a motorcycle rider preparing for a long road trip, only more secure.

A smile spread across Ryowyn's face. "Oh my," she exclaimed. "I could stay here all day."

Alyssa exposed her teeth again and let out a deep rumbling sound that reminded Morgan of ice thawing on Lake Commando. If that was the dragon's purr, she'd hate to hear its roar.

"I am pleased to hear that, Ryowyn," Alyssa said. "There's one for each of you. And although I'd never admit to this in my human form, I should be large enough for all four of you to sit single file."

Morgan needed no further invitation. She tossed a blanket up to Ryowyn and climbed up to join her.

"You seem quite at ease with all this, Ryowyn," she said. "Have you seen blankets that transform into saddles before?"

The princess tilted her head as if surprised by such a thought. "No, but…I have a tail that transforms into two legs."

A nervous laugh burst from Morgan's lips. "Right. Another wonder of the Fourwinds."

She took the blanket and held it open. It was much lighter than it looked, more like the weight of a sheet than a blanket. She took a deep breath and spread it behind Ryowyn. The fabric quickly transformed into an identical saddle. After tightening her backpack's shoulder straps, she sat down and understood Ryowyn's initial reaction.

"You're right, Alyssa. This is far better than a horse saddle."

The Ice Dragon chuckled. "As with their mead and so many other things, the elves create only the highest quality."

Morgan looked down at her mother, who was watching expectantly like a little girl waiting for her turn to ride the pony. Morgan climbed down and tossed the other two blankets up to Ryowyn.

"I think you'll like this, Mom."

When Ryowyn finished spreading the last two blankets, the four saddles were ready. The stirrups and handholds looked reliable, but Morgan wondered if additional harnesses might make them more secure once they took to the air. Despite her skepticism, she wasn't about to question elves and druids.

"Ryowyn and I will ride in the front two, Mom," she said. "You and Nyrianne will be more protected behind us. Will you be strong enough to carry all of us, Alyssa?"

A tiny cloud puffed from the dragon's nostrils. "Like you, Morgan, I am much stronger than I appear."

Alyssa lowered a wing as close to the ground as possible, and Morgan helped Julie and Nyrianne climb onto her back. When they were all seated, the dragon rose slowly to a standing position and spread her wings.

"Is everyone ready?"

All four women voiced their consent, but Julie was more enthusiastic than the others.

The Ice Dragon lifted her wings high above them, bent her knees, and pushed off the ground. The sudden lurch was much like a plane lifting off a runway. Alyssa spread her wings wide and, with a deep *whoosh*, thrust them downward as she rose several feet in the air. Each successive flap of her powerful wings took them higher into the clear afternoon sky.

The four women bowed their heads as if united in a prayer for safety and clung to their saddle handles. No one spoke, and Morgan suspected that they, too, were all holding their breath.

When they were about two hundred feet off the ground, Alyssa lowered her head and flew forward while slowly increasing altitude and speed.

Morgan noted two features of dragon riding that she had not expected. First, as much as Alyssa's wings moved, her body remained incredibly stable. This made the ride far more secure than riding horseback. Second, it had not occurred to Morgan to worry about the wind as they increased in speed. All four women had tied their hair in ponytails, but it was amazing how little the wind whipped either their hair or clothing. As Morgan studied Alyssa's movements, she realized that the large flared horns that framed her scaly head acted as a massive windshield. Alyssa positioned her head perfectly, deflecting the air currents over the women.

"How fast are we going?" Julie shouted.

"I can't say for sure," Alyssa said, "but I'll need to go about as fast as you would drive on a highway back home. You should be well protected, but let me know if it gets too windy."

She kept her altitude low for the first leg of the journey, at least until they were out of the Rainia Valley. The southern route took them through the Hillron Mountains, and Alyssa glided deftly and silently between the majestic peaks. Morgan gazed at the rugged beauty, too awestruck to be afraid.

Alyssa was right: Morgan felt completely safe in the elven saddle. The footholds were a perfect height, allowing each rider to stretch her legs as needed. The handles offered a secure and comfortable grip.

When the mountain landscape tapered off into foothills, Alyssa took them higher. By the time they were soaring above the Clover Fields, the four passengers were comfortable enough to look down.

"That herd looks very strange from up here," Morgan observed.

Alyssa increased altitude again. "Your vision is not as keen as mine. Those are not animals but gnomes. And by the way they're traveling, I'd say they've been infected with Phyriad."

As the sun dipped behind the western mountains, patches of trees came together in a dense forest below. The trees were probably huge, but from high above, they looked like a miniature model landscape. Rivers and creeks of various sizes wove through the region as if someone had dropped random lengths of silver string between the trees.

Alyssa turned her head back. "That area used to be known as the River Country," she said. "Joe was born there, but it's been many years since his people abandoned these lands and moved south. We're getting closer to the Maidstone now."

She began a gradual descent as they approached a narrow canyon. A few minutes later, an increasingly loud rumble silenced all conversation. Clouds of mist billowed as water spilled over seven waterfalls, crashing into the canyon. Morgan recognized the area but could not locate the exact spot where she, Will, Rowe, and Bremer had crossed on their way to the Waerdreath. Adrenalin surged through her at the memory, but there was no time for reminiscing.

Pockets of humid air awakened her to the present as Alyssa took them down in a gradual, slightly unsteady spiraling path toward the canyon. On a broad ledge partway down the towering cliffs, the Maidstone tower loomed. Alyssa banked toward it.

Water droplets spattered Morgan's face, and she tightened the cowl of her hood. The scene triggered a childhood memory of when her grandparents had taken her on a helicopter ride above Niagara Falls. The roar and the rising mist here reminded her of that trip, but this canyon was much narrower, even though the volume of water seemed similar.

Alyssa followed the canyon's path, then dropped suddenly. Morgan's stomach lurched. She gripped the handles, not to guide the dragon but simply to hang on. Down they went, descending along the shadowy, wet cliff until Alyssa leveled out just above the dark tower. She shot forward in a sweeping motion that took them past the Maidstone for a closer look before landing.

The tower was nestled on a protruding ledge over halfway up the dark cliff. It was impossible to see where the fortress stopped and the cliff began, making it look as though the tower were merely part of a much larger structure. The rugged land around the tower was overgrown with tall grass, yellow-flowered weeds, and patches of wild blackberry. Morgan's eyes widened as they descended. The area was probably over an acre in size, but it looked much too small to land in. Alyssa's leathery wings fluttered and rumbled like distant thunder as great currents of misty air rose up from the canyon.

"This'll be a little bumpy," she said. "Hang on."

Morgan squinted and pressed her chest against the saddle. The other three did the same.

Alyssa made numerous adjustments to the pitch of her wings, and despite the turbulence and waterfalls crashing near them, she maintained a steady descent. Her powerful wings swept forward suddenly, and with a final lurch, she touched ground.

Morgan turned to check on her mother.

"I'm fine," Julie said. "I've had my share of rough landings; that wasn't too bad."

Twilight veiled the area in patchy shadows. In the evening sky, a few stars flickered into view. Morgan stood, stretched her back, then helped her mother to the ground. Ryowyn descended from the opposite side with Nyrianne.

Julie smiled at Morgan and stretched her arms as if they were arriving at a tropical resort after the best flight she'd ever had. Ryowyn sat on a large rock beside Nyrianne.

"Well, that was exciting," the old woman said. "But I'm glad to be back on solid ground."

Morgan nodded and took a few steps away to scan the area, taking note of the ominous tower. There was still enough light to see the muted colors of the grass and trees, but the round tower was all gray and black from base to conical roof. The vines that clung to the tower were so thick in places that Morgan could barely see the weathered stone blocks beneath. "Not the kind of place to take a family vacation."

Julie caught up with Morgan and took hold of her arms, squaring to face her. Her smile had faded into a familiar sternness that suggested a mother-daughter talk was about to begin.

"I don't know what we'll find inside this place, kiddo. But no matter what happens, I want you to know that I admire your courage and your commitment." Her cheeks twitched, and she reached out to smooth her hand over Morgan's hair. "This hasn't been an easy transition for us…losing your father, and"—she sniffed as a tear spilled from her eye—"and coming to this strange place. But you've grown so much these past few weeks. I've always been proud of your accomplishments, but I want you to know that I'm very proud of the wonderful person you are."

Morgan expected more, but Julie was silent as she gazed into her eyes until it became slightly awkward.

"Um…thanks, Mom."

Julie offered a quick hug and spoke quietly in her ear. "And I love the way you care for Rowe. I can see it's been hard between you two recently, but don't give up." She pushed back but held Morgan's shoulders. "I'm with you all the way."

Ryowyn had come closer and must have overheard Julie's last statement. "So am I, Morgan. We're in this together."

Morgan glanced around. "Where's Alyssa?"

From around the tower, Alyssa appeared in human form striding toward them, her sandaled feet barely making a sound. She wore a white V-necked dress that flowed just below her knees. The fine material rippled in the breeze and lifted slightly, revealing light-blue skintight leggings. Morgan noticed the same material covering Alyssa's arms and upper chest and wondered if it was a full bodysuit.

"I think I'd be feeling pretty confident if I were wearing *that* suit," Ryowyn said with a smirk. Morgan caught the twinkle in her eye, and they exchanged a knowing smile.

The convivial mood vanished, and Ryowyn crouched suddenly as if ready for an attack. If her coral-studded suit were not enough to dispel anyone's thoughts of the princess being weak or timid, she shot her arm out to one side, giving everyone a start. All eyes widened when a long trident appeared in her hand. The weapon was tipped with a sharp spike, flanked by two gently curved silver blades.

Ryowyn nodded her head in the direction of a scarecrow-like figure behind Alyssa. The scrawny male body hung from a long, overhanging tree limb, his head held in a cage that was attached to the branch by a thick chain. Morgan gasped when she noticed his unmoving red eyes.

"That is a seer," Alyssa explained. "Natas sees everything he sees. But I froze his eyes, so he cannot see."

"But Will told me he killed the seer when he was here," Ryowyn said.

Alyssa gave a hesitant nod. "Well, he did. But the Maidstone is too important to Natas, so he would have quickly replaced that seer with a new one."

"How long do we have until Natas realizes what you did?" Ryowyn asked.

Alyssa's forehead wrinkled as she studied the darkening sky. "At best, I'd say we're good until dawn."

"Where are we?" Nyrianne asked, wiping beads of mist from her face with the colorful shawl she wore over her shoulders.

Julie slipped her arm around the old woman's elbow, and they both straightened slightly. "Remember, we came here to find the antidote for Phyriad to help our friends. You told me it was inside this tower. Does any of this look familiar to you?"

Nyrianne drummed her pursed lips with her fingertips and blinked slowly as she examined the area. There was nothing in the way of recognition in her eyes until she noticed the tower.

"We shouldn't be here," Nyrianne said, shaking her head slowly as her wide eyes fixed upon the wide front entrance that led into the dark tower. "This place requires fortitude…so much fortitude. And I'm so old. We shouldn't be here."

"Probably not," Julie agreed. "But do you remember that our friends Rowe and Will are infected with Phyriad, and they're very sick? They will die unless we help them. Could you show us where to find the cure, Nyrianne?"

"Oh," Nyrianne said, her features softening. "I remember Will. Such a kind boy."

Alyssa took a few cautious steps toward the tower. Her hands flexed open and closed as she scanned the sky.

"What is it, Alyssa?" Ryowyn said. "What do you see?"

"We need to get inside. Every time I use magic, Natas senses my presence. I've used ice on the seer, but in the Maidstone, I must be more cautious."

"Come, Nyrianne," Julie said. "I think you'll remember everything once we're inside."

Morgan took Nyrianne's other arm to help Julie, and everyone followed Alyssa toward the archway of stone blocks protruding from the tower's base. The entrance was a black hole.

"I can't believe we're going in there," Morgan whispered, staring at the ghastly centuries-old structure.

As they approached the archway, Julie almost dropped the warden rod when the small crystal at the top flared to life. The light intensified, and she pointed it away from her face, lighting the way ahead for a dozen feet.

Morgan released Nyrianne to Julie's care and hesitated at the entrance with Alyssa. Julie and Nyrianne caught up a moment later, with Ryowyn taking up the rear. When the five women were gathered close together, Alyssa strode into the dank-smelling corridor, leading them into the unknown.

CHAPTER 20
CHASING RIVERS

The city of Rainia was a hive of activity. Construction, which had been the primary industry for several months, came to an abrupt halt when the Red Dragon attacked and scorched the eastern watchtower and a few buildings. Workers had scrambled to find family members and shelter. The fires had injured several people, but thankfully, no one died. Just when the flames threatened to spread and do significant damage, the miraculous rain conjured by the mer queen quenched all fears.

People emerged from homes and shops, sharing stories with their neighbors as they tried to piece together what had happened. Many had seen the Red Dragon overhead. Some shared firsthand experiences of the fire and smoke, and most agreed that the timely storm cloud that darkened the sky had spared the city. Citizens who lived near the northern watchtower brought news that the Red Dragon had fallen and that General Raric had returned. Some said that Raric was actually the dragon, magically transformed, but those who had not been there dismissed such tales.

Individual accounts morphed into rumors that would lay a

foundation for legends told by old-timers years from now. For now, the skies were clear again, free of mysterious clouds and fire-breathing dragons. All eyes focused on the ground and the task of rebuilding the city.

Joe listened to fragments of stories as he accompanied Ryodan back to the lake before returning to the Crow's Nest. On his way to the castle, he stopped in the rolling field north of the city to watch the southern sky. He alone saw the Ice Dragon as she carried the four women out of the Rainia Valley on their journey to the Maidstone.

It was late afternoon when Joe found the private room near the Crow's Nest infirmary where Twell had taken Raric. The general was lying in a large bed. He was still clad in the dragon armor, which wrapped tightly around his body. His half-lidded eyes were slowly opening. Captain Culthison and Brynlee Mason sat in chairs on opposite sides of the bed. Raric squinted, looking at the three of them through the fog of sleep.

"Not the little boy I used to know," Brynlee said with a twinkle in her eyes. "But still the adventurer, I see." She turned to Joe with a warm smile. "Raric the Rascal, we used to call him. I spent most of my time caring for his sister, Alarra, but I filled in whenever his governess was ill. Raric was an ambitious and hard worker who exceeded his father's expectations in all things. But he always preferred new adventures…" She touched Raric's thick forearm. "What was it your mother would say?"

"She said I was 'chasing rivers,'" Raric mumbled. "And look where those rivers led me."

He tilted his head toward Culthison and spoke to Joe. "The captain has briefed me about Enders Brigade and the fate of the gnome army." His eyes clouded, and his rugged chin quivered. "My memory is so foggy, but I understand I have killed many soldiers."

Joe stood at the end of the bench and tapped the hardwood floor once with his staff. "No. Scarlas is responsible for those deaths. You, General Raric, stopped the trail of blood today. What matters now is whether you choose to stop chasing and simply follow the river you are in."

"And what does that look like?" Raric said, his words dripping with bitterness. "I may have killed Uluk the Shadowfallen, but I almost destroyed the entire gnome race. And this beautiful valley. Despite any thread of hope you might cling to, Johanissan, Natas still reigns and Phyriad continues to infect the Fourwinds."

"The gnomes are not completely destroyed," Joe said. "While we don't know how many of the North Gnome Army were infected, we have heard rumors that a substantial group of gnome refugees is on its way here."

Culthison sat forward in his chair. "If this is true, we must welcome them. Brigadier Bayard promised the gnome commander, Yossar, that they could find sanctuary here."

Joe gripped his staff and pressed his lips in a fine line before answering. "As the only remaining Callum Sage in the valley, I will do what I can. Rowe and Will are sick and quarantined in a safe location. Morgan has left for the Maidstone to find a cure. I will personally see to it that the gnome refugees are welcomed here, Captain." He shifted his gaze to the general. "I believe Rainia is not only a place of refuge but the birthplace of a new civilization."

Raric sat up slowly. "Perhaps I could go to the Maidstone to help Morgan and the others."

"It might come to that," Joe said. "But you must first return to the Druid Forest. Margrave should be able to help you control your dragon powers. He was quite concerned that you had left too soon after the melding process."

"Is it safe for me to turn back into the Red Dragon?"

Joe scanned the general's body. "I cannot say for certain. But after the strength you showed today, I believe you could safely assume the dragon form and fly to the Druid Forest."

Raric leaned back against the headboard. "Thank you, Johanis-san. Will you accompany me again?"

"No, I need to be at the North Crow Gate if—or *when*—the gnomes arrive. Will and Morgan are not here to…clear them, and I suspect not everyone will receive them as well as I will. But if Margrave needs me, please come back, and I will join you."

Brynlee offered the general a cup of water. The lines around her eyes deepened as her gentle smile returned. "Raric the Rascal. Hardly in one place for a day, and he's already planning another adventure. Not unlike my own son."

⚜

After a full day walking with Marlay Bonicle, Bremer had already grown tired of the wizard's constant chattering. It was as if the old man had been sleeping so long and missed so much of what had been happening in the Fourwinds, he suddenly felt the need to make up for lost conversations. One more reason Bremer preferred to travel alone. Most people talked too much for his liking, but this crazy wizard was almost nonstop. He was the sort of person who asked questions but never seemed too interested in his listener's responses.

"So, you've been to the Waerdreath? Did you know that castle was built with blocks carved from the volcanic island it sits upon?

I suppose you did if you traveled with a Callum Sage. Wait…did you say you were once a Callum Sage?"

Bremer grunted.

"Yes, yes. My apologies. But I wager you didn't know that some of that volcanic rock can also be found in the Maidstone tower? How is this possible? Who could have transported such heavy stones all that way? I have my own theories. Would you like to hear them?"

"Not really."

"Well, my brother, Addolay, always disagreed with me on this, but—"

Bremer held up a hand, and the wizard clapped his mouth shut. "It's getting dark, Marlay. This is a good spot to camp for the night. I'll gather firewood."

A few minutes later, Bremer returned from the small grove nearby to find Marlay warming his hands over a small fire. The flames flickered around four large rocks that seemed hastily pushed together in a tight circle.

"No need for firewood or flint with me around," Marlay said, pushing his shoulders back. "I'm sorry if you wasted some energy collecting wood. Really, Bremer, you should learn to wait for a response after you speak. I could have told you…"

Whatever Marlay said after that fell on deaf ears. Bremer focused on frying up some of the bacon, potatoes, onions, and carrots that Meagan had gathered from the storeroom of the Cauldron's Stew.

After dinner, they unpacked their bedrolls and spread them out on the moss beneath four tall firs. The wizard was snoring within seconds.

Finally, Bremer thought, *some peace and quiet. Almost.*

The grove nightlife slowly drowned out the wizard's heavy

breathing. Crickets and chittering chipmunks formed a united chorus but were soon silenced by the solo appearance of an owl hooting to claim its territory. Bremer breathed in the cool air, grateful for the steady fire that required no fuel source. He gazed at the ocean of stars above and suddenly realized that the grove had grown silent.

The dragon had glided down without a sound until it flapped its massive wings once before landing less than fifty feet away.

Bremer was on his feet in a second. Before he could draw a sword, there was a flash of white light. Bremer covered his face with his arm, and when he looked back, a tall man stood where the dragon had been.

"General Raric?"

"We meet again, Bremer Mason."

"How did you…? Are you the—?"

"Red Dragon. Yes. As you see, a lot has happened since we both awoke from the elven healing tents. And I see you travel with interesting company."

Behind Bremer, Marlay stirred and rolled over with his face toward them. He opened his eyes, closed them for a second, then recoiled, eyes wide.

"Is this the wizard, Marlay Bonicle?" Raric asked.

Marlay remained on the ground but gave a curt nod.

"I saw you the other day as I flew over Acttun."

"Flew? *Really?*" Marlay rose to his knees. "Fascinating."

Raric took a step toward Bremer. "I just came from the Crow's Nest. I'm sorry to tell you, Bremer, but your friends Rowe and Will have been infected with Phyriad. I was hoping this wizard might help them."

"So was I." Bremer scowled at Marlay. "But he cannot. I was with

Rowe and Will in Acttun and was quite sure they were infected. This wizard assures me that a druid named Margrave will know of a cure. We're on our way to the Hollowtangle to find him."

Raric's eyes narrowed. "Margrave?" His head tilted to one side. "It's a long walk to the Druid Forest."

The wizard stood and brushed a twig from his cloak. "What did you mean when you said you *flew* over Acttun?"

"It's a long story," Raric said. "But I doubt a wizard of your reputation would be surprised to hear that the druid Margrave performed a dragon melding using the hide of the Red Dragon. I have been fighting an inner battle to control the dragon soul within me. We seem to be equally matched, but I'm on my way to see Margrave, hoping he will show me how to win this battle."

Marlay pulled his orange hat over his ears and ventured a few steps toward Raric. "Dragon melding…yes, yes." He tugged his wispy beard. "I've studied dragon melding but never thought it possible. Leave it to Margrave to actually attempt it."

"Well," Raric said, lifting his eyebrows and shoulders in unison. "I didn't give him much choice."

"How are Rowe and Will?" Bremer asked. "Did you see them?"

"I did not, but I understand their cloaks are slowing the sickness. They're resting in the old outpost cabin in the mountains above the castle."

Bremer rubbed the top of his head. "I hope it works. What about Morgan? She still at the wall?"

"Morgan and her mother have gone to the Maidstone in search of a possible antidote for Phyriad."

Bremer dropped his hands to his sides. "Now, there's a foolhardy idea. And she thought going to Acttun was risky! They'll never be able to cross those lands alone. They'll be attacked by Phyriad-infected creatures…or the South Gnome Army."

"They won't have to worry about the gnome army, I can assure you. And they are not crossing on land. The Ice Dragon flew them to the Maidstone. And two others went with them, but I didn't recognize the names."

Marlay was fully awake now. He rubbed his hands together and licked his lips as if preparing to enjoy a delicious dinner. "Fascinating! I would love to learn more about your experience. What was your name again?"

"General Raric."

"General! Now, this *does* get interesting. Was the melding as painful a process as they say? Are you aware of your surroundings when in dragon form? When you fly, can you—"

"Not now, Marlay," Bremer interrupted. His head was abuzz with thoughts of Morgan in the Maidstone and of Rowe and Will in the cabin getting sicker every day. There was so much to do, so many miles to cover, and so little time. The wizard's questions were important, but Bremer couldn't shake the sense that a measure of good fortune had brought Raric to them at the same time they were all seeking Margrave.

"We'll have to leave Morgan's fate in the hands of the Ice Dragon for now. But…would you…" Bremer fumbled for words, unaccustomed as he was to be asking for help. "I mean, since you're going there anyway…could you take us to the Druid Forest? The time saved could make all the difference for Rowe and Will."

Raric stiffened, and his eyes flared as if he were angry or offended at the audacity of Bremer's request. Or maybe he was wrestling the dragon within, a beast that would rather bring chaos than healing. Bremer was familiar with the turmoil that inner demons could stir up. But Raric's reply surprised him.

"Our paths seem intertwined, Bremer. We're both chasing the same river. I cannot promise a smooth or safe journey, but the two of you are welcome to ride with me."

CHAPTER 21

INTO THE MAIDSTONE

The entrance to the Maidstone was uninviting, to say the least. The narrow passage muffled the rumbling waterfalls outside. A damp stone floor and dripping walls kept the temperature much colder than outside the tower. Morgan was comfortable beneath her Trannalun cloak but noticed her mother and Nyrianne huddled close behind her as Julie held forth the warden rod. The light from the top of the staff cast a soft glow on the rough volcanic-ash-black walls and the smooth, timeworn slab underfoot. Alyssa led them confidently into the tower, but Morgan slowed, feeling as if they were trespassing. She drew her sword, expecting to be turned away.

As they approached an open area, the dark rugged walls transitioned to a light-tan color. They were cold and smooth to the touch, not wood or drywall, Morgan thought, but more synthetic.

Alyssa stopped when everyone was through the entrance passage and inside the large foyer. A low, droning sound from beyond the room filled the space.

"What's that sound?" Julie asked.

"The waterfalls?" Ryowyn suggested.

"Sounds more like a motor," Morgan said.

Ryowyn cocked her head. "A what?"

"That's something that gives heat and light to buildings where I'm from." Morgan remembered Will describing old turbine engines he had seen when he'd hiked up to the Maidstone. The noise was not excessively loud, but it had been a while since she had heard electric-powered sounds inside a building. Generators and air conditioners created a similar constant drone, but there was nothing like that in the Fourwinds. The room had more in common with buildings in a city back home than those she'd seen in the Fourwinds.

Julie shone the light around. To their left was a narrow hall, its walls streaked with dried blood, possibly from the creature that Will had shot. The floor sloped downward and led to a small-windowed door, but the light could not penetrate the utter darkness beyond. Across the foyer, a crudely cut hole opened like a gaping maw waiting to swallow its next victim. On the walls to either side of the opening hung small cauldrons.

Morgan gasped.

Julie held the staff up and took a step toward the opening. "What is it?"

Thick hoses connected the cauldrons to the wall. The distinct smell of iron filled the air.

Morgan's stomach tightened. "I've seen those before." She swallowed, trying to relieve her dry throat. "Larger ones at the cabin in the Arden Forest and small ones like this at the Waerdreath." She glanced at the others' faces. Alyssa and Julie seemed intrigued, Ryowyn looked appalled, but Nyrianne was calm.

"Is this place familiar to you, Nyrianne?" Morgan asked.

"Why, yes, of course." The old woman's head flinched back slightly, and she nodded. "One never forgets the Maidstone."

Morgan wanted to avoid talking about the cauldrons, but Alyssa and Nyrianne were wandering toward the cave-like entrance.

Julie's knees bent slightly as she crept forward. "What's in these pots?" she asked. "And what are they for?"

Nyrianne grabbed Julie's arm, and everyone stopped walking. "You don't want to know that, dear."

There was something about the change in the old woman's tone and the frightened look in her eyes that convinced Morgan to finally get some answers.

"Nyrianne," Morgan said, repeating her previous comment more clearly. "I have seen these before. I know what's inside." She glanced at Alyssa, looking for support. "But I need to know—and I think we all need to know—as much as we can about this place if we're gonna find what we're looking for and help our friends."

Nyrianne's eyes darted from face to face. She took a step away from Morgan, and away from the cauldrons.

"You may speak freely, Nyrianne," Alyssa said in a quiet voice. "You are among friends."

The old woman folded her hands in front of her and lowered her head. After a moment, she brushed a hand across her cheek. Her voice quivered as she spoke.

"Long ago—a lifetime, it seems—I conducted experiments… I—I do not remember everything, I'm afraid." Nyrianne was staring at the cauldrons now. "Did you know that the parts that are vital to sustaining human life can also empower other things? For some purposes, blood is enough. Yes… We drew just enough blood from General Raric while he was nailed to the cross to power the Illiack, allowing him to see many events throughout the Fourwinds. And Natas could see through his eyes."

"The seer outside," Ryowyn said. "Are these cauldrons allowing Natas to see what he sees?"

"Well, of course, dear. If you look around, you will find a cord between these cauldrons and the seer's tree." She winked at Alyssa. "Except that his eyes are temporarily blinded with ice."

Julie's mouth hung open, and her eyebrows arched, creating deep lines in her forehead. "What was that you said about human life powering other things? How did…" She shook her head slowly.

Nyrianne's eyes narrowed as she turned to Julie. "The harvesters are very skillful with the knife," she said.

Morgan and Julie exchanged a horrified look. "Yes," Morgan said. "We know."

"Quite by accident," Nyrianne continued, "Natas discovered that when certain cauldrons were filled with the blood and organs of a person recently killed, the resulting magic could ensure his control over passageways to other times and other worlds. And as he discovered, there were many passageways out there. So, he sent harvesters to the ones he knew of to unleash his diabolical contagion. Imagine entire worlds populated by creatures transformed into the image of Natas. He would be king among the gods." She trailed off and shifted her weight suddenly. "You know, Julie, I always wanted to go to your time, but I never made it."

Morgan took a deep breath, trying to keep Nyrianne focused. "So, if there were cauldrons like these in each place, would Natas be able to see there too?"

Nyrianne tilted her head and scratched a cheek. "Yes, of course. He would need a seer, but I suppose a harvester could serve that purpose." She pointed at the cauldrons. "Two are needed for each seer. But to empower a passageway, the runes are essential. We don't understand why or who created them, but we do know that the markings on each cauldron are identical."

Morgan's mind reeled. If this were true, she realized, the four cauldrons at the cabin in the Arden Forest would allow Natas to have two seers roaming the world.

"Do these cauldrons mean there's a passageway to another world here in the Maidstone?" Ryowyn asked.

Nyrianne grinned. "You catch on pretty quick, my dear."

"We would be wise to avoid it," Alyssa said.

"There, you see?" Nyrianne opened her arms in a flourish. "I do remember *some* things. The caretaker of the Maidstone is the only other person who knows about the power of the cauldrons." She looked around the room. "I wonder if Illume is home."

Morgan raised her eyebrows at Ryowyn.

"Was Illume your friend?" Ryowyn asked.

"Oh no, dear child. He's a very bad man."

"Why do you say that?"

"Oh, the harvesters use stealthy and careful methods. But Illume enjoys taking parts from one race—perhaps the legs from a minotaur—and attaching them to the hips of another. His skills are without equal, but his unnaturally long life has turned him into a monster. Very bad indeed. He should never have found the horn of Thaudas. Dreadful things happen to those who steal from unicorns. Too much power for one man."

Ryowyn approached Nyrianne and lowered her voice. "Illume is not here anymore." She pointed at the bloodstained hallway. "He's dead, Nyrianne."

Nyrianne huffed and squinted as if she doubted Ryowyn's story. "So, we don't have to worry about Illume?"

"That's right," Alyssa said. "Will was here and took the horn from Illume. With his horn restored, Thaudas healed Ryowyn. And now we can do the same for Will, for Rowe, and perhaps many others."

"The winged unicorn cannot heal Will now, or anyone infected with Phyriad," Nyrianne said matter-of-factly. "Thaudas can save an ailing life, but Phyriad does not kill; it transforms."

"I understand," Alyssa said. "That's why we're here: to find the antidote."

"But what about all the beasts Illume created?" Nyrianne said.

There was a pause in the conversation as everyone stared at the old woman.

"Can you take us to find the antidote for Phyriad without being seen by these beasts?" Alyssa asked.

"The antidote is guarded." Nyrianne's tone changed again, from slow and clear to curt and veiled. She seemed to drift in and out of lucidness.

"So, you know where the antidote is?" Julie asked.

Nyrianne wore a mischievous look as if she were enjoying their dependence on her. "I might."

Morgan lifted her sword and ventured across the sloped floor toward the windowed door. Alyssa and Ryowyn followed.

"Careful, child. If Illume is dead, then his abominations no longer have a master. It would be wise to step cautiously—even with that sword."

"We cannot stay here," Alyssa said.

Julie shone the light toward the door, but Morgan still could not see past it. She turned back.

"Oh, what a pretty stick you have, dear," Nyrianne said to Julie, reaching for the warden rod.

Julie flinched and stepped away from the old woman.

"Don't worry," Nyrianne said. "I just like to admire pretty things." She glowered at Alyssa. "And I can tell you there is nothing pretty beyond that door. Come this way."

She hobbled toward the dark opening next to the cauldrons, then drifted to the right where the wall became dark and rough.

"They really should cover this up with a nice tapestry," Nyrianne said.

Morgan and Alyssa exchanged a nervous glance. If the old woman was having this much trouble keeping a clear head already, could she be trusted to lead them to the antidote? Morgan sighed. For now, at least, Nyrianne was their best option.

Julie stepped beside Nyrianne. "Tapestries would be beautiful, and perhaps we can come back and do that after we've saved our friends' lives."

Nyrianne spread both hands over the rough wall, tracing her gnarled fingers along the edges as if searching for something.

Ryowyn gasped. "Look!"

A thin line of glowing light outlined a doorway in the rock.

"Oh!" Nyrianne exclaimed. "There you are." She leaned forward, pushing against the wall as she whispered a short, incoherent phrase.

A deep thump reverberated in the foyer, and a section of rock slid sideways. Without turning, Nyrianne walked through the three-foot-wide opening. Julie pointed the light inside and followed, beckoning the others with her free hand.

Morgan expected to enter another room but instead discovered a spiral staircase that reminded her of the passage that led to the Records of Time in the Crow's Nest. The steps went downward for about one story and opened into a hallway.

The air was stale. Dust-coated debris littered the floor. Chunks of stone filled parts of the compact space, as if the walls had caved in years before. Nyrianne navigated a narrow path through the rubble, at times needing to climb over sections on hands and knees.

The glow of the warden rod revealed other objects amid the rocks. Morgan thought they looked like strands of electrical wire, pipes, and broken metal. But that was impossible. It was probably old vines and dead branches, she reasoned.

When they reached the end of the caved-in area, the walls and floor became smooth, albeit still very dusty. Nyrianne stopped to brush her dress, and a little cloud billowed around her. Julie coughed as she held the light for the others until they all stood on solid ground.

The hallway widened toward the left but ended about ten feet away in a wall of rubble. Julie spun around, and the light revealed a long corridor heading in the opposite direction.

"This way, child," Nyrianne said.

"What kind of place is this?" Ryowyn said. She kicked a flat, perfectly square object lying on the floor, and Morgan's suspicions were confirmed. She looked up. In the smooth ceiling, a few tiles were missing. Broken light fixtures dangled precariously from short wires. As she walked beneath them, her boots crunched shards of shattered fluorescent tubes.

They hadn't taken twenty steps when they came to another pile of broken rock. Julie raised the staff. The way forward was completely blocked. Nyrianne continued, slowing only to sidestep a few ceiling tiles and broken lights. A dozen feet from the blockage, she stopped and faced the wall.

Morgan stepped beside her and gasped when she saw two openings. "It's an elevator!"

Broken boulders filled one shaft, but the other was clear of debris. Julie leaned forward and shone the light into the open shaft. A series of thick cables disappeared into the darkness below. The pungent smell of burnt oil and grease reminded Morgan of the small auto repair shop in Cochrane where her dad used to take his old Honda Civic.

Nyrianne pressed the round elevator call button. "Wait till you see this." She stepped back and started whistling a tune.

After a moment of silence, Julie placed a hand on Nyrianne's shoulder. "I—I don't think the elevator is working, Nyrianne."

"Oh dear. I was afraid of that. I was hoping to show you this wondrous contraption. Probably built by elves long ago." The corners of her mouth sagged. "I suppose we'll have to take the stairs. But nineteen levels are an awful journey for these old bones."

Morgan glanced at the others to make sure they had heard the same thing.

"Do you mean we have to go down nineteen stories?" Alyssa said.

Nyrianne huffed. "Well, of course."

"Are you sure we'll find the antidote to help Will and Rowe down there?" Ryowyn asked.

Nyrianne clapped her hands together. "Oh yes! Dear Will." She shuffled over to the left of the elevators and opened a narrow door. "Come now; what are we waiting for?"

CHAPTER 22

THE GNOME REMNANT

In less than a week, the security level in the Rainia Valley had shifted from a moderate threat to high alert. The Red Dragon that Will, Morgan, and Rowe had spotted from the North Crow Gate proved a significant distraction from building defenses to keep the spread of Phyriad from entering the valley. That distraction almost destroyed Rainia and threatened all life in the valley. But that was yesterday. Now that the dragon was under Raric's control—or so it seemed—a new day began. With the rising sun, workers and soldiers returned to rebuilding towns and guarding the border.

Joe had arisen before the dawn, and as he walked from the Crow's Nest to the North Crow Gate, he sensed that this new day was far from normal. Those he thought to be the protectors of the valley—the Callum Sages—were gone. Will and Rowe had been successful in retrieving the thunderclaps that had brought down the Red Dragon. But they were paying the price for their efforts. Joe was reluctant to go near them and risk infection, but he resolved to visit the cabin soon. And now Morgan, who had proven herself invaluable in defending the valley, was off to the Maidstone in search of something that might save Will and Rowe. The burden of responsibility weighed heavily on Joe.

At a large rock by the roadside, he sat and massage his feet. He was getting too old for these adventures. Finding Will and Morgan back in Cochrane had sparked hope in him. He had hoped the young Callum Sages would take over the work he had done years ago in the Fourwinds. He had hoped that Rowe of the Nest would train them. He had hoped…but since he'd returned to the Fourwinds, a new enemy rose each day to defy his hopes.

Joe stood and breathed in the morning air. The sun warmed his face. On the branch of a nearby fir tree, a few blackbirds chirped the same tune they sang every morning. Life awakened all around him. And as far as he knew, Will, Morgan, and Rowe were all still alive. While they lived, hope endured.

He started down the road again, and less than ten minutes later, a horse-drawn cart approached from behind him.

"I'm headin' to the North Crow Gate," the driver called. "Can I offer you a ride?"

"Thank you." Joe smiled and climbed into the back of the cart. Whatever challenges this day brought, he refused to give up while hope lived.

That sentiment stayed with Joe until they were a few hundred feet from the wall. Soldiers rushed up the main stairs, swords drawn and bows nocked. Angry outbursts and threatening shouts sent hope cowering to a safe corner of Joe's heart.

At the top of the stairs, he found Twell and a group of archers with arrows pointing down at the road leading from the Epping Forest to the closed gate. An unarmed gnome stood in the shade with hands held high. Beside him, another gnome knelt beside a third gnome with an arrow lodged in his thigh.

"What's going on?" Joe asked.

Twell flicked his head toward Joe but kept his arrow trained on the gnomes. "They say they come in peace, Johanissan. But we've watched their army moving through the trees all morning. I don't trust them."

"But these three are unarmed, Commander. I see no threat."

Twell lowered his bow slightly. "But we have no way of knowing if they're infected with Phyriad. How will we know without Morgan and Will?"

Joe studied the gnomes' faces. He had seen the effects of Phyriad on the mer at the Niasa Sea, and these three showed no outward symptoms. Nevertheless, he knew that to proceed without caution would be unwise.

"Let me go to them." Joe placed a hand on Twell's shoulder. "I have an idea, but please, lower your weapons until they're actually needed."

Twell hesitated, then grumbled as he lowered his bow. "At ease, soldiers."

A minute later, the main gates opened, and Joe walked toward the three gnomes. One hand clutched his staff, which offered him the extra support his trembling legs needed. He held the other hand high in greeting, trying to look as unthreatening as possible. He hoped his posture and his white hair would help communicate peace to these three and to any gnome soldiers who might be hiding in the trees, ready to attack. Again, he hoped.

"I apologize for the hostile greeting you received," Joe said to the gnomes. "They will not shoot again."

The standing gnome lowered his arms, but his large eyes flickered back and forth from Joe to the soldiers on the wall.

Joe stopped about ten feet from the gnomes. "Do you come from the Nameless Forest?"

The wounded gnome nodded with a pained grimace. "Seeking refuge from the Iron Dragon, we are."

"How many of you are there?"

"Not a thousand remain," the kneeling gnome said as he tightened a rag around his comrade's bleeding leg. "And injured is our commander."

"Are you Commander Yossar?" Joe asked the wounded gnome.

"I am not, but take you to him we can."

"That would be good. There's someone I need you to see before we let you into the valley. Or…someone who needs to see *you*, I should say."

The two gnomes helped the wounded gnome up, draping his arms around their shoulders for support. Slowly, they returned down the road back through the Epping Forest. Joe kept his distance, not wanting to lose any of the trust he'd gained with these three. And the slower pace was perfect as far as he was concerned.

They rounded a few bends in the road before coming to a small meadow where the gnomes stopped. The field was empty, but under the canopy of the surrounding forest, a wall of gnome soldiers stretched back as far as Joe could see.

"An emissary we have," one of the three gnomes called. "But help we need."

Two gnomes rushed from the trees and carried the wounded gnome into the shadows. The other two followed, leaving Joe standing alone in the field.

A moment later, a tall gnome emerged from the trees, leaning on a walking stick as he limped toward Joe. The gnome was not only taller but older than the other three. He wore less protection over his wrinkled and tanned skin, and wisps of blond hair fluttered in the breeze.

"Frightened you need not be," the gnome said. "Finished with battle we are, and seek only refuge for our few survivors."

"My deepest condolences for your losses," Joe said with a gentle nod. "My name is Johanissan of the River Country, Callum Sage, and…emissary from the Crow's Nest." The last title sounded odd in his ears, but he wanted to assure the gnomes he was here to help.

"Commander Yossar I am," the elderly gnome said, pointing to his chest. "Brigadier Bayard told us sanctuary we might find in your valley. As I promised him, not a sick gnome among us there be. Hungry and tired only. And now one wounded."

"I'm sorry about the poor reception for your three scouts. As you can imagine, the arrangement made by Bayard came as a shock to many of our people. Since receiving the news, we've had heated debates over the matter. I understand you've seen the effects of Phyriad on your people, so I don't have to explain what's at stake here. We must be ruthless in the defense of the Rainia Valley."

"Speak for us Commander Bayard will."

Joe leaned on his staff. "I'm sorry, but Bayard did not survive the battle with Uluk the Shadowfallen. But his successor, Captain Culthison, has spoken for you."

Yossar ambled forward until he was two feet away. Joe hadn't expected to look the commander in the eye; he'd never met such a tall gnome. Nor had he seen such pride and determination in one's eyes. Not to mention the glimmer of hope.

"Our leaders have discussed our potential cohabitation, and we're committed to doing what is best for the residents of the Rainia

Valley," Joe said. "It is the only protected place in the Fourwinds that we know of. We understand that it was bush gnomes who attacked the South Crow Gate, and we are aware of the dubious dealings of Uluk the Shadowfallen. We also believe that you have been pawns in Natas's plan to rule the Fourwinds. But a long-standing hatred remains between humans and gnomes. Your armies sacked many towns, including Longcross near the Stoneberg, and you completely destroyed Hammerclaw down to its foundations."

Yossar tilted his head. "And yet, of olden days no one speaks, when humans drove gnomes from our land and into the west?"

Joe hung his head. There was no bitterness in Yossar's tone, only the sadness of a broken spirit. "As I said, it is a long-standing hatred. But I have hope that somehow we can return the land to something we nurture and share rather than something we seize and control."

Yossar was nodding as he repositioned his walking stick. If he was in pain, his stoic expression masked it well. "Hear my story, Johanissan of the River Country. A time there was, before I had breath, when farmed the Clover Fields the highland gnomes did. Songs we sing about those harvests, and tales of wagons buckling beneath the weight of colorful vegetables.

"But then war arrived, and then walls. Desolate the lands became. Refused to sustain us the soil did—despite our efforts. Starved we did. Wrong we might have been for not maintaining a strong military like our cousins, the bush gnomes, did. Instead, found fertile land beyond your Stoneberg we did, but not enough. And so, agreement we made with Uluk: fight his battles against your people in exchange for the Clover Fields. Deceived us he did."

Yossar bent down and scooped up a handful of dirt. "Full of regret I am when I think of the death and destruction we caused.

But farmers we are, and peaceful at heart. And beautiful this soil is." He stood straight, and the dirt trickled between his fingers. Joe breathed in the aroma of dust, dead leaves and decay, and the hope of new life. Some grains spilled onto his boots.

"At your feet does the fate of my people lie, Johanissan. This promise I offer: if grace us with land Rainia does, more fresh produce than they can imagine will the highland gnomes share."

Joe smiled. He had no intention of turning away the gnome refugees before today, and now he had no problem welcoming them. "You make a very convincing argument, Commander." He reached out his free hand, and Yossar clutched it.

"But," Joe continued, "we have a strict set of protocols before we allow anyone passage through the North Crow Gate. It's a tedious process, but you can assure your people that we use the same scrutiny for everyone who seeks entry. This is to ensure our survival. It will feel like we're distrustful—and some people will be. There are widows in the valley who will want you dead. Regardless, leave your weapons at the gate. They must see that you have come to give and not take."

"My promise you already have. At your mercy we are."

"All right, then. How many are with you?" It was a jarring question, but there was only one way to ask such a thing.

"This morning, there be eight hundred forty-one."

Joe braced himself with his staff. On one hand, the thought of leading so many into the valley was staggering. But considering Yossar's army was originally estimated at twelve thousand, the number of dead gnome soldiers was mind-numbing.

"How long before you're ready to move?" Joe asked.

"Supplies we have very little, so ready to march we are at any moment."

Joe turned and looked beyond the trees to the mountains north of the Crow's Nest. "Before we begin the protocols at the gate, I must take you to someone who needs a close look at each of you."

Yossar turned to the trees, waved his hand, and the wall of gnomes trudged into the field. The weary crowd funneled into a long line two or three soldiers wide as they followed their commander and Joe along a narrow, hidden path through the Epping Forest.

An hour later, they left the cover of trees and followed a rocky trail into the mountains. They stopped once by a small stream for rest and water, but there was very little conversation.

By midafternoon, they arrived at their destination. The outpost cabin stood on a ridge above a small meadow. It was a beautiful vacation getaway, if not for the present occupants.

"Hello!" Joe called.

The front door swung open, and Will stepped out. Even from a distance, his pale, sweaty face glowed in the daylight. His body shook as he coughed and struggled to speak.

"Joe! It's so good to see you!" Will leaned against a post under the overhanging roof. "And you brought some friends."

"Good to see you, *Masitaw.*"

It had been a long time since Joe called Will by the nickname his mother had used when he was a child. It certainly seemed appropriate today. *Masitaw* could be translated roughly to *fighter* or *he struggles*. The determined grin on Will's sickly face told Joe that at least the boy's mind was still fighting, even if his body was weakening.

"How's Rowe?" Joe asked.

"Neither of us are up to entertaining visitors these days." He hacked again. "Rowe's sleeping. His fever spiked pretty high last night. I'm mostly just coughing, but man, does my skin ever itch.

I feel like my entire body's on fire." Will folded his arms tight to his chest and hunched his shoulders.

"Are the cloaks helping to slow the effects?" Joe asked.

"From what I've seen of Phyriad's impact on others, I'd say so."

Joe walked along the side of the cabin, staying about thirty feet away. The gnomes followed, filling up the large open field.

"These brave gnome soldiers defied the Shadowfallen and are now seeking refuge in the valley," Joe said. "But I wanted you to… *see* each one of them first." He pointed two fingers to his eyes, then raised his eyebrows, hoping Will would understand he wanted to know if there were any harvesters among them.

Will nodded right away and gave a thumbs-up.

Joe continued around the front of the cabin in a wide circle until all the gnomes were within Will's sight. He kept conversation light, knowing Will had little energy and was working quickly to scan the crowd.

"Do you and Rowe have enough food?"

"More than we can eat…not that we're eating that much." After several minutes, he added, "I wish I could offer our friends here something. They are a fine-looking group of gnomes."

Joe exhaled the breath he didn't know he'd been holding. He was relieved to learn there were no harvesters disguised among the gnomes. But now that he knew, he wondered what he would have done had there been any. Rowe was in no condition to kill harvesters.

"Thank you for your time and insight, Will. As promised, I must get these soldiers through the North Crow Gate before sundown. I hope to be back to visit soon…unless Morgan and the others find the antidote first."

Will hacked a few times, then offered a feeble wave. "Thanks,

Joe. I hope you don't have to come back. Next time, let's meet at the Recovery in Rainia."

Joe chuckled to himself as he led the long, silent company of gnome soldiers back to the North Crow Gate. Will certainly loved the Recovery Inn, and the idea sounded fine to Joe. He added to his list of hopes a successful journey and swift return for Morgan and the others.

CHAPTER 23
Secrets Far Below

"I counted nineteen stories."

From deep beneath the top level of the Maidstone, Julie's words echoed in the stairwell. With each flight down, the air had grown warmer and staler. Dust choked Morgan's throat, and she coughed as she followed her mother's upward gaze in the light of the warden rod. The gloomy stairs reminded her of an old apartment building where she used to visit a childhood friend. The children had always preferred the challenge of taking the stairs over the elevator. When she was tall enough, Morgan had loved to look over the handrail down through the virtually endless concrete steps. The children would call out to one another, enjoying the eerie echo. But in this dismal place, she would have welcomed an elevator.

Alyssa had stopped them every five floors to maintain their bearings and pause for a brief rest, but Nyrianne had said they only needed to go down nineteen. *Only* nineteen. Morgan had grown tired of the rhythmic shuffling of boots on concrete steps somewhere around eight. Now, after nineteen floors, Morgan did a quick check to see how everyone was managing so far. Alyssa was breathing normally and appeared ready for another nineteen flights. Ryowyn coughed lightly, took a small drink, then offered the leather canteen to the others. Julie's hair had come loose, and there were dark circles under her eyes. Nyrianne actually seemed stronger—physically, at least.

The five women gathered around a closed metal door with green paint still visible in places. It had been worked over with hammers or rocks or whatever people in the Maidstone used to try to smash through locked doors. But despite the dents and gouges, nothing had come close to penetrating this door. The handle had broken off, but three flush-mounted dead bolts held the door secure.

Ryowyn pressed both hands against the metal. "Any place this deep must have some terrible secrets. It feels alive."

The deep, droning sound they had heard in the foyer above had grown louder as they'd descended and was reverberating through the walls. Morgan leaned in beside Ryowyn and put her ear to the door.

"What do you hear?" Julie asked.

Morgan stepped aside. "You tell me."

Julie pressed her cheek to the door, and her eyes widened. "Sounds like…Hoover Dam. Remember when we took the tour after you won that fencing tournament in Las Vegas?"

"Well, maybe not *that* loud," Morgan said. "But similar."

"I wonder if they're producing power from the waterfalls. That'd be helpful."

"How's that?" Morgan asked.

Julie's expression brightened. "It would mean functioning climate controls, which would bode well for any vaccines stored in this place."

"We must be getting close," Alyssa said. "Nyrianne, how did you get through this door when you were here? Did you have a key?"

Nyrianne started to shake her head, then nodded once.

"Do you still have the keys?" Julie asked.

Again, the old woman nodded.

Julie placed a hand over her heart and smiled. "Great, Nyrianne. Where are they?"

"Oh, sweet child, I would never risk bringing those keys on such a dangerous adventure. Goodness, no; they're much too valuable to warrant such risk."

Julie's hand fell to her side. "But how do we get through this door without the key? Looks like brute force hasn't been too successful."

Nyrianne examined the door for a few seconds, then stared at Julie. "Yes…force is needed. Why not just use your staff?"

Julie lifted the warden rod slightly. "I—I don't think—"

"Like this," Nyrianne said, motioning for Julie to hold it with both hands, parallel with the floor, waist high. She then thrust her hands forward three times, as if she were jabbing each lock with the end of the staff.

Julie shot a skeptical glance at the others.

"I'm sorry," Ryowyn said. "My father never said much about it. I only know that the staff is a protector."

"It can't hurt to try, Mom."

Alyssa seemed more confident and waved her hands for everyone to stand back.

Julie raised the warden rod as Nyrianne had instructed, with the lighted end pointing away from the door. The light grew brighter, and Julie's hands trembled. She drew in a sharp breath and jabbed the top lock.

The tip of the rod sparked, and the dead bolt exploded from

the door, clanging to the floor on the other side. The spark shot through the rod to Julie's hands, and she nearly dropped the staff. Her back straightened, and her mouthed popped open as if she'd gotten a small electrical shock. But her face was beaming like that of someone who had just jumped into a cool lake on a hot summer day. Morgan remembered the exhilarating sensation when she had first held the sword that she and her mother found in their attic.

Without hesitation, Julie repeated the jabbing maneuver two more times. When all three locks were gone, the door creaked inward on rusty hinges.

Alyssa pushed it open wide, and the warden rod glowed even brighter, illuminating the short hallway.

"I—I'm not doing anything," Julie said quietly. "This thing has a mind of its own."

"Try to imagine there are batteries in the handle," Morgan suggested.

Julie examined the rod. "You mean this thing doesn't take a slew of D batteries?"

Morgan chuckled. "Something happened to you back there, didn't it, Mom? Something inside you."

"Yes, how'd you know?"

"I've had similar experiences when I use the sword. Can you describe it?"

Julie shuddered. "It was distinct, powerful, and otherworldly. A rush of energy shot through my body and concentrated in my hands. Then it flowed through to the rod. I couldn't let go. After the rod sparked, the sensation left me. I could hardly breathe."

"It's the first time you've experienced magic in the Fourwinds, Mom."

"Magic?"

"I know it sounds strange, but think of all the things you've seen since coming here. And I have a feeling it's not that strange to you after all you and Dad experienced in Africa."

Morgan put her arm around her mother, but Julie just shook her head as she walked, staring at the floor. Once again, Morgan was amazed at her mother's strength and resilience. The Fourwinds was a strange place, but what she'd seen of the Maidstone already was far more mysterious. She just hoped they would find what they needed soon and escape without too much trouble.

Closed doors lined both sides of the hallway, but Alyssa increased her pace toward a long counter in the middle of a junction where the hallway divided. Ryowyn was a few steps behind, trident raised.

"This looks like a nurses' station or a reception desk," Julie said, turning to Alyssa. "What is this place?"

"Mom! Remember that hospital in Kiev?" Morgan asked. "Where you took me when I sprained my wrist?"

Julie's eyes widened as she nodded. "It does remind me of that."

"Feels like we just stepped through the Gateway in the Records of Time and returned to our world," Morgan said.

"Oh, child," Nyrianne said. "There are many gateways…many passageways. No need to travel back to the Crow's Nest."

Morgan waited for further explanation, but she wasn't sure how lucid Nyrianne was at the moment.

"She's right," Alyssa said. "About the gateways, at least. But we're still in the Fourwinds."

She spoke with a confidence that piqued Morgan's curiosity. "How do you know, Alyssa?"

"The Ice Dragon is a wanderer," Nyrianne said with a cackle. "And a hard thing to track. Not like that kind, kind boy, Will," Nyrianne murmured.

"I can tell you this," Alyssa said. "This facility was built long ago, before this land was known as the Fourwinds. The Maidstone was constructed during the breaking of the old world to protect this secret lab."

Morgan wiped her forehead with the back of her wrist. "Breaking of the old world?"

Alyssa waited until Morgan held her gaze. "In your world, it was neither peaceful nor long ago. Quite the opposite, in fact. Life in the Fourwinds was just beginning, and in your world, it was—"

"Ending," Morgan finished. She stared at Alyssa in silence.

"So, you're saying that"—Julie sputtered a nervous laugh—"that we're in the future?"

"No," Alyssa said. "You are in the present, living out what has already transpired since you, Will, Morgan, and Joe left your time." She released a puff of air, put a hand on her hip, and cast her gaze down each hallway. "I'm sorry. That probably doesn't help. I wish I could explain it more clearly. The druids are much better at this sort of thing."

"That's unbelievable," Julie said, her hand poised over her open mouth. "If this is from somewhere in our world, I can't imagine where it would be. And I've traveled a lot."

Her eyes were wild as she started searching the counter. Decades-old dust covered the station, and papers cluttered the lower counter beyond a small glass divider.

"Whoever built this," Morgan suggested, "they haven't been here for a long time."

Julie blew dust from a binder. "I think this was some kind of military medical facility."

"U-S-A-M-R-I-I-D," Morgan read. "What's that?"

"It stands for *United States Army Medical Research Institute of*

Infectious Diseases. When we lived in Cleveland, I worked with a lab tech who had served in the army. She told me about research they did to investigate disease outbreaks and biological threats to the military." Her mouth hung open for a moment, and her eyes widened. "They were responsible for creating numerous new drugs…and vaccines."

"What's a vaccine?" Ryowyn asked.

"It's a…" Morgan searched for words that the mer princess might use. "An *elixir* given to someone to prevent them from catching a certain illness."

"And some drugs can reverse the effects of an illness," Julie added.

Ryowyn's face brightened. "So, these people created an elixir that could heal Will and Rowe?"

Julie shrugged as she watched Nyrianne walk away from the counter toward a closed double door.

"Let's see where she goes," Alyssa whispered.

They all joined Nyrianne by the door. Morgan leaned close and listened.

"I hear…*voices*," she whispered. "And sounds of…equipment."

"Nyrianne, do we need to pass through this door to find the cure for Phyriad?" Julie asked.

Nyrianne nodded.

"Where does this doorway lead?" Alyssa asked.

"Well, into the depths of Illume's nightmare, of course."

Julie glanced at Alyssa, then turned to Nyrianne. "But this is the way we need to go?"

"Oh yes. Through these doors, then…let me see, one left and two rights." She raised her eyes to the ceiling. "Or was it two lefts and one right?"

Julie handed the warden rod to Ryowyn and pulled a package of surgical masks from her pack. "I borrowed these from Lady Minto Hospital. From here on in, let's assume everything is contagious. If this was once a research center, we don't know what we'll find beyond these doors." She secured her mask in place, then helped Nyrianne position the elastic bands behind her head.

Morgan noticed Ryowyn's confusion and remembered that the mer probably didn't know about medical concepts like vaccines, germs, and airborne diseases. "These masks should prevent us from getting sick."

"I don't imagine you have a key for this door either?" Alyssa asked.

Nyrianne shrugged and held up empty palms.

There was only one lock on this door, and Morgan knew they had only one option.

"Use the staff again, Mom." Morgan drew her sword. "I'll go through first with Ryowyn."

Julie gripped the warden rod with both hands. "So, we're just gonna fight our way through whatever's beyond this door?"

"Just do it before we all lose our nerve." Morgan bent her knees slightly, holding the sword low and across her body. "We'll be fine."

Ryowyn stepped behind Morgan, the blades of her trident a few feet in front of them.

"Oh, dear God," Julie whispered, holding the staff at waist level.

She struck the lock, and a spark of magic flashed. There was a deep thump, and the lock disappeared into the room beyond. Morgan kicked, and both doors flew open.

In the middle of the dimly lit room was a long surgical table surrounded by trays of stainless-steel tools. IV tubes hung from a portable pole at the head of the surgical table, and several machines beeped and blinked. An unidentifiable creature covered in iron-gray scales lay facedown on the table with a long, deep incision in its back. Morgan gasped, trying to press the mask closer to her nose, but the stench would not be denied.

On another table, a giant humanoid creature with dragon-like features lay on its back. It appeared to be dead and was secured to the table with wide leather straps. Its body was a mishmash of scales, horns, and talons. Fangs protruded below a short snout. Two rows of small, pointed horns topped glassy dark eyes and spread over a bald head. Its left arm had been replaced with a much larger arm covered in dark hair. The right arm was distinctly human, but curved talons extended from unusually long fingers.

The light from the warden rod flickered, and Morgan turned to see her mother trembling. Behind Julie, tucked into a corner, was another table with a massive corpse on it. The hideous creature reminded Morgan of the harvester she had slain in Cochrane. But this harvester was several days dead. Both legs were missing, and a part of its wings had been removed from its back.

"Welcome to Illume's nightmare," Nyrianne said softly.

Morgan's stomach turned, and her head grew light. This was much worse than a nightmare.

Ryowyn must have noticed Morgan's reaction because she came alongside her and offered an encouraging hand. The princess was surprisingly resilient, and her touch was like soothing medicine. She offered the same touch to Julie.

Nyrianne strolled across the room and through another set of double doors as if everything here were perfectly normal.

Large round lights illuminated the next room and centered on a surgical table surrounded by more whirring and beeping machines. Morgan spun around with sword raised, expecting an attack. But the only occupant of the room was another scaly humanoid creature lying facedown on the table. Stainless-steel tools, some caked with dried blood, littered a small tray next to the head of the table. A long tube connected the creature to a ventilator making a strange grinding sound. Two pumps were beeping and flashing their warning that the IV bags were empty. It was as though everyone had just disappeared mid-surgery.

"Does any of this look familiar from your nursing experience, Julie?" Alyssa asked.

"Familiar, but smaller and far more advanced than anything I've ever seen or read about." Julie's voice was quiet, and her throat sounded parched.

"Which way from here?" Morgan asked.

Nyrianne stood next to the body on the table. "I was going to ask the dracar for directions, but he's dead."

"Sorry, Nyrianne, but what did you just call that creature?"

"I once thought that certain people who had been exposed to Phyriad were immune," Nyrianne said, "but I was wrong. They just reacted differently. Weeks after being exposed, they transformed into something…unexpected. They developed scales over their skin, but also"—she pointed to her own eyes—"the whites of their eyes suddenly turned red. When their eyes changed, so did their hearts. After a few months, you would never believe they had ever been human. They looked like wild dragon creatures, but they were highly intelligent. So, Natas trained them for his own purposes. These are the dracar."

Alyssa pointed to a side counter where a large pair of leathery wings were connected to a machine. "What are those for?"

Nyrianne scoffed. "Natas wants the dracar to fly, but the experiments have failed…so far. He has trained some to continue the work."

There was a scuffling noise outside the room that sounded like someone pushing a wheeled cart down a hallway.

"Let's focus on finding that antidote," Morgan said.

"Right," Julie agreed. "If this is a surgical ward, we may be close. Vaccines are often stored in refrigerators near blood and plasma."

Alyssa stood at the double doors on the opposite side of the room. There were narrow windows in both doors, but they were blacked out. She pushed one door open a crack and peered out.

Muffled conversation and footsteps drifted in. They were not alone.

Alyssa closed the door. "It looks busy out there," she said. "More doors and hallways. We should remember this room in case we have to retrace our steps."

Morgan walked slowly to the door, but Nyrianne strode past her. The old woman pushed the metal crash bar, and the door swung wide open. Nyrianne disappeared into the hall.

The other women glanced at one another, then followed.

Nyrianne hobbled toward a long U-shaped counter. Behind it, three dracar wearing matching plain white T-shirts and light-green linen pants stared wide-eyed at Nyrianne. All their exposed skin, including their hairless heads, was covered in small, dark scales. Their red eyes narrowed with each step the old woman took toward them. The dracar cowered slightly when Morgan and Ryowyn joined her, weapons raised in front of them.

"Sweet children," Nyrianne announced. "We're looking for…" She turned back and raised her eyebrows at Julie. "What is it we came here for?"

Julie kept her distance. "A—a vaccine…an antidote…f-for Phyriad."

One dracar slammed its hands onto the counter and spoke in short, sharp sounds that varied from high-pitched to deep bass tones.

Nyrianne approached the counter and touched the dracar's reptilian arm. "I'm sorry, my dear, but I cannot understand dracar. Could you just point us in the right direction?" She jabbed her own arm with a finger, indicating that they were looking for something that required injection. It was a start.

The dracar shifted its head toward the left for a split second before shaking it rapidly.

"Oh, now don't lie to me," Nyrianne said. "To the left, is it? Thank you, dear."

Morgan and the others followed the old woman. When they came to an intersecting hallway, two larger dracar dressed in the same uniforms as the creatures behind the counter whipped past them, pushing a wheeled surgical bed. In their haste, they almost knocked Nyrianne over. On the bed was a body lying facedown, secured with thick leather straps. One dracar was pulling an IV pole while the other studied a flashing screen at the foot of the bed. They were so preoccupied with their tasks that neither gave the strangers a second look.

Nyrianne led the way, shuffling across the intersecting hallway. They passed two more junctions, then turned down a narrower, shadowy hallway. Many of the ceiling tiles here were missing, and all but one light bulb was dark. Empty surgical beds filled most of the hall.

All five women worked to push aside beds and clear a path toward a metal door with an unlit *EXIT* sign above.

They were about ten feet away when a harsh cry sounded from the direction they'd come. Another joined in until it sounded like an ear-piercing alarm.

Morgan stopped and turned while the others continued on. "Ryowyn, I might need you."

"The door's locked!" Julie shouted.

The two dracar they had passed at the intersection rounded the corner and skidded to a stop. Their red eyes were wide, and their fanged mouths drooled.

The sword of Avarthrill flashed in the dim light, and the mer trident gleamed.

"Get that door open, Mom," Morgan called. "And make it quick!"

CHAPTER 24
A Shaky Welcome

A warm late-afternoon breeze swept across the road to the North Crow Gate. There were still a few hours until the sun set, but Joe wanted to be inside the wall with all 841 gnomes well before nightfall. Those on watch at the gate were on high alert day and night, but darkness compounded the possibility of Phyriad-infected invaders. So far, they had seen none, but no one wanted to take any chances.

Joe was ready to address Twell's reluctance to admit the gnome soldiers, but the words in his head didn't sound convincing. To complicate matters, Joe was hot, tired of walking, and hungry. He was in no condition to argue with the commander.

As he came within sight of the wall, however, Joe's steps lightened. Captain Culthison was standing beside Twell. Dench was there too, towering over both men. Joe raised a hand in greeting, and the captain and the half-orc were the only ones on the wall who returned the gesture. There were no arrows pointed at the gnomes this time, but many soldiers had bows in hand.

Commander Yossar walked beside Joe, keeping a slow and

steady pace. The gnome soldiers followed in complete silence with hands on their heads.

"Surrender is unnecessary," Joe said. "You're not prisoners of war."

Yossar kept his chin up and shoulders back. "A gesture of humility it is, not humiliation."

The gnomes wore layers of clothing and strips of cloth to protect their sensitive skin from the sun. Many wore wide-brimmed hats. Except for their trusted commander, they all kept their eyes to the ground, burdened with fatigue, hunger, and remorse. Joe could not imagine the fear and despair he would face if he were in their boots.

Before anyone exchanged a word, the main gates opened. Apparently, Culthison and those who had fought with him and Commander Bayard had convinced Twell to receive the gnome refugees. Joe's little speech was unnecessary, after all.

As he approached, Joe studied the mixed expressions of soldiers on the wall. Some of those from Enders Brigade appeared sympathetic, and a few even had moist eyes. They knew this remnant from the North Gnome Army had renounced their loyalty to Uluk the Shadowfallen. Enders Brigade had witnessed the army's surrender and considered themselves allies with the highland gnomes.

But the soldiers from Marauders Brigade had difficulty accepting such an alliance. They had raced to help in the battle at the South Crow Gate only to discover that they were almost too late to save the valley. For the past two weeks, they had been preparing for battle with the South Gnome Army—a battle that might never happen, if what Raric said about that army's encounter with the Red Dragon were true.

The remnant of the North Gnome Army made quite an impression as they shuffled along in their straight rows down the dirty road through the stronghold. Normally, there was a tremendous amount of activity around the North Crow Gate, but today all was still. The wind rustled softly through the forest and carried the dust of the highland gnomes into the Rainia Valley. All around the wall, the combination of relief and tension, of sorrow and anger, of mercy and fear, left everyone speechless.

When the last of the gnomes had entered the valley, the massive gate creaked shut. As it did, Joe heard the first of many complaints from the human soldiers. He glanced up to see someone spit disdainfully.

"Filthy vermin," someone mumbled.

"They don't belong here," said another.

"Not true," an Enders Brigade soldier argued. "They defied the Shadowfallen."

More voices chimed in.

"These gnomes aren't the enemy."

"Bah! They're all the same, cut from the same defiled cloth."

Joe's face grew warm, but he dared not lash out in anger. Fortunately, the jeering was cut short.

"Silence!" Twell barked. "Back to your posts. Now!"

Culthison and Dench came alongside Joe and Yossar. Many of the gnomes nearby cowered in the presence of the half-orc, their bulbous eyes growing even wider.

"It's okay," Joe called out as he reached up to pat Dench's back. "Dench is as good a friend as you'll find in this valley."

"Me stand wit' you, Johanissan," Dench said.

Most soldiers responded to Twell's command. The murmuring and bickering grew faint as Joe led the gnomes due south down a well-maintained road.

Over the next hour, they met a few travelers, and Joe offered a smile and a friendly wave. Although he was well-known and liked in the valley, most ignored him today as they stared at the strange new visitors.

Joe leaned close to Yossar. "This will take time, my friend. But you will find shelter and a home here."

"Thankful I am today for these large trees."

Joe smiled, knowing how powerful a simple word of gratitude could be. "We timed it well; sunset always casts long shadows by this great forest. And there's a deep well up ahead where all those wagons are stationed."

At first, Joe thought the wagons were part of a supply caravan traveling from the Crow's Nest, but then he saw Gloriana and a gathering of boys and girls helping her set up tables. Joe shook his head in awe as he watched her tie back her wild gray hair and give instructions. That woman had a gift for organizing volunteer teams while still finding time for the quietest child or loneliest old man.

Yossar was struggling to keep up even with Joe's pace.

"We're almost there," Joe said. "There is water and, if I know Gloriana at all, enough food in those wagons for everyone. We'll take a short break, then make the final push to your new home."

Gloriana stopped what she was doing and came to greet Joe, offering the famous hug she gave to all her friends.

The gnomes kept their distance from the wagons. Most sat or lay down in the cool grass.

"This is Commander Yossar and his…friends." He almost said *army*, but if they ever hoped to find welcome here, the gnomes would need to lose that old identity and become friends.

Without a hint of reservation, Gloriana caught up Yossar in a hug. The commander stiffened but didn't back away. She took his shoulders in her hands and turned him to face the North Crow

Gate, now barely visible in the distance, especially with the rugged beauty of the Hillron Mountains as a backdrop.

"That is your past," Gloriana said. "And, for better or worse, that chapter has ended." She turned him to face south toward the sparkling Rainia Lake and beyond to lush rolling fields and patches of smaller forests.

"Beautiful it is," Yossar said.

"That is your future," Gloriana continued. "And the pages are blank."

Without another word, she joined the children, who stood ready to help hand out food. As hungry and thirsty as the gnomes must have been, many of the stronger ones helped distribute the food and water to others before serving themselves.

Joe found a patch of grass and watched Yossar join in the serving. He wondered if the gnomes knew they had such an exceptional leader, but based on the way they had followed their commander thus far, they probably did.

Gloriana brought Joe a chunk of bread and steaming stew in a dented metal bowl. "It's not much, but—"

"It's perfect," Joe said, hearing his stomach growl its thanks. He dipped the bread in the bowl and took a large bite as Gloriana sat beside him.

"It was a good thing you did back there, Johanissan. I know it's what you do and who you are, but all the same…it was good."

Joe swallowed his food and surveyed the crowd of gnomes. "Is the Rainia Valley ready for this?"

"There are stiff necks here, but there's also a lot of bighearted people. We all know it's the right thing to do, but this is unheard of. I keep thinking of Rowe's speech at the gathering last week. If we can't figure out a way to focus on our commonalities instead of our differences, this might not work." She placed a hand on his shoulder. "But I sure love that we're trying."

"Yes, it will be a rocky road."

"Well, I managed to scrounge up seven wagons of food and supplies. They're rolling south as we speak. I also twisted some arms and called in a few favors to get tents set up."

Joe turned to face her, holding the bread over his bowl.

"Don't look at me like that," she said. "You know we've been preparing for this for a while. I just didn't know it would be today."

"And you say what *I* did was a good thing?"

Gloriana laughed. "We're all in this together."

Joe enjoyed another mouthful of stew. Already, he felt energized. "I saw Will," he said.

Gloriana's forehead wrinkled. "How did he look?"

"Actually, pretty good. He was a bit pale and has a nasty cough, but nothing too serious…so far."

"How was Rowe?"

"Didn't see him. I guess he's fighting a fever. Will said their cloaks are so hot you would burn yourself if you touched them."

"After all Rowe's been through." Gloriana sighed. "If there was ever someone who deserved to ride off into the sunset, it's him. And poor Morgan. She must be worried sick."

"Well, I imagine she's preoccupied with other matters at the moment."

Gloriana shivered despite the warm afternoon. "The Maidstone. I'm so glad she has her mother and Ryowyn with her."

Joe scraped his bowl clean with the last of his bread. "I'm sure Alyssa will help too, although I can't say the same about Nyrianne. She's…unpredictable."

"Speaking of unpredictable, have you heard news of Bremer? His mother has been asking me about him."

Joe chuckled. "No. And I don't expect to either." He grabbed his staff and pushed himself to his feet. He turned to offer a hand to Gloriana, but she was already up on her own. "All my hope now lies in Morgan and the others. If they can find something for Will and Rowe, things will be a whole lot better here."

Yossar was walking toward them, and the gnomes were forming lines again.

"Looks like it's time to move on," Gloriana said.

Yossar stood a few feet away and offered her a curt bow. His face was stern, but his large eyes glistened. "Grateful we are."

"Not much farther now," Joe said. "Beyond the lake, like Gloriana said, a new chapter begins."

CHAPTER 25
THE ANTIDOTE

The warden rod sparked, and with a loud *pop*, the door lock broke.

It would have been a welcomed sound, a way of escape from the freakish surgical ward, but it came about thirty seconds too late. Morgan had thought the two dracar they'd seen earlier pushing a surgical bed were nurses or orderlies. Now, they looked more like trained soldiers. Their red eyes glared at Morgan and Ryowyn, who challenged them with sword and trident.

One dracar held a quarterstaff with intricate metal caps on both ends. The other hefted a long polearm topped with a wide blade, which it promptly used to slash a surgical bed, slicing clean through the dense mattress.

"I'll take the one with the staff," Ryowyn said, bending her knees in a ready stance.

"Morgan!" Julie shouted from the other end of the hall.

Morgan fixed her eyes on the dracar with the polearm. "Kinda busy, Mom!"

The dracar jabbed its blade at Morgan, but she easily sidestepped.

As she did, she pushed a wheeled bed at the dracar, momentarily knocking it off-balance.

Taking advantage of the distraction, Ryowyn lunged at the other dracar with her trident. She brought her weapon up in a quick sweeping motion, striking the quarterstaff so hard it flew from its hands, hit the ceiling, then clanged to the floor. The weapon crackled, and short bolts of lightning lanced from one end. Almost everything metal in the hallway sparked as if the air were suddenly charged. Ryowyn raised her arm to shield her eyes.

As the dracar reached for its fallen weapon, Morgan lunged. But the other dracar had recovered to return the volley. The wheeled bed crashed into her legs, and she stumbled sideways, pushing another bed between her and the dracar.

In two swift motions, Ryowyn shuffled forward and drove her trident into the chest of Morgan's opponent. The dracar crumpled to the floor in a pool of dark-red blood.

A streak of blue lightning shot from the remaining dracar's quarterstaff, striking Ryowyn's side. She dropped her weapon and began to shake as if she were having a seizure. Her legs gave out, and she fell to her knees.

As she went down, Morgan launched into a perfect balestra, lunging past the creature's guard. Back home, her fencing opponents respected her most for this move. The dracar parried, but Morgan finished the duel with a riposte. She jabbed the creature's shoulder.

The dracar retreated one step, then shot another bolt from its weapon. A discharge of power struck Morgan's Trannalun cloak and instantly rebounded back at the dracar. The quarterstaff splintered like lightning striking a small tree. The dracar cried out in an ear-piercing scream and flew backward against the wall, its lifeless form smoking.

Morgan spun around to help Ryowyn up off her knees. "Are you all right? That blast killed the dracar, but—"

"My father fashioned this armor," Ryowyn said, rubbing her side as she drew in long, slow breaths. "It's very strong. But that can't happen too many more times."

More footfalls and the strange alarm sounded from around the corner.

"We've gotta go!" Morgan yelled as they both rushed to the door where the other women waited.

Morgan closed the door behind them. "The lock's broken! We need to block this door with something, or they'll be on us in a minute."

"You have a warden rod," Nyrianne said quietly.

Morgan heard the old woman's voice, but since her eyes had not yet adjusted to the dim light, she could not see her.

"How can it help us?" Julie asked.

Nyrianne sighed and stepped into the soft light of the warden rod. "Ah, so kind and generous, but with so little training… You've used the rod to break, but it's primary purpose—as the princess said earlier—is to protect. Trace the frame."

"But—" Julie said.

"Just trace the doorframe, Mom. Quick!"

The alarm in the hall beyond grew louder, punctuated by shouting. Someone had discovered the two dead dracar.

Julie raised the rod and used the tip to trace the outline of the closed door. A flash of light sparked from the rod, and the dead bolt hole sealed over. The door vibrated with a series of *thunk-thunking* sounds as if multiple dead bolts were locking on all four sides.

All sound from the hallway ceased.

Julie dropped to her knees and gaped at the warden rod in her hands. "I—I… How did…"

Morgan wrapped her arm around her mother's shoulders. "This must drive your scientific mind wild, Mom."

Nyrianne and Alyssa were already walking down the new hallway lit by a few pale-blue ceiling lights. It was quiet here except for a faint humming noise, and the air was cool and fresh.

Morgan inhaled deeply. "Can we remove our masks yet?"

"Let's keep them on for now," Julie said.

They followed the hallway for about fifty feet until it opened into a two-story, concrete-walled rectangular room. They were standing on the second floor, at the top of a narrow staircase that led straight down to a shadowy area below. A metal railing ran along a four-foot-wide catwalk on two sides of the second floor. Across the room was another entrance identical to the one they had just come through. On the two sides, accessible only by the catwalks, were multiple closed doors, evenly spaced apart. Each door had a narrow glass window at eye level.

The room's design reminded Morgan of the courtyard of a quaint hotel her family had once stayed at where all the doors opened to a central swimming pool area. But these doors were closed, and there certainly was no inviting pool in a sunny courtyard. And this was no vacation. Morgan discarded the hotel image in her mind; the area was more like a gloomy dark-gray prison ward.

Julie gasped, pointing to a wall on the level below where a dark opening made the shadowy room seem bright by comparison. "Is that…?"

"That is the passageway—the gateway—we spoke of," Alyssa said.

Nyrianne tugged at Julie's sleeve. "Oh, we cannot go down there."

Morgan had been studying the second floor, but now she stared at the shimmering black hole, mesmerized. Where would this passageway lead? Maybe they could use it to escape this underground labyrinth. What if it led to Cochrane? If so, maybe they could find the Arden Forest and reenter the Fourwinds through the Gateway to the Records of Time? She shook her head. That was a lot of *what-ifs* and *maybes*.

Alyssa placed a hand over Morgan's. "Do not look long into the darkness. That journey cannot end well. We still have a job to do."

"But how will we get out of here?"

Alyssa squared to face her. "I am accustomed to finding my way through underground spaces, Morgan. Remember where we first met?"

Morgan blinked and met Alyssa's gaze. "The Tuxan Mines. I was so disoriented down there and would've been lost—or killed by minotaurs—without Rowe. It's amazing how you found us in all those tunnels, but you arrived just in time. I'm so glad you're here now, Alyssa."

Nyrianne broke away from the others and followed the catwalk to the right. She stopped in front of the first door.

"Is that it, Nyrianne?" Julie asked. "Is that where they keep the vaccines?"

The old woman didn't respond but peered into the small, lightly frosted window.

"If those rooms are refrigerated," Morgan said, "wouldn't that be a good place to search?"

"What if there are more dracar inside the rooms?" Ryowyn said, raising her trident.

"I doubt anyone works here," Julie said. "This is more like a storage facility."

"And there are no signs of activity," Alyssa added. "We would have heard or seen something by now."

They walked along the catwalk to the first door where Nyrianne stood. Above the small window were large dark symbols that looked like hieroglyphs. As they walked closer, Morgan noticed faded numbers *1001* above the door.

"Okay," she said. "Let's start here."

Ryowyn held her weapon ready as Morgan drew her sword and checked the door handle. It was unlocked. She pushed it open, and a blast of chilly air escaped.

The room was quiet and flooded with blue light. The second Morgan crossed the threshold, lights came on, making the room bright as day. She squinted, sweeping the air with her sword as Julie and Alyssa entered behind her. The room was empty except for a wall of metal cabinets with stainless-steel counters and tall glass door cupboards above.

Julie went to work right away. "Look for anything you can read in the cabinets. We need to find some documentation to confirm that the antidote will do what we hope it will—assuming we find an antidote."

They searched the cabinets but found nothing. Every shelf was bare.

Julie had a determined look in her eyes and a spring in her step. She led the way to the next room. Similar hieroglyphs marked the door, but the faded number above read *1002*.

A search of that room yielded the same result.

By the time they reached the fifth door, Julie's determined look had withered. Morgan grabbed the door handle and pushed, but this room was locked. Julie's eyes widened, and without waiting for instruction or invitation, she punched the lock with the warden rod.

The lights blinked on as they stepped inside. The room was furnished with identical cabinets, but on one counter lay a clipboard. Julie sprang toward it and flipped through the sheets of paper. Her shoulders slumped.

"It's all written in those strange characters," she said. "I can't read any of it."

"There must be something in here," Alyssa said, opening a lower cabinet door.

"We'll leave you to it," Morgan said, pointing to the door with her sword. "We'll be right outside…in case you need us."

Outside the room, Nyrianne had sat on the floor with her back to the wall. Morgan watched with envy as the old woman's eyes fluttered shut and her head slumped. Even a ten-minute nap would be nice right now.

Ryowyn planted the end of her trident on the floor and stood outside the door, looking very guard-like and mysterious, especially with the surgical mask veiling much of her soft facial features.

Morgan smiled but then noticed the princess massaging her side. "Are you sure you're okay?"

"I'm fine. Just a little tender. But I might have a scar to match Will's."

Morgan furrowed her brow at the memory. "Hopefully it's not *that* bad. When those bush gnomes attacked us and shot Will, we all thought he was dead. Even Rowe gave up hope for a few minutes. But then he woke up. I assumed it was his cloak that saved him, but later, Rowe told me you'd offered your life in exchange for Will's."

Ryowyn's eyes teared up. "And then he did the same for me, rescuing me from that horrible lake and coming to the Maidstone all by himself."

"And here you are again, willing to sacrifice your life to save Will."

Ryowyn stared at Morgan. "Of course I am. That's what love does. You're doing the same for Rowe."

Morgan gazed at the sword in her hand and shuffled her feet. Was she really doing this for Rowe? Or was she trying to prove herself again? Or was it something else, mixed up inside her?

"What's wrong?" Ryowyn asked.

"I don't think I'm as unselfish as you are. I want to be, but…I keep thinking of my last conversation with Rowe. I tried to get closer to him, but he's got so much on his plate. I know he's struggling to do the best he can. And he was right; he was the best person to get the thunderclaps.

"I can be so selfish sometimes, but I want to be there for him— like you were for Will. I'm just not sure I could…" She trailed off, afraid to say the word aloud. Dying for a loved one sounded so romantic in books and movies, but was she willing to sacrifice her life for Rowe's, or for any of theirs?

Ryowyn shifted the trident from one hand to the other and broadened her stance. "My father told me something long ago that has never left me. He said you don't become the person you want to be by thinking about it or wishing for it. You face each day's opportunities and live like that person. And slowly—but sometimes suddenly—you see who you truly are."

Morgan looked up, her eyes burning. "Sounds like something *my* father would say."

"You are not a selfish person, Morgan. You care for children, for families broken by war, for strangers. I know your friendship with Will has helped him become the person I love. I'm grateful for that. And I've seen how you care for your mother. That same care is growing for Rowe." She pointed to the sword. "That weapon might wield ancient magic, but it's not powerful enough to help us find something to heal Will and Rowe and then get us out of here. But I believe your love and friendship is more than enough."

Morgan sniffed. "You're a good friend, Ryowyn. Will's a lucky guy."

Ryowyn tucked her thick white hair behind her ear. "I don't know what you mean by lucky, but we are both fortunate to have found each other. Will is kind. He supports what I do and who I am. He listens to me and makes me laugh. And when I'm close to him, I come alive. Sometimes at night, he will stroke my hair and touch—"

"Okay," Morgan said with a short laugh. "I don't need to hear all the details."

Ryowyn wasn't laughing. "Why not?"

"Where I'm from—or maybe the way I was raised—we didn't talk about intimate details like that."

"But that's what life is all about. If we cannot share intimacy and our deepest feelings with those close to us…well, what else is there?"

Morgan opened her mouth but couldn't think of a response.

"You're a strong person, Morgan. Being vulnerable doesn't make you weak. It might make you stronger."

"Well, you're pretty tough, too, from what I've seen. What you did for Will, then being trapped in Lake Commando, helping Mom with the wounded soldiers…and you're quite handy with that weapon."

Ryowyn held the trident in both hands, turning it over as she studied the detailed carvings of waves etched into the handle. "This kind of fighting is not my strength."

Morgan snorted softly. "Since we're being honest, we might as well admit that we'll have to fight our way out of this place."

"Where did you learn to use a sword?"

"I've had a saber in my hand since I was a child. I had some very good trainers and coaches. But all the fencing—the sword fighting—that I did back home was for sport. Here in the Fourwinds, I've had to fight for my life. What about you?"

"My father insisted that I train with my brother, Wrathan. But I never imagined I would use it in a fight for my life."

"I don't think any of us expected to be in this position. Fighting harvesters is bad enough, but now there's dracar."

"But the dracar are experimenting on harvesters. And maybe even other dracar. If they're all working for Natas, why are they destroying each other?"

Morgan thought about that for a moment. "It's crazy. But even if they're fighting each other, it doesn't seem like *any* of them would be on our side."

"And that is why," Ryowyn continued, "we must unify the various peoples in the Rainia Valley."

Morgan studied Ryowyn's fierce blue eyes and solid stance. She realized that it had been quite a while since she'd consciously noticed the princess's teal-colored skin and snowy-white hair. She'd come to see her as a friend despite their stark differences. And now she noticed the leader in her friend.

From somewhere beyond the outer room came a series of sharp, piercing shouts.

Morgan poked her head inside the storage room. "Almost done in there? Something's coming!"

Julie was reading from a navy-blue binder, her fingers running down the page. "*Zoster N1X1.* All the symptoms of the virus described here match what we've heard about Phyriad." She looked up as Morgan and Ryowyn joined her at the counter. "*Zoster* is another word for *shingles*, a virus that causes a painful skin rash. The N1X1 must be the mutation of the virus." She continued reading.

Morgan glanced at Alyssa, who shrugged. "And…? What does that mean, Mom?"

"Back home, there's a vaccine for shingles, so maybe… Here it is! Alyssa, find something that says *Venzal*."

Alyssa opened a metal cabinet door. "I think I saw that earlier. Yes, here it is." She brought a small red pack that resembled a travel first-aid kit to Julie, who opened it and pulled out a thick plastic tube.

"Is that an EpiPen?" Morgan asked.

"Very good, kiddo. Technically, it's not epinephrine inside, but it is an auto-injector, which works the same as an EpiPen. Whatever the formula is, the manual says it can reverse early symptoms of Phyriad."

There was a shuffling noise outside the door.

"We need to get back out there," Ryowyn said to Morgan as they helped Alyssa empty the cabinet.

"How many are there, Alyssa?" Julie asked.

"Oh dear. There's only ten of these packs."

"Can we hurry, please, Mom?"

"Let's load them up," Julie said as she continued reading from the binder. "It talks about a vaccine here…"

A deep, throaty howl suddenly filled the large area outside the room. The four women spun to face the door.

Morgan raised her sword and scrambled to the door. "Take whatever you need, Mom. We've gotta go!"

Alyssa stuffed the last of the red cases into her leather pack. Julie tossed the binder into her pack and hoisted it over her shoulders.

"Julie said she needed five more minutes!" Nyrianne yelled.

Morgan scanned the area to see who the old woman was talking to, but her eyes had not yet adjusted to the half-light.

From the entry at the opposite end of the room, a harvester emerged. In one clawed hand, it held a burning torch but no weapon. The creature's powerful leg, arm, and chest muscles rippled as it turned and growled at the women.

Each harvester Morgan had seen had distinguishing features, but this one was almost identical to the one she had killed back in Cochrane on the shores of Lake Commando. But surely this was a coincidence or some kind of trick. That harvester had killed her father and taken his form. The deception had almost fooled Morgan. She would never forget how her father's eyes had somehow shone through the harvester's as she'd thrust her sword through its chest. And she would never forget that harvester's name. Like Abaddon, this harvester glared at Morgan like a demon from the pit of hell. Her arms went weak, and she lowered her sword.

Instead of fleeing, as Morgan was about to suggest, Nyrianne walked toward the monster and shouted, "Why can't you leave Julie alone until she finishes? Go back to where you came from!"

Before the creature took another step, a reverberating bolt of lightning shot from Nyrianne's outstretched hands. Morgan and the others recoiled, covering their ears. The shock wave crackled above the opening to the first floor, lifted the harvester from its feet, and threw it backward. Its head struck the doorjamb, and shards of concrete crumbled around the limp body. If the harvester wasn't dead, it would be unconscious for a long time.

Nyrianne turned to face the others. "I suppose we should leave now," she said in a calm, matter-of-fact voice.

"We can't go that way," Morgan said, pointing to the harvester's body. She ran along the catwalk toward the doorway they had entered.

A burst of shouting echoed from down the hallway.

"We need to go down," Alyssa said.

They were out of options, but no one questioned the idea. Their only hope was to find an exit on the first floor. Alyssa and Julie helped Nyrianne down the metal stairs, and Morgan and Ryowyn followed, weapons ready.

As they ran past the dark passageway, Morgan hesitated. The possibility of escaping immediately was alluring, especially now that they'd found the antidote for Will and Rowe. She stepped toward the opening. Where would this lead?

Alyssa grabbed Morgan's cloak sleeve and pulled her away. "No, Morgan! This way."

At the far end of the room, a dozen feet from the passageway, they all stopped in front of a steel door.

Julie cracked the lock with the warden rod.

When all five women had passed through the doorway, Julie sealed it in the same way she had done earlier. As before, Morgan's ears rang in the sudden silence.

The warden rod glowed brighter, revealing yet another hallway that faded to darkness to their right and left. Morgan spun on her heels, trying to decide which direction to run.

CHAPTER 26

A Druid's Wisdom

In a small patch of long grass deep within the Hollowtangle forest, the Red Dragon touched down. The morning sun had not yet removed the night's chill, and dewdrops clung to the lush field. The arrival of the imposing creature had scattered local wildlife and silenced even the boldest songbird. Dragons were rightly feared, even in this part of the forest. But it was the presence of two humans that pushed all woodland creatures deeper into the Hollowtangle.

"How did you find a place to land in this dense forest?" Bremer asked, adjusting the scabbard at his side as he scanned the area. When he turned around, Raric stood where the dragon had been a moment before.

The general was tall and imposing, clad in scaly red armor. "I've been here before," he said. "Not that I remembered how to get here, but somehow I must have known…" He trailed off as if searching for an elusive answer.

"I haven't seen this place in a great long while." Marlay was looking around like someone who had returned to his favorite childhood fishing hole.

As Raric led the way to the edge of the Druid Forest, Bremer was aware of movement throughout the wall of trees, thorns, and saplings. The forest was abuzz with insects, chittering squirrels, and the padding paws of larger creatures that kept him on edge.

"I don't trust druids," Bremer mumbled.

"There is wisdom in such sentiment, Bremer Mason."

The deep voice came from the dark thicket, and the druid Margrave appeared as simply and silently as a leaf dropping from a tree. *Or a snake shedding its skin,* Bremer thought.

"How do you know my—"

Margrave waved a dismissive hand at Bremer. "By reputation only, master rogue."

The tall druid flicked his long, dark hair from his face, and a few moths fluttered from his large antlers. His broad torso was clothed with a mossy green vest, and tree bark trousers covered his legs. He wore nothing on his feet and carried only a tall, sturdy walking staff, which seemed alive with green sprouts. The druid did not appear surprised by the visitors.

"Marlay Bonicle," Margrave said. "Welcome back."

The wizard ran a hand over his wispy beard and tried to smooth his robes. Despite his age, he had a childlike curiosity that almost made him appear slow at times. But Bremer knew something of Marlay's history and had already seen him in action defending Acttun. He was every bit as formidable as the druid.

"You haven't changed a bit, Margrave," the wizard said, his bushy eyebrows rising as he spoke.

"Nor have you," Margrave said. "And I see—"

"Margrave, I need your help," Raric interrupted, getting straight to the point.

"Of course you do, General. You left far too soon last time." Margrave stepped closer, examining the dragon armor. "Even I am surprised to see you still alive."

"But you *can* help me?"

Margrave puffed his chest and lifted his short-bearded chin. "I will teach you to control the dragon armor, but not to help *you*. No. The Iron Dragon must be stopped, and you are one of many important pieces. I need only a few hours to give you what you need to face Natas. But you must not face him alone."

The druid turned to Marlay. "Now, then. What brings a legendary wizard all the way from Acttun? A plague is spreading across the land, and you seek council from a druid?"

"Well, I was bored," Marlay said while casually scanning the forest. "And he has a couple of sick friends. I thought you could—"

Again, Margrave waved dismissively. If the druid weren't so powerful, Bremer would have cut off that annoying hand by now.

"I have long considered whether humans have outlived their stay in the Fourwinds," Margrave said. "Two less might help make it a better place."

"But these two are among the last of the Callum Sages," Marlay said.

The druid's thick gray eyebrows rose. "Rowe of the Nest has fallen?"

"Rowe and another long-lost Callum Sage named Will Owens. They were infected with Phyriad while trying to steal my thunderclaps at the asylum."

"Owens?" Margrave said, stroking his beard. "That name is familiar…"

Bremer stepped toward the druid. "His mother is—or, so Rowe tells me—the Ice Dragon."

Margrave stared at Bremer as if seeing him for the first time.

"If you can help us find a cure for Phyriad," Bremer continued, "you'll be doing more than simply preserving the human race."

Without a word, Margrave led them to the thicket wall, which slowly opened to form a doorway into the Druid Forest. They walked in silence for a few moments, surrounded by a symphony of birdsong, buzzing, chirps, squeaks, caws, and distant roars. Bremer wondered if every animal in the Hollowtangle had converged upon the Druid Forest.

Margrave walked along, scratching his short beard, deep in thought. After a few minutes, he continued. "It is a commonly held belief that Phyriad was found not so much *inside* the Maidstone but below it. The elixir that has spread across the Fourwinds was developed under the guiding hand of a young sorceress who became a powerful queen."

"Sidara?" Bremer said. "That witch almost killed us in the Waerdreath."

Margrave was eyeing the wizard. "You knew this young sorceress, Marlay. For it was you who brought her to the Maidstone."

Marlay's jaw dropped slightly. "Nyrianne? But I took her there for protection, so…so she could develop her gifts."

"And so she did. But her gifts were stolen, twisted, and abused by Natas. And so, she became the Dark Queen."

"Until Will destroyed her," Bremer said.

Margrave gave him a sideways glance. "Perhaps."

Marlay walked along in stunned silence. Bremer was familiar with guilt, but to feel the weight of responsibility for the creation of an evil queen must be unbearable.

"Why are you telling us this?" Bremer asked. "We need something to heal our friends—and maybe many others—not stories about a past we cannot change."

The druid wagged his large head. "What Sidara did not know is that after she left to rule the Waerdreath, her team of sorcerers developed an antidote for Phyriad."

"An antidote?" Marlay said, his face brightening. "Inside the Maidstone?"

The druid's head dipped. "If it is still there, that's where you will find what you seek."

"So, it's true," Bremer said, recalling what Raric had said about Morgan going to the Maidstone.

"We must go at once," Marlay said.

"Do not be hasty," Margrave said. "You two need rest while I work with Raric."

They stepped around a thicket of trees to see two moss beds nearly a foot thick. Multicolored blankets were folded neatly at the foot of each bed.

Although it was not yet midday, Margrave bid Bremer and Marlay good night and led Raric across a meadow to a shallow firepit surrounded by two large moss-covered chairs.

✦

Early the following morning, Bremer was enjoying the warmth of the sun and the sweet taste of cherries, but watching Margrave's odd routine was far more satisfying.

The druid stood naked as the day he came to be in this world in front of a wall of vines between two ancient oaks. Numerous items of clothing and armor hung from the vines. He started with a pair of brown leather pants embedded with long, flat strips of metal armor. He then pulled on a pair of leather boots, which he carefully laced up to just below his knees. As he was donning a thin shirt, Marlay joined Bremer.

The wizard plucked a cherry from Bremer's bowl. "You snore very loudly, you know."

Bremer spat a pit at Marlay's feet. "How else do you expect me to process all that dwarven ale?"

Marlay tried to steal another cherry, but Bremer pulled the bowl away.

"Ale?" Marlay griped. "Where did you get ale?"

"You fell asleep too quickly. And for far too long, I might add." Bremer burped and tapped his chest with a fist. "The druid has a mighty fine selection, considering his humble abode. After Raric left, Margrave was quite the host. I think my opinion of druids might be changing."

Marlay spun around. "Raric is gone? Where? Why? How'll we get out of here?"

Bremer rubbed his forehead. "How can you wake up with so many questions?"

"How can you drink so much and sleep so little?"

Margrave draped a layer of silky-thin chain metal over his shirt as Bremer popped another cherry in his mouth. "The druid is quite the teacher," Bremer said. "That, or the general is an excellent student. Yeah, come to think of it, it's more likely that Raric is a good student."

"I can hear you both," Margrave said, buttoning a tight leather vest, "but you know that, don't you, rogue?"

Bremer winked at Marlay. "Will we need to leave without you, druid? Or are you just about ready for battle?"

"We're leaving?" Marlay asked. "Where? How?"

"So full of questions," Bremer said, handing the cherry bowl to the wizard. "Fill up on these instead."

"Times being what they are," Margrave said. "I'll be guiding you to the Maidstone." He picked up a pair of crafted wooden handles topped with egg-shaped spiked iron balls. He then tied them to his belt and took up his long staff. "Ready to go, wizard?"

"What about Raric?" Marlay asked. "Is he coming back? We could use a dragon, don't you think?"

Margrave shook his head. "I asked Raric to test his new skills by flying back to the Rainia Valley. His task is to pick up Johanissan and anyone else he deems useful, then meet us at the Maidstone."

"Johanissan of the River Country?" Marlay said as he pulled on his orange hat. "Now there's a Callum Sage I remember. You see, Bremer, I haven't been out of the game that long."

Bremer sighed as he followed Margrave along a narrow path. "Johanissan is actually quite old, Marlay. You'll probably get along very well."

Beyond the meadow, they entered a forest populated with ancient oak trees. Small birds, butterflies, squirrels, rabbits, and even a few deer kept pace with Margrave. Bremer assumed that they were loyal to the druid but also curious about the strangers with him. Margrave's head swiveled as if taking in the beauty and life around him for the first time. Bremer rarely took time to stop and enjoy a forest, river, or meadow, but if ever he did, this would be the ideal spot. Instead, he remained focused on the path and on finding a way to help Rowe and Will. Marlay followed, spitting cherry pits along the way.

They came to the base of one of the largest trees Bremer had ever seen. Most of the oaks had knots and a few burls, but this one also had a large hollow that opened from the ground to about six feet up the trunk. Bremer was just thinking that the hole almost looked like a doorway when Margrave ducked inside it. Bremer and Marlay followed into the darkness.

As big as the oak was from the outside, the inside was even more spacious. Bremer and Marlay followed the soft glow of the druid's staff, unable to see anything else. Initially, the air was warm and dry but gradually turned cool and moist. They began in silence, but within minutes, a steady rumble filled the dark tunnel. And as the noise increased to a roar, the damp air turned into a wall of mist.

Margrave's staff dimmed, replaced by a circle of light ahead of them. As they approached it, the circle became a doorway. Long, leafy vines hung over the opening, dripping with water. Margrave pushed through the green curtain, and they ventured out into the sunlight.

Bremer recognized the area, although he couldn't comprehend how the druid's secret passage had taken them there so quickly. He wiped the dripping water from his brow and followed Margrave to the foot of a towering bluff. A narrow path switchbacked upward along the cliff's edge. At the top, shrouded in sparkling mist, was the cone-shaped roof of the Maidstone tower.

"That's a long way up," Bremer said. "Are you sure you're up for the hike, wizard?"

"Worry about yourself, rogue. I've got plenty of spark in me."

As the three travelers studied the only available path, a large, dark object cast a momentary shadow across the cliff.

"I thought I saw…a dragon," Marlay said. "Could that be Raric?"

"It seems a bit soon for Raric," Margrave said.

Bremer looked up again but saw nothing. "Was it red or gray?"

"Could have been either. Or neither. Or maybe it was just an eagle. But no, I'm fairly certain it was a dragon."

CHAPTER 27

HARVESTERS' LAIR

In the gloom of yet another unknown hallway far beneath the Maidstone, Morgan waited for Alyssa or Nyrianne to offer an idea of which direction to take. She glanced at her mother and Ryowyn, who seemed to be expecting the same guidance from her. They had escaped a harvester, thanks to a surprising attack from Nyrianne, and had what they hoped to be an antidote for Phyriad. Now, they just needed to find a way out.

Before anyone could offer a suggestion, something growled from the shadows to their right.

Julie pointed the warden rod light in the direction of the sound and screamed.

Glowing red eyes emerged from the shadows, and a hairless wolflike creature took a cautious step toward them. Muscles rippled beneath the tight skin of its forelegs.

Ryowyn pointed her trident toward the beast, and Morgan raised her Trannalun cloak to protect her mother.

The creature bared its fangs and snarled.

Nyrianne raised her hands as if she were preparing another magical blast of lightning.

But the creature did not attack. Instead, it turned and raced down the hall to the right on all fours, claws clacking against the stone floor.

"Now, there's a creature that knows when it's outmatched," Nyrianne said with a snicker. She planted her fists on her hips.

"Partly true," Alyssa said. "But I don't think it was running away from us. That was a guardian. It's gone to inform its master."

Alyssa took a few steps to the left, and Julie followed as the warden rod brightened. Smooth stainless-steel walls lined the narrow hallway. On either side was a closed door.

"These look like walk-in freezers," Julie said. She pulled open the first door and peeked inside.

"Wait for us, Mom," Morgan said, stepping behind her. "You don't know what's in there." She turned to Ryowyn. "Keep watch; we'll just be a minute."

The room was freezing. On three walls were shelves capable of storing months' worth of supplies, but they were all empty. In the middle of the room was an overturned rolling cart surrounded by small glass vials that appeared to have shattered when someone—or something—had knocked it over.

"There's writing on the racks of this cart," Morgan said.

Julie bent to her knees to read a label. She gasped. "*Venzal.* This could be more of the antidote. Or maybe a vaccine." She carefully picked through the shards. "See if you can find any still intact."

Most of the vials were broken, and some had traces of frozen liquid puddled around them.

"Here's one," Julie said. "And another."

After a minute of searching, they had only found two unbroken vials.

"Are you sure this is for Phyriad?" Morgan asked.

"No, but I'm hoping that manual I took says something about it. And a vaccine like that would need to be kept frozen."

They stepped back into the hallway. "But how will we keep these frozen?" Morgan asked.

"Leave that to me," Alyssa said. "Morgan, hand me a bag of nuts."

Morgan removed a small leather sack from Julie's backpack. Alyssa divided the remaining nuts, then slipped the two vials into the sack and tightened the leather cord. She wrapped both hands around it, and a few seconds later, the bag was covered in ice.

"I will keep this safe, Julie." Alyssa slipped the cord around her neck and tucked the frozen bag below the neckline of her dress.

"That looks cold, dear," Nyrianne said.

Alyssa winked. "Not to me."

"Let's check the other freezer," Julie said. "There might be more vials."

She pulled the door open, shone the light inside, then scrambled backward.

Morgan saw the harvester before anyone could scream. She drew her sword and waited for the creature to attack. But it didn't. The bearlike head hung low, eyes open but glazed and unmoving. Its scaly, muscular arms and legs didn't flinch. A long reptilian tail, lined with small horns, was stretched across the floor. Two leathery wings hung limply from its upper back.

Morgan bent her knees and stepped cautiously inside, sword in front of her.

The harvester was motionless.

"Bring the light in," Morgan said. "I think it's dead."

Alyssa helped Julie to the doorway, but they stopped short of entering.

Ryowyn stepped in with her trident poised for attack. "Another one in the corner!"

The two harvester corpses hung from large meat hooks mounted to a sliding rail near the ceiling. Black ichor congealed around their necks.

"More victims for the experiments," Nyrianne said from the hallway. "Dracar and harvesters depend on one another, but they do not get along well."

Morgan forced a laugh. "That's an understatement," she said. "Sorry, Mom. No sign of vaccines in here."

A scuffle of boots on stone, punctuated by angry shrieks, filled the hallway from the direction in which the wolflike beast had run.

"We need to find a way out of here," Morgan said as she slammed the freezer door.

They rushed down the hallway and quickly came to the end. A single metallic door more than seven feet tall blocked the way forward. In a place where modern technology and architecture had seemed so out of place, this door was older than anything Morgan had seen in the Fourwinds. It appeared to have been crafted from iron using hand tools and a great deal of care. There were no simple dead bolt locks for Julie to break with the warden rod.

Behind them, the hallway flooded with dracar, some wielding polearms. The wolflike creature was with them, drooling and snarling. The angry mob stopped about thirty feet from the women.

Morgan and Ryowyn held their weapons ready, but Morgan knew there were too many to fight this time. "What are they waiting for?"

Ryowyn shifted her stance. "They—they look…frightened."

"Of what?"

Ryowyn glanced back at the door.

"I hope they aren't afraid of what's on the other side," Morgan said as the dracar stepped backward.

"I think this could be the lock," Julie said, pointing to a metal circle on the door about three inches in diameter. "Shall I try to break it?"

"I would not go through that door if I were you," Nyrianne said in a chilling tone.

"There's nowhere else to go," Morgan said. Her voice sounded harsh in her ears, but she was growing tired of the old woman's odd pronouncements and lack of helpful direction. "We cannot fight all these dracar."

The creatures stared with unreadable red eyes. A tall dracar pushed through the crowd and took a single step toward the women. A deep scar marred its face, and part of its upper lip was missing, revealing sharp fangs. The creature seemed to be grinning. It moved to a panel on the wall, opened a small door, and pulled a short lever.

A crude steel wall dropped from a slot in the ceiling, crashing to the floor with a powerful thud that shook the walls. When the dust settled, the women were completely sealed off from the dracar.

"Huh," Julie said. "I didn't see that coming."

"Now there's only one way to go," Alyssa said, eyeing Nyrianne as if daring her to suggest otherwise. She stood in front of the ominous iron door.

What are these fishhook markings above the door?" Julie asked.

Morgan stood next to her mother and looked to where she was pointing. "That's the Mark of Natas. Rowe said that whoever lives beyond a doorway with the Mark above it has pledged their loyalty to Natas."

"Shine the light up at the ceiling again," Ryowyn said to Julie as she pointed. "There, look!" In another slot on the ceiling, there was another wall ready to drop.

"The dracar must be terrified about whatever is beyond this door," Alyssa said.

"Why are you afraid to go through it, Nyrianne?" Morgan asked.

The old woman cocked her head to one side. "Afraid? Nyrianne is many things, but not afraid."

"Then it's okay for me to break the lock?" Julie asked. "Nyrianne? Are you all right with that?"

"The genesis of the harvesters lies beyond this door," Nyrianne said. "They have made their home beneath the Maidstone for many years."

Morgan walked over to the new wall that had entrapped them. She examined it but didn't see a single gap or possibility of opening it from their side. Glancing down at the damaged stone floor, she shook her head.

"We're out of options," she said. "I say break the lock, Mom."

Julie struck the lock, driving it from the door with a powerful high-pitched snap.

Morgan and Ryowyn held their weapons ready as Alyssa pulled the door open.

A blast of musty air greeted them from the dark cavern. Everyone gagged at the smell of decay and rot.

The light from the warden rod revealed walls cut crudely into the mountain. The droning sound that had grown louder as the women journeyed beneath the Maidstone now reached a crescendo. With each step into the cave, the dank air grew warmer.

Julie's staff flared, illuminating a long, jagged tunnel. It was wide enough for the five women to walk side by side, but they all needed to crouch slightly. Despite the noisy turbines, large drops of what Morgan hoped was only water plopped from the low ceiling into numerous puddles.

"This is a foul place," Nyrianne said. "We should not be here."

"We need to get out of the Maidstone, Nyrianne," Julie said, taking her arm. "Do you know another way?"

If the old woman had heard the question, she ignored it.

As dark and endless as the tunnel seemed, it soon opened into a giant cavern that resembled the inside of a large cylindrical tower that rose several stories before disappearing into the darkness above them. Morgan stretched her back and gazed upward. Faint lights winked on and off, revealing small apartments…or cells. Each level had large sections missing as if the place had been slowly crumbling over the years with no one bothering to repair the damage. Rocks and debris covered the floor, and Morgan took careful steps to avoid tripping. A shuffling of activity from above, punctuated by an occasional cry, blended with the rhythm of the turbine engine noise.

"Keep to the edges," Morgan said, realizing that they were in plain view should anyone be looking down.

They walked beneath a long overhang until they found a double-door opening that led to a flight of primitive stone stairs. At the top was a long hallway lined with countless barred gates. A few groans echoed off the rough granite walls, drowning out all other sounds.

Julie stepped forward, and her light expanded until it reached the first tiny prison cell. A puff of dust followed a light scuffling sound and rose through the bars.

Morgan pointed her sword at the gate as she bent down for

a look inside. Huddled in the back corner of the six-foot-square cell was a disheveled teenaged girl. Her bloodshot eyes widened, and her entire gaunt body trembled. She was the first human they had seen in this place without red eyes. But her arms and legs were covered with a thick, dark rash.

"It's okay," Julie said. "We won't hurt you."

"You…you're not m-m-monsters," the girl said, her voice cracking.

Nyrianne huffed. "Well, dearie, that depends on who you ask."

"We're not monsters," Ryowyn said flatly, glaring at Nyrianne.

"Th-there were s-s-so many," the girl said.

"Where have they all gone?" Nyrianne asked.

"I—I dunno. Left a few days ago." The girl inched away from the wall but remained guarded, glancing at each woman's face.

It was then that Morgan noticed the slumped, lifeless wings that had been grafted to her back.

"Are—are you here to f-f-free us?"

Morgan gasped at the wretched state and horrible smell of the girl. But she wanted to help. She thought about asking her mother to strike the lock with the warden rod, but she needed to be sure it was safe before they did anything.

She rushed over and peered into the next cell where a man was lying facedown on a small cot. The wound below his shoulders where wings had been grafted to his back was oozing with blood, pus, and filth. The area was swollen in a large hump. He didn't move.

Julie stepped behind Morgan and raised a hand to her mask, pressing it to her nose. "Who would do such a thing?" she whispered.

The next cell housed someone that was more dracar than human. "And why are they in prison cells?" Morgan asked.

"This is no prison," Julie stated. "It's a crude post-op facility."

Before they could inspect another cell, a gate slammed open in a nearby hallway, and a man shouted in terror.

Morgan stood, ready for an attack, but Alyssa was standing next to an open cell across the hall.

"Quick," she said. "Everyone inside!"

The five women crowded into the empty cell, with Alyssa and Morgan entering last. Alyssa eased the gate closed. The warden rod went dark.

A dim light pierced the shadowy hallway, and a harvester stood on hind legs holding a flickering torch. Morgan clutched the grip of her sword, but Alyssa stayed her hand. A collective whimper rose from a few other cells until the monster stopped in front of a single gate. The whimpering was replaced by a single terrified shriek so eerie it could have been male or female. The harvester unlocked the gate, flung it open, and reached inside. Morgan couldn't see what was happening, but the prisoner went silent. The harvester dragged a limp body from the cell by the foot.

"I'm glad I couldn't see that," Julie whispered as the warden rod light automatically glowed again as if responding to their need.

They crawled out of the cell and stood in the hallway. A few faces appeared from behind the bars of each cell, and grimy hands reached out. All of the prisoners had red eyes.

"We have to help these people," Julie said.

Nyrianne put her arm around Julie. "Not people, dear. It is too late for them once they become dracar."

"There's nothing we can do," Morgan whispered, her words sounding foreign to her.

Julie tapped the lock of the first girl's cell with the warden rod, but nothing happened.

"That will not work on these locks," Nyrianne said. "Different sort of magic. Only harvesters can open them."

Julie ignored the old woman and was about to hit the lock again when the girl grasped the gate bars and hissed, flashing sharp teeth. Her eyes were now brilliant red.

Julie stumbled back against the empty cell.

Morgan grabbed her mother, pulling her away from the misery.

As they hurried down the hallway, Julie choked back a sob. "Is there no way out of this nightmare?"

"Oh, but this is the way out," Nyrianne said as she limped along behind them. "Up, up, up."

They came to a closed door illuminated by a wall-mounted torch, and Alyssa pulled it open. When they entered the empty hallway, the door closed, cutting off the groans and cries of the dracar prisoners.

Julie brushed her eyes with her palm.

Nyrianne stroked Julie's long hair. "So kind," she said. "Like the boy, Will, wanting to save everyone." Her arm fell to her side. "But dracar cannot be saved."

After a few minutes of trudging through the empty hallway, Morgan's thighs burned. "We're moving upward," she said.

"I think this is a long, spiraling hallway," Alyssa added. "And up is where we want to go."

Julie and Nyrianne walked in silence, slow but steady.

"You doin' okay, Mom?"

Julie was panting. "My legs are tired, but if this leads us out, I'll be fine."

Ryowyn came between Julie and Nyrianne and linked arms as they walked together. A moment later, their pace quickened.

Julie clasped the princess's forearm. "Thank you, Ryowyn. That helps."

They continued up the hallway for several minutes and finally reached the top. A solid metal door that seemed to take them out of the cylindrical structure blocked the only way forward. As was becoming their custom, Alyssa tested the handle while Morgan and Ryowyn stood with their weapons ready. This door was unlocked, so Julie's staff was not needed. The rusty hinges squealed, and a waft of stale air greeted them.

After walking down a long hallway, they passed through an open doorway. Julie lifted the warden rod, and the light revealed another large cavern. The rough walls rose nearly thirty feet to an arched ceiling. Enormous steel warehouse racks lined both walls and disappeared far back into the darkness of the cavern. The racks were empty, but three wooden crates, each about three feet square, sat in a neat row, side by side in the center of the room. Morgan scanned the area, but it appeared to be unoccupied.

Behind them, light flickered and danced in the hallway. Someone had been following them. Heavy footfalls scuffed the floor, and two bulky harvesters entered the hallway, each carrying a burning torch.

Morgan rushed back to close the door to the cavern, but it wouldn't budge, as if it hadn't moved for a millennium. Ryowyn and Alyssa rushed to help, but it was too late.

One harvester stretched its lizard-like neck forward and hissed at the women. The torch fell from its claws, and the creature dropped onto all fours. It launched forward with unbelievable speed.

Ryowyn charged past Morgan into the hallway to confront the attacker. The harvester sprang at her, but she drove her trident into its broad chest. The center spike punched through its hide, and

Ryowyn shuffled back a step, removing the trident and spinning it over her head before slashing a curved blade across the harvester's face. The creature roared and stumbled back an awkward step.

Morgan rushed past Ryowyn and plunged her blade into the harvester's neck. Magic erupted within her and rushed like a hurricane through her hands. She grunted and gasped for breath as the sword vibrated and flashed green sparks. The creature tried to swipe at Morgan with long, jagged talons, but Ryowyn spun around again with her trident. The harvester's hand dropped to the floor as the sword's magic continued to burn the life from the creature.

Morgan held her sword in the dying harvester's body as the second harvester closed the distance. It leapt through the air with shocking speed, gnashing its yellowed fangs. Ryowyn reared back a moment too late. The creature struck her shoulder with a powerful clawed hand. Her armor absorbed the worst of it, but the blow knocked her against the wall, and she went down hard.

Seeing Ryowyn fallen, Morgan pulled her blade free and shouted her rage as she lunged toward the second harvester.

The creature was quicker and more agile than any harvester she had faced. It dodged to avoid each of her jabs, her blade ringing off the exoskeleton that protected its lean arms. But this harvester was also more vicious in its slashing attacks, providing no room for Morgan to pierce its gaunt torso. She turned, allowing the harvester to rake the Trannalun cloak, which saved her life.

In an attempt to lure the creature closer, Morgan bent her knees, pretending to be wounded. The harvester stopped slashing for a second, and she spun around, slashing its hideous face. The creature roared as thick black ichor gushed from its eyes. Morgan lunged and drove her sword through its chest.

Small, dark humanoid shapes emerged from down the hallway,

followed by a tall harvester that looked identical to the one that Nyrianne had slain earlier.

The harvester bent to pick up a torch and scowled at Morgan.

"Back to the cavern!" Morgan shouted as Ryowyn rose to her feet.

They stumbled through the doorway just as Alyssa took hold of the iron door. With little effort, she slammed it shut.

Julie required no invitation to use the warden rod. It sparked and flared like a welding torch as she sealed the edges. The others shielded their eyes against the brightness, but Julie held fast, grunting and straining as the magic did its work. When it was finished, she fell to her knees. The staff clanged to the floor, and its light returned to a soft glow.

The door shook with heavy pounding and the high-pitched ringing of metal objects attempting to break the seal. Morgan and Ryowyn stood ready, but the door showed no sign of yielding. They all remained quiet, and after several minutes, the pounding stopped altogether.

Morgan crouched next to her mother, who was sitting with her head between her knees, taking deep breaths.

"You all right, Mom?" She brushed her mother's hair from her face. "I know it takes so much out of you."

"You mean the, uh, the…magic? It's the same for you, isn't it?"

Morgan nodded as she helped her to her feet.

"Which way now?" Julie asked.

"Let's make sure we're alone," Alyssa suggested.

Guided by the light of Julie's staff, Alyssa walked around the room, examining the empty warehouse racks and vaulted ceiling. Morgan and Ryowyn followed close behind, weapons poised in case of a surprise attack. Despite layers of dust and debris, the empty warehouse racks, and the three crates, the large room was empty.

Morgan was curious about the three crates, but Alyssa had a more appealing idea.

"Let's take some time to rest here."

CHAPTER 28

A WAY OUT

Morgan's head bobbed, and she awoke with a start. She rubbed her bleary eyes and focused on the glow of the warden rod. Remembering where she was, she jumped to her feet and brushed dirt from her Trannalun cloak. Ryowyn and Nyrianne had fallen asleep next to her against a wall and were now awake in a sitting position. The older woman let out a loud yawn as Morgan helped the mer princess to her feet.

Alyssa and Julie stood beside the three large wooden crates in the center of the room. Julie pointed her rod to something on the floor, moving the light around. Morgan and Ryowyn joined them, and Julie lowered the warden rod light to the dusty floor. Clearly marked wheel tracks led to the crates and in every direction.

"Forklift?" Morgan suggested.

"That's what we thought," Julie said. "Whatever these three crates are, there used to be a lot more on those shelves. The tire tracks are everywhere, like this was a busy place not long ago."

"Look at this," Alyssa said, pointing to the single word scrawled on the top of a crate: *Indian.*

"What's inside?" Morgan asked, examining the crate from all sides.

Alyssa shrugged. "We were waiting for you."

The three-foot-square crate was nailed together, and thin gaps between the smooth boards made it difficult to see inside. Morgan used the tip of her sword to loosen the solid lid, and Alyssa pulled it off with her hands.

Inside was a large glass sphere full of liquid, frothing with thousands of small minnow-like creatures. Everyone jumped back, startled.

As Morgan leaned in for another look, she could see tiny razor fins and rows of sharp teeth. The creatures were gnashing at one another and appeared to be bleeding, but there was not a single dead one among them.

She grabbed the lid to shut away the sickening sight, but Ryowyn stopped her.

"Wait," the princess said. "Remember the story that Johanissan told us about the attack on the Niasa Sea? These are the creatures that infected two-thirds of my people."

Morgan studied her for a moment, and suddenly, she realized what the word on the crate meant.

"Ocean," she breathed. "Indian *Ocean*."

"Look at this, Morgan," Julie said, shining the light on the top of the second crate. "It's marked *Pacific*."

"And this one," Alyssa added, standing over the third crate, "is marked *Caspian*."

Morgan inhaled sharply and held her breath. She rubbed her arm, feeling a sudden chill.

"I don't understand," Ryowyn said. "What do those words mean?"

"Those are the names of major bodies of water," Morgan said. "The Pacific Ocean and the Caspian Sea."

Julie shone the light toward the empty shelves. "Where did all the other crates go?"

"I think we can guess *where* they went," Morgan said. "But *how* did they get to those places throughout the world?"

There was a moment of silence as they all considered the possibilities. Then Alyssa spoke. "That passageway."

"Yes," Morgan said. "That explains the spiraling ramp from here down to the hallway and through the large door to the passageway. A forklift could easily get down there."

"So, that's where all the harvesters went," Nyrianne said. "The bearers of Phyriad. Across the Fourwinds *and* beyond."

After a long moment of staggering silence, Julie retrieved her backpack containing the auto-injectors from a pallet where she had left it. She cradled the pack in her arms. "We cannot reverse the effects of a global virus," she said quietly. "But we have here a measure of hope. Saving Will and Rowe might only be the beginning."

Morgan tossed the crate lid on the floor and drew her sword. "Well, here's to doing what we can. Stand back, everyone." She punched the sphere with the pommel, and the glass shattered. Liquid seeped through the thin slits in the wooden crate and spread across the stone floor.

Trapped inside the crate, the creatures flopped and floundered, struggling to survive outside the liquid.

Julie and Ryowyn backed away, cringing in disgust and horror.

When all the flopping sounds stopped, Alyssa waved her hands in front of her, and the crate turned into a large block of ice.

Morgan and Alyssa repeated the procedure on the other two crates.

"If Natas is not yet aware of our presence here," Alyssa said, "he certainly is now. I have used far too much magic today."

"Did you find a way out while we were sleeping?" Morgan asked.

"Follow me." Alyssa walked down the corridor between the empty warehouse racks.

After only fifty paces, they came to a smooth granite wall.

"Dead end," Morgan said.

Alyssa turned to Julie. "Raise the staff higher."

As Julie lifted the warden rod, a series of thin lines glowed on the wall and joined to form the shape of a narrow door.

Alyssa pushed the wall, and the door swung open. "A warden rod contains a variety of magic, including the ability to reveal secret doors."

Cobwebs hung so thick that Morgan couldn't see more than twelve inches past the doorway. She'd just started to have second thoughts about entering when the pounding on the door through which they'd entered the room resumed.

"Sounds like the harvester has returned with something stronger," Nyrianne said.

Morgan stepped forward. "Let me go first." She brushed the webs aside with her sword and entered. Julie followed close, holding the staff up as high as the jagged ceiling would allow. Ryowyn guided Nyrianne in, and as soon as Alyssa entered, the secret door closed behind them.

The narrow passage led straight through the granite. The air was still and quiet, and the way forward was impossible to see because of the density of spiderwebs. Breathing became laborious. Morgan continued to wave her sword in front of her, slashing webs. After several minutes, her legs began to tingle, and her hands trembled. Lines of sweat tickled her forehead. Suddenly, her sword clanged against a rock wall. She raked the webs with her left hand, searching for a way forward.

"Crap!" Morgan cried, her breaths coming in short puffs. "I can't stand tight spaces."

Julie approached with the light. "Easy, kiddo. Let me slip past you." She raised it higher, and the warden rod revealed the glowing outline of another secret door. Morgan pushed as Alyssa had done before, and the stone wall made a grinding noise as it inched forward against the floor. The door clicked and swung open.

Morgan burst into the open space, dropped her sword, and bent over with her hands on her knees. She ripped off her mask and gulped the fresh air.

"I'm sorry, everyone," she said. "I panicked."

Julie wrapped her arm around Morgan's shoulder and offered her a canteen. "You're okay now, Morgan. I haven't seen you like that since you started high school."

Morgan sipped some water. "Thanks, Mom. I just need to get outta this place."

"We're all starting to lose it," Julie said. "But look where we are."

Before them were four gaping elevator doors. A soft glow emanated from the shafts, but all were missing the doors. Morgan peered inside. A concrete wall separated each shaft. Two had collapsed and were filled with rock and rubble. Another smelled of something rotten, causing her stomach to churn. Inside the fourth were dangling cables similar to the shaft they had seen when they'd entered the Maidstone.

"Looks like we're taking the stairs again," Julie said.

Ryowyn wandered a few steps down the hallway and opened a metal door. "Over here."

Morgan stepped through and raced up a flight of stairs until she realized she was in complete darkness. As in the cobwebbed passage, her breathing became short again with the growing sense that the walls were closing in around her. The harder she gasped for air, the tighter her chest became. She longed to get out of this place but needed the light her mother carried.

Ryowyn caught up with her and grabbed her Trannalun cloak. "Stop, Morgan! We need to stay together. We're almost there. Remember why we're here."

Morgan met her friend's stern gaze.

"What is it, Morgan? What's wrong?"

"What if we don't make it? Or, what if we do, and the antidote doesn't work? I didn't leave Rowe on a good note…and there's so much I wanted to say…"

Ryowyn stepped forward and caught Morgan up in a hug. "Easy, Morgan. Don't give up now."

As the mer princess held her, Morgan's anxiety melted away. Her breathing slowed, her head cleared, and her limbs felt stronger. She held her a moment longer until the others caught up.

"I'm sorry, Ryowyn," Morgan said.

"Stop apologizing," Nyrianne said as she climbed the stairs ahead of them. "People will start thinking that you're guilty of something."

"Or that you're Canadian," Julie said with a chuckle.

The square stairwell led them upward. At each level was a landing and a closed metal door with a small square glass window. Most were dark, but light shone through a few windows. A red light glowed above every door.

Morgan wondered if they might find either more of the antidote or more dracar. She resisted the pressure of her curiosity and fear and pressed on. The risk of stopping now was too great; they already had the antidote. Ryowyn's words echoed in her mind: *Remember why we're here.*

Eventually, they came to a level where the concrete steps transitioned to metal. Morgan picked up her pace, realizing they must be close to the top.

Far below, a door opened, and the sound of muddled voices and clanging metal echoed in the stairwell.

"Keep moving," Morgan hissed.

Nyrianne lagged behind, and Julie and Alyssa stayed with her. Morgan stopped on a landing. She was now one flight ahead of the others, and there were no more steps to climb. She peered through the small window in the door and saw burning torches mounted on the walls.

"I think we're back in the main foyer of the tower where we first entered," she said. "But it looks like someone's been here."

"You go ahead and scout," Ryowyn said. "I'll stay with the others, and we'll catch up."

Morgan entered the foyer, crouching low with her sword held waist high in front of her. On the opposite side of the room, the runes on the two cauldrons glowed. Fresh air brushed her cheek, and a longing for more overwhelmed her. She rushed through the main entryway, inhaling deeply.

As soon as she stepped outside the Maidstone, she skidded to an awkward stop and froze in stark terror.

CHAPTER 29

BATTLE AT THE MAIDSTONE

At least a dozen dracar soldiers stood about ten yards outside the Maidstone entrance. Their lean bodies were covered with small dark scales that shimmered in the morning sunlight. There might have been as many as fifteen dracar, but Morgan had no time to count. All she knew was that each one carried long polearms similar to the weapons used by the dracar that she and Ryowyn had faced in the surgery hall beneath the Maidstone. Watching this organized troop now, Morgan suddenly realized why they had not encountered more dracar soldiers on their way out. Why chase the five women through the labyrinth below when the dracar could simply wait for them at the only exit?

Now that Morgan had emerged, however, none of the dracar seemed interested in her. In fact, they were all facing away from the Maidstone. Something beyond the ledge had captured their attention. The blades on their polearms gleamed as a few ventured farther from the tower. Morgan craned her neck to see beyond them and quickly spotted a tall dark-haired man with a set of antlers on his head—whether they were real or a headpiece was difficult to discern. He was dressed for battle and armed with a short-handled mace in one hand and a long-handled one in the other. Behind him, there was a flash of movement, and another man dressed in black sprang onto the ledge and rushed to attack.

"Morgan!" Bremer shouted. "Stay back!"

The rogue threw a pair of knives into the chests of the two dracar nearest him before drawing swords in both hands. The antlered man crushed a third dracar skull with his short mace. With the longer weapon, he parried an attack from another dracar.

Despite Bremer's apparent lack of confidence in Morgan, she knew that she had to help. She and Ryowyn had defeated the two dracar they had faced as they journeyed through the Maidstone, but the odds out here seemed to favor the dracar. While the creatures focused on Bremer and the stranger with the antlers, unaware of an attack from behind, Morgan drew her sword and killed the one closest to her.

The other dracar whirled to face her, and two more fell to the ground with Bremer's knives in their necks.

With opponents on two sides, the remaining dracar repositioned themselves so they were facing their three enemies.

Bremer and his odd-looking companion paused. They had used up the element of surprise and now needed to act strategically.

Morgan ran to Bremer's side. Her blade dripped with black ichor. The dracar brandished their polearms but did not attack.

Bremer scowled. "Morgan, I told you—"

"There's no time to pick a dream team," she countered. "Ryowyn and I already took out two of these things inside the Maidstone."

Bremer's eyes narrowed as if he were unconvinced. "Well, I…" he mumbled, keeping his eyes on his opponents as he moved his feet.

The dracar shuffled into a tight group, chattering among themselves with their strange low-pitched sounds as if discussing a plan of attack.

Morgan ventured a quick look at the tall, dark-haired man next to Bremer, now realizing that the antlers were very much attached to his head. "Who's this?"

"Druid Margrave, this is—" Bremer began.

"A Callum Sage," Margrave interrupted, his eyes widening ever so slightly. "I do not recognize the face, but that sword is familiar."

Morgan returned her gaze to the creatures. "I'll try not to take that personally," she said.

A single dracar broke from the group, its weapon aimed at Margrave. The druid lifted his shorter mace and flexed his grip on the handle. A narrow spike shot from the metal head, slamming deep into the attacker's chest. The body flew backward from the violent impact. Those remaining hesitated and spread out.

"They're unfamiliar with people fighting back," Margrave said, waving both maces in front of him. "Their primary weapon is fear, so they don't know what to do with us."

Two dracar lashed out at Bremer. He sidestepped the first polearm, cutting the weapon in half before stabbing the other dracar below the armpit. Spinning around, Bremer slashed the defenseless dracar across the neck.

The surviving dracar stomped their feet and cried out in their shrill language. They pressed forward, jabbing relentlessly but keeping their distance. Morgan parried, deflecting an aggressive thrust. She shuffled her feet, easily fighting off each advance, but saw no opportunity to counterattack.

Bremer deflected a polearm with one sword while plunging the second deep into an unprotected chest. Margrave sidestepped an attack and bashed a dracar's shoulder, throwing it off-balance. Morgan delivered the death blow with a high outside cut.

"Well done, Sage," Margrave said as he rushed forward to engage another dracar. His footwork was so fluid, he might have been dancing. Morgan had never met a druid, but she was thankful he was on her side.

Bremer was dueling with a pair of dracar when he tripped over a tree root. He stumbled back, and the dracar attacked in a desperate flurry. While Bremer scrambled to regain his footing, Morgan stabbed one dracar as Margrave attacked the other.

Another dracar lunged toward Morgan, and she parried with a downward cut that knocked the wooden polearm from the dracar's hands. The sword shot up in front of her, light and fluid, as if it were one with her arm and responsive to her every thought. She abandoned defensive maneuvers and released herself to the power of the sword.

The next few seconds passed in a blur. Years of training had taught Morgan to read her opponent's moves and respond with calculated lunges, parries, and ripostes. Now, she stared at the sword in her hands. The blade glowed with green magic. The thought of a weapon controlling her actions sent a chill through her body. Her skin tingled with energy. She couldn't remember what offensive moves she had used to kill the last three dracar, which were now bleeding and lifeless in the long grass. She lowered her bloodied sword and heaved deep breaths.

"The sword of Avarthrill," Margrave said in a respectful voice that one might use in the presence of royalty. "I must say, I recall seeing it in the hands of someone much…bigger. Although, you wield it with as much strength and authority."

Sheathing both his swords, Bremer sat down on a large rock

and ripped off a section of his shirt. A thin line of blood stained his shoulder. Morgan wiped her blade in the grass, returned the sword to its scabbard, and helped Bremer tie the cloth around his shoulder. The slash was bleeding but was not as deep as she had feared.

"The first time I met you," Bremer said between huffs, "that sword was firmly in its sheath, and you were surrounded by holgs. You're not the same frightened girl I found in that forest."

Morgan tried to laugh, but the sound came out as a light grunt. "This place has a way of growing people up."

There was only a moment of silence before another man pulled himself onto the ledge from the trail that switchbacked up the cliff. He appeared to be unarmed and wore a flowing green robe and an orange hat. Morgan tensed and gripped her sword.

"Hold on, Morgan," Bremer said as he stood. "That's the wizard Marlay. He's with us."

"Great timing, wizard," Margrave called out, his voice dripping with sarcasm. "Your presence would've been helpful a moment ago."

Marlay didn't slow down until he was almost upon them. Bremer grabbed his arms and held him fast. "Slow down, Marlay. What happened?"

The wizard's face was white, and he gasped for air as he turned to look back at the bluff. By his terrified expression, Morgan expected to see something chasing him.

"I held him off…" Marlay huffed. "Distracted him for a moment… But he's coming back!"

"Take a breath, wizard," Bremer said. "Who—"

Words poured from Marlay's mouth as if he couldn't get them out fast enough. "The dragon flew directly over us while we were climbing the trail! With the waterfalls crashing down all around, you couldn't hear me yelling and didn't notice the danger. You'd be dead had I not intervened!" He turned and pointed upward with a shaky finger.

The Iron Dragon swooped around a mountain peak before dropping into a dive toward them. Dark clouds followed like a regent's personal guard, casting gloomy shadows around the Maidstone. Natas circled the tower with a terrifying roar, and the blue sky darkened. Those on the ground froze in their momentarily stunned positions.

"Run!" Marlay shouted.

The single word jarred them into action, and all four raced to the Maidstone entrance. Margrave, Morgan, and Bremer entered the shadowy doorway and gazed at the sky. Marlay remained out front, stretching his arms above him as he started murmuring a low, guttural chant.

The dragon was in full attack mode, looking much the same as the Red Dragon when it had attacked Rainia. Natas opened his massive jaws wide as if he were about to breathe fire into the Maidstone entrance.

Marlay raised his voice and, splaying his hands, shouted the final words of his spell. The light seemed to bend around the wizard. He squeezed his eyes shut.

Instead of the blast of fire Morgan had expected, a torrent of yellowish-brown liquid from the dragon's maw streamed toward Marlay. Morgan gasped and was about to turn her head from what she expected to be a gruesome sight. But when the liquid was about ten feet from Marlay, it struck a translucent barrier. The wizard held his trembling hands up as the protective shield radiated a vibrant green glow. The color was similar to Morgan's sword when it burned through a harvester, although the magic barrier was brighter and much larger. The shield held but drooped as the liquid sizzled with a long, ear-piercing hiss.

Natas completed his strafing run and shot beyond the tower.

"That's deadly acid," Margrave shouted. "Make the shield thicker, Marlay!"

"No time, druid," the wizard called back. "And this won't survive another attack!"

From high above, the dragon roared. Morgan lost sight of the enormous creature, but the booming cry resounded in her chest and chilled her to the bone.

A moment later, Natas reappeared and launched a cone-shaped spray of acid. The attack was lower and more calculated than the first run and would easily scorch the entire ledge. This time, Marlay would be helpless.

But before the acid reached the ledge, a blazing column of fire descended from the sky and consumed the liquid. Morgan gasped when she spotted the source of the counterattack.

The Red Dragon flared his massive wings in front of Natas and launched another eruption of flames that forced the Iron Dragon to bank hard and drop into the canyon out of sight.

Morgan exhaled, releasing some of the tension that gripped her.

Raric managed a hasty, barely controlled landing about fifty feet from the Maidstone. The impact caused loose rocks to break away from the cliffs around the tower.

Joe and Ryodan Ayoust scrambled off the Red Dragon's back and stumbled to the ground. When they were clear, Raric made a few quick steps, dislodging several rocks before dropping over the cliff in the direction that Natas had flown.

Joe fell to his knees and vomited. Judging by the stains on his sleeve, it wasn't the first time. Even the mer king needed a moment to recover from their harrowing landing.

Morgan, Bremer, and Margrave sprinted away from the safety of the entrance and into the open field to help Joe and Ryodan. Marlay followed, chanting and slowly waving his arms above his head. As he did, the barrier thickened and expanded above them.

"Look!" Morgan said, pointing at two distant dragons in the sky. "Raric is chasing Natas away. We have to get back to the tower!"

"No!" Margrave shouted. "Natas has created a decoy, and Raric is chasing an illusion."

"There!" Bremer cried out, pointing east. "Beyond the ridgeline!"

Natas dropped from the ridge above the Maidstone. He opened his maw, and a stream of acid shot down toward the group huddled under Marlay's shield. Part cloud and part liquid, the acid expanded before hammering Marlay's shield, sizzling and steaming upon impact. Morgan covered her nose at the pungent chemical odor. Acid splashed around the shield, scorching grass, bushes, and a few small trees, which burned and crumbled to blackened piles of dust.

"I cannot hold much longer!" Marlay grunted, gritting his teeth.

The acid flow stopped. Natas's huge wings made a deep *whoosh* sound as he soared in a wide circle high above them. His furious roar resounded in Morgan's chest. She wondered if the Iron Dragon had ever faced such opposition, but she had a feeling it would only serve to further enrage the beast.

"We need the thunderclap!" she cried.

Marlay's eyes flared. "You have a thunderclap? You might have mentioned that sooner, girl!"

Morgan glanced at the tower entrance. "Alyssa has it; she should've been here by now."

Ryodan rose to his feet and bellowed, "We have to distract Natas until either she arrives or the Red Dragon returns."

The mer king's eyes turned white as snow as he raised one arm toward the nearest waterfall. He began a low chant, and his body shook as he called to the raging water. Morgan had seen the mer queen summon the waters of Rainia Lake, and hope sparked within her. Perhaps Ryodan could extinguish the Iron Dragon's acid the way Almithara had snuffed out the fires in Rainia.

But the ancient waterfall resisted as if refusing to bend to another's will.

A thunderous roll of mocking laughter echoed off the cliffs, followed by a deep growl that sent another shiver through Morgan's body. The booming voice was more powerful than anything she had ever heard. It seemed to come from everywhere at once, making the waterfalls seem like babbling brooks. Morgan knew its source immediately.

"Your foolish efforts to stop me will fail," the Iron Dragon rumbled. "And what a fitting place to meet your end."

Natas swooped lower, then angled sharply upward again as if toying with the group, fueling their fears. As he circled around again, now less than two hundred feet above, Joe set his staff on the ground and stood next to Ryodan. He rubbed his hands together, then launched a burst of razor-sharp ice crystals at Natas.

The dragon shot a defensive blast of acid at the icy daggers, shattering them in midair. Everyone huddled under Marlay's shield as large drops of acid rained down.

"Your powers have weakened, old man," Natas mocked. "The days of the Callum Sages are over." He roared again and circled once around the tower.

Margrave dropped his weapons and raised both hands, and a

second later, he was holding a ball of fire about the size of a basketball. He hurled it at Natas as the dragon glided past, but the fireball bounced harmlessly off the armored chest and dissipated into tiny sparks.

Natas howled with rage, flapping his huge, leathery wings about twenty yards overhead. "The most powerful druid in the land finally emerges from hiding, and this is the best he can do?"

While Margrave was conjuring his fiery ball, Bremer had retrieved an arrow from his quiver. With Natas distracted by the druid's attack, Bremer pulled back the string of the dark elf's bow and tracked the dragon's flight pattern for a brief second before releasing. The arrow pinged harmlessly off the dragon's scaly hide.

"How dare you use that bow against me, thief!" Natas howled. "You stole it from my servant, but you lack the power to wield it."

Morgan noticed her sword trembling in her loose grip. She looked up at the enormous Iron Dragon as the downward thrust of its wings whipped dust, dead leaves, and twigs around her. She shielded her face in her elbow, looking down at the blade, which now glowed with magical green light. Normally, the sight would fill her with courage, but standing in the shadow of such a powerful enemy, despair blurred her vision. If her brave companions could not stand against Natas, her small weapon would be even more futile. Despite her fear, Morgan thought she saw the dragon's eyes narrow upon seeing the sword.

Natas beat his powerful wings again, rising higher. His massive chest heaved in and out.

"Get ready for another blast, wizard," Margrave said.

Marlay's outstretched arms trembled. "This is all I've got!"

Morgan glanced at the Maidstone entrance again. At this point, running back to the safety of the tower would be futile.

She wondered what was taking the others so long and prayed for Alyssa to show up with the thunderclap. Until then, she had to trust Marlay's shield.

Before Natas could launch another blast of acid, Ryodan drove the end of his trident into the ground. Raising his other arm, he shouted at the waterfall in a language Morgan could not comprehend. The mer king stepped out from under Marlay's protective barrier. Morgan started to cry out but then noticed another small, translucent shield surrounding Ryodan. His eyes flashed like a welder's torch as he swept his arms in an upward motion. As he did, Natas shot another blast down on them.

Ryodan cried out as acid burned through his warding magic and seared his armor. But the mer king pushed through the pain. He ripped the trident from the ground with one hand and launched it at Natas. With his other hand, he stretched toward the waterfall in a final effort before the acid reached his exposed skin.

Ryodan's spell finally worked. A blast of river water lanced from the waterfall, driving the Iron Dragon upward. Gusts of wind soaked the area in a turbulent shower and saturated the group huddled together around the mer king, who had fallen to his knees.

When the torrent slowed, Morgan raised her eyes, expecting another attack from Natas. Instead, she saw the Red Dragon racing toward him. Natas dropped beyond the ridgeline and disappeared, with Raric in pursuit.

Alyssa was now standing in the entrance with Julie, Ryowyn, and Nyrianne behind her. "Get to the Maidstone! Now!"

While Bremer, Joe, and Margrave helped Ryodan to his feet, Morgan ran ahead to the entrance. She focused on the leather satchel slung over Alyssa's shoulder.

Ryowyn's eyes widened when she saw her father stumbling, and she started to run out toward him.

Alyssa grabbed her arm. "It's okay, Ryowyn. They're helping your father! Let's get back inside."

Marlay's shield had weakened under the force of Ryodan's water spell, but he worked to build it up again when he rejoined everyone near the entrance. Slowly, the size of his magical shield increased.

"Follow me," Alyssa said, heading back inside.

Everyone except the wizard hurried through the narrow entrance and stopped in the large foyer. Bremer and Margrave lay Ryodan down on the floor, and Ryowyn fell to her knees beside him. The mer king was unconscious and breathing with staggered gasps.

"What took you so long?" Morgan asked Alyssa.

"Two dracar met us in the stairwell right after you left," Alyssa explained. "Ryowyn killed one, and the other fled, screaming its warning cry."

A scuffle of footsteps sounded from the stairwell that the women had used to find their way out of the Maidstone depths.

"The dracar are coming," Nyrianne said, her voice strangely calm.

Morgan and Bremer readied their swords, and Margrave lifted his maces. Joe squared his shoulders and planted his staff protectively in front of Ryodan and his daughter.

"Can't we go back outside?" Julie asked.

"No," Alyssa said. "Too dangerous. The Iron Dragon is out there. Some of you need to stay here and face the dracar, but I need Morgan and Bremer to come outside with me."

Ryowyn stood beside Joe, pointing her trident at the stairwell door. "I'm staying with my father."

Alyssa turned and walked through the entryway, and Bremer followed.

Morgan looked at her mother and Joe, who both nodded to her, and she ran after Bremer.

Outside, Marlay stood guard with his protective shield in full force. Overhead, dragon roars and fiery blasts pierced the steady rumble of waterfalls as Raric and Natas battled. Through the cheerless clouds, they tumbled in midair, locking talons as they snapped at each other.

Alyssa removed her satchel and set it on the ground. The ice around it melted instantly, and the thunderclap peeked through the opening.

Morgan stared at the weapon. "But we have no ballista to launch it."

Alyssa put a hand on Bremer's shoulder. "Bremer Mason, we will need you and that bow."

Bremer shook his head gloomily, like a fighter who had advanced to the championship round only to be defeated by an impossibly strong opponent. "I've tried that already. The bow is useless against him."

"You didn't have the thunderclap," Alyssa said. "This might rub you the wrong way, but you need to trust Morgan and work together." She turned to Marlay. "If you have any advice, wizard, feel free to chime in."

"The bow of Onathe Wyeth should be powerful enough, but a single thunderclap cannot kill the Iron Dragon. It might not even be enough to knock it from the sky temporarily. You'll need a more powerful weapon and deeper magic to defeat Natas."

"That's why Raric and I must fight Natas until he's weakened. Then we'll use something more powerful." Alyssa glanced at Morgan's sword, which she held low.

Morgan swallowed hard. "But…but how can I…?" She shook

her head. "No, I can't fight Natas; none of us can. Even Ryodan couldn't."

A few hundred feet above them, Raric soared past again, this time with Natas in pursuit. The Iron Dragon breathed a stream of acid, but Raric banked to avoid the deadly blast. Natas flew out of sight.

Alyssa moved her face to within inches of Morgan's and clasped her shoulders. "You do not fight alone, Morgan. You have powerful allies. You're a Callum Sage, and you have the sword of Avarthrill. Do not underestimate the power within you or the strength of those around you. Remember what I told you and Will: if one falls, the other must carry the banner. If we stand together, we'll win this battle."

Alyssa spun around and sprinted toward the ledge, leapt into the air, and fell out of sight. Morgan gasped and rushed to the edge of the cliff. A second later, the Ice Dragon rose into view, her massive wings lifting her above the ridgeline. Morgan stepped back as the wind whipped her hair.

Before Alyssa could gain momentum, the Iron Dragon sky-rocketed from the canyon and careened into her. The impact was bone jarring. It drove them both upward for several feet before they tumbled down toward the canyon floor. Skipping once off the river, the two dragons crashed into the rocky ground and rolled into a sheer cliff. The earth shook, breaking rocks from the canyon walls.

Alyssa had landed high on Natas's back and could not clamp her jaws firmly around his neck. Natas shook her free, and both creatures scrambled to their feet like caged wild animals. Their long talons scratched deep grooves in the rocky ground. Natas's booming roar overpowered Alyssa's, but the Iron Dragon was slightly smaller than the Ice Dragon. Both appeared to be driven by the insatiable desire to kill the other.

Natas feinted left and right like an overgrown but nimble fencer waiting for the best opportunity to attack. He lunged, breathing a barrel of acid as he did. Alyssa stopped it with a frigid blast of air. Natas pressed forward, shooting several short blasts that kept her on the defensive. She stumbled backward, and Natas rushed her, nearly getting his jaws clamped over her long neck. His attack forced her to retreat as his gnashing teeth sought flesh. She leapt back and spread her wings, struggling to break free of the relentless assault. Sharp talons raked her neck, breaking several scales. Blood seeped from the wound. Alyssa roared and fought wildly, but Natas continued to force her back. If he pinned her against the cliff, she would have no way of escape.

High above the river, a few hundred yards from where Morgan, Bremer, and Marlay watched, the Red Dragon roared and plummeted toward the other dragons. Alyssa took advantage of the brief distraction, dodging a biting attack from Natas and shuffling away from the cliff toward the river. She was now in the clear, but her feet slipped on the wet rocks at the river's edge. Natas snapped once more before turning to face the incoming Red Dragon.

Raric splashed into the river, dousing the entire area. Alyssa shot a blast of frigid air at Natas while water dripped from his scales. Raric rose from the river and towered above the partially frozen Iron Dragon. Snatching up the long tail, Raric jerked Natas off his feet and threw him into the cliff wall. Several icy gray horns shattered, sending debris and rocks all around. The Iron Dragon staggered but rose slowly to his feet.

Turning to follow up with another attack, Raric slipped and nearly went down.

Despite his injuries, Natas inhaled, then launched a cloud of acid at Raric, who was still struggling for a firm foothold.

Alyssa was quick to react. Breathing a gale of dense, frosty air, she blew the cloud of acid across the river.

Natas bounded toward a bend in the canyon, his wings beginning to unfold. Raric recovered his footing and breathed a fiery blast just as the Iron Dragon rounded the bend. Natas escaped the brunt of the flames, but some ignited the Iron Dragon's hind leg.

Leaping forward, Raric took several bounding steps before throwing himself skyward. Alyssa spread her great wings and ascended directly behind him.

"Better get that thunderclap ready," Marlay said.

Bremer traced a rune on his quiver with his finger, and a hollow, headless arrow appeared.

Morgan slid the rod of the thunderclap into the arrow shaft. It was a tight fit, as if the arrow had been designed for the weapon. "When we're ready, I'll twist the tip here, and it's ready to launch."

"Hope it works," Bremer grumbled.

"Aim as close to Natas as you can," Marlay explained. "You don't have to hit him. Just try to avoid the others."

Natas was struggling for altitude through the swirling mists of the raging waterfalls. Rounding the gentle bend, he turned his long neck and opened his huge maw. The moment Raric flew around the bend, burning acid struck his neck.

Alyssa changed course to avoid getting hit, leaving the other dragons to rise high above her.

Both Raric and Natas appeared to be tiring. The Iron Dragon's right rear leg was burned so badly that it flopped awkwardly. Dark blood oozed from an open wound. Smoke streamed from the Red

Dragon's neck. But despite their wounds, they chased one another, matching blasts of fire and acid as they ascended from the canyon.

Banking around a tall, narrow rock formation, Natas rose, but he wasn't fast enough. The Red Dragon caught up to him, biting at his already injured leg and nearly tearing it off. Natas fired another long breath of acidic fog—only, this one was in front of him. He zigzagged wildly as if desperate for a way of escape.

Raric fired another explosion of flames that scorched Natas's back before he disappeared into the fog. Natas veered toward the Maidstone while Raric shot up and turned to avoid flying into the dense, poisonous fog. But he was too late. For a second, the Red Dragon disappeared in the cloud of acid, then dropped, barely able to slow his fall. He caught a current of air before coming to a rough landing on the riverbank far below. His legs gave out, and his massive head collapsed onto the rocks.

Morgan's heart sank. "Get up, Raric," she pleaded quietly. "Please, get up."

But the Red Dragon lay still and vulnerable beside the river.

Morgan spotted Natas beyond the fog gliding past the Maidstone toward the riverbank. Although the Iron Dragon's leg was limp and several horns were broken, the beast was still an intimidating sight. He seemed bent on finishing the Red Dragon.

Bremer drew back the bowstring.

"No, wait!" Morgan said, pointing at Alyssa, who appeared right behind Natas.

The Ice Dragon slammed headfirst into Natas, her jaws clamping around his neck. The Iron Dragon screeched. With a powerful flap of her wings, Alyssa slowed their descent. Natas scratched savagely at her body. She released her hold and darted in the opposite direction.

Morgan twisted the narrow band near the thunderclap head, and the weapon crackled to life. "Now!"

Bremer released the bowstring, and the thunderclap screamed through the air, glowing bright blue. It zipped past the Iron Dragon's huge head, and he tilted his wings to avoid a direct hit. When the weapon was about halfway over Natas's body, a bolt of lightning flashed between the thunderclap and the dragon's scales. A deafening crack charged the air, louder and brighter than any thunderstorm Morgan had ever experienced.

She covered her eyes, and when she looked again, Natas was faltering in midair. He flapped his wings feebly once or twice, then dropped like a stone to the river.

Alyssa had banked around, avoiding the weapon's trajectory. She flew up and landed on the ledge, lowering a wing to the ground.

"Climb on my back, Morgan! No time for a saddle—we only have a few minutes. Bremer, Marlay, get inside and help the others."

Morgan scrambled up the wing onto the dragon's back and clung to a large horn. Her stomach lurched as Alyssa dropped over the edge. The waterfall mists instantly soaked them both.

Seconds later, Alyssa glided to a soft landing beside the river. Morgan slid from the dragon's back and stood on shaky legs. She gulped moist air, trying to keep the sparse contents in her stomach down. But the stench of bloodied and burned dragon flesh stung her nostrils, and she vomited.

When she looked up, she noticed the Red Dragon still lying near the riverbank about twenty yards away. The Iron Dragon was closer to where Alyssa had landed. Like Raric, Natas wasn't moving.

In the wake of the fierce dragon battle, the rumbling waterfalls returned the area to a wild yet comparatively peaceful state.

"Is he dead?" Morgan asked.

Alyssa lowered her head and her icy eyes narrowed. "No. We must kill him."

"But…how?" Morgan knew the answer already, but it seemed impossible. She placed a hand on the hilt of her sword.

"Remember the first harvester you killed," Alyssa said. "That seemed impossible too, didn't it?"

Morgan slowly drew her sword, taking a single cautious step toward the Iron Dragon. "But that was self-defense. I had no other option."

"If you delay now, self-defense will not be an option."

Morgan studied the Iron Dragon's hide. "But the scales are so dense…"

"Raric opened a wound in his leg. Let the sword work its magic."

The vicious gash in Natas's hind leg was a gruesome sight. The smell turned Morgan's stomach again as she approached. She winced and held her breath. But as deadly and terrifying as Natas had been only moments ago, she found it difficult to attack a creature while it was unconscious. She gripped the sword of Avarthrill with both hands, staring at the gaping wound.

"You can do this, Morgan," Alyssa urged. "It is the only way."

Without warning, Natas's eyes flicked open, and his long neck shot toward Alyssa. She raised her front claw in defense, but Natas's jaws clamped over it. Alyssa howled in pain.

"No!" Morgan screamed, raising the sword over her head.

She plunged the blade deep into the open wound and held it fast. Dark blood spattered and sizzled. Her body tingled as if she were holding a live wire instead of a sword.

The ancient blade crackled and sparked, searing the Iron Dragon's flesh. Natas released his hold on Alyssa's claw and shrieked. The deep, reverberating wail made Morgan's ears ring, and she screamed as she held the sword in the wound. Natas tried to swing his head around to the source of his pain, but the magic had already raced through his body, paralyzing him.

Morgan squeezed her eyes shut. Fleeing at this point would be useless; she could never outrun the Iron Dragon, even in his wounded state. She had no choice but to wait until either Natas found the strength to swallow her whole or the sword proved its worth.

What seemed like hours was over in minutes. Morgan risked a glance and saw the Iron Dragon's eyes flash green before his head thumped to the rocky ground. Through long, sharp teeth, Natas released a pronounced hiss that pierced the stillness and then faded in a final puff of steam. Morgan shut her eyes again, unable to move. Several minutes later, the crackling of the sword ceased, and all was quiet except for the timeless rumble of the seven waterfalls.

Long after Natas stopped breathing, Morgan held the sword steady. When she finally opened her eyes, the Ice Dragon was standing next to her. Alyssa's kind eyes reflected both pain and pride. Around them, the saturated air was already soaking a large pile of ash. A light rain began to fall, and the remains of the Iron Dragon slowly blended with the muddy earth.

Alyssa lowered her head and spoke the words that caused Morgan to fall to her knees.

"It's over, Morgan."

CHAPTER 30

ANOTHER BATTLE BEGINS

Beside the rushing river, the Red Dragon stirred. A puff of smoke rose from his nostrils. His legs twitched, but his eyes remained closed. Morgan glanced in his direction, then gaped at the gigantic pile of ash.

"He's gone, Morgan," Alyssa said. "Natas is defeated."

The thought was impossible to imagine. Morgan took a few faltering steps backward, half expecting the Iron Dragon to somehow magically rise from the ashes. She looked at the other two dragons and gazed up at the Maidstone tower.

"Mom…"

"We need to get back to them," Alyssa said. "Raric will be fine, I'm sure, and will find us when he wakes."

Morgan sheathed her sword and climbed onto the Ice Dragon's back. Alyssa extended her wings and rose through the mists. Morgan clung to slick horn as the waterfall spray washed over her, awakening her to the reality of what they had just accomplished. Alyssa's words rang in her ears: *Natas is defeated.*

A minute later, they were back on the ledge. Marlay stood at the Maidstone entrance, his arms folded across his chest. He was smiling at Morgan.

"I wouldn't believe it if I hadn't seen it with my own eyes," the wizard said, slowly shaking his head. "The end of Natas."

"That is only the first step," Alyssa said. "Our battle against the spread of Phyriad has just begun."

Marlay nodded. "Ah, but first steps are most important."

Without waiting for Alyssa to transform, Morgan ran to the entrance. Marlay pulled a sunstone from his pocket, and together they walked through the murky passage.

Ryodan lay in the same place on the foyer floor, unconscious and drawing shallow breaths. In the dim light cast by the flickering wall-mounted torches, they could see Margrave on his knees, working on the mer king. Small blue flames floated in the air around Ryodan's injuries as the druid moved his hands methodically and muttered words Morgan could not understand. Joe also knelt beside Ryodan, his broad, bare chest peeking through the gap in his brown cloak. He had used his soaked undershirt to clean away the acid that had burned through some of Ryodan's armor.

More than half a dozen dracar bodies lay broken and bleeding throughout the foyer.

"Where's everyone else?" Alyssa asked, entering a few seconds behind Morgan and Marlay.

"They went through that door and down the stairs, I think," Joe said. His long white hair was a tangled mess, and there were dark circles under his weary-looking eyes. "The fighting stopped a few minutes ago. Bremer and Ryowyn chased a few of these creatures, and your mother went with them carrying the warden rod."

"Let's go," Morgan said, running to the stairwell door.

Alyssa followed, and the wizard held up his sunstone as Morgan swung the door open. She drew her sword and entered the stairwell.

They stepped over a dead dracar and discovered about four others sprawled along the stairs down to the next level. Morgan hoped that was a sign that Bremer and Ryowyn had fought off the attack and kept her mother and Nyrianne alive. But why hadn't they returned?

The door to the first level was ajar, propped open by a dracar corpse with a deep gash in its neck. Muffled sounds and a loud crash from the hallway beyond suggested they were on the right path.

They jogged down the hallway to a junction and stopped next to what looked like a sprawling nurse's station—only, this one had been thoroughly trashed. A shout came from the left, and Morgan stepped around the corner.

Bremer stood with an arrow drawn in the bow of Onathe Wyeth, aimed at a harvester with its back to the wall. The creature's reptilian eyes glared at Bremer, and black ichor dripped from its exposed fangs. A large clawed hand wrapped around Julie's neck. Her wide eyes stared pleadingly at Bremer, then flicked to Morgan. The warden rod lay on the floor a few feet from her.

Morgan flinched, wanting to run and help, but she knew that a single misstep would mean the death of her mother.

Sitting against a wall between Bremer and Morgan, Ryowyn was leaning awkwardly to the side. The princess's right eye was bruised and swollen, and a line of blood on her cheek glistened in the muted light. Nyrianne was nowhere in sight.

The harvester growled upon seeing the three additional intruders. Julie whimpered as the creature tightened its hold.

Bremer's bowstring thumped. The arrow pierced the harvester's cheek and thwacked into the wall behind it, pinning its head. The creature released its grip on Julie's neck. She dropped to her knees and scrambled away, gasping for breath.

As the harvester gripped the arrow, Alyssa waved a hand, sending four long shards of ice that looked like bolts shot from a ballista. As each one struck the harvester, they shattered on impact. All that remained of the creature was a large dark stain splattered against the wall.

Morgan hurried across the smooth floor and slid to her knees, reaching for her mother. "Can you walk, Mom? We need to get out of here before—"

From farther down the hallway, another door slammed open, and a dark figure filled the frame of a double doorway. The same harvester that Nyrianne had attacked earlier now flexed its muscular arms as it hefted a long spear and stepped forward, surveying the scene.

Nyrianne appeared from beyond the nurse's station and casually approached the harvester.

"Excuse me," she said, "but I seem to be lost."

The harvester was close enough to kill her. Instead, it brought the spear tip to her neck and lifted her chin until she was looking into its grim face. The creature narrowed its eyes as if it recognized her and dared her to make the first move.

Morgan had seen what Nyrianne could do to a harvester, but the woman had slipped into one of her confused states and seemed unthreatened.

"I don't suppose you could direct me to the alchemists' lab?" Nyrianne said.

The harvester tilted its head to one side.

In the silence that followed, Marlay walked slowly toward Nyrianne. His mouth hung open as if he, too, had recognized the old woman. When he was about ten feet from her, he paused midstride.

"Stop!" Marlay shouted, raising a hand at the creature as he uttered several words similar to the ones he'd used outside.

The harvester froze as if suddenly paralyzed and glared at the wizard. It was completely still, and only its eyes moved.

The color drained from Marlay's face, but it was not the harvester he was staring at.

"It cannot be," the wizard breathed as he walked toward Nyrianne. "Impossible."

"Wait, Marlay," Bremer said. "Stop, you old fool."

The wizard took another step as if he hadn't heard the warning. His quiet voice cracked. "Nyrianne?"

The old woman moved away from the harvester. She and Marlay now seemed oblivious to the imminent danger.

"Professor Bonicle?" she said. "I'm so sorry for being late, Professor. It seems I've lost my way."

A single tear rolled down Marlay's cheek. "That is quite all right, Nyrianne. It seems I've found you."

Nyrianne continued walking toward Marlay until they were face-to-face. The harvester remained by the doorway, snarling and straining against unseen bonds.

Bremer put another arrow in his bow, but with Marlay and Nyrianne between him and the harvester, he lacked a clear shot.

"Well and good, then, Nyrianne," Marlay said as he turned and slid an arm around the old woman, leading her to Alyssa. "Now, you go with Alyssa, and I'll meet you upstairs. There's something I need to finish up here."

After Alyssa led Nyrianne out of the hallway, the wizard spun around, his face set in stone. Bremer lowered the bow.

Marlay pointed at the harvester, and the wizard's eyes darkened. His voice deepened as he strode toward the petrified creature. "You will beg for death, but that won't come for a great long while."

The harvester's eyes grew wide as Marlay stopped in front of him. The old wizard used his outstretched finger to move the spear to the side with no resistance. He placed his open hand on the harvester's chest, closed his eyes, and whispered a few incoherent words. After a moment, the harvester's eyes widened further as the wizard raised his voice.

"This spell is one that I affectionately refer to as the Hand of Marlay."

Terror spread across the harvester's face. The spear clanged to the floor, and the creature's arms pressed to its sides as if bound by invisible chains.

No one moved for a moment as if they were expecting the harvester to break Marlay's spell. Then Julie coughed, her throat sounding hoarse. She picked up the warden rod from the floor and used it to push herself to her feet. Morgan held her other arm, and together they started to leave the hallway. Bremer helped Ryowyn slowly stand. Judging by the way she was bent slightly and holding her side, she probably had some broken ribs.

Marlay opened his arms in a wide gesture, allowing the others to pass. "It is safe for us to leave now."

Morgan led Julie toward the nurse's station, her eyes locked on the harvester. As they all shuffled around the corner, Marlay stopped for a final look at the harvester.

"Good day," he said before turning to leave.

Joe met them at the door at the top of the stairs. He glanced at each face, and put his arm around Ryowyn, leading her to where the mer king lay. Alyssa and Nyrianne were standing nearby, their heads bowed.

Ryowyn gasped at the sight of her fallen father. She fell to her knees, tears forming as she rested her hands on his still chest.

The druid Margrave was kneeling by Ryodan's side. "I am sorry, child. I did all I could to save him, but the Iron Dragon's poison was too deep."

Ryowyn's small form shook as she wrapped her arms around her father's chest.

Morgan looked at her mother through watery eyes. Julie hugged her tightly, and Joe took them both in his arms.

"I'm so sorry," Marlay said after a moment.

Morgan looked up, assuming he was offering condolences to Ryowyn. But the wizard, with tears in his eyes, was speaking to Nyrianne.

The old woman held the wizard's gaze for a moment. Her eyes were more focused than Morgan had ever seen them, and much sadder. She opened her arms, and Marlay stepped into her embrace.

"I know now that you had no idea what you were doing when you brought me here as a child," Nyrianne said in one of her rare lucid moments. "What happened to me, and the evil that spread throughout the land…" She looked down at the grieving mer princess and the dead king. "And even what happened here today as a result. None of this is your fault, Marlay, despite the story you may be telling yourself."

Nyrianne's voice was so soothing that the sharp pain in Morgan's heart subsided, if only a little.

"Will you forgive me?" Marlay managed between sobs.

"If there was anything to forgive, then I would forgive it."

Nyrianne pressed her cheek against his. She met Morgan's gaze, and her eyes twinkled. "A wise young man once taught me that."

"I wanted so much for you, child," Marlay said.

Nyrianne patted his back. "I know."

Joe led Morgan and Julie a few steps away from Ryowyn to give her space to grieve.

"Did you find it?" Joe asked, keeping his voice low.

Morgan nodded solemnly, pointing to the supply pack that Julie was carrying.

"We have about a hundred doses of an antidote for Phyriad," Julie said.

Bremer was standing off by himself but overheard Julie's response and stepped closer. "Should we go back for more?"

"There *is* no more," Julie said. "According to the files I saw, the two rooms we searched were the only ones with anything associated with Phyriad. We also found a couple of vials that might be a vaccine, but I'll need to read more about it. And perhaps do some tests."

"But do we have enough to help Rowe and Will?" Bremer asked.

"The single doses we found should work for anyone infected within the past ten days."

"I don't like it when people say *should*," Bremer grumbled.

Julie's brow remained furrowed. "I also read about a booster intended for those infected within a month, or for anyone not responding to the first treatment. But we found none of that."

"Then let's hope we have what we need," Joe said.

From the stairwell, far below the foyer, came a loud banging as if someone were pounding on a door.

"It's time we leave this place," Alyssa said.

Julie raised the warden rod and illuminated the dark entryway.

Bremer and Margrave carefully lifted Ryodan's body, and Alyssa and Morgan led the way out of the Maidstone while the others followed in a somber procession.

General Raric was outside sitting on a large rock. He was in his human form, and a nasty red burn mark scarred his neck and upper chest.

"Judging by that pile of ash," he said to Alyssa, "I assume that Natas is dead. But how?"

"The sword of Avarthrill burned the life from the Iron Dragon," Alyssa answered. "But only through the combined efforts of each one here was such a feat possible." She lowered her voice. "King Ryodan made the ultimate sacrifice."

Raric stood slowly and sighed as he watched Bremer and Margrave lay the mer king on the ground.

"It will be a tight fit," Alyssa announced once they were all outside. "but I will take Ryowyn, her father, Morgan, Julie, and Nyrianne. I'll fly Ryowyn and her father to Rainia Lake. Then we'll go to the outpost cabin to administer the antidote to Will and Rowe."

"Oh," Nyrianne said, "I'm so looking forward to seeing Will again."

"And so am I, Nyrianne," Alyssa said. "Raric, can you take Bremer, Joe, and—"

"I am fine to return to my forest by myself," Margrave said. "No dragon riding for me."

Marlay glanced at Nyrianne. "I would like to come to Rainia," he said. "If that is acceptable."

"Of course," Morgan said. "You'll be welcome there."

The wizard's eyes softened, and he bowed his head. "I'm grateful."

Ryowyn rose and slowly walked over to Morgan. "Please bring my Will home to me soon."

Morgan squeezed her hand. "The very second he's well enough. If we can make him wait that long."

"What about the Maidstone?" Julie asked. "Who knows how many dracar are still alive down there? Do we leave them to continue their vile experiments?"

"It's possible they will disperse now that Natas is dead," Joe suggested.

"I say we burn it," Bremer said. "If we have everything we need, why leave such an evil place standing?"

"But what about those prisoners?" Julie asked.

Bremer scoffed. "Anything alive down there is fighting against us or is already so infected that they're beyond the reach of the antidote you found. Let's burn the place to the foundations and be done with all of it."

As horrible as the idea sounded, Morgan realized there was nothing they could do to help the prisoners. "You saw the surgery rooms, Mom. And all those prisoners—even the girl—were either dead or dracar. Not sure anyone could survive down there, even if we had a way to reverse the effects of Phyriad."

Julie hung her head and exhaled. "I suppose you're right. I just don't want to give up hope."

"And that's why we need you in the Rainia Valley," Joe said. "And all those who will keep that flame alive."

"Speaking of flames," Raric said. "I can look after burning the Maidstone. But then I need to get back and rest." He strode over to the ledge. "Get away from the tower."

Bremer and Margrave lifted Ryodan again, and everyone moved

across the meadow to the bluffs, as far from the Maidstone as they could go. Bremer found a small grassy patch to lay Ryodan.

Without a word, Margrave continued walking to the narrow switchback path that connected the Maidstone with the valley below.

"So, this is farewell then, druid?" Marlay said.

Margrave stopped and turned. "For now, it is, wizard. Should you find yourself in the Hollowtangle, you have an open invitation to visit the Druid Forest."

"If it's still standing," Marlay said with a grimace.

The druid glowered. "If the dracar come for my little corner of the Fourwinds, I will make them pay in ways you could not begin to imagine." He turned away and walked down the narrow path.

When they turned around, Alyssa was standing in the form of the Ice Dragon. High above the Maidstone, the Red Dragon circled.

Next to Alyssa were the four elven saddle blankets. Morgan looked at Ryowyn but knew that the princess would not have the strength to leave her father's side to help, so she climbed the dragon's back alone.

"Bremer," she said. "Throw me those blankets." As she had done before, Morgan spread the blankets, which transformed into four saddles.

"Now, that would be a handy addition to *our* dragon," Marlay mused.

"I will carry Ryodan safely in my claw," Alyssa said.

Morgan helped Julie and Nyrianne into their saddles, then climbed down to Ryowyn, who had not taken her eyes off her father. She marveled at the princess's strength. If it were Julie's body they were taking back to the valley, Morgan would have been an emotional mess. But Ryowyn had experienced things beyond Morgan's worst nightmares. Even so, the princess remained quiet and distant as the reality of life without her father gently worked its way into her broken heart. Morgan wanted to give her friend—who was now more like a sister—all the space she needed to grieve. For now, she helped Ryowyn take the first step by getting her into the elven saddle.

Alyssa spread her ice-white wings, stepped over the ledge, and immediately caught a current of air that carried her upward.

The Red Dragon landed near the Maidstone entryway, double-checking to make sure everyone was clear. He lowered his head and placed his enormous muzzle against the entryway. After drawing a deep breath, he released a long, rumbling exhale of fire. Flames roared into the Maidstone. A few cracks in the windowless tower glowed, starting near the base and gradually spreading to the top. Within seconds, the conical roof was ablaze as fire continued to rush from the Red Dragon. The inferno inside the tower burst through the top opening with a thunderous roar. Ancient stone blocks broke away from the structure, falling into the mists below.

Morgan and the other women watched in awe as the tower crumbled. But they would not see the complete collapse of the Maidstone. Alyssa adjusted her wings and took them in a south-easterly direction.

As they journeyed back to the Rainia Valley, Morgan and Julie craned their necks for one last glimpse of the Maidstone. In a way, leaving that awful place seemed like an ending. But Morgan turned her head back to the eastern horizon and the distant outline of the Hillron Mountains. For Rowe and Will, the journey was not over. And it was far from certain.

CHAPTER 31
Not Out of
the Woods Yet

The bunk bed creaked as Will rolled onto his side and covered his exposed leg with his Trannalun cloak. Despite the afternoon sunlight peeking through a narrow curtain gap in the front window of the outpost cabin, he was shivering. Through mucus-crusted eyelids, he scanned the small room. He listened, daring to hope that the sound he had heard outside was not just another dream. Ryowyn and Morgan had walked through the cabin door so many times in his imagination, he wondered if his fever was starting to pry apart his loosening grip on reality. Conversation with Rowe had ceased sometime yesterday due to their foggy fevers and the limited number of waking hours. Loneliness was his new companion.

Outside, the front steps creaked. Will rubbed his eyes and blinked. That sound was not imagined. The door latch clicked, and the door swung slowly open. Will shielded his eyes as sunlight poured into the cabin. Two silhouettes filled the doorway.

"I hope you're here to either kill me or heal me." Will's voice was raspy, and he wheezed a deep breath.

The two figures entered but stopped just inside the doorway. Will blinked again. They certainly seemed real.

"We're here to heal you, Will," Morgan said. Her voice sounded muffled, and he noticed she was wearing a surgical mask. Julie, also wearing a mask, stepped in behind Morgan.

Hope filled Will's heart. His breathing became shallow, and his chest pounded. "That's the first good news I've had in days. In case you're wondering, I don't feel so good."

He propped himself up on an elbow and ran his tongue over his raw, chapped lips. He couldn't breathe through his congested nose, and deeper breaths through his mouth stirred something in his chest. He coughed and hacked, then spat a mouthful of greenish phlegm into the metal bucket beside his bed.

"Sorry about that," he said.

"That's okay," Morgan said, shrinking back. "You look worse than you sound."

"I'll bet I feel worse than I look."

Julie dropped a large red bag on the counter and kept her distance despite the masks they wore. "Well," she said, "we might have something for that."

Will was certain now that he wasn't dreaming. He tried to sit up but only had the strength to prop himself up on an elbow. He scratched the scaly rash on his forearm.

Morgan had turned her gaze to Rowe's bed. Her eyes were glistening.

"He's still alive," Will said. "He was up a little while ago, but his coughing is worse than mine." He rubbed his eyes with the palms of his hands. "I have a crushing headache behind my eyeballs. Do you happen to have any aspirin in that pack? Extra strength?"

"Maybe something better," Morgan said. "We think we found the cure. It's in some kind of EpiPen injector needle."

"From the information we found," Julie added, "one shot should have you back in the saddle in a day or so."

"That's great," Will said. "If you need a test patient, I'm ready to go. But…" He glanced at the door. "Where's Mom and Ryowyn?"

Morgan's shoulders slumped.

"What is it, Morgan?" Will coughed and spat into the bucket. "What's going on?"

"They're both fine," Morgan explained. "We killed Natas."

Will gaped at the women. He ran a hand over his greasy, tangled hair. His highest hope was that the women would find a cure. Defeating the Iron Dragon was more than he could have imagined.

"But," Morgan continued, "we only found a hundred doses of the cure for Phyriad. So, one battle ends, and another begins."

"That's incredible," Will said. "But what about Ry—"

Morgan held up her hands. "Ryowyn's fine. She has a few scratches like the rest of us, but we took her to Rainia Lake so she could bring her people news. She's okay." Morgan was now fidgeting with her hands.

"What news?" Will asked.

Morgan looked at her mother, who offered her a nod.

"Just tell him," Julie said.

Morgan gazed at the floor. "It's a long story. Natas attacked as we came out of the Maidstone. The battle was hectic and violent. Raric—or, the Red Dragon—joined us, with Bremer and Joe, and also a wizard, a druid, and…Ryowyn's father." She looked up. "I'm so sorry, Will, but Ryodan was killed."

Will cocked his head and tugged his congested ear. He'd heard the words, but they didn't register in his mind.

She nodded solemnly. "I'm sorry, Will."

The hope that had begun to form in Will's heart melted. He slumped back onto his bed and rested his cheek on the pillow. Ryodan had accepted him into their family. Despite being king, he'd gone out of his way to welcome Will. Within a very short period, Will had found a new father figure, and Ryodan seemed pleased with his new son-in-law.

Will closed his eyes, squeezing out hot tears.

After a moment, Julie spoke. "When you're ready, we'll let your mother administer the antidote."

Will raised his head. "Mom's here?"

"She's been waiting outside until you were ready," Morgan said.

Will sat up again, wiping the crust and tears from his eyes. "Well, I'm as ready as I'll ever be."

Julie stepped outside and returned a moment later with Alyssa. "Morgan and I are wearing masks and staying back because I'm still not sure how this disease spreads. Alyssa tells me she is immune to Phyriad, but I feel more comfortable taking precautions."

His mother stood in the room, more beautiful than he remembered. Her simple smile was as genuine as it had been every day when he came home from school.

Julie handed her a mask and a pair of latex gloves. Alyssa put them on and pulled up a chair and sat beside Will's bed. She placed a gloved hand on his cheek, and the corners of her eyes crinkled in a smile. "You have your father's eyes. So handsome."

"I'm sorry, Mom."

"For what?" she asked, folding her hands in her lap.

"For all the pain you had to go through. I know you had to

leave me and Dad back in Cochrane to stand against Natas. I can't imagine how hard it was for you."

He turned his head and coughed again, drier this time. Alyssa handed him a cup of water from the bedside table.

"Try not to talk too much for now," she said. "Let's get you better first."

She pushed up his cloak sleeve until most of his arm was exposed. He flinched and looked at the others, wondering how they might react. But none of them cowered or turned away from the ugly rash.

"Make sure you find a clear section of skin," Julie said. "Or as clear as possible. If the rash is too thick, the needle won't penetrate."

"He's completely covered," Alyssa said with a sigh. "But there's some up near his shoulder that's not bad." She placed the end of the tube against his skin and pressed the other end, holding it steady for a few seconds before she pulled it away.

"That's it?" Will asked.

"How'd that feel?" Julie asked from the doorway.

"Burns like fire."

Julie sat at the table and scribbled something in a blue binder. "Tell me as soon as it starts to change. We need data, and since you're not going anywhere, I'll be asking you about when and how you were infected, and how you're feeling from hour to hour. We need to build out a baseline for expectations."

Will pulled his sleeve back down and massaged his shoulder. "Whatever I can do for research."

"You're so much like your father," Alyssa said.

"I miss him, Mom."

"I do too. I think of him every day."

"Can you tell me what happened that day?"

Alyssa nodded quietly as she walked over to Rowe's bunk with another needle. "I think you're ready to hear some details, Will." She sat in the chair beside Rowe and cleared her throat before continuing. "Your father and I were attacked by two harvesters while we were snowmobiling on the Frederick House River. They were in their true shape, but I was caught in human form. I couldn't fight them, but I was able to drag one into a hole in the ice. There, I transformed into the Ice Dragon, and when I broke through the ice, I watched the other harvester strike your father on the head."

"That explains the gash," Will said. "He couldn't remember what happened."

Alyssa shook her head. "I thought I had lost him, so I killed the harvesters. In that moment, staring at your unconscious father, I knew I couldn't protect the two of you, not while the Iron Dragon was sending his demons to do his bidding. I had to try and stop Natas. So, I returned to the Fourwinds, but discovered that he had become more powerful than ever—too powerful for one dragon to face alone. Natas knew I'd returned, and my presence slowed his plans and made him more cautious. But it also made him more determined. I went underground, trying to influence events and encourage various races to stand against the Iron Dragon. Never did I think I'd be gone from you for so long, but the work here was too great, and I eventually became desperate. Then you and Morgan showed up, and despite my concern for you, I began to feel hopeful again."

"I wouldn't say things got better. Just look at this place. We've seen war; crazy, evil demons; powerful, corrupt leaders; and a plague that threatens to destroy us. And we're not out of the woods yet." He coughed and spat into the bucket.

Alyssa leaned close to Rowe. "That's true. But I still believe the Callum Sages are the best hope for the Fourwinds."

"I think Rowe's worse off than me," Will said. "His rash has spread more, and he hasn't been able to keep any food down in the past day. And I think his fever is pretty bad cuz I don't understand a word he says anymore."

"Can you wake him?" Julie asked.

Alyssa placed a hand on his arm. Rowe stirred, then rolled over and blinked a few times.

"Hey, partner," Will said. "We've got company."

Morgan gasped, and Julie put a hand on her shoulder.

"Rowe," Morgan said. "We…we found a cure."

Rowe's eyes drifted toward her, but they were milky and seemed unfocused. He groaned.

"Morgan's here, Rowe," Alyssa said. "But she can't come close until you're better. I have something that should help. I just need your arm." She pulled his sleeve up and examined his bare arm. "It's completely covered."

"Try the other arm," Julie said.

Alyssa rolled up his other sleeve. "There's a small patch that's not as bad…"

"That'll have to do," Julie said.

While Alyssa administered the needle, Rowe lay on his back, motionless.

"Rowe," Morgan said in a wavering voice. "Can you hear me?"

The room was quiet except for Rowe's heavy breathing. Outside, the surrounding trees were alive with birdsong.

Alyssa stood and walked back to Morgan.

"Are we too late?" Morgan whispered.

Will sat up. His joints were on fire, and his head still ached.

"I don't think so," he said. "I already feel…different. Not better, but…warm and relaxed."

Rowe moaned and rolled over with a deep, barking cough.

Julie wrote in the binder. "According to what I read here earlier, the antidote will either work within a few hours, or…" She tapped the pen against her chin.

"I'd like to wash a bit," Will said, pushing himself to his feet. As soon as he stood, the room started spinning, and he sat down again.

"You need to rest," Julie said.

"I'll go get water," Morgan said, turning and leaving the cabin.

Will lay down, listening to his mother and Julie speaking quietly.

"She needs to stay with him," Alyssa said. "You know she won't be able to leave him."

Julie fumbled through her backpack. "I know, but we can't risk having her infected too." She pulled out a small box of latex gloves and another containing surgical masks and placed them on the table. "I thought we'd use all of these in the Maidstone, but maybe—"

"They might help," Alyssa interrupted. "But there's no guarantee. We have to believe the antidote will work."

Morgan returned a moment later with two full pails. Water sloshed onto the wood-planked floor as she set one down. Her eyes were red and puffy. She grabbed a clean cloth from the table and took one step toward Rowe's bed.

"I have to stay with him, Mom. You would have done the same for Dad."

Julie sighed. "No need to defend your case. I know you too well." She took a fresh auto-injector from her pocket. "Keep this with you at all times, and if you exhibit any symptoms, promise me you'll use this."

"I know how to use an EpiPen, Mom."

"Well, it's similar but a bit different. Jab this end into your thigh, press the yellow button, and hold for ten seconds."

Morgan moved a chair beside Rowe's bed and brought the pail of water. She leaned forward and spoke in tender whispers as she washed his face. When she pulled up his cloak sleeves, she gasped. The sound of the cloth rubbing against his arms was like wiping sandpaper or tree bark.

Alyssa offered Will the same service. He had splashed water on his face a couple of times over the past few days, but having his mother care for him flooded him with childlike comfort. He hoped Rowe was feeling the same.

The tension in Rowe's jaw relaxed. He mumbled incoherently as Morgan washed his arms and chest. But his eyes remained closed. She kept whispering to him as she washed one section of his body at a time, trying to keep his cloak against his skin as much as possible.

"He's so warm," Morgan said.

"That could be a positive sign," Julie said. She sat at the table, taking notes as she listened and observed.

Will fell asleep to the sound of pen on paper and washcloths dripping into pails of water.

When he awoke, he stretched his arms, then tried to slide his legs over the side of his bed. Alyssa didn't stop him but stood from her chair to help support his legs as he stood.

"I need some air," he said with a gentle cough. He expected another wad of phlegm, but his chest offered only a slight rattle. "I can't believe how much better I feel."

"Are you sure you're up for it?" Alyssa asked.

"It's amazing," Julie said. "You *do* look a bit better."

He glanced at Rowe, who was still sleeping in his bed. Morgan had fallen asleep in the chair beside him.

Alyssa led Will through the front door, and he shielded his eyes against the bright sunlight.

"It's morning?"

Alyssa smiled. "You slept all night, son."

Will stretched as he gazed out over the tops of the Epping Forest, scanning the vast beauty of the Misty Gorge and the Rainia Valley. His joints were stiff but didn't ache as much. He closed his eyes as the morning sun warmed his cheeks.

"So beautiful," Alyssa said as Will sat in a large wooden chair on the porch.

"I'm feeling better, but I'm trying to figure out if it's just a boost of energy from seeing you or if the cure's actually beginning to work."

"Julie said you could start feeling better within a few hours, and you slept all night."

Will studied his mother as she sat in the chair beside him. She really was beautiful. Her long, dark hair swayed in the gentle breeze, and her blue eyes sparkled like the sun on the Niasa Sea.

"I'm in no hurry, Mom. But whenever you're ready, I'm curious about the whole dragon thing."

"Okay," Alyssa said, scooting her chair around to face him. She leaned forward, her arms resting on her knees. "Remember all the adventure and fantasy stories we used to read together?"

Will smiled. "How could I forget? Those were the best years of my life. Some of those stories were so crazy, but you made others seem so real, it was hard for a small boy to separate fact from fiction."

"Well, I hope you haven't separated things too cleanly."

Will swept his hand across the stunning vista. "If I did, all this has messed me up again."

Alyssa chuckled. "To get an idea about where our family comes from, you first have to understand a very old history, which I will teach you in the days to come. But for now, let me say that our bloodline is a powerful one, with ancient magic that can take one of three forms. Your great-grandfather Joe can harness ice from air. Your grandfather could see through all forms of illusion, and shape-shifters like harvesters. My form of magic allows me to transform into what you saw before. I'm an Ice Dragon, and so, too, will be your firstborn grandchild."

Will stared off into the horizon. Memories flashed in his mind's eye: of sitting on the porch in Cochrane, watching Lessers and the harvester; of Joe in the Arden Forest, locking the harvester in ice; of seeing more harvesters in the Crow's Nest and the North Crow Gate; and of another vague incident that slowly took shape. It was nighttime less than a week ago, and he was riding on the back of a dragon—a white dragon—and they were soaring over the Epping Forest.

After a moment, Alyssa squeezed his hand. "Are you okay?"

Will blinked and licked his cracked lips. "Why is it that nothing seems to surprise me anymore?"

Morgan came outside with two cups of water. Will took one and gulped down the entire contents.

"You look much better," she said.

"How about Rowe? Is he awake?"

"Not yet, but his breathing sounds better. And he's groaning less."

Will slumped back in his chair. "I wish I could have gone to the Maidstone with you guys. I feel so useless here."

"We all did our part," Morgan said. "Just think where we'd

be if you and Rowe hadn't gone to Acttun. Those thunderclaps brought down the Red Dragon and helped free Raric so he could control his dragon side. We couldn't have fought Natas without him. And when Bremer stayed in Acttun, he found the old wizard named Marlay Bonicle, the one Rowe told us about. Bremer and Marlay then found a druid named Margrave, and together they helped us fight the Iron Dragon. It was a thunderclap that finally knocked Natas from the sky."

"And your sword that killed him," Alyssa added. "But there are no solo heroes in this story."

Will rubbed the back of his head. "Wizards, and druids, and dragons…oh my."

They all laughed at his storybook reference.

"It *is* kinda like a crazy dream," Morgan said.

Will grinned, still weak but more alive than he'd been in many days. "One thing's for sure," he said, taking his mother's hand again. "Wherever we are, I'm glad to be back with you guys. There really is no place like home."

CHAPTER 32
RETURN TO RAINIA

While Alyssa had taken a direct route from the Maidstone to the Rainia Valley, the Red Dragon took time to soar above the burning tower, circling wide to allow his passengers a full view of the destruction. Joe sat comfortably between a pair of smooth horns on the dragon's back, holding tight to the one in front. Behind him, Bremer and Marlay clutched similar horns. Joe had ridden a few horses in his life but had only ridden bareback once. Riding a dragon without a saddle was much easier than riding a horse without a saddle. It would be a challenge, but it was much better than returning to the valley on foot.

The wizard Marlay, however, didn't hesitate to express his discomfort.

"While I appreciate your efforts to accommodate the three of us, General Raric, I must say that I do not think my old bones are up to the journey without better seating arrangements. I cannot speak for our friend Johanissan, but I think he might agree."

Joe said nothing, clutching the horn with one hand and his

staff in the other. His long white hair whipped around his face. Bremer, as usual, was a closed book.

A section of the burning Maidstone tower broke away, creating a small rockslide that tumbled into the canyon.

"I could drop you back down there, wizard, if you're so uncomfortable," Raric suggested.

"No, no," Marlay replied, wrapping his arms around a horn. "Just get us to the Rainia Valley as fast as you can."

"Could you take us over Fairbay?" Joe asked. "I don't want to land, but I'm curious to see if there's any activity around the town since Phyriad was released into the sea."

"It's a bit out of the way," Raric said. "But I like the idea of seeing what's happening throughout the land."

They flew in a northeasterly direction and soon were high above the vast blue expanse of the Niasa Sea.

Joe studied the shoreline, remembering the tragic attack on the mer soldiers. "I was at the Gryton Mines the day the gnomes—slaves of Uluk—released a large flask full of small creatures into the sea. It was a dark day. Phyriad quickly infected all marine life, including about two-thirds of the mer army. It was a mad frenzy. Mer soldiers transformed before my eyes. Ryowyn's brother, Prince Wrathan, was among them."

"And now the mer are without a king," Bremer mused.

As Raric flew over the abandoned and ruined village of Fairbay, no one said a word.

Joe turned for another look at what remained of his favorite place in the Fourwinds. Something broke from the surface of the water and disappeared with a splash.

"Did anyone else see that?" he asked.

"Yes," Bremer said. "What was it?"

"It almost looked like a merman, but it wasn't blue. It was… no, maybe it was just in the shadows."

"I saw it too, Johanissan. It was definitely iron-gray."

"Natas is gone," Raric said, "but the effects of his influence survive. We have our work cut out for us in the days and months to come."

"If we're taking detours, could we fly over the Upper Plains of Ashron?" Marlay asked. "We don't need to go all the way to Acttun, but I'm curious about that infected horde that attacked the city."

"I was planning to do just that," Raric said. "I cannot imagine what has happened to Dwenlin Thah or Acttun."

After they passed the foothills near the sea, they flew over the open plains. Marlay pointed out a small group of people wandering around, and Raric rose higher. Joe assumed they were all infected, and he didn't mind being as far from them as possible. The farther east they went, the more groups they saw. There seemed to be no organized effort, and no one was in a hurry to get anywhere. Instead, they roamed the plains like sheep without a shepherd.

"I think I've seen enough," Raric said.

He flew due south, west of the Misty Gorge. As they passed over the charred remains of a temporary army camp, Raric said nothing. Marlay started to make a comment, but Bremer punched his leg and put a finger to his lips. Joe nodded his agreement. The South Gnome Army had suffered a heavy loss in the Red Dragon's reckless, fiery attack, and too many burdens were already threatening to overwhelm General Raric. An added layer of guilt could smother him.

By late afternoon, they entered the Rainia Valley.

"Why is there a wall on the edge of that huge canyon?" Marlay asked.

"That's the South Crow Gate," Joe said. "And that canyon is new. There used to be a major thoroughfare connecting the valley with the Southlands. But after three days of intense fighting between the gnome army and the defenders of the Rainia Valley, your friend Nyrianne brought the battle to a decisive conclusion."

"Well, well," the wizard said. "Nyrianne and I certainly will have some catching up to do."

They approached the southern shores of Rainia Lake, and Raric dropped over the trees, keeping his distance from Rainia or any human settlement. He came to a quick but tolerably smooth landing. Joe and the others climbed down, grateful to be on solid ground again.

"Turn your backs," Raric said, "or you'll be blinded for life."

Even with his back turned, Joe saw the reflection of the bright-red flash in the trees. When he turned around, General Raric stood in human form stretching his arms over his head.

"Couldn't have landed any closer to the middle of nowhere?" Bremer grumbled.

"Sorry," Raric said. "The last time I entered the valley, they shot me down with those thunderclaps. You wouldn't have appreciated that kind of a landing."

Joe looked to the north, beyond Rainia Lake, to the majestic shelf of rock known as the Hillron Mountains. Nestled near the base was the faint outline of the Crow's Nest castle. The rugged beauty stood in sharp contrast to the horrors of the Maidstone, the devastation of Fairbay, and the chaotic nightmares that roamed the rest of the Fourwinds.

"So, you said we have our work cut out for us, General," Joe said. "And I agree. But where do we go from here?"

"I'm sure you all have your own affairs to attend to. But I need to find Captain Culthison and Commander Henowing. I presume they are either at the North Crow Gate or the Crow's Nest, but we might find them in Rainia. It's a long walk, but much better than showing up in a heavily guarded valley as a dragon."

"Thank you for returning us safely," Joe said. "I'd like to check on the gnomes. Their new settlement is not far from here."

Raric tapped his chin with a finger. "If you can spare the time, I could use your support in Rainia."

Joe leaned on his staff. "Of course. I also need to find Ryowyn and her mother. I'm sure they will be with their people in mourning. There will be a grand funeral planned for their king."

They followed an overgrown road that led north, struggling to stay in step with Raric, whose heavy footsteps pounded the earth.

"What about you, Bremer?" Raric asked. "What will you do now?"

"Well, this might sound crazy, but ever since you talked about all the work to be done throughout the land, I've been thinking. What would it take to get you to fly me to the Waerdreath?"

"What?" Raric exclaimed. "Of all the crazy things you've said or done, that is by far the maddest."

"You wouldn't need to stay with me, of course. And, who knows, I might even find more of the antidote. When I was there last, I spoke with an alchemist named Fadua—"

"Fadua!" Marlay exclaimed. "I trained him as a boy. I heard he went on to do great things. I should love to see him again."

"I'm afraid that won't be possible," Bremer said. "When I met him, he was locked in the dungeons beneath the castle. He was very helpful, though, so I helped…relieve his suffering."

Marlay was nodding, his bushy brows furrowed. "That is unfortunate. But I agree, rogue, the Waerdreath certainly would be a likely location for an antidote."

"There's something you're not telling us, Bremer," Raric said. "Why so eager to go back to that dreadful place?"

"When we were there, the Waerdreath captured my imagination. I don't like secrets, General, and that place is full of them. We spent most of our time wandering through passages hidden behind walls. I want to make sure there's no one lingering in the castle who might still be loyal to the Iron Dragon, unaware that he's dead. With Sidara, Uluk, *and* Natas gone, that place just needs a bit of…housecleaning, and then I'd be free to explore."

Raric chuckled. "I did not expect that answer, Bremer. The former Callum Sage, master rogue, and now duke of the Waerdreath?"

Marlay burst into laughter. "Maybe I could help in your transformation. I could be the Wizard of the Waerdreath."

Bremer drew a dagger from his belt, not bothering to stifle the menacing sound.

After all they had been though, Joe knew he would never hurt the great wizard. But he also understood that there were only a few ways to shut him up.

Marlay stopped laughing instantly and held up both hands. "Easy there, rogue. I was joking."

Raric was still chuckling. "I don't think he shares your sense of humor, Marlay. He's quite serious about the Waerdreath."

They came to a fork in the road, and Bremer stopped. Without explanation, he turned down the path that led to the west.

"Where will I find you?" Raric called after him.

Bremer turned his head slightly and kept walking. "Don't worry, General. I'll find *you*."

Joe, Marlay, and Raric watched the secretive man in black for a moment before continuing north along the old road to Rainia.

That evening, as they entered the city limits, Marlay parted ways with Joe and Raric. He explained that he hoped to find Nyrianne somewhere in the city.

"We have much to discuss," the wizard said. "About the past *and* the future."

The city of Rainia was buzzing with news of the return of General Raric. Captain Culthison and Commander Henowing had arrived earlier with a small guard from the Crow's Nest. It didn't take long for them to find the general.

"We need to find a private meeting place, Commander," Raric said.

Twell led them to the northern watchtower at the edge of the city where they all huddled into a vacant room. There were no chairs, so they all stood around a small square table.

"Has Morgan returned, Commander?" Raric asked.

"I have not seen her, sir," Twell answered, "but it's possible she went to see Rowe first."

Raric tilted his head slightly. "Any news about Rowe and Will?"

"Nothing, sir."

"If I may speak freely, sir," Culthison said, his eyes glistening, "it is good to have you back."

"Of course, you may speak freely, Captain," Raric said. "In fact, it is very important that I also speak freely with all of you." He inhaled deeply and scanned the expectant faces around him. "We've returned from the Maidstone with what we believe is a cure for Phyriad."

A collective gasp seemed to suck air from the windowless room.

Raric raised a hand to quiet the murmurs. "It will be tested on Rowe and Will, and if it is successful, we will need to increase security to protect the small amount of the antidote we have.

"How small, sir?" Culthison asked.

Raric let out a long sigh. "Apparently, we only have enough to treat about a hundred people. Captain, I want you to look after personal security for Morgan's mother, Julie. We have to protect that antidote. Whatever she needs, you will be there for her."

"Yes, sir."

"And now for a personal matter. I've been told about the damage done by these hands… I've requested name and rank of every soldier, including family members, harmed or killed by the Red Dragon." His voice cracked. "It is a small but important first step toward redemption."

"The men understand the sacrifice you made to defeat Uluk, Commander General," Culthison said. "What you transformed into was not you. We know that."

"I appreciate the sentiment," Raric said. "But not everyone will share it. For now, I need you to order the ballista operators not to fire at either the Red Dragon or the Ice Dragon. They are now your allies as we seek to restore order and peace to the Fourwinds."

"I like the sound of that, sir."

"One more thing," Raric said. "Ryodan, king of the mer…is dead."

"No," Culthison groaned, glancing at Joe. "Not after all they've been through."

Joe sighed heavily. "King Ryodan risked his life by facing the acid breath weapon of the Iron Dragon so we could live. I'm going to see the queen and princess after this meeting. It's very important that we all support them."

Twell Henowing was watching Joe as if waiting for him to

elaborate. Joe recalled the commander's resistance to him letting the gnomes into the valley and wondered if he felt the same about the mer.

"There will be a funeral for the mer king very soon," Raric said. "Let's make sure we honor him, Commander. I expect both Marauders and Enders Brigades to be well represented on that day."

Twell's jaw clenched as he held Raric's stern gaze for a moment. "Yes, sir."

Raric nodded once and concluded the meeting. "So, we have four items for immediate implementation. First, maintain security at the North Crow Gate. Second, prepare for the mer king's funeral. Third, help Julie to safeguard the antidote. And finally, make sure everyone knows that the Red Dragon and the Ice Dragon are our allies. If we are to stop the spread of Phyriad, we must allow them to move freely in and over this valley."

CHAPTER 33
A Slippery Path

After sitting on the porch for about an hour in the morning, Will had enjoyed a long nap, then returned to his chair on the porch. At his request, they were spending as much time outside the stale cabin as possible. He inhaled the warm afternoon air, and for the first time since he and Rowe arrived at the cabin, he smelled something. His sinuses were still congested, but his nostrils were miraculously clear. He breathed in the sweet aroma of flowers—he wished he knew their names—and the faint scent of hay and manure from the small stable. Even the smell of manure brought a smile to his face.

"I can't believe how clear my head is, Mom. My headache is gone, my eyes aren't burning anymore, and I can breathe."

"I can't believe your rash is gone," Julie said, scribbling notes in her binder. "I've seen medications work fast, but this is remarkable."

"I'd say we found the antidote," Alyssa said as she examined Will's arms.

Julie frowned. "Maybe. I don't understand why it was so effective on Will but Rowe is still in bed."

"Trust me," Will said. "He looks better today than he did before you showed up with those needles."

Alyssa placed a thermometer under Will's tongue.

"If your temperature is still normal, I can officially clear you to go home to your cottage on the lake," Julie said.

"Where'd you get dis?" Will asked, the thermometer wobbling between his lips.

Alyssa smiled and pushed his chin up to close his mouth.

"Well, there aren't as many medical tools here as I'd like," Julie said, "but I did bring a few essentials from home. Now, keep that mouth closed for a few minutes if you can."

Will peered through the front window at Morgan caring for Rowe. A steady flow of fresh pails of water and clean cloths had made a vast improvement on Rowe's outward appearance, but he was still coughing up too much phlegm. His skin rash remained, although Morgan was working to stop him from scratching in his sleep. His fever was everyone's biggest concern. Alyssa had frozen some water so Morgan could place small ice-wrapped towels in Rowe's armpits. But despite their efforts, the fever remained.

Julie folded her arms in front of her. "If his fever gets too high for too long, we risk irreversible brain damage."

Will shuddered to think what they would do without Rowe's encyclopedic brain.

"At least Morgan seems unaffected by being so close," Alyssa said. "Most people develop symptoms anywhere between a couple of minutes and a couple of hours."

Alyssa removed the thermometer from Will's mouth and checked the reading. "You're still looking really good, Will."

"Thanks. I doubt it's an airborne disease. Rowe and I were bitten by Phyriad-infected creatures."

"Your cases are unique," Alyssa said. "It seems as though the magic of your Trannalun cloaks has limited the effects in your bodies to severe flu-like symptoms and a nasty rash."

"From what I've read," Julie added, "and from the few cases we've heard of, this disease spreads either by entering the bloodstream or by people consuming contaminated food or water. So, it's very important that we continue to keep things clean and sterilized. You'll find a small pack of alcohol wipes to clean the thermometer, Alyssa. But I have a limited supply. We'll need to find other ways to sterilize items at the infirmary. I'll be quite busy training Gloriana and all the volunteers over the next few days. And I'll be documenting everything."

"Maybe we should think about heading back to the valley so you can get started as soon as possible," Will suggested. "And… maybe I could go with you?"

Julie shrugged. "I don't see why not. You mostly need rest and nutrition, and you can get both of those at your cottage. As long as you promise me no contact with anyone for two more days."

Will rubbed his hands together. "I can manage that. I just feel bad not being there for Ryowyn."

"I'm sure she understands," Alyssa said. "She'll be excited to see you."

"There's someone else who wants to see you," Julie said. "Someone who came with us to the Maidstone."

Will paused, watching the two women. "I remember Mom said another name, but I forgot to ask. My head was pretty fuzzy the day you left. Who is it?"

"Nyrianne," Alyssa said. "She was the strange old woman who helped defeat the gnome army at the South Crow Gate."

Will scratched his head. "Rowe told me about that. But why'd she go to the Maidstone with you?"

Alyssa glanced at Julie. "It's a long story, Will. Nyrianne was familiar with the Maidstone…and with Phyriad. You met her in a very different form…at the Waerdreath."

Will's mind raced. The only woman he met in that castle was the Elf Queen. "Cinhalla? The Elf Queen is in the valley?"

"No," Alyssa said. "Not Cinhalla but another queen. A dark queen."

Will clenched both hands into fists. "Are you telling me that Nyrianne, the old woman who saved the Rainia Valley is…Sidara?"

"*Was* Sidara. Your act of compassion and forgiveness at the Waerdreath freed her."

"Maybe so, but…now I see the extent of her evil. I experienced Phyriad firsthand. You all risked your lives. And Ryodan is dead."

Alyssa placed her hands on his shoulders. "This will be a difficult journey for you. Forgiveness is a magnificent gift, but it can be a slippery path."

Will met his mother's gaze and shrugged. "This whole adventure's been a slippery path."

⁕

There was no packing or preparation needed before leaving the cabin. After Alyssa removed the boundary collar from Will's neck, she transformed into the Ice Dragon, and they were ready to leave. Julie gave final instructions to Morgan, emphasizing precautions like keeping her mask on, avoiding touching her mouth, and not drinking from the same cup as Rowe.

"I know, Mom," Morgan said as Julie and Will climbed into the elven saddle. "Don't worry."

"We'll be back to check on you tomorrow," Julie said.

As Alyssa soared above the Epping Forest, Will noticed the gray apelike holgs waving their clubs from high atop the trees. The memory of their violent attack when Will, Morgan, and Rowe began their journey to the Waerdreath was a bit blurry because of the concussion he had suffered after falling from his horse. But the sharp fangs and bloodthirsty screams were still fresh in his mind. If not for Rowe's quick thinking and skill with the sword, Will would not be alive.

He owed his friend his life. And here he was now, leaving Rowe to suffer and struggle for survival. But he was in good hands with Morgan, and Julie promised to check in on him daily. Will shook off his guilt and concentrated on preparing to be with Ryowyn and her mother.

Alyssa banked away from the forest and dropped below the tree line where late-afternoon shadows stretched across the valley floor. "If it's okay with you, Will, I'll drop off Julie first. She needs to get the antidote into safe storage."

"No problem. I'm just happy to be out of that cabin and heading home."

The roads connecting the North Crow Gate and the city of Rainia with the Crow's Nest were still busy with supply wagons, small groups of soldiers on horseback, and a few peddlers' carts. Most people stopped to stare at the dragon overhead, but no one looked frightened.

Alyssa leveled out above a stretch of tall grass that was far enough away from any roads to avoid too much attention. She landed smoothly, and by the time about twenty soldiers on horseback appeared, she was back in her human form.

A middle-aged soldier with brown hair tied back in a short

ponytail and a thin beard tracing his rugged jawline dismounted and removed his riding gloves. He smoothed back a few stray hairs over the top of his head and bowed slightly.

"Julie Finley, it's good to see you again."

"Captain Culthison, you're looking much better than when I saw you last."

"The infirmary was in excellent hands while you were away, but we're glad…I mean, *they* will be glad to have you back."

Julie smiled, and Culthison lowered his eyes and fidgeted with his gloves.

Will looked at Julie in a new light. The captain was attracted to her, he realized. Will wasn't surprised. After all, Morgan had caught his attention when he had first met her while she was jogging down his street.

"General Raric has placed me in charge of making sure you have whatever you need to safeguard the new supplies you have."

Julie handed him one of the backpacks. "The general made a wise choice, Captain. I was concerned about what to do with these."

"We have made room in the main castle vault."

A soldier brought over a pair of horses, but Julie, Alyssa, and Will declined.

"I'm ready for a nice walk," Julie said. "And Will and Alyssa are not coming to the castle right now."

"Of course, as you wish." Culthison signaled to the soldiers, and they all dismounted.

"Is there anything else we can do for you, my lady?"

"Well, first of all, you can start by calling me Julie. But I wonder if you could send someone ahead to find the little girl Gloriana was looking after while we were away. Her name's Lillie. That little monster has me wrapped around her cute little finger."

Culthison smiled. "Actually, I just ran into Gloriana and Lillie before I left the castle. I told them I was coming to find you, and Lillie's eyes lit up."

"So, how are things at the North Crow Gate, Captain?" Will asked. "Have there been any new arrivals?"

"Johanissan led a large group of gnomes in. He said you had cleared them. Commander Henowing was reluctant, but we sorted it out. Pretty sad how few made it, but I recognized the gnome commander. I met him at the Nameless Forest with my former commander. We made a deal with them, so I couldn't refuse them entry."

"Allowing them entry must have troubled some soldiers, Captain," Will said, glancing at his mother. "Forgiveness is a difficult path. Where are the gnomes now?"

"They've settled along the southern shores of Rania Lake. The soil is rich there, and all they want to do is farm. Can't wait to see their produce."

A covered wagon rode up and stopped at the roadside. A little girl leapt out of the back. She looked at Julie and squealed with delight.

Julie caught the girl up in her arms. "Lillie!"

"Where's Morgan?" Lillie asked as Julie twirled her in the air.

"Hey! What's wrong with me, you little rascal?" Julie laughed. "Morgan is taking care of Rowe. He's a little sick, but they'll be back soon. She told me to give you some kisses for her." She buried her face in Lillie's neck, which resulted in more squeals and giggles.

"Are you staying in the castle tonight?" Lillie asked.

"I am, sweetie. With you, I hope."

Daylight was fading when Will arrived at the cottage. The journey back to the valley had sapped his limited energy, even though he'd done little walking. The antidote may have cured him of Phyriad, but he still needed to recover his strength after being down for almost a week. He thought about going straight to bed but longed to find Ryowyn first.

Sliding from the saddle, he rounded the cottage and saw two figures standing by the dock.

"Will!" Ryowyn called as she ran into his arms.

Her body shook with sobs as he held her close. Ryowyn's touch was magical in the truest sense of the word, but for Will, it meant the completion of his healing. He buried his hands in her soft, moon-kissed hair. A cool evening breeze enveloped them in pine-scented, salty air but could not come between them. Will wrapped his arms tighter around her, squeezing her so close he thought she might break. But Ryowyn returned the embrace, firm and tender and full of life-giving energy.

When at last she released her hold, Ryowyn took his face in her hands and kissed him firmly on the mouth. He enjoyed the flood of warmth that flowed from his lips to his toes in a split second.

He pulled away. "I was supposed to wait a couple days before touching anyone!"

"You're not infected, Will. I can feel it." She choked back a sob, and a fresh tear dripped from her chin onto his arm. "I'm so glad you're here."

Will glanced at Almithara, who was sitting in a simple wooden chair by the dock. She was, as ever, the picture of regality, even in sorrow.

"I wish I could have… If only I…" Will had thought about what he might say, but words now failed him.

Ryowyn took his hand and led him to her mother's side. The queen's deep-blue eyes were dry but radiated compassion and tenderness, and her voice echoed that softness as she rose to greet him.

"I am sorry I could not come to you in your time of sickness, Will Owens, as I did in Fairbay."

Will smiled as he reflected on his second visit to the Recovery Inn. He had suffered so much at the hands of bush gnomes in the Clover Fields. If not for Bremer, Will would have eventually died like an abused dog in one of the cages. And if not for the timely arrival of Thaudas, the winged unicorn, Will would have died alone on the banks of an unknown river.

"There's always someone to rescue me," he said. "I used to be too proud to admit that fact, but I keep bumping up against it."

"There are times to give and times to receive," Almithara said. "A time to live and a time to die. For us, life continues to offer fresh opportunities. But for Ryodan—" Her cheek twitched slightly. "He loved you as a son, Will."

"And I loved him as a father."

In a surprising gesture, the queen opened her arms and drew Will and Ryowyn into a long embrace.

"Our mourning rituals will soon be complete. Then we will remember the king—your father—and our new life will begin."

CHAPTER 34

SECOND CHANCES

The bedroom window offered Will an unobstructed view of a small patch of lush forest outside the peaceful cottage by the lake. Swooping branches of an expansive maple displayed large green leaves that danced in the afternoon breeze, mingling with three stately alders and a wispy pine. Will sat upright in his bed, watching small birds, squirrels, and an array of flying insects zip and scurry in random directions. Life was simple here, despite its diversity. There was no agenda to follow, no schedule to keep. And no power-hungry creature attempting to rule them all. The disorderly rhythm of everyday life continued in this small hamlet, oblivious to the turmoil that had threatened to upset the balance of life beyond the valley.

For the first time since arriving in the Fourwinds, Will sensed that some form of peace was within reach. He didn't expect a problem-free existence, but the view from his window provided a glimpse of a beautiful, if not messy, life.

Besides the beauty outside the window, Will had been enjoying the sound of Ryowyn's soft, steady breathing; the fresh scent of her flowing white hair; and the smooth curves of her teal-skinned body.

A front porch floorboard creaked, and Ryowyn stirred. Her eyes fluttered, and she raised her head from the pillow.

Will handed her a cup of water, and she sat up and drained the contents. "Let's stay in bed forever," she said.

"Someone's here." He leaned down and kissed her forehead. "I think it's Joe, and he's not alone." He pulled on a pair of soft linen pants and a thin short-sleeved shirt.

"Weren't you going to meet him later?"

"It's okay. I'll go see what's up. You rest."

Will stepped into the front room and saw Joe and Alyssa standing outside, leaning against the porch railing. As soon as Will met Joe's eyes, Joe held the door open for Alyssa.

"Well, good morning, sunshine," Joe said as he closed the door quietly behind him.

Will enjoyed a brief but firm hug. Human interaction and physical contact felt like the warmth of the sun after a long winter. "News travels faster than I thought around here."

The wrinkles on Joe's weathered face deepened as he grinned. "As soon as I heard you were well, I had to come see you." He stepped back and examined Will from head to toe. "After seeing you…what was it? Five days ago? You were so sick. But now you look like you didn't even have a minor cold."

"The antidote did wonders for me. I know it was a needle with some kind of drug in it, but I'd swear it was magic."

Joe leaned against the counter as Will poured three mugs of water. "Well, I wouldn't discount that as a possibility," he said with a wink at Alyssa.

Will lifted his mug. "Here's to the wonders of modern magic."

Joe touched his mug to Will's, and they all drank. Will lowered his cup, and the smile on Joe's face faded.

"You're not here for a social visit, are you?" Will said.

Joe straightened his back. "All the gnomes I brought to you at the cabin are now settling in the vacant lands south of the lake. I think that spot will work well for them."

Will's stomach tightened. He was a little uncomfortable knowing the gnomes were now in the Rainia Valley but thankful they were far enough away that he wouldn't need to interact with them for the moment.

"That's good," he said. "They're lucky to have found a new home."

"Technically, they're not all there right now. I brought someone with me."

"I didn't think you were alone."

"This might be hard for you, Will, but I want you to meet him."

Will set his mug down and placed both hands on the counter. He suddenly felt the need for extra support.

"I know you suffered under the hands of some cruel gnomes at the Clover Fields. But they're not all bad. Remember Ellywick?"

Will nodded. How could he forget? When he and Morgan first arrived in the Fourwinds, it was Rowe's dear friend and mentor, an old gnome named Ellywick, who had cared for them and given them a healing basil-scented concoction to ease the transition into their new reality.

"Why did you bring a gnome here? I could have gone to meet them."

"His name is Yossar. He was commander of the North Gnome Army until recently. Now he's more interested in farming. I brought him here for two reasons. The first concerns the future of the Fourwinds, and the second concerns the fate of our friend Rowe."

"Rowe? What d'you mean?"

"The gnomes had heard rumors of a cure for Phyriad months before we started looking for it. Not long ago, while Yossar's army was passing by the Hollowtangle on their way north, he commissioned a small team to enter the Maidstone and steal Phyriad. Only two of the original twelve gnomes survived that mission. But they returned to Yossar with what they thought was the cure."

"So, what did they steal?"

"Yossar showed me the box yesterday because he couldn't read the labels. What they stole was twenty-five doses that look similar to the ones Julie found. But the label description clearly says that it's actually a booster for the original antidote. If so, this could be what we need to get Rowe back on his feet."

Will rubbed his hands together. "Do you have the booster with you now?"

"When I told Yossar about you and Rowe, he offered to give all twenty-five doses to me."

That sounded too good to be true for Will. "Just like that? At what cost?"

"No cost. He didn't ask for anything. He genuinely wants to take steps toward reconciliation."

It still seemed too easy. "Okay, but why bring him here?"

"Despite how you may feel, Will, many people look to you as we navigate a new reality in the Fourwinds. Look at what your relationship with Ryowyn has done to bring human and mer together. I believe that if you were to lead the way to forgiveness, considering the suffering you endured under the gnomes at the Clover Fields, we'd be on our way to establishing a harmonious society here in the valley."

Will scratched his chin and peered out the front window to evade his mother's gaze. Why was everyone talking about forgiveness? Wasn't he the one who'd released Sidara by offering her forgiveness? And shouldn't people have to live with the consequences of their actions, even if they've been forgiven? He couldn't see the gnome leader, but knowing he was sitting outside his door caused his stomach to churn.

"Just so we're clear," Will said slowly, "you want me to forgive the commander of the gnome army. The same guy who probably ordered the Clover Fields to be built, allowing the suffering and death of so many people? The guy who commissioned, and possibly trained, a leader like Grudum, the slave camp leader who almost killed me?"

Joe stood in silence for a moment but did not look away from Will. Alyssa sipped her water.

"I dunno, Joe. Doing this makes breaking into the Waerdreath and offering forgiveness to Sidara seem like a simple walk around Lake Commando. If you have the booster, why can't we just take it to Rowe right now?"

"I've become friends with Yossar, and I hope we'll be friends for a long time. We talked about the Clover Fields and the atrocities that took place there. I told him about what I saw when his soldiers released Phyriad into the Niasa Sea. He knows about the destruction of Fairbay that resulted and how that forced the mer survivors to relocate to this lake. He is filled with deep regret and sorrow. And I believe he is sincere.

"When I told him you had suffered in the Clover Fields and that you and Ryowyn were both in Fairbay when it fell, he wanted to do something. Then he realized that they had the booster that could help your friend. That created an opportunity to meet with you personally."

"We should speak with this person, Will." Ryowyn was standing at the edge of the front room with her arms folded across her chest. She strode toward Will, her long, plain white dress flowing around her bare feet. "Have you offered our guests anything besides water? You must try this sweet bread that Gloriana gave us, Joe."

Joe accepted a slice. "Thank you, Ryowyn." He swallowed a small bite and lowered his voice. "Truth be told, I think Yossar will give us the boosters even if you refuse to meet him. And I doubt he would hold it against you. If you're angry, that's understandable. You've been through deep pain. But I think you know that forgiveness isn't something you'd do for me or for Rowe or even for the healing of the Fourwinds." He tapped a finger against Will's chest. "Forgiveness is something that begins the healing process in here."

"It's one thing to believe something in theory, son," Alyssa said. "But when we develop actual relationships with people, our beliefs are sometimes challenged. That's how we grow as individuals and as a peaceful society."

Will looked at Ryowyn, hoping she might offer some insight. "What d'you think?"

She took the plate of bread, walked to the front door, and held it open. "I think you all talk too much."

At the far end of the long porch was a tall gnome down on one knee, with his ponytailed head bent low. His prominent, slightly pointed ears were scarred and notched, likely from many battles. It was impossible to tell how much clothing he was wearing, but it was certainly more than necessary on this warm morning. At his hip was a large satchel that hung from his shoulder by a wide leather strap.

"Will and Ryowyn, this is Commander Yossar," Joe said.

The gnome looked up and ran a long-fingered hand over his

gray-streaked beard. "Commander no more, since dissolved our army is. But Yossar I am." He bowed his head again. "And at your mercy."

The gesture took Will by surprise. The last time he'd seen a gnome, Will was the one low to the ground, groveling for mercy. "Please…please stand."

Ryowyn took Yossar's hand and helped him to his feet. "You are welcome here, Yossar. To our home and to this valley." She gestured to the chairs on the dock. Everyone followed her and slowly took their seats. In the initial awkward silence, gentle waves lapped the shore. Ryowyn offered sweet bread to everyone, then set the plate down on the dock by her feet.

Will noticed that Yossar accepted a piece of bread but did not eat.

"Joe tells me that your people have settled in the south," Ryowyn said.

"Begun to turn the soil we have," Yossar said, "and seed we have, thanks to Joe."

Ryowyn leaned forward. "That's wonderful. Our council has been discussing ways to produce enough food for the growing population."

"With this soil, double the population you could, and still no problem producing enough and more. Trade with anyone we will, to earn our stay."

"But that's where you have it wrong, Yossar." Will's conflicted thoughts tumbled over each other like the waves on the shore. "You could never earn your stay, not after all that's happened. Nor could we. We've all received mercy from unexpected places. When I was on my way to the Clover Fields, a highland gnome named Panigim showed me mercy and offered me a drink of water."

Yossar stared at Will with his mouth open.

"What's wrong?" Joe asked.

"Panigim…my overseer she was, second-in-command. And a dear friend."

Will shook his head. "It must've been a different Panigim. The gnome I met was a servant."

"White hair?" Yossar asked. "And spoke often of farming and her hatred for bush gnomes?"

"Yes, but how… Why was she—"

"Humble servants our best leaders are."

"I'd like to thank her for her kindness," Will said. "Did she come here with you?"

"Killed by harvesters protecting Phyriad she was. The first of many."

Will had heard enough. He had been deeply impacted by Panigim's kindness, gruff as she was, and he was drawn to Yossar.

"This cycle of violence has to end," Will said. "What if we were the first generation to stop judging each other by our past offenses?"

Yossar removed a glove and held out his hand. Will grasped it.

With tears welling in his large eyes, Yossar squeezed Will's hand and nodded. "Bury the memories of war we will. All pain before our new life in the Rainia Valley will no longer exist for my people."

Ryowyn sniffed.

"Told me about your father's death Joe did," Yossar said to her. "Sad for you I am."

A breath caught in Will's throat. The gnome leader was not afraid to speak of death, whether of the mer king's or of Panigim's. The word was so cold and final. He still couldn't believe Ryodan was…gone…no longer with them…passed away. All those words were true, but the word *death* opened something new in Will's heart. It was a dark place, but not a lonely one.

Ryowyn lowered her head and wiped her eyes. "Thank you for sharing our sadness, Yossar."

After a moment, the gnome rose to his feet. "One more question I have. Our new settlement we would like to call Ashron, to honor the memory of those who died at Fairbay."

"I think that would be appropriate," Joe said.

Yossar removed the satchel from his shoulder. "For your friend, Rowe, this is. And whoever else needs it."

Will reached out to receive the leather bag. "I'm forever in your debt."

Yossar snatched it back. "No debts between us. Accept this you must in the spirit for which it is given."

"Sorry, that's a careless saying my people have. I meant to say… I'm forever…grateful."

Yossar nodded and gave Will the satchel. "When Phyriad first spread through our camp at the Nameless Forest, tried to use this we did. But too many were sick, and no effect did it have on the few that received it. Now we learn that useless it is without your antidote."

"This is for anyone in need," Will said. "Including your people. If anyone shows signs of the illness, please let us know. We will all work to share now."

Joe leaned forward in his chair. "This will be a difficult process. Not everyone will be so eager for peace."

"Better than not trying at all it is," Yossar said. "Not as slaves or to earn favor do we now work. But for the pleasure of being true to who we are."

"Looks like we're ready for another trip to the outpost cabin," Alyssa said. "Let's hope it's our last. Julie is at the Crow's Nest today, so we'll pick her up on the way. She will need to be part of this. Will you come with us, Ryowyn?"

"No, I must return to my mother to complete our mourning rituals."

Joe stood, leaning on his staff. "This meeting was more than I expected. You three give me hope for the future."

Around the side of the cottage, footsteps scuffed the dry ground. All heads turned to see Nyrianne shuffling toward them. No one seemed surprised to see her.

"Dear, sweet Will," Nyrianne said. "Such a kind boy you have, Alyssa."

There was very little about the old woman that reminded Will of Sidara, the Dark Queen he had faced a few weeks ago. But he knew it was her. And as she hobbled toward the dock, arms outstretched, he realized there was nothing about his response that reminded him of the fearful person he was a few months ago. But he knew it was him.

⁂

Will climbed off the Ice Dragon's back, clutching the leather satchel containing the booster. He helped Julie down, then walked toward the cabin. He wanted to get the booster to Rowe quickly, but his legs were shaky, and his feet felt heavy. A knot formed in his stomach. The cabin's location was picturesque, but Will's memory of it was tainted with Phyriad. As he and Julie neared the door, Alyssa came to his side in her human form and wrapped her arm around his waist.

Morgan met them at the door. She pulled the mask from her face, revealing cheeks that were pale and drawn. Her bloodshot, dark-rimmed eyes needed no explanation.

"Will? I didn't expect to see you back here," she said.

"You won't believe this, Morgan, but the gnome commander, Yossar, had the boosters. Turns out he never trusted Natas. They meant to steal the antidote but ended up with the boosters instead." He opened the satchel for Julie, who reached in and removed a pen injector. It was similar to the antidote injector but with a red button.

"This should help Rowe," Julie said.

Will thought she sounded hopeful and upbeat, but her words had little effect on Morgan. She hitched her shoulder, sighed, and returned to the dark cabin. Once inside, she handed Will and Julie masks and retied her own.

It took a moment for Will's eyes to adjust to the dark. He remembered how the light had made his headache worse. The closed curtains and shutters had helped.

Rowe was lying on his back, wheezing with labored breaths. Each exhale trailed off with a distinct rattle. The sights and smells brought back dreary memories for Will. But he didn't remember Rowe ever sounding so bad.

"Rowe, it's Julie. I have another injection to give you. This is a booster shot that will increase the effectiveness of the first one we gave you. It will make you better."

Morgan rolled up the sleeve of Rowe's cloak that enveloped him like a red cocoon. Julie studied the bark-like skin, searching for the softest part, then pressed the injector pen tight against his shoulder.

Rowe remained still and unresponsive.

Julie pushed the button with her thumb and waited. When she removed the injector, Morgan slipped his arm back inside the fiery cloak and pressed the garment against him. She brushed his sweaty hair to the side and followed Alyssa, Julie, and Will out to the front porch.

"You should eat something, dear," Alyssa said while unloading her backpack. "Gloriana baked you fresh bread, roasted grouse, and potatoes."

Morgan said nothing as Alyssa fixed her a plate of food. Julie wrote a few notes in her binder.

"And you need to get some rest," Will said as Morgan pulled off her mask and latex gloves. Her hair was a tangled mess.

"I'm exhausted," Morgan said. "But he gets worse at night. There are times I have to lift him off the pillow so he can draw a breath."

Will couldn't believe she was still standing. "After all you went through at the Maidstone, and then to spend all this time with Rowe… Thanks for all you've done for us," he said.

"This smells so good," Morgan said as she picked at the food on the plate. "It's been hard getting Rowe to eat anything. He's so weak."

"Tell you what," Alyssa said. "After I take your mom and Will to the valley, I'll come back and take tonight's shift with Rowe. You need to sleep."

Morgan swallowed a mouthful of potato. "Oh, Alyssa, I want to be polite and tell you I'll be fine, but I'd be lying."

"I'll be back in a few hours," Alyssa said. "I'm holding on to the hope that this will be our last night here."

CHAPTER 35

REUNION

Even if the moon and stars had not shone for the past two evenings, Morgan wouldn't have noticed. She had spent most of her time sitting with Rowe, listening to his staggered, slurry breathing, snorts, moans, and mumblings. But tonight, a few hours after receiving the booster shot, his breathing was noticeably clearer. Morgan sat with him for almost two hours, afraid that he'd stopped breathing because he was so quiet, so still. Finally, when she realized there was nothing more to do for him but let him sleep, she went outside to breathe in the fresh mountain air. Through a thin blanket of clouds, the moon and stars shone, faithful as ever.

She was just drifting off to sleep in a chair on the front porch when a sudden swooping sound interrupted the stillness. Morgan sat to attention, and a moment later, Alyssa appeared from the other side of the stable.

"You're outside," Alyssa said. "That's a good sign."

Morgan exhaled, relieved to hear a human voice again. "I hope so. He's sleeping better than I've seen so far."

"Sorry I took longer than expected. When I dropped off Will

⊰ 351 ⊱

in Ashron, Yossar—the former gnome commander—insisted on a guided tour before dark." She sat in the chair beside Morgan. "Those gnomes are already hard at work. There were dozens of leveled building sites with stacks of lumber and supplies. The fields were plowed, and gnomes were planting kale, radishes, and a few other crops whose names I didn't recognize. They should be ready for a fall harvest. Yossar said it was too late for most vegetables this year, but they're planting whatever they can. They also have plans for orchards. Considering the hardship those gnomes have suffered, there's a real sense of excitement. It's going to be quite a community."

Morgan stretched her arms in front of her as she chewed her bottom lip. She wanted to be happy for the gnomes. But whenever she thought of them, images of angry warriors shooting small arrows as they scaled the South Crow Gate flashed in her mind's eye. People told her that those were *bush* gnomes, and the remnant now living in the valley were *highland* gnomes. But she couldn't paint either group with a broad brush. She had seen enough to know that there was good and bad in every group, and in everyone.

"You're unsure about the gnomes, aren't you?" Alyssa asked.

"Sorry. I know we need to welcome everyone, but I can't stop thinking about the death toll at the South Crow Gate. Many good people died at the hands of gnomes."

"And many good gnomes have died at the hands of human soldiers."

Morgan rubbed her temples, then combed both hands through her thick, tangled hair. "I know, Alyssa. I know. But…how is Will dealing with it? He almost died in the gnome slave camp."

"He's actually planning to spend the day with them tomorrow, planting seeds—literally and symbolically. He and Ryowyn had a real connection with Yossar before we came here with the booster for Rowe. They're on the road to forgiveness and healing. It's pretty amazing what's happening."

"Forgiveness? Just like that?"

"Well, no one expects it to be a smooth road ahead. But what other choice do we have?"

Rowe's bed creaked, and he coughed lightly.

Morgan gripped the arms of the chair to get up, but Alyssa stopped her.

"Why don't you sleep out here tonight? I'll stay inside with Rowe."

Morgan sighed. "I don't think I have the energy to argue with that idea. Thank you."

✦

The next morning, Morgan awoke to see a few small birds pecking and skittering across the porch. She stretched beneath her thick blanket, and the birds cheeped and flitted away. Despite the rough sleeping conditions, she felt more rested than she had in days, or maybe even weeks.

It was still overcast, but the clouds parted for a few minutes, and the sun made a brave attempt to warm the earth. But the clouds returned, and shadows crept across the meadow until they had chased away the sunlight. A few poplar trees nearby swayed in a sudden gust as the wind shifted, and their emerald leaves faded to sage green in the muted light. A minute later, a few raindrops pattered on the porch roof.

In what looked to be the beginning of a dreary day, hope shone somewhere deep inside Morgan's heart. The winds of change were blowing. It wouldn't be all sunshine ahead, or smooth roads, as

Alyssa had said last night. But there was something different about today, a change as subtle as turning a corner, or coming up for air after being underwater, or seeing tints of red, orange, and yellow in a tree that was all green yesterday.

Alyssa rounded the stable carrying two pails of water. Her face was raised to the sky, and her mouth was open as if she were trying to catch as many of the scattered raindrops as possible. She was in no hurry whatsoever.

Morgan sat upright, wondering how long Rowe had been left alone inside.

"Good morning," Alyssa said. "Refreshing, isn't it?"

Morgan clambered to her feet. "What's happened?" Fear rose up to challenge the hope that had awakened her. She burst through the cabin door, unsure of what to expect.

Alyssa followed. "Wait, Morgan. He's—"

Rowe was sitting upright in his bed, reading a book and sipping from a steaming mug. A broad smile illuminated his face like sunrise on a weathered mountainside, sparkling in his clear sky-blue eyes.

He coughed lightly. "There's the face that's been brightening my dark dreams. I hope you finally got some sleep last night." His voice was weak and croaky, but at least he was speaking in complete sentences.

Morgan put a fresh surgical mask on and strode across the room to Rowe's bed. "You look so… Your rash, it's…" She spun around to see Alyssa grinning and nodding her head. "I can't believe the difference from yesterday."

The miraculous healing that Will experienced was already evident in Rowe. The congestion in his nose had cleared, his cough was less productive, and the rash on his skin had already started to recede. He licked his lips and offered a weak but unforced smile.

"Thank you for all you did for me," he said. "Especially after what you've been through. Alyssa told me a bit of your story, and I can't wait to hear more."

Morgan wanted to hug him, but she was still cautious and unsure if he were contagious.

Alyssa set the pails down near the cookstove. "It is remarkable how he's responded to the booster. Now we just need to get his strength back. I made some soup from the leftover food that Gloriana supplied."

Rowe set his book on his lap. "That sounds great. I feel like I could eat all day."

Alyssa flashed a smile and came to the bedside. "I need to get back to the Crow's Nest now. You two should have everything you need until I return tomorrow. One more day's rest—and a bit of exercise if you're up to it—and we'll all be back together."

"Thank you, Alyssa," Rowe said, "for everything."

Alyssa gave Rowe's shoulder a squeeze and offered Morgan a tender hug before leaving. She paused at the front door. "Oh, and, Morgan, I don't think you'll need your surgical mask or gloves anymore."

Morgan walked outside with Alyssa to see her off. She stood alone on the front porch for a moment, watching the shape of the Ice Dragon disappear through the gray clouds. Thunder rolled over the mountains, and a steady rain sent her back inside.

"Looks like a great day to stay indoors," Morgan said, adding a few sticks to the cookstove.

She looked up to see Rowe watching her. Her fear that he might not survive another day had fled, and hope swelled in her heart. After a moment, she swallowed, realizing her open mouth was dry.

Rowe moved his book to the side table. "Looks like you have something to say."

Morgan brushed some dirt from her hands and sighed. "I have a lot of things to say. And I hope I finally have time to say them."

Rowe coughed and gestured to the chair beside his bed. "I want to hear all about your trip to the Maidstone."

Morgan stirred the small pot of soup on the cookstove as she began to tell him all about the exciting adventure, beginning with the Red Dragon's attack on Rainia and the subsequent journey the four women had riding on the Ice Dragon. She spared few details.

"When we reached the Maidstone," she continued, "the fun was over."

Now it was Rowe who sat in silence with his mouth open. "Sounds much better than our flight from the Waerdreath."

Morgan nodded. "But the Maidstone was worse than Sidara's castle."

The soup was starting to bubble, so Morgan poured out two bowls and brought one to Rowe. She pulled the chair that was next to his bed back a few inches. Although she had removed the mask and gloves, Morgan was still reluctant to get too close to Rowe. She sat down with her bowl and continued her story.

As Rowe devoured his soup, she told him about the journey down nineteen stories and the encounters with dracar, harvesters, and human prisoners. When she came to the part where they found the antidote, she paused.

"There's so much about that place that reminded me of my old life. If it weren't for the creatures, I would have thought we'd slipped through the Gateway into my old world. The construction of the rooms, the lights and technology… Does that make any sense to you?"

Rowe's spoon hovered over his bowl. He had a blank look on his face. "Not really, but I can't say it surprises me." His eyes narrowed as he leaned forward. "Did the Maidstone stir a longing in you to return to your old world?"

Morgan held up a hand. "Oh no. Quite the opposite, in fact. More than ever, I know now that this is my home." She gazed into her bowl, moving her spoon absentmindedly between the medley of vegetable chunks. "When we found the antidote, it really hit me what we were doing, and what we were risking."

Rowe set his empty bowl on top of his book on the small table. He sat up straighter and said nothing, nodding slowly as he waited for her to speak.

She took a sip of broth and continued. "I had a teacher once who told me that real living begins when you discover something that you'd be willing to die for. Before I came to the Fourwinds, I thought I'd figured that out. I had my fencing achievements, my career plans, and a supportive family. But inside the Maidstone, all that faded away. There were so many times we could have died down there."

Rowe coughed lightly into his elbow. "What did you discover that made you want to live?"

Morgan held his gaze for a moment. He seemed genuinely interested, not only for her sake but also for himself, as if he were searching for a reason to rise from his sickbed.

She nested her half-empty bowl inside his and collected the spoons. "Hearing Ryowyn talk about Will made me realize why we were there. I don't want to sound all heroic, but if we didn't get out alive and bring you the antidote…" She trailed off.

"Then we wouldn't be having this conversation," he said quietly.

"Yes, but…" Morgan sighed and pursed her lips. *Why is it so hard to just say what I feel?* she thought.

Rowe stretched his arms and yawned.

"You need to rest," Morgan said, somewhat relieved to have more time to collect her thoughts. "We can talk more later."

Rowe lowered himself beneath the blanket. "Sorry, Morgan. I really want to hear more, but I think I need to sleep." He yawned again and pressed his cheek against the pillow. "So good to see you," he mumbled as he slipped into a peaceful sleep.

The rain continued for the rest of the morning, thrumming gently on the tin roof before spilling over clogged gutters and splashing into puddles around the cabin. Inside was warm and cozy, even with the front window slightly open to flush away the stale, sick air. Morgan cleaned up their dishes, then sat quietly with her thoughts as Rowe slept. She nodded off once or twice, but even the slightest snore or movement from Rowe kept her from a satisfying sleep.

When he awoke late in the afternoon, Rowe appeared significantly stronger and more alert. He rose from his bed, cautiously at first, but was soon moving about the cabin, stoking the fire, and helping to chop carrots, potatoes, and onions for another batch of soup.

After their early-evening meal, the rain tapered off. Rowe wiped his bowl clean with a chunk of Gloriana's crusty bread and brushed a few crumbs from his light beard. He stood up and stretched, and his chapped lips cracked as a contented smile touched his rosy cheeks.

"How about a walk?" he suggested.

Morgan studied his face and glanced at his legs to see if they were wobbly. His body seemed quite strong, and his steady gaze was determined.

"Well, Alyssa mentioned exercise," she said reluctantly. "I think it's a bit too soon for a long hike, but a short walk might be okay."

They wrapped themselves in their Trannalun cloaks and ventured beyond the small stable to a wide path that led into the forest. The rain had stopped falling but continued to drip from the saturated branches. Morgan inhaled the fresh smell of mountain pines. Rowe ventured a deep breath too and did so without a single cough. He reached out a hand, but she hesitated.

"I think it's fine, Morgan. Even if there is a trace of Phyriad in me, it won't spread by holding hands. Apart from still being a bit weak, I feel as normal as I did before I went to Acttun."

Morgan nodded and took his hand as they walked down the path. "Remember the last thing we talked about before you left for Acttun?"

Rowe's brows knit together, and he scratched his chin. "I think you were worried about my safety. But I also remember you saying I was…distant…and preoccupied."

Morgan felt her cheeks warm. "I *was* worried, you know, but I know that going to Acttun was for the best." She glanced at him. "I can't imagine what we would've done without those thunderclaps."

He squeezed her hand lightly. "Let's not go there. What matters is that they worked, and we're here now. But about those things you said to me—"

She released his hand and squared to face him. "You're strong, Rowe. Probably the strongest man I've ever met. It's one of the things I love about you."

"I could say the same about you."

She sniffed. "But it's that kind of go-it-alone ambition we

share that also limits us. We're both strong, but where would we be without the others…and without each other?"

Rowe held her gaze for a moment. There was a longing in his eyes that reflected her own. "Lost," he breathed.

He took her hand again, and they continued walking. A few lower branches encroached on the trail as it narrowed. Morgan pressed close to Rowe and pulled her hood over her head to avoid the water dripping from the trees. His body was warm and firm despite his words about feeling weak. He reached up and shook a branch above them, causing Morgan to run off ahead to keep from getting wet.

She turned and glared, but his boyish grin made her smile. "That wasn't very nice!"

He shrugged his shoulders, failing to erase the grin. "Just demonstrating the waterproof quality of Trannalun cloaks."

They were in a small clearing, and Morgan walked backward, wagging her finger at him as he strolled toward her. She bumped into a large, mossy boulder, and her back pressed against it. Rowe stepped close and gently pushed back her hood. His hands smoothed her hair and settled at the back of her head.

"Well, okay," she said with a smile as she looked into his eyes. "I guess I forgive you."

His thumping chest rose and fell a few times before he looked up to the dusky sky. She licked her lips and swallowed, wondering if it was safe to kiss him.

"It's getting dark," he said, moving away from her. "We should head back."

Morgan bit her bottom lip and walked beside him in silence back the way they had come.

"Wait," she said, stopping suddenly. "There's something I didn't finish saying this morning."

Rowe stopped and folded his hands in front of him.

She took a deep breath. "I had lots of time to think as I watched you recover, Rowe."

"And what did you think about?"

"When you got infected and ended up here, and Alyssa told us about a possible antidote in the Maidstone, I knew I had to go. Nothing could stop me. I thought I was just being headstrong, but yesterday I realized there's more to it than stubbornness. I'm a fighter, Rowe. I've always fought for my own goals, to win at any cost to be successful."

Rowe reached out and squeezed her hand. "And I love the fighter in you."

She wrapped both hands around his. "It wasn't until Ryodan died that I realized how close I came to losing Mom in the Maidstone. Or any of the others. We took a huge risk. Part of me assumed that we'd fly to the Maidstone, find the antidote, get back here, and everything would be fine. But as I watched you these past few days, I realized how close I came to losing you too. Life seems so fragile now."

A rain cloud darkened the sky, and a few large drops fell. Morgan brushed one from her cheek and continued.

"Now that Natas is dead, and you're better, I'm wondering what *normal* life will look like for us."

Rowe huffed. "I'm not sure I can promise anyone a normal life. Or if I even know what that is." His head bowed. "You didn't lose me, Morgan. But I admit I was slipping away, even before Acttun. I'm sorry. After we survived the battle at the South Crow Gate, I was so afraid of losing you too."

She cupped his cheek until he met her eyes again. "We'll get through this. It won't be easy, and there will be more than just physical scars that need healing. Whatever lies ahead, and for however long we have, I want to be with you through it all, wherever the path leads."

His shoulders relaxed, and she took a step closer until she was inches from his face. Before she could say or do anything else, thunder rolled, and the clouds released another downpour.

Rowe tugged her hand, and they laughed together as they ran, dodging puddles all the way back to the cabin.

Inside, Morgan set two chairs in front of the cookstove and draped their cloaks over the chair backs. Rowe added a few split birch logs and left the firebox door open. Small flames crackled and licked the dry wood.

Rowe poured two glasses of mead and sat next to Morgan. "Do you remember the night we met?"

She laughed. "It wasn't *that* long ago."

Rowe swirled the golden liquid in his glass. "It wasn't, but I sometimes forget what life was like before you arrived."

She raised her glass. "Elven mead wasn't part of my life before I came here, but it helped my healing and transition that first night."

"And here we are again, sharing elven mead. But now I'm the one healing and moving into a new chapter of life." He took a sip. "We exchanged our favorite memories that night. I got a glimpse into your life."

"And now we have *shared* memories."

He sighed heavily. "I just wish there weren't so many dark ones."

She took his hand and traced the lines in his palm with her fingertip, then pressed her hand over his rough callouses as their fingers interlocked. His presence soothed her like the warmth of the fire.

A log popped and collapsed in the glowing embers. Morgan sipped her mead as she watched the mesmerizing flames.

"I'm gonna keep fighting, Rowe. But now I'm not just fighting for me. I'm fighting for a better life for everyone in the valley, for my friends, my family, and…for us."

He set his glass down on the floor and turned to face her. His eyes were so big and expectant, as though her every word were the most important thing in the world to him. His cheeks, framed by a scraggly beard and messy hair, were rosy and full.

"I've been on my own for a long time, Morgan. I've made countless decisions and fought many battles. I always assumed that my lot in life would be one of lonely service. But when I met you, something changed. I wanted to be with you, to open myself up to you." He snorted softly and shook his head. "You say I'm strong, but you've also seen my weaknesses. I'm not good at letting others get too close, but knowing that you plan to stay, I'm willing to work on it."

Morgan studied his face: the stern lines on his forehead, his dazzling but sad blue eyes, his clenched jaw, and small dimples barely visible beneath his beard. Despite her familiarity with these features, there was still so much about him that she didn't know—and maybe some things she didn't *want* to know. But after all they'd been through, she was willing to take the risk.

He inhaled and his mouth opened slightly, but before he could say anything else, she pressed her lips against his. His skin smelled smoky but invitingly familiar, like coming home. After a moment, she drew back and gazed into his eyes, then kissed his forehead.

Rowe stood and moved his chair closer so they were side by side.

He sat down again, rested his head on her shoulder, and kissed her neck. His breath was hot, his lips dry, and his beard scratched her skin, but she didn't care. The path ahead might be rough, but they would walk it together.

After a few minutes, Rowe's breathing became heavy and deep. He would sleep much better in bed, she knew, but for now, Morgan nestled her cheek against the top of his head and watched the flames slowly fade to a steady glow.

CHAPTER 36
FAREWELL

The next afternoon, Morgan and Rowe stood hand in hand on the southern shore of Rainia Lake, huddled together with a crowd of both new and familiar faces. The rain had stopped during the night, but the clouds had lingered all morning as if they weren't quite finished with what they'd started.

Morgan had visited many strange sites in the Fourwinds and encountered races she'd never imagined, but never had she seen such a diverse group gathered in one place. They all came together for one purpose. The death of Ryodan Ayoust was a significant loss for the mer, but it also represented the tremendous loss shared by everyone gathered this day. While they honored the life of Ryodan and his sacrifice, they also remembered all who had fought for another day of freedom.

Bremer and his mother, Brynlee, were at Rowe's side. The rogue was clean-shaven, and his black leather coat was fully buttoned. If she didn't know Bremer, Morgan would have mistaken him for a prominent shopkeeper in town.

Julie stood at Morgan's other side, with Lillie between them.

The little orphaned girl clutched their hands and beamed up at them. In truth, since the day Morgan had taken her in from the streets, Lillie was anything but an orphan. She was now a cherished member of their family.

Commander Twell Henowing and a large contingent of Marauders Brigade gathered nearby, looking sharp and attentive in their blue-and-gold uniforms. Captain Culthison stood with a smaller group of Enders Brigade, each soldier wearing fully buttoned brown vests marked with a wolf's paw insignia. More soldiers would have joined them, but recovery had not come so easily for everyone.

Morgan shifted slightly, turning from side to side to take in the full gamut of the gathering. Directly behind Rowe, with a large hand on his shoulder, was Dench and about twenty other half-orcs. Farther back, sitting in a large field, their long, scaly necks stretched high and proud, were the Ice Dragon and the Red Dragon. Although Raric had been reluctant, Alyssa insisted that the valley residents needed to get used to the fact that dragons were part of this new community.

Despite Alyssa's desire for integration, most people were understandably uncomfortable. So far, only those involved in the journey to the Maidstone and back could recognize the true value of these two dragons. Which is why an odd-looking couple—the wizard Marlay and his long-lost student, Nyrianne, who for the moment seemed quite lucid—chose to sit next to the dragons.

Farther up on the hillside was a large gathering of gnomes. While there were representatives from the human and half-orc communities, it looked as though every gnome that had come to the valley were gathered there. Disregarding the pain that daylight caused them, the gnomes had all arrived in their finest clothing to offer their respects.

Joe stood beside Yossar, his white hair tied in a ponytail, and his staff held straight and proud. If Morgan knew the old Callum Sage at all, he was with Yossar out of pure friendship rather than a public display of solidarity.

The entire mer community was present. The lake rippled with dozens of them, floating in stationary positions with only their heads and shoulders above water. Standing on the shore and facing the silent crowd was a small company of mer soldiers dressed in polished orange coral armor. Their long tridents gleamed, even in the dreary gray afternoon.

Will and Ryowyn stood beside the stalwart mer queen, Almithara, who was about to address those who had come to show their respects and bid a final farewell to Ryodan Ayoust, king of the mer.

A closed casket made of tightly woven reeds bobbed in the shallows behind Almithara.

"Life is full of many wondrous events," the queen began, her voice surprisingly strong and confident. "But perhaps the two most wondrous of all are the day we enter this life and the day we leave it. The king's life was full of wonder. Through joys and sorrows, victories and defeats, days of abundance and days of hardship"—she swallowed hard—"Ryodan Ayoust lived fully every day. He loved deeply, though many thought him hard and overbearing. Such is the way of kings to those who see from a distance. But those who knew him best saw his generous, fiercely loyal heart.

"There are many tales I could tell of how Ryodan selflessly defended his people. Bards like to exaggerate them, but many are true. Most of you know the story that led us to this lake. In the violent attack on the Niasa Sea, our home for over twelve generations, the king fought bravely until there was nothing left to do but flee for our lives.

"At the Maidstone, Ryodan fought for something larger than himself, something larger than the merpeople, even larger than the Fourwinds. There, Ryodan fought alongside humans and dragons to defeat a powerful enemy so that goodness and freedom could live. In doing so, the king sacrificed his life. And because of that sacrifice, and the bravery of some who stand among us, we gather together today.

"We gather with sadness in our hearts, but we are not without hope. For Ryodan's death represents the sacrifice and loss of many others. They were our friends, our loved ones. Their sacrifice is a gift to us all. And it is a gift to future generations who will be able to live in a peaceful world. From what I see today, it will be a diverse and potentially harmonious world. But peace never comes without effort, and rarely without sacrifice.

"And so, we say farewell to Ryodan Ayoust, son of Ryothun Ayoust, protector of all that lives and moves beneath the waves, defender of the waters, and king of the mer. As we honor him, we also remember those close to your own hearts. We commit Ryodan's body to the waters below and to the waters above, knowing that his spirit will be carried away to mingle with those who have gone before him. The waters fall and return to the sky in an endless cycle that nurtures and sustains life."

The queen raised her hands over the lake, and a small whirlpool formed around the floating casket. The water twisted and churned and slowly rose, lifting the casket in a thick column. The mer in the lake moved their arms in unison, sending waves that fed the column, pushing the casket higher and higher. Within seconds, the column was a mighty geyser that shot up into the low-lying clouds. The water column stopped flowing, and a moment later, the casket dropped from the sky and splashed into the lake. It floated on the surface, open and empty.

No one on the shore spoke or dared to move.

Without a crack of thunder to warn those gathered in and around the lake, the clouds released a gentle rain. Moments later, Morgan's saturated hair clung to her head. Droplets trickled down her face to soak her clothing. Even so, she stood still, basking in the collective silence and stillness of mer, gnome, dragon, half-orc, and human.

A single sound broke the silence. Still clutching Morgan's hand, Lillie started giggling. She tugged her arm, and Morgan looked down.

"We're all taking a baff," the little girl said. "Now everyone will be clean."

EPILOGUE

Long after dark, Will and Ryowyn walked the main street of Rainia and entered the new Recovery Ale House and Inn. The eatery was filled to capacity and humming with conversation mingled with bursts of laughter and clinking glasses. Although the couple was becoming well-known throughout the valley, the presence of a red-cloaked Callum Sage holding the hand of a teal-skinned mermaid still captured the attention of many long-term residents. A few patrons seated at tables curled their lips and turned away. Those reactions didn't surprise Will. He was no stranger to sneers and whispers behind his back from his dark days in Cochrane.

Despite the few negative reactions, the young couple made their way across the room without incident, and the majority of patrons offered smiles and friendly waves. Some stopped them with kind words, firm handshakes, and unwavering eye contact.

Only three days had passed since the races gathered as one people for Ryodan's funeral, and already the signs were pointing to a more harmonious future. Will expected no miracles, but the camaraderie evident in this room filled him with hope.

Jessman was standing at the bar, and when he saw Will, he waved and joined them. "Will, lad, good to see ya. And wee Ryowyn, yer always welcome here. How are ya both?"

"Fine, thanks, Jessman." Will shook the big man's hand. "Business looks good."

"Yes, but still lots of work to do. Hansla picked a good location, although I've no idea how he knew this would become the main road through the city."

Will chuckled. "I think your success has more to do with Hansla's cooking, Homas's fine brew, and your warm hospitality."

Jessman laughed heartily and slapped Will's shoulder. "Ain't that the truth, lad?" His smile dissolved, and he leaned close to Will. "Still have'na seen any gnomes in here yet, though. Not sayin' I'm opposed to it, mind ya. Just don't know how it'll affect business."

"One step at a time, Jessman," Ryowyn said. "And we'll take them together."

Jessman beamed. "Ah, bless me, yer as wise as yer father was, Ryowyn. But how'd ya end up with this lad?"

"I keep asking myself the same question," Will said, scanning the room. "I'm looking for Rowe. He said he'd be—"

"They're all in the back room. Rowe said he needed a quiet space for meetin', and I think the noise gives him a headache."

Jessman led them past the busy kitchen. Hansla was flipping something in a sizzling frying pan with one hand while he stirred a large pot with the other. He nodded at Will and Ryowyn. Homas was there too, but he was busy scolding a barmaid. Jessman continued down the narrow hallway to a closed door. He knocked twice and clicked the latch open.

Seated around an oval-shaped table in the middle of the small room were Rowe, Morgan, Julie, and Joe. The table was cleared except for a single lantern that illuminated the four expectant faces. Their shadows danced on the empty walls.

"Sorry we're late," Ryowyn said.

Morgan gestured to the only two unoccupied chairs. "You're not. Homas just brought us drinks."

Will and Ryowyn sat and scooted their chairs up to the table.

"What's in the bottle?" Will asked. He could tell by the somber mood in the room that a drink might help make the meeting go easier.

Jessman poured a glass for Will. "Homas has been workin' on this all week. He calls it *Barrage*. It's made from his dark whiskey and a carefully guarded secret ingredient." He offered a glass to Ryowyn, but she declined.

Will sipped from his glass, savored the warm liquid in his mouth for a moment, and swallowed. "My compliments to Homas once again."

"I'll pass that along, lad." Jessman started closing the door behind him. "Let me know if ya need anythin' else."

When the door closed, Rowe raised a large mug. "I thought you might like *Barrage*."

Will touched his glass to Rowe's. "You're not having any?"

"Nothing fancy for me. I prefer my dark ale."

Morgan leaned forward with her elbows on the table, hands folded in front of her. "Well, I wish this was just a social gathering, but we've got pressing matters to discuss. Thank you all for coming on short notice."

Will had rarely seen her in business mode. It was usually Rowe who took charge. But he was sitting back in his chair, nursing his ale, his eyes fixed on Morgan.

"We spotted a few more infected people roaming the Epping

Forest today. Not sure if they were humans or gnomes. They were unarmed, unorganized, and they kept their distance from the North Crow Gate. But Twell has expressed concern."

"Did the soldiers shoot at them?" Joe asked.

"No, but they were ready."

"Why shoot them?" Julie asked. "I mean, if they pose no risk to the wall?"

"Well, a handful is one thing," Will said. "But what happens when a few turns into a few hundred or, given enough time, perhaps a few *thousand*?"

"It would take a huge, organized army to breach the North Crow Gate," Morgan said. "My concern is what happens if *one* infected person finds a way in. Are we prepared for an outbreak here?"

Will's chair creaked as he shifted uncomfortably.

Julie placed an auto-injector on the table. It was identical to the one she'd given to Will and Rowe.

"What's this?" Joe asked.

Julie leaned forward and tapped the device with a finger. "We have a limited supply of this antidote. We know it's successful; Will and Rowe can vouch for that. But Phyriad spreads quickly. If there's an outbreak, we'll run out of these in no time."

"But we can't go back for more," Ryowyn said.

"No, we can't. But I'd like to work with Marlay to see if we can replicate the formula and create an antidote that we can administer orally. These needles are single use only. By combining my knowledge of science with Marlay's knowledge of…"

"Alchemy," Rowe said in a quiet voice.

"Yes, alchemy. I think we'll be able to do it, but it will take time and experiments."

"But what about people who have been infected for a long time?" Ryowyn asked. "The antidote won't work on them."

Julie's head dipped as she nodded. "I'm afraid the best we can do is protect those who are not infected. We don't have the skill or equipment to create a drug to reverse the effects."

"Unless Marlay could conjure something," Joe suggested.

Julie winced and shrugged her shoulders. "It's a long shot. Even so, I'm not giving up hope. I've seen some wild things here that have blown away my ideas of what's possible."

Morgan sighed. "We have another problem." She turned to Rowe.

"The Crow's Nest is vulnerable," he said, circling the rim of his mug with a finger.

Joe sat back in his chair, and Will thought of the word before Joe said it: "The Gateway."

"That's right," Morgan said. "Before the South Crow Gate battle, when Mom and I were in the Records of Time, we watched two harvesters carry a small bag into the Gateway. If they were carrying Phyriad—"

"I have no doubt they were," Rowe interjected.

"—then who knows what's happened on the other side."

Will shifted in his chair again. "And if they plan on returning… they could come back guns a' blazing."

"It might be worse than two harvesters," Morgan added. "When we were in the Maidstone, we found a few remaining jars of Phyriad marked for locations throughout our world. There were empty shelves and tire tracks that led us to believe the harvesters had already delivered multiple shipments of Phyriad long before we got there. It might be more widespread in our world than it is here. We think Raric burned the cauldrons that powered the passageway we saw deep in the Maidstone, but we can't risk an attack from the Gateway in the Records of Time."

"Can we destroy the Gateway?" Will asked. It seemed strange to hear himself closing off the possibility of returning to Cochrane. But everyone and everything he wanted or needed was here now.

"It doesn't sound like we have a choice," Julie said.

Rowe pushed his mug away and looked at the faces around him. "You *do* have a choice. With the exception of me and Ryowyn—and perhaps Johanissan—you all have a life back there."

"You mean *had* a life back there," Will said.

"We don't have to destroy the Gateway," Rowe continued. "There is a way to seal it off. It will not be permanent, but it will be difficult to break. You will be choosing a new life here in the valley and entrusting the fate of your old world to others."

"So, what do you need from us?" Morgan asked.

Rowe pushed his chair back and stood. "I need two Callum Sages to pass through the Gateway with me to seal it off from the other side first. Then we'll return, and I'll seal the Gateway from this side."

"I'm in agreement," Joe said. "But as a retired Callum Sage, I cannot go back. And I have work to do with my new friends in Ashron."

Julie removed the antidote auto-injector from the table and tucked it away in her pack. "I don't understand what all that means, Rowe, but I trust you."

Will studied the determined look on Morgan's face. She sat on the edge of her seat with her lips pursed and her back straight as if she were ready to leave immediately.

"I guess that leaves you and me," Will said to her. "When do we leave?"

Shortly after dawn the next morning, the three red-cloaked Callum Sages stood outside the cabin surveying the quiet Arden Forest. Rowe held his sword low at his side, panting heavily. The sword of Avarthrill was raised in front of Morgan, who appeared unaffected by the passage through the Gateway. Will holstered his 1911 handgun and bent over, trying to stop the spinning sensation in his head.

"When we get back," he said, "remind me to ask Dench for more sword-fighting lessons. These bullets won't last forever."

"I hope you never need another weapon," Rowe said. "Shades! I hope none of us ever have to use our weapons again. But I cannot imagine such a world."

Will snorted. "I don't think it exists."

Morgan was pacing around the clearing. "No sign of harvesters. Or anyone. What do we need to do, Rowe?"

"Well, as Alyssa told us, full cauldrons are needed for harvesters to get through. Let's empty these four and hide three of them deep in the forest, as far apart from each other as we can get them. After that, we'll have plenty of time to return before the Gateway will be sealed from this side. We need to take one cauldron back with us. As long as it stays empty in the Records of Time, the Gateway will be inaccessible from either side."

"I don't like the sound of that," Will said, remembering the splash of blood and gore when he'd previously overturned a cauldron. "What happens if the single cauldron we take back to the Fourwinds doesn't *stay* empty?"

"Then someone will have a brief window of time to pass through again into this forest."

Morgan leaned against a small tree. "And if they find the three cauldrons here?"

"I think you know the answer to that," Rowe said.

"Can't we destroy the cauldrons?" Will asked.

Rowe shook his head. "They have been forged with powerful magic. I have not heard or read of anything capable of destroying them."

Morgan sheathed her sword and faced Will. "Looks like you finally get to finish what you started the first time we were here."

Will thought back to when they had discovered the cabin and Joe had instructed them to empty the cauldrons that hung from each of the four corners. Will only had time to empty one before a harvester forced him and Morgan back into the cabin where they were separated from Joe and fell through the Gateway to the Fourwinds.

"You say that like I've been longing for the opportunity."

Morgan wasn't smiling. "What do you mean by 'plenty of time,' Rowe? How long will we have to get back?"

"I cannot say for certain, but I'd estimate about three hours."

"Sounds good," Will said as he approached a cauldron, rubbing his hands together. "This shouldn't take long. From my experience, I suggest we remove them slowly from the hooks, then empty them close to the ground. Unless you want the vile contents splashed all over your nice clean cloaks."

With no harvesters to threaten them this time, they emptied the cauldrons within a few minutes. Rowe set one by the cabin door, and then each of them took one of the others and split up, walking in different directions until they could no longer see each other.

"That's far enough," Rowe shouted. "If you can bury your cauldron, do it. If not, try to cover it with leaves and brush."

"Don't call it *my* cauldron," Morgan shouted back. "I'm happy to bury it."

Several minutes later, they met back at the cabin. Will found himself breathing heavily even though he hadn't done that much work. He wiped his sleeve across his forehead. The lingering effects of Phyriad in his system had disappeared a few days ago, so he knew it wasn't that. Either his nerves were rattled from dealing with the cauldrons or his lungs had adapted to the cleaner air of the Fourwinds.

"Not one of my favorite things to do before breakfast," he said, burying his nose in his elbow.

"But it's done," Morgan said. "Let's get outta here."

As they approached the cabin door, there was a loud snap in the forest. They all spun around and drew their weapons.

"I thought you said there was nothing out there," Will hissed.

"I didn't see anything," Morgan said. "Maybe it was a raccoon or a deer."

Will pointed his gun in the direction of the sound. "Who's there? Show yourself, or I'll shoot."

The forest was silent.

Will took a few steps forward, crunching twigs and dry leaves underfoot.

A small human body appeared from behind a large maple tree, hands held high.

Will turned to Morgan and Rowe. "It's a boy."

When Will looked back, the boy was dashing through the forest in the opposite direction.

"Wait!" Will shouted as he ran after him.

"We have to get back," Rowe called. "We don't have time for this!"

The boy zigzagged through the woods. Just when Will thought he might lose sight of him, the boy tripped on an exposed root and went down. Will caught up, holstered his gun, and raised his empty hands. "It's okay, I won't hurt you."

Morgan and Rowe caught up, and the boy's eyes bulged when he saw their swords. They quickly sheathed them and followed Will's lead, holding up their hands.

The boy was probably not more than eight years old. His dark hair was wild, and it looked like he hadn't had a bath or change of clothes for days.

"I know you," Morgan said. "You live on my street. Ethan, isn't it?"

The boy nodded.

"What are you doing out here, Ethan?" Will asked. "Where's your family?"

Large tears welled in Ethan's eyes. Morgan bent down to his level. "We're not gonna hurt you. We want to help. Are you alone?"

Ethan stared at Morgan and slowly shook his head. "Only five left."

"Five what?" Will said. "People?"

Ethan rose to his feet. "Follow me."

It took them about an hour to follow the pathway to the trailhead. Ethan then led them down the Arden Road to a lumberyard, which appeared to be unoccupied. Behind a tall stack of two-by-twelves was a small shed.

Ethan tapped the door three times. "It's me," he said.

A woman opened the door and gasped when she saw the boy with three strangers.

"I found them, Mom."

Behind the woman, a young man appeared, gaping at Will.

"Todd?" Will said.

The young man pushed past the woman and threw his arms around Will. "Sorry, Aunt Sarah," Todd said to the woman. "Will, I'm sorry I ever doubted you, buddy."

Will folded his arms loosely around his childhood friend. Not only was he shocked to see Todd here, he couldn't believe the warm smile and watery eyes. The last time he had seen Todd was about three years ago when Will told him he had been seeing strange creatures walking out of the Arden Forest. Todd had laughed it off as a joke at first. But when Will insisted, Todd became angry and then embarrassed by his friendship with Will. They quickly drifted apart.

"Bring them inside," a man's voice called.

Todd grabbed Will's cloak and pulled him into the shed. Morgan and Rowe followed.

"Morgan Finley!" The man who had invited them in was leaning against a post. He had a sling around his shoulder holding his right arm tight against his chest.

Morgan gasped and ran to him. "Coach!" She hugged him briefly as another woman emerged from the shadows. Both of them had the same bedraggled appearance as Ethan.

Morgan turned to Rowe. "This is the man who taught me most about swordplay, and this is his wife, Mrs. DeFinney."

"Swordplay?" Coach said. "Since when did you start calling fencing *swordplay*?"

Rowe shook Coach's hand. "I am honored to meet you, sir. And you too, Lady DeFinney."

"Please," Coach's wife said, blushing. "Call me Laura."

Coach gaped at Rowe, glanced at the swords on his and Morgan's hips, then raised his eyebrows at Morgan. "Where have you been?"

"It's a long story," Morgan said as she hugged Laura.

Will spun around, his mind reeling. "Why are you all here? What's happened?"

"We were all at the lake about a month ago and saw you three fighting those strange creatures," Todd explained. "I knew then that I'd been wrong about you, Will. When you first told me about your visions a few years ago, I should have stuck with you, even if I didn't understand it all." He wiped the back of his hand across his nose. "I'm so sorry for treating you the way I did. Coach was the only one I'd told about your visions, so I knew I could trust him not to think I was crazy."

"I'm happy for this reunion of friends," Rowe interjected. "But, Will, we don't have much time before the Gateway closes."

"Right! I forgot."

Morgan grabbed Rowe's sleeve. "Wait a sec, Rowe. Coach, what happened after we left?"

"We were trying to get the town back together in the days following the fires that nearly destroyed everything. But as soon as we had the flames under control, the majority of people hightailed it outta town."

"And it was the *vast* majority," Laura added. "We were down to less than a hundred. Cochrane was like a ghost town."

Todd thrust his hands into his pockets. "My parents left too, but I knew I had to stay and find you. Mom said I could stay with Aunt Sarah and Ethan, but the smoke had done too much damage to their house. So, Coach and Mrs. DeFinney—"

Laura raised a finger and cleared her throat.

"Sorry," Todd continued. "Coach and…*Laura* live next door to Aunt Sarah, and they said we could all stay with them."

"Within two days," Coach said, "people were getting a really bad flu and developing rashes. They wouldn't stay in their beds, and most of them headed south. Very few hung around town."

Rowe stepped back. "And you're sure none of you are sick?"

Coach nodded. "Apart from being frightened and hungry, we're all fine."

"We've been scrounging for food and fresh water," Todd said, "but things have gotten worse in the past week." He pulled a phone from his pocket. "I talked to my parents a few days ago. Dad wasn't feeling well, and Mom had a high fever. I haven't been able to reach them since. We had internet for a while, then it failed. Then two days ago, our cellular service quit. We had electricity, but yesterday, even that died. It's like we're off the grid."

"We've lost contact with everyone," Coach said.

"Until today," Todd added. "I can't believe you're here."

Will ran a hand through his hair. "It's amazing each of you is here. What are the odds of finding such a group together?"

Laura placed a hand on Will's shoulder. "Not that amazing, really. When someone's lost, good friends try to find them. Todd was determined to find you, Will. And Coach would never give up on you, Morgan."

Ethan stood beside his mother, Sarah. She put her arm around the boy and smiled at Will. "And we promised my sister we'd look after Todd."

Rowe started toward the door. "We really need to leave. *Now*."

Morgan caught up with him. "We have to take them with us."

Rowe's shoulders slumped, but the corner of his mouth twitched in a slight smile. "How did I know you'd say that, Morgan?"

Will knew she was right. They would probably be safer in the Rainia Valley. But he also wondered how well they would adapt to life in the Fourwinds. For him, the decision to return was easy;

he had a new life and loved ones waiting in the Fourwinds. But these people had family, friends, jobs, and a familiar lifestyle here. At least, they'd *had* all that.

"If we close the Gateway," Will said to Rowe, "how will they be able to return when things calm down?"

Rowe paused before answering, studying both Will and Morgan as if confused about why they didn't understand. "First of all, the Gateway is now under our control. It would be risky, but if we needed to return here one day, we could reopen it. I am more concerned with what is happening here. What makes you think the situation will calm down or return to normal, Will?"

"You're right, Rowe," Morgan said. She tried to keep her voice down, but the room was too small to hide their conversation from the others. "Those containers we saw in the Maidstone were marked for places all around the world. Phyriad could be spreading. As it does, who knows what'll happen? We've seen how it affected the Fourwinds. Millions of people here could soon be infected. And it sounds like Phyriad has already infected Cochrane. There's nowhere else to hide."

"Are you saying the illness we experienced here is spreading around the world?" Laura asked.

Morgan nodded. "I'm sorry. As far as we know, there's no cure and no—"

"But you know of a safe place?" Coach interrupted. "What's this *Gateway* you're talking about? Where have you been, Morgan?"

Several possible answers came to Morgan's mind, but none of them seemed adequate. "I—I wish I had an easy answer, Coach. I don't. But if you come with us…well, you'll see." She glanced at Rowe, who smiled at her.

"It won't be an easy transition," Will added, "but where we're going is safer than here."

"You are welcome to join us," Rowe said. "We have shelter, food and water, and the finest elven mead."

Coach arched his eyebrows. "Sorry, the finest what?"

"He said you'll find all you need," Will said, trying to avoid more questions than necessary. "But you will have to leave behind life as you know it."

Coach put his arm around Laura. "There's just the two of us now."

Sarah bent down next to Ethan. "My son is all I have left," she said. "And…my sister."

"Can I at least go to find my parents?" Todd asked. "They were staying in Toronto but…" He trailed off, and the look on his face suggested he already knew the answer.

Will moved closer to his old friend. The thought of separation from parents stirred familiar, unwelcome pain. And knowing they were sick made it worse. "We just… Sorry, Todd. We don't have time." He blinked and scratched the corner of his eye, trying to suppress the welling emotion that was also reflected in his friend's face.

"But will I see them again?" Todd pressed. "Why are you talking about disease and war? What does that mean?"

For a moment, no one spoke. Will felt like he'd swallowed a rock. His throat tightened.

"If I've learned anything over the past month or so," he said, "it's that there are many things beyond my control. There are no easy answers, Todd." He turned to Morgan and Rowe. "But even when it feels like all hope is lost, I always have a family who loves and cares for me."

"That's right," Morgan added. "We can't do this alone. We're stronger as a team."

Coach chuckled softly. "That doesn't sound like the Morgan Finley I used to know."

Rowe stood by the door and cleared his throat. "So, are you all willing to come with us?"

"I trust you, Morgan," Coach said, eliciting nods from Laura, Sarah, and Ethan.

"I—I dunno," Todd said. "But…I believe you, Will."

On the hike back through the Arden Forest, Will and Morgan tried to describe the Fourwinds to their friends. There was no use hiding the truth because the reality of their new home would be shocking enough. Morgan warned them that some would find the transition next to impossible. Will tried to explain the Gateway but received more questions and skeptical looks for his efforts. The adults agreed that they were probably going to a remote cabin where they would hide away until things settled down and returned to a new normal. As Will spoke, Todd was quiet as if reluctant to doubt his friend again. Only the boy, Ethan, believed.

"We're going to another world," Ethan said. "Mom used to read stories about faraway places, but I never thought I'd go to one."

The sun was directly overhead when the three Callum Sages and five refugees from Cochrane arrived at the cabin. The dark veins in the logs still throbbed, albeit much slower than before, like a dying pulse.

"We still have time," Rowe said, carefully picking up the cauldron by its handle. "But quickly, everyone." He gathered them in front of the door. "Hold each other's hands or the clothing of the person in front of you. I will lead the way through the cabin door, and Will and Morgan will come last. Whatever happens, do not let go of each other."

One by one, they passed through the door and into the Gateway. When it came to Todd's aunt Sarah, she lost her grip on Ethan's hand and vanished. Terror flashed in the boy's eyes as he gaped at Morgan and Will. They were the only three who had not yet entered the Gateway.

"It's okay, Ethan," Morgan said, gripping the sword of Avarthrill. "Your mom is safe with the others. Will and I know the way from here. We'll get you safely to your mom and your new home."

Will squeezed the boy's hand. "We'll stay with you, Ethan. No guarantees of happily ever after, but we're part of your family now. And that's a good thing."

Morgan was scanning the forest as if taking in its horrible memories one last time. "This is where it all began," she said.

Will looked down at the boy clutching their hands, his wide eyes full of hope for a better tomorrow. "And this is where it begins again."

He paused for a final look at the Arden Forest, considering life as it once was, and as it might have been.

The Gateway's waning power tugged gently on their Trannalun cloaks, and Will and Morgan slipped into a life that was yet to be.

GLOSSARY OF TERMS AND NAMES

Abaddon: harvester who passed through the Gateway in Book 1

Acttun: \akt-un\ an eastern city in the Fourwinds, home of artists, fortunetellers, seers, wielders, warlocks, magicians, sorcerers, wizards, and more

Acttun Academy: school in Acttun for training wizards

Addolay Bonicle: wizard; Marlay's brother deceased (prior to Book 1)

Aerodice Mountains: western range in the Fourwinds that separates gnome and human realms

Alarra: of the House of Aldor, High Queen of Dwenlin Thah; Raric's sister

Almithara Ayoust: mer queen; Ryowyn's mother

Alyssa: the Ice Dragon; Will's mother

Arden Forest: fictional name of the large forest outside Will's home of Cochrane

Arman Bayard: brigadier, commander of Enders Brigade; deceased (Book 2)

Ashron: new gnome community in the fertile southern Rainia Valley

Avarthrill, sword of: mysterious magical weapon found and wielded by Morgan Finley

Blackie: Lillie's horse
Bremer Mason: Rowe's friend; former Callum Sage; rogue
Brynlee Mason: \brin-lee\ Queen Alarra's governess; Bremer's mother

Cauldron's Stew, the: eatery and inn in Acttun
Chicora Mountains: range north of the Rainia Valley; home of the Tuxan Mines
Cinhalla: \keen-halah\ the Elf Queen; Queen of the Northern Elves
Clover Fields: farmlands east of Hammerclaw; formerly used by gnome army as prison camp
Coach DeFinney: Morgan's old fencing coach
Crow's Nest, the: castle in the Rainia Valley; home of the Records of Time and the Gateway
Culthison: captain of Enders Brigade's Second Dragoon Company, now in command after the death of Commander Bayard

Dadore: \da-dor\ alchemy student who survived the battle at the South Crow Gate
Dench: half-orc; half of Rowe's personal guard
Dracar: humans transformed into reptilian creatures and trained to serve Natas in the Maidstone
Dragon War: battle in the Fourwinds three years before time of Book 1 in which General Raric killed Scarlas the Red Dragon
Dwenlin Thah: capital city of the Fourwinds; throne of the High Queen Alarra

Ellywick: gnome, healer; deceased (Book 1)

Enders Brigade: part of the human army in the Fourwinds; commanded by Twell Henowing; usually based in Dwenlin Thah; insignia is a wolf's paw print

Epping Forest: wooded area east of the Misty Gorge, stretching from north of the Rainia Valley to the central valley; home of very tall, ancient trees and the tree-dwelling, apelike species known as holgs

Ethan: boy who lives on Morgan's street in Cochrane, approx. 8 years old

Fadua: \fad-wah\ an alchemist imprisoned by Sidara in the Waerdreath dungeons; deceased (Book 2)

Gateway, the: magical passageway/portal from the Fourwinds (Records of Time) into the contemporary world (specifically, a cabin in the Arden Forest near Will's home)

Gloriana: worker and friend of Rowe who lives at the Crow's Nest

Grant Finley: pastor, Julie's late husband

Grudum: \groo-dum\ gnome guard at the Clover Fields; deceased (Book 2)

Gryton Mines: iron mines located along northern shore of the Niasa Sea

Half-orc: ostracized race born of union of orc and humans living east of the Hillron Mountains; tolerated in the Fourwinds but friends and allies of Callum Sages

Hammerclaw: stronghold city in the south-central region of the Fourwinds; commanded by the Iron Lord

Hansla: works as cook at Recovery Ale House and Inn

Hillron Mountains: range south and east of the Rainia Valley; home of the half-orc community

Histories, the: books documenting the history of the Fourwinds; studied and preserved by the Callum Sages; kept in the Records of Time

Holgs: apelike creatures that live in the treetops of the Epping Forest

Hollowtangle: large forest west of the Niasa Sea; home of the Druid Forest and the Maidstone tower; former home to the People of the River Country

Homas: works at Recovery Ale House and Inn

Illious: \ill-ee-us\ Master Alchemist; deceased (Book 2)

Illume: caretaker at the Maidstone; deceased (Book 2)

Interrupted: Tonna's horse

Iron Dragon: also known as Natas, the so-called mythical creature of chaos

Jessman: bartender at the Recovery Ale House and Inn

Joe/Johanissan: Callum Sage from the River Country; Will's great-grandfather

Julie Finley: Morgan's mother

Kalmar: mer soldier who took over as captain after the death of Prince Wrathan

Kydaris: alchemy student; friend of Dadore; deceased (Book 2)

Larionoff: Morgan's opponent at World Fencing Championships

Laura DeFinney: Coach's wife

Lessers: small, mischievous demon-like creatures from between worlds that infiltrate the contemporary world; visible only to Will

Lillie: orphan girl in the Crow's Nest; considers Morgan her mother
Little Hammerclaw: new town built on the Foglan River on the northeastern shore of Rainia Lake
Longcross: village near the Stoneberg

Marauders Brigade: part of the Fourwinds army almost trying to defend Hammerclaw; recommissioned by General Raric and sent to help defend the Rainia Valley
Margrave: druid who lives in the Druid Forest (in the Hollowtangle)
Mark of Natas; the Mark: symbol of those loyal to Natas; looks like three fishhooks
Marlay Bonicle: wizard from the Acttun Academy
Meagan: server at the Cauldron's Stew in Acttun; friend of Rowe and Bremer
Misty Gorge: canyon west of the Rainia Valley; Serpentine River flows through it
Mofard Flats; the Flats: area between the Upper Plains of Ashron and Dwenlin Thah; used as army staging/training area
Moonwalker: powerful armored creature over eight feet tall, sometimes used by gnome army; usually wields spiked iron ball as preferred weapon
Morgan Finley: Callum Sage; world fencing champion

Nameless Forest: small wooded area north of the Hollowtangle
Natas: mythical creature of chaos; the Iron Dragon
Niasa Sea: former saltwater home of the merpeople
Nyrianne: grandmotherly woman; former student of Marlay; *see*: Sidara

Onathe Wyeth: dark elf; deceased (Book 1)

Panigim: Overseer of the gnome army; deceased (Book 2)

Phyriad: \fear-ee-ad\ a substance found in the Maidstone and used by Natas to create an infectious elixir that transforms living beings into dragon-like creatures

Plains of Ashron: large region west of the Niasa Sea, divided into Upper and Lower

Raric: commander general of the human army; the new Red Dragon

Records of Time: library tower in the Crow's Nest, traditionally protected by the Callum Sages

Recovery Ale House and Inn: eatery and inn located in Fairbay

River Country: home of Johanissan; abandoned

Rowe of the Nest: Callum Sage

Ryodan Ayoust: \rye-o-dan\ mer king; Ryowyn's father

Ryowyn Ayoust: \rye-o-win\ mer princess

Sarah: Cochrane resident; Ethan's mother, Todd's aunt

Scarlas: the former Red Dragon

Serpentine River: long and winding river that flows from the Hillron Mountains, through the Misty Gorge, and into the Niasa Sea

Shalem priests: a devout sect in Acttun; caretakers of the asylum

Sidara: Dark Queen; *see*: Nyrianne

Springfield 1911: a semiautomatic pistol; Will's preferred weapon

Stoneberg: wall between the eastern and western regions of the Fourwinds; commissioned by Queen Alarra's great-great-grandfather; key to its iron gate has often changed hands

Thaudas: half winged horse, half unicorn (black); rescued Will in Book 2

Todd: friend of Will's in Cochrane who doubted his visions

Tonna: first messenger, Enders Brigade

Tranas: councilman at the Crow's Nest; close friend of Rowe; died in the battle to defend the South Crow Gate (Book 2)

Trannalun cloak: worn only by Callum Sages; powerful magic woven into red fabric to protect and heal the owner

Tuxan Mines: located beneath the Chicora Mountains; worked by the Tuxan dwarves

Twell Henowing: first lieutenant of Enders Brigade, promoted to brigadier/commander of the Marauders

Uluk the Shadowfallen: Dark Queen Sidara's minion; offspring of a fallen angel and a woman; deceased (Book 2)

Urk: goblin; friend of Bremer

Will Owens: Callum Sage

Wrathan: mer prince; deceased (Book 2)

Yossar: Highland gnome commander

Did you enjoy *Into the Maidstone?*

We're looking for a group of loyal readers who will help us continue writing stories like these.

Honest reviews help bring our books to the attention of other readers. If you enjoyed this book, we would be grateful if you could spend a few minutes leaving a review (as short as you like) at Amazon (or other online retailer) and on Goodreads.

What's Next?

Visit
www.MaidstoneChronicles.com

Featuring:
• Regular Giveaways for Fantasy Book Lovers
• Forthcoming Book Releases
• Author Details
• Details on our "Buy a Book / Give a Book" program
(for each book we sell, we're donating student workbooks
for classrooms in Haiti to help kids there learn to read and write)
• Social Media Links

**Everyone on our email list has a chance to win
in our regular giveaways of popular fantasy books.**

Thanks for reading and engaging with us!
— *Shane and Darryl*